Sarah's Patchwork

Sarah's Patchwork

STEPHANIE GRACE WHITSON

FIC
WHITSON
1998

A
JANET
THOMA
BOOK

THOMAS NELSON PUBLISHERS
Nashville
Printed in the United States of America

Published in Nashville, Tennessee, by Thomas Nelson, Inc., Publishers.

The Bible version used in this publication is the KING JAMES VERSION.

Author's Note: The poem "The Patchwork Quilt," which appears in the Prologue, was written by Natalie Whitted Price. Every attempt was made to trace copyright or publishing permission for the use of this poem, but was unsucessful.

Library of Congress Cataloging-in-Publication Data

Whitson, Stephanie Grace.
    Sarah's patchwork / Stephanie G. Whitson.
      p. cm.
    ISBN 0-7852-7185-6
    I. Title.
PS3573.H555S27 1998
813'.54—dc21   97-50431
                                               CIP

Printed in the United States of America.

1 2 3 4 5 6 QPK 03 02 01 00 99 98

To Bob
my leader, my example
my beloved, my friend

Acknowledgments

Dear Mom, Tomorrow Saturday and Sunday are off. Max and I disided to do our school on our own. Max has already done his school and I have to. you can write tommorrow and you can write Saturday and Sunday if you want to write. We are going to make lunch for you so you don't have to worry about anything. We hope this will help! Love, Shannon and Max.

This note appeared one morning on my desk. It was arranged on a serving tray along with a small bouquet of silk flowers, a booklet style menu, and this announcement perched on an easel.

Today's special is.
Good Peeda with ledas and caret's and cheez. 3 layer's. With ranch dressing and then microwave so the cheez is melted in every bight. on the side is the wonderful Fruit Star which look's like a star only it is Fruit. Cewee banana Apple celery caret's and orange and and pink orange and green orange. and on the side you get some chip's your Choice drink you get some good juice to wash down the fruit chip's and pedda. Desert menu is on Page 2 if you would like any! You also get served a cup of coffee. (no extra charge!) If this is what you would like just circle yes.

YES.NO.
if you do not want this please take look at our menu.

I won't bore you with the menu, except for two entries—"leave a good tip" and "don't you just love having kids?"

Yes, I do love having kids, and I need to acknowledge once again all the sacrifices my family makes to allow me to write. Thank you, dearly beloved.

Thank you, readers, for your continued encouragement and your prayers.

Thank you, Sara, for listening patiently when I whine.

Postscript for those of you who know that we home school our children: Yes, I did take note of the need to spend some extra time on spelling this year!

Prologue

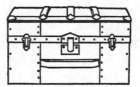

1947

lutching the envelope in her hand, Lorna mounted the wide staircase to the second floor of the old manse. At the top of the stairs she paused momentarily, wondering what it would be like now without Aunt Sarah to share the window seat. They had sat there so often, peering through the leaded glass to the garden below, watching for signs of spring, laughing at the antics of new kittens on the lawn, enjoying the moonlight as it filtered through the ancient burr oak trees that lined the brick wall surrounding the property.

A strident voice called from downstairs. "Lor-NUH."

Lorna grimaced and answered with just a tinge of impatience in her voice. "Yes, Mother."

"Where *are* you, Lorna? Upstairs already?" The sound of something dropping in the hall echoed up the stairs. "Oh, I suppose you're anxious to read that letter." With a loud sigh, Lorna's mother added, "I'm just putting my bag here in the hall. I've a terrible headache and I'm going to lie down on the couch in the parlor." The voice dropped to a low moan. "Oh . . . my *head* . . ."

Lorna forced empathy into her voice. "I'll be right down, Mother—"

"No, no—it's all right, Lorna. I'll just lie down—alone —for a while—"

Lorna had already started down the stairs, having left the envelope on the window seat. "Don't be silly, Mother. I'll draw the blinds in the parlor and get a cool cloth for your head . . . maybe some lemonade?"

"That would be nice, dear. Thank you." Edna Biddle sank onto the hideous gray sofa, delivered only yesterday by Harry Miller himself of Miller and Rains Department Store. "I'll just have a nap—and leave you to your letter. I'm sure you'd rather read it privately."

Ignoring the hint, Lorna began to draw the blinds in the parlor, banishing every shred of the spring morning's dazzling sunshine from the room. She slipped out of the room quickly and padded down the hall to the back of the house and the vast kitchen where she began The Ritual: One: chip ice. Two: slice fresh lemons. Three: retrieve reamer from butler's pantry. Four: extract lemon juice. Five: add water and sugar. Six: chip more ice. Seven: retrieve fresh linen cloth, dampen with water, and lay atop ice in crockery bowl.

Arranging the items on a white tray, Lorna completed The Ritual with the all-important step eight: proceed to bedside with just the right amount of compassion and empathy. "I'm sorry you have another headache, Mother. You've had a stressful morning. A nap will do you good."

Edna was already reclining on the sofa. Placing the back of one hand across her forehead, she sighed. "Well, at least we know we still have a home. Thank God for that."

"Aunt Sarah would never have turned us out, Mother. You must know that."

Raising up on one elbow, Edna reached for the glass of lemonade and sipped slowly before responding. "I *didn't* know, Lorna. I didn't know at all. Of course we've been faithful to care for Aunt Sarah all these years. Still, she could have done whatever she wanted. And as eccentric as she'd become, nothing would have surprised me."

Edna lay back on the couch and closed her eyes again before continuing. "I was relieved to hear Judge Rimes read the will. Relieved that Aunt Sarah *had* a will. A bit surprised—" Edna forced pleasure into her voice— "surprised, but so pleased, dear, to know that at least *your* devotion has been rewarded."

Lorna nodded solemnly. "I still can't believe she gave the trunk to me."

Edna opened her eyes. "Oh, Lorna. I wasn't talking about *that*. Who cares about an old trunk filled with musty quilts and baubles? The *house*, Lorna. She left you the house." Edna patted Lorna's hand. "Indisputably yours—as soon as you are of age." Edna's eyes roamed upward. "It's quite an albatross . . . terribly outdated . . . but at least your father can rest in peace knowing that his wife and daughter are provided for." Quickly Edna added, "Of course, *he* would have provided for us, too, if he'd been able." She sighed heavily. "If only the war hadn't taken him from us—"

While her mother dramatized, Lorna raised her dark eyes to the fine molding that graced the parlor. At the first opportunity she interrupted her mother's musings. "Is your headache better, Mother?"

"I think so, dear, thank you."

Lorna rose to go. "You take a good nap. I'll be upstairs if you need me."

Edna nestled into the sofa's overstuffed cushion. She was snoring softly before Lorna reached the top of the stairs. Bending to retrieve the envelope, Lorna turned to open the ornate oak door that led into the room that had been Aunt Sarah's for nearly half a century.

The room was bathed in light. Everything from the cream-colored walls and the whitewashed furniture to the soft yellow and cornflower blue quilt on the daybed reflected the sunshine. The floor creaked as Lorna walked across the room and opened narrow French doors onto a small, private second-story porch. The cheerfulness of the room had an odd effect on her. Looking down at the envelope clutched in her left hand, she fought against the tears pressing against her eyelids. Her eyes came to rest on the rocker tucked into the corner by the French doors. Beside the rocker sat a workbasket, still-unfinished quilt blocks peeking out from beneath its leather-covered lid. A cream-colored shawl was draped over the back of the rocker. But the rocker was empty, and its emptiness conquered Lorna's resolve. She slid to the floor by the rocker. Pulling the shawl to her, she buried her face in its softness and gave way to tears.

"Oh, Aunt Sarah," Lorna whispered through her tears, "who will understand me now? Who will I talk to? I miss you so much already, and you've only been gone a short while." She was interrupted by her own sobs. Groping for the envelope, she managed to continue. "I don't care about the house, Aunt Sarah. I'd rather have you back. You always understood. Mother never understands." Lorna shook her head, willing her tears to stop. "No, I won't let Mother ruin this. I'm going to stay in here all afternoon and read this letter and just pretend you've gone over to quilt with the ladies at the church."

Her hand shaking, Lorna glanced down at the envelope Judge Rimes had given her that morning. "It isn't really an addendum to the will," he had explained as Edna looked on, one eyebrow raised. "It's a personal note for you, Miss Biddle. I was instructed to give it to you only upon my client's death." Lorna had accepted the envelope with a trembling hand, biting her lip as she saw Aunt Sarah's beautiful Spencerian handwriting. *For Lorna, when I am gone.*

Now, Lorna sat on the rag rug in Aunt Sarah's room and opened the envelope carefully. It contained only a few lines written by Aunt Sarah's hand.

Dearest, precious Lorna, child of my heart—You have said your good-byes to old Aunt Sarah. You have learned from the judge that the manse is yours, and now perhaps Edna will finally accept that my devotion to you both is sure.

But one thing remains, Lorna. The trunk in my room. I have shared its memories with no one but you. I don't know how it is that a child can understand things so completely, Lorna, but from the moment you were born you were my kindred spirit.

I love you, dear Lorna. And now that I am gone, I want you to have the trunk, and all the precious memories it represents. Once you asked if you could use the stories in the trunk, and I declined. I wanted to keep them, to cherish them and to leave them untarnished by others' comments and criticisms. But now I am gone, and I want you to use the trunk to inspire you. If you think that these things will help you, if you think they will make your dream of becoming a writer come true, then use the memories in the trunk. God bless you, dear Lorna. May His hand guide yours to share the memories in such a way that everyone who reads the stories will know that He truly does make all things beautiful in His time, that with God's help we can transform yesterday's tears into treasures.

Lorna sat with Aunt Sarah's note in her lap, staring across the room at the trunk that had arrived in Lincoln,

Nebraska, over a half-century ago. She knew its contents by heart. Only a few years ago, when Lorna was an eleven-year-old fretting over a rainy day, Aunt Sarah had opened the trunk for her and invited her to take something out.

"You choose anything you want, dear. I'll tell you a story, and we'll see if the rain doesn't pass over before too long."

Lorna had lifted the top tray and set it aside, letting out an excited "Oh!" at the sight of an exquisite crazy quilt. She ran her hand over the featherstitching, exclaiming, "Someone brought one of these to the church rummage sale last week. I wanted it, but Mother wouldn't let me buy it."

Aunt Sarah had nodded with understanding. "Your mother likes the latest fashion, Lorna. Crazy quilts haven't been popular since long before you were born."

"But it's beautiful, Aunt Sarah. Did you make it?"

Aunt Sarah had nodded. "Yes."

"Then that's the story I want to hear. Tell me about the quilt."

Aunt Sarah laughed. "Oh, I can't tell about the quilt in only one afternoon, Lorna. There's an entire book in this quilt." Her blue eyes sparkled. "But if you point to one square of fabric, I'll tell you a *chapter* in the book."

"This one!" Lorna didn't hesitate to point out a shiny swatch of claret silk.

Aunt Sarah smiled mysteriously. "I don't know, Lorna. You may not be old enough to hear about the claret silk." Sarah's reluctance made Lorna all the more insistent on hearing the story, so Aunt Sarah sat down in her rocker, picked up a half-finished quilt block, and began to talk.

When the story was finished, Lorna sat quietly fingering the silk. Her dark eyes were serious. "Mother doesn't know that about you, does she?"

Sarah shook her head. "No, dear. I've never told that story before."

"Not even to my father when he was still here?"

"Not even to your father."

Lorna smiled quietly. Once again, her dark brown eyes looked into Aunt Sarah's blue eyes. Once again, their hearts touched, crossing the generations between them. "I won't tell anyone, Aunt Sarah."

"I know that, Lorna. My stories are just for you. Perhaps someday you will use them in your writing—but not yet."

Lorna had nodded. Sunlight pouring through the window made the colors in the quilt dance. With a start, Lorna realized that the rain had stopped. "Do I have to wait for the next rainy day before I can hear another story, Aunt Sarah?"

Aunt Sarah laid aside her needlework and chuckled. "Land sakes, child. If we wait for rain I'll never get all the stories told. There's enough stories in that quilt alone to have kept Noah entertained on the ark. And that's only one of the quilts in the trunk. And there's more than just quilts in there, too."

Lorna peered inside the trunk. Removing the crazy quilt had uncovered the bodice of an exquisite gown made of the same claret silk that had caught her eye in the quilt. But Aunt Sarah had folded the crazy quilt and bent to lay it back in the trunk. Replacing the top tray, she closed the lid.

After that day, nearly every private moment that Aunt Sarah and Lorna shared had revolved around the trunk. When her mother went to play bridge, Lorna collected a story. When the old peach tree near the carriage house was laden with fruit and Aunt Sarah was making jam, Lorna collected a story. When Edna went to circle meeting, Lorna collected a story.

"Just remember, dear," Aunt Sarah sometimes reminded, "the stories are for you. I'm giving them like a gift. You keep them to yourself. Enjoy them."

Lorna had done more than enjoy them. She had treasured them, relived them, collected and preserved them. Just as her mother sought out china elephants to add to the shelf over the television in the parlor, so Lorna sought new stories from Aunt Sarah. She kept them faithfully, anticipating the day when Sarah would allow her to write them down.

And now, with her mother asleep on the sofa downstairs and the afternoon ahead of her, Lorna had been given permission to use Aunt Sarah's stories. Going to the trunk, she opened it and lifted out the tray. The crazy quilt lay just as Aunt Sarah had left it, its folds cushioned with tissue paper. Lorna knew what lay beneath it. There was the bodice of a wedding gown . . . another quilt called the Whig Rose . . . a cathedral-length wedding veil . . . yards of lace . . . a photo album. As she lifted the crazy quilt out of the trunk and spread it across Aunt Sarah's bed, Lorna noticed a piece of paper pinned to one corner. A poem titled "The Patchwork Quilt" was on the paper. Across the top, Aunt Sarah had written, *Given as a recitation at Women's Club November 12, 1922. Written by Natalie Whitted Price.*

Lorna read the poem:

Did Gran'ma ever tell you about the patch-work quilt
    That lies across the sofa in her room?
It was made from scraps of dresses that she wore
    when she was young,
    And some of them were woven on a loom.
Sometimes when it is raining and I can't play out
    of doors,
    She lets me spread it out upon the floor,
And as I choose the pieces I'd like to hear about,

She tells me of the dresses that she wore.

It isn't just the dresses that Gran'ma tells about,
   It's the things that happen'd when she had
      them on,
And almost ev'ry piece that's in that dear old
      patch-work quilt,
   Holds the mem'ry of a sorrow or a song,
Oh, things were very wonderful when
      Gran'mama was young,
   You ought to hear her tell about it all,
The ladies all were beautiful, the children all
      were good,
   And the men were all so gallant and so tall.

She calls the quilt her mem'ry bed, and ev'ry little
      piece,
   Is a flower blooming in its scented fold
There are red ones for the roses and blues for
      "don't forgets"
   And yellow ones for sun-flowers of gold,
There's one she calls sweet lavender that smells
      like baby-clothes
   And one of purple like the sunset skies,
I never ask about these, or the grey one like the
      rain,
   For when I do, dear Gran'ma always cries.

My Gran'ma told me once that life is just a
      patch-work quilt,
   Of births and deaths and marriages and things
And that sometimes when you're looking for a
      lovely piece of red
   You only find a knot of faded strings,
But she says the red is redder when it's by a piece
      of brown,

And grey is not so grey by sunny gold.
Oh, I hope I'll have a lovely patch-work quilt
like Gran'mama's
To show to little children when I'm old.

Across the bottom of the page, Aunt Sarah had written, *Lorna, now you have a lovely patchwork quilt. And now you may tell the stories.*

Leaving the quilt lying across the bed, Lorna crept down the hall to her own room. Retrieving a pencil and a notebook, she made her way back to Aunt Sarah's room, pausing at the top of the stairs to listen for her mother. Edna was still asleep.

And so Lorna told the stories. It was years before anyone wanted to read about the claret silk, the madder brown, the black cashmere, the old rose calico . . . years when Lorna wrote and rewrote; years when she lived her own patchwork of sorrows and songs. And as she lived, Lorna began to understand. And as she understood she rewrote. And each time she rewrote, the telling was better, until one day she stopped rewriting and sent the story away, and when it came back it was a book and the name of the book was *Sarah's Patchwork*.

CHAPTER 1

Red Plaid Flannel

"Remember, O Lord, what is come upon us. . . .
We are orphans and fatherless."
Lamentations 5:1, 3

Thirteen-year-old Sarah Biddle rocked back and forth in a broken chair, clutching her wailing infant sister against her. In the dim light she could see the cot where her mother lay, so thin her form barely showed beneath the threadbare coverlet. Sarah's attempts to wash it in the barrel used to collect rainwater in the back alley had failed to clean it. Once a soft yellow, the coverlet had turned dirty gray, the same shade of gray that streaked the walls of the room they occupied.

The baby's cries had no effect on the still form other than to cause it to turn its face toward the wall. It had been days since Ivy had been able to respond to her children. Too ill to produce milk for her baby, she had moved farther and farther away from all three of her children, both mentally and physically. Now her still form lay pressed against the wall as she tried to cross the last few steps from her awful reality into another place—a better place. It was surely better, for no hell could be worse than where she and the children were now.

1

"Tom," Sarah whispered, "Tom—you asleep?" From the corner where he lay curled up on a pile of newspapers, Tom answered. "Nah, I not sleepin'." Tom pushed himself to a sitting position and hunkered into the corner.

"Get me the sugar bowl, Tom. Emma's just got to let Ma get some sleep."

Tom stood up stiffly, shivering as he limped across the room to a packing crate the family used as their table. Retrieving a chipped bowl, he handed it to Sarah and stood by her chair, watching as she licked her finger, dipped it into the sugar bowl, and stuck it in the wailing infant's mouth. The wailing ceased momentarily, and Sarah rocked, intoning, "There now, there now," until finally Emma went to sleep.

"You done good, Tom, to get the sugar. It'll help keep Emma quiet for a while."

Relieved of the guilt he had felt earlier in the day when he stole the sugar, Tom smiled at Sarah. Loud footsteps sounded in the hallway just outside the door. Grimacing with the effort, Tom forced his crooked leg into action. He hurried to his pile of papers in the corner of the room, plopping down and turning his face to the wall just as the door was wrenched open.

Mason Biddle glanced at Sarah and headed for the cot where Ivy lay. His huge hands were gentle as he pulled the coverlet up under her chin, patted her bony shoulder, stroked her hair. When he noticed a blush of pink in her cheeks he felt a flicker of joy, but then his hand touched her face and he realized that Ivy's cheeks were flushed with fever, not life.

"She needs a doctor," Sarah said matter-of-factly.

Mason turned to her angrily. Reaching into his pocket he drew out two wormy apples and tossed them into Sarah's lap. "I picked those up out of the street, Sarah. Only meal we'll get today. I've got no job, and nobody seems to want to hire me. There's no money for a doctor. We'll just have to get by."

The baby stirred, and quickly Sarah covered her finger with sugar and put it in the baby's mouth to keep her from crying. Looking down at the floor, Sarah frowned. Tom lay huddled in his corner, trying very hard not to make any movement that would cause his newspaper mattress to rustle and remind his father of his existence.

Standing up, Mason surveyed the room. "I'm going out." Before Sarah could protest he added, "Not drinking, Sarah. I'm going to get help." Turning toward the cot, Mason added in a voice that approached tenderness, "Ivy, you hear me? I'm going to get help."

Late in the afternoon, Mason sat on the bottom step of the tenement house, his head in his hands. He had walked the streets the entire day looking for work. Like thousands of other immigrants, he had found nothing. Then he heard something rare. A kind voice was speaking to a tangle of filthy boys who had been begging on the street corner. "Come with me, lads, and we'll fix you up. You'll not have to beg again. Winter's coming on. How does a warm, clean bed sound? Regular meals, too. Nothing fancy, but good food. And a home. If things work out, you'll go west. Good homes are waiting for fine, strong young men like you."

Mason stood up abruptly. Walking up behind the man, he spun him around, half growling, "What d'ya mean, talking such tales to these boys? There's no such better life for the likes of them—or me." Mason reached out, intending to shove the stranger away, but the man thrust out his own hand and grasped Mason's in a firm handshake.

"Brace, sir. Charles Loring Brace. Founder and director of the Children's Aid Society. We help the children of the street. We find homes for them in the West—homes, good jobs, new lives." Brace looked keenly into Mason's eyes.

"Most of our children are orphans. But occasionally we help families."

Mason stared back dumbly at the stranger for a long moment. Something inside him gave way. He mumbled, "I got a sick wife with a baby she can't feed and two half-starved children. All day I been walking the streets looking for work. All day they been waiting—" Mason fought to keep the desperation from his voice, but he lost the battle. "I can't go back until I can bring help."

"Why don't you come back to the Society with me," Brace offered. "Come and see what we might be able to do." He turned to the small group of boys who had stayed to watch the interchange, hoping for a fight. "You lads come along, too. See if you don't think the Society offers you a good chance."

A few of the boys laughed harshly and walked away, but six of the younger ones huddled together, their eyes on the ground, waiting for Brace to lead them away.

Mason hesitated. Something of the proud young man who had deserted his father's farm in Surrey and crossed the wide seas with a new bride still remained. "I'm not asking for charity," he insisted.

"Of course not," Brace said quietly. With supernatural effort he looked past Mason's filthy shirt and matted hair. "Let us get these boys rounded up and you can see for yourself what kind of help it is we offer." With a final word of encouragement to the boys, Brace headed off up the street.

Mason followed close behind.

It was early evening before Sarah heard her father's footsteps. The day had seemed long. The sugar bowl was empty, and Sarah's stomach complained of hunger. She had given one apple to Tom, and when she was unable to rouse her mother, had insisted that Tom eat the second apple as well. She had held Emma all day, rocking often in a vain attempt to soothe the infant's cries. At some point someone in the next room had pounded on the wall, screaming in a language Sarah didn't know. But she understood. She used up all the sugar to keep Emma quiet, pacing the floor until she was so exhausted she dropped into the broken chair, falling asleep with her baby sister in her arms.

When the door opened, Sarah looked up without emotion. Her father's large frame filled the doorway, and it wasn't until he had entered the room that Sarah realized he had someone with him. She was so tiny that the top of her head was several inches shy of Mason Biddle's chest. Mason crossed the room to his wife's cot and choked back emotion as he settled beside her. "Ivy, I brought help." There was no response.

"I am Mrs. Hurd, dear." The woman was looking at Sarah with so much kindness that Sarah blinked back tears of relief. "I am with the Children's Aid Society here in New York." She glanced about the room. "I have come to take your baby sister somewhere where she can be fed and cared for."

"Take Emma?" Sarah echoed. Her eyes sought out her father. He sat on the edge of Ivy's cot and looked at Sarah, nodding.

Newspapers rustled as Tom stood up.

Mrs. Hurd turned toward him. "You're Tom. Don't worry. We'll take good care of Emma until your mother is well again." Looking meaningfully at Mason, she continued, "You can come visit Emma whenever you like. Your father knows where to come. And when your mother is better, Emma can come home."

Sarah opened her mouth to protest, but before she could say anything, Mason Biddle's huge hands were pulling Emma from her arms, handing her to Mrs. Hurd. "You promise me she'll be cared for." He nodded toward the cot. "When Ivy's well, we'll be wanting her back. Soon .

as I find work I'll pay for her care, too. I'm not giving my children away."

"Of course not, Mr. Biddle. I understand perfectly," Mrs. Hurd said as she hurried toward the door. She was gone amid loud protests from Sarah and Tom. When the door closed behind Mrs. Hurd, the accusing eyes of his two remaining children were too much for Mason. Scooping up his sick wife, he headed for the door. "And now, Sarah, we're going to find a doctor. We'll walk to every hospital in New York if we have to. Someone has to help us. Someone has to."

Late that night Mason Biddle staggered into the New York City Hospital with Ivy cradled in his arms. Near dawn of the next morning he staggered out with the realization that he had no way to see that his wife was properly buried. He clutched Sarah and Tom by the hand as he made his way to the Children's Aid Society. When he arrived he called out for Mrs. Hurd, beating on the door until a large woman with stringy braids and a ridiculously small mouth answered. "Mrs. Hurd is not a resident matron, sir. She won't be in until later this morning."

Mason forced himself through the door, ordering Sarah and Tom to wait on the doorstep. When he came out, hopelessness had settled over him. He sat on the steps next to Sarah and Tom and without emotion declared, "You're staying here. I'm going to find a place where we can all be together." Mason crouched down in front of Sarah and looked up into her disbelieving eyes. "I will find that place and I will come for you. Until then, you be real good and do what these people say. They'll feed you and see that you have clean clothes. Winter's almost here. You'll be warm." He turned to Tom. "No more shivering under a pile of newspapers, son."

Sarah heard her father's words, but it would be days before the import of what she was hearing settled in. For the moment, she was numb with grief and shock. The matron called for them to come inside. Tom and Sarah stood in the doorway and watched until the red plaid shirt Mason had always worn faded out of sight. Sarah thought he would look back, would wave and call out another promise to return. But he didn't.

It was the last time Tom and Sarah Biddle saw their father.

CHAPTER 2

Cinnamon Pink

"Pure religion and undefiled before God and the Father is this, to visit the fatherless and widows in their affliction, and to keep himself unspotted from the world."
James 1:27

There it was, in *Surrender Book Number Eight* on Mrs. Hurd's desk: the name *Mason Biddle*. Across from the signature someone else had written the names *Sarah, Thomas,* and *Emma*. Sarah looked at her father's signature in disbelief. Mrs. Hurd put a hand on Sarah's shoulder. "He had to do it, dear. There was no other way. It broke his heart, but he knew that by surrendering you to the Children's Aid Society, he was giving you a future he never could."

Sarah said in a near whisper, "But he never said goodbye." Then her blue eyes looked piercingly at Mrs. Hurd. "You haven't heard from him? Not once all winter?"

Mrs. Hurd shook her head sadly. "I wasn't present when he came back to sign the surrender book."

Mrs. Hurd gently led Sarah to a bench along the wall of the office and sat next to her. "I don't think he could bear to see you, dear. First, he had to let Emma come here. Then your mother died. And finally he brought you and Tom. But he never meant it to be permanent. Once he realized there was no other way, he probably just couldn't bear one more good-bye."

Sarah lowered her head to hide her tears. Her hands pulled at her pinafore.

"Sarah, think for a moment of all the vagrant children you have seen in the city," Mrs. Hurd said. "Some say there are ten thousand now. A thousand immigrants pour into the city every day. There isn't enough work for them all. You've seen the girls on the streets selling rags or matches. Walk down by the wharf and there are young girls singing, hoping someone will pay them for their sweet voices." Mrs. Hurd shook her head sadly. "The things that can happen to those poor children, Sarah— your father protected you from that when he brought you here. Our founder, Mr. Brace, has made it his life's work to try to help boys and girls like you and Tom and little Emma find new homes with families who can care for you."

Mrs. Hurd put her arm around Sarah before continuing. "Sarah, your father brought you to us because he didn't want you to have a life of misery and shame." Gently, she lifted Sarah's chin and looked at her. "You may not believe it right now, but your father loved you very much. It was his *love* that made him bring you here, Sarah. I'm certain it was the most difficult thing that he ever did, leaving you here with us."

Sarah looked down at her hands. They were clean. She and Tom were well fed. They had been warm, just like their father had promised. Sarah remembered the previous winter. The family had crowded onto a filthy mattress in a rat-infested tenement to try to keep warm. Mason Biddle had brought home rags and newspapers. Ivy had fashioned a makeshift comforter, sewing the rags together with string and then stuffing the piece with wads of newspaper. Sarah remembered the nights when rats ran through her hair. She remembered trying to scrub herself clean with water her father brought in a little pail from the river. She looked down at the blue dress she wore now. It was crisp and clean.

Sarah looked up at Mrs. Hurd. "He did the best he could, I guess," she said quietly, her voice trembling. She looked away for a moment. "Could we stay together—all three of us? Would someone take us three?"

"We will do our best to see that you stay together, Sarah—if not in the same home, at least in the same community where you can see one another often. We will try our best." Quickly, Mrs. Hurd added, "And I promise you, Sarah, we will keep a record of where you go. You can write to us. We will keep your letters. And if your father ever returns or ever contacts us for information about his children, we will tell him where you are. I promise."

Sarah stood up and crossed over to the desk where *Surrender Book Number Eight* lay open. Raising one finger to her lips she then lowered it to touch Mason Biddle's signature. *I'll be good, Pa,* she promised. She closed the book and turned to Mrs. Hurd. "Can I see Tom now, Mrs. Hurd? I need to explain it to Tom."

"Why wasn't I told about this?" Clara Hurd's voice was barely under control as she burst through Matron Baxter's office door.

Baxter looked up from her desk. "Told about what, Clara?"

"You placed Emma Biddle. You placed her without so much as a word to me—and what's worse, you didn't tell Sarah or Tom."

"Sarah and Tom are going west tomorrow to find a new home. You know as well as I do that we cannot depend upon the placing agents to care for infants. Our practice is to send the *older* children west." Baxter laid down her pen and looked up at Clara Hurd. Understanding shone in her eyes. "I know it's a bad situation, Clara. This entire work is composed of bad situations, but our mission is to make the best of them. The couple who took Emma Biddle are wealthy, leading citizens. Whatever motivated them to come to us, I'll never know, but I have no doubt they will give that child the best home imaginable. Probably better than either you or I had, in fact."

"But why didn't you tell Sarah and Tom?"

"I didn't want there to be a scene. I planned on telling them in the morning before they boarded the train. A sleepless night would do nothing to increase their chances of early adoption. Heaven knows it will be difficult enough for Tom, what with his being crippled."

Mrs. Hurd sat down opposite Matron Baxter, her shoulders slumped, her head bowed dejectedly. "How will I ever tell Sarah? Her one desire was to keep her brother and sister with her. She's been very brave about everything, but she's lost so much—"

"*All* of our children have lost much, Mrs. Hurd," Baxter said matter-of-factly. "We must do the best we can for them." Her voice softened. "We cannot let ourselves become so deeply involved. If our hearts break for every one of them, we will be of no use in this work.

"I didn't give Emma up lightly, Clara. But the couple who came—the woman fairly melted when she saw Emma. I was instantly struck by the child's resemblance to her. She scooped that baby up out of her crib and covered her with kisses. The gentleman was nearly overcome as well. Later they told me that Emma reminded them both of the child they had lost. They had been informed by the woman's physician that their only hope now for a family was to adopt. They carried Emma Biddle outside to a carriage fine enough to grace any castle in England. If I told you their names, you would recognize them. And you would approve."

"If they are wealthy, surely they could have given a home to Sarah and Tom as well," Mrs. Hurd offered.

Matron Baxter shook her head. "They specifically wanted an infant. I did my best to convince them to take Sarah and Tom and keep the children together. But you know the prevailing mind-set. So many people believe that these orphans have a bad bloodline, that they come from inferior stock and will not do well because of inferior blood. Emma's resemblance to their own lost infant was her salvation. But it was apparent that I risked Emma's placement by insisting that they adopt three children instead of one. I conceded. In spite of the fact that they give some credence to the 'bad blood' nonsense when it comes to the older children, they are good, kind people. They asked for confidentiality, and it has been granted. I entered false names in the record, and I did it without one regret."

Matron Baxter's expression pleaded with Mrs. Hurd as she concluded. "Clara, Emma Biddle will have as good a life as the Society has ever provided. Most of these children go west to work. We know the work is hard. We know that not every situation is ideal. As careful as we are, we know that some placements will be dismal failures. But we do our best. It was a joy for me to see one of our infants go to a loving couple. I am as certain as I can be that at least one child who has been in my care will have a good home. If you cannot bear to tell Sarah and Tom that their sister has a wonderful new home, I will do it."

Clara Hurd shook her head. "No. I'll tell them." She rose slowly and headed out the door. "But could you make the customary announcement about the trip west tonight? I can't face Sarah yet. I need to think this through. I'll be here in the morning to say good-bye, and I'll tell her then."

"Of course." Matron Baxter raised her considerable bulk from her chair and followed Mrs. Hurd into the hall. Clara took her hat and cloak and went out the door to a sleepless night at her home.

Matron Baxter entered the children's dormitory and made the announcement: "Girls—those of you with beds along the east wall—listen carefully. We have just today received a gift of clothing from the women's sewing society at the Methodist Episcopal Church on Forty-eighth Street. Each of you will receive something new to wear tomorrow and a change of clothes as well. Tomorrow morning you will rise very early and board a train. You'll be going west to your new homes."

Matron Baxter turned to go, but someone touched her shoulder. It was Sarah Biddle. Baxter didn't wait for her to speak. "Don't worry, Sarah. Mr. Tice has just gone into the boy's dormitory to make the same announcement to a group of boys. Tom will be among them. I promise." Baxter hurried out the door, pretending not to hear Sarah's question about her baby sister.

As Matron Baxter walked away, something sounded an alarm deep inside Sarah, but she pushed it out of her consciousness and returned to her bed. A few minutes later a resident matron turned out the dormitory lights, and ten young girls were left in darkness to wait through the longest night of their lives.

The anguish in Sarah Biddle's voice nearly broke Clara Hurd's resolve to be reassuring and cheerful about Emma's placement. It was 5 A.M. Sarah had taken only a moment to admire her new cinnamon pink dress before hurrying down to the dining room to eat breakfast with Tom. The two had barely finished when they were summoned to Matron Baxter's office. When Sarah saw that Matron Baxter was absent and that only Clara Hurd was in the office, the warning that had sounded inside her the night before came back.

"Where's Emma?" Sarah demanded. "Where's our sister? I want to hold her on the train."

Clara Hurd looked from child to child and gripped the edge of Matron Baxter's desk to keep her hands from shaking. She had spent the night rehearsing what she would say, but standing before Sarah and Tom Biddle and seeing the desperation in their faces, Clara lost her resolve, forgot her speech, and blurted out in a miserable voice, "Matron Baxter has informed me that only yesterday Emma was placed in a fine home here in the city."

The impact of the words on Sarah was instant. Speechless, she clutched Tom. It seemed like hours before she was able to speak. When she found her voice, she fairly shouted at Clara, "I want her back. You git her back. We're not gittin' on the train without our sister."

Clara shook her head sadly. "Sarah, Tom, it's for the best. We can't take infants west. We don't have the facilities to care for them—"

"I said *I'd* take care of her," Sarah retorted.

"How could you, Sarah? How could you mix bottles, keep them clean, change diapers? You've got Tom to look out for, and he's only four. Caring for Tom *and* an infant would be too much."

"You're just makin' excuses."

Tom began to cry. Sarah's lower lip trembled, but she bit it hard, fighting back her own tears. Clara held both hands out to the children. "Sarah. Tom. Matron Baxter said that a wealthy young couple came yesterday. When they saw Emma, they covered her with kisses. They instantly fell in love with her. They can't have children of their own—"

Tom interrupted. "They could have took me and Sarah, too. We'd be good. Then they'd have three children."

"And a wonderful three they would have had too." Clara's eyes pleaded with Sarah as she continued. "And Matron Baxter tried to convince them. But they wanted a baby—and only one child. You wouldn't have wanted us to deny Emma a home with such wonderful people, would you?"

Sarah pondered the question. "They *kissed* her?"

Mrs. Hurd nodded. "They said Emma looked just like the baby they had lost."

"They're rich?"

"Mrs. Baxter said they had a carriage as fine as any she'd seen. She said they are well known. Such wealthy families usually go through other channels when they want to adopt, but for some reason they came to us. Perhaps it was God's miraculous way of providing for Emma. Perhaps He knew she needed to stay here in New York." Seeing doubt in Sarah's eyes, Mrs. Hurd returned to her original theme. "Mrs. Baxter knew the minute she heard the couple's name that they could give baby Emma a fine home."

Sarah thought the information over. She had learned over the months at the Society to deal with realities that no child should ever have to face. But this reality was new. For the first time in her life, she had been told that she was not wanted. The information thrust pain into a part of her that had never been hurt before. With a little cry, she sank into the chair opposite Mrs. Hurd. She pulled Tom into her lap and clung to him, pondering Emma's absence from her life. She saw her father's name as it had appeared in *Surrender Book Number Eight*. In her mind, she wrote her own name under it. Across from her name, she wrote *Emma Biddle*.

Moments passed. Clara Hurd walked around the massive desk that separated her from the children, knelt on the floor beside them, and reached out to embrace them.

Sarah looked at her sharply and hung on to Tom more tightly. "Guess it's just you and me now, Tom."

Tom murmured into her shoulder, "They gonna take me away, too, Sarah? You won't let them take me away, too, will you?"

A flash of bitterness crossed Sarah's face as she looked at Clara Hurd. "You're stayin' with me, Tom. I got you now, and I ain't never lettin' go of you. You stay with me and they can't take you away. We let Emma go. That's what caused it. I should have kept Emma with us." She looked at Clara Hurd accusingly as she continued. "I trusted them, Tom. But I know not to do that anymore."

Clara opened her mouth to say something, but Sarah stood up abruptly. Holding Tom's hand she walked to the door, opened it, and left without another word.

At the sound of the heavy door closing firmly, Clara Hurd buried her face in her hands and wept.

CHAPTER 3

Lavender Calico

"I will say unto God my rock,
Why hast thou forgotten me?"
Psalm 42:9

Clutching her suitcase in one hand and Tom in the other, Sarah Biddle marched resolutely onto the passenger train that would take them west. She and Tom were part of a group of seventeen children who would journey together under the care of two agents, Mr. W. B. Tice, and Mrs. Ophelia Granwich.

When Sarah first saw Mr. Tice, she thought she would never stop looking up. He was the tallest man she had ever seen. He spoke to the children gently, making a game of lifting the smaller ones up onto the train platform. When he saw Tom limping along, he reached for him, but Sarah half shouted, "I'll help him. He's my brother."

"So you're Sarah Biddle," Mr. Tice said quietly. Leaning down he said, "All right, then. You help Tom up and I'll take your luggage." Sarah grunted with the effort but managed to haul Tom up behind her. Once inside, she hurried Tom to the back of the train car where an empty seat would enable them to sit side by side.

Ophelia Granwich came onto the train car huffing and puffing with the exertion of managing her large frame. In a shrill voice she demanded quiet and then began explaining the details of the trip. "Now, children, we are on our way to the state of Nebraska. We will be on this train for three days and two nights before we stop to meet families who may want to adopt you. At each of these stops, there has been a local committee already working to find homes for you. In each city we will meet with prospective families—sometimes in churches, sometimes in courthouses. Mr. Tice and I will not leave you with anyone you don't want to be with. You must be honest with us if you feel uncomfortable about someone who wants to take you home."

A whistle blew and the train lurched ahead. Mrs. Granwich grabbed her hat with one hand and the edge of a seat with the other. A few children giggled at her sudden loss of dignity. While the train pulled ahead, Mrs. Granwich concluded her speech. "We will eat and sleep on the train. It is a long journey. Let's have no nonsense to make our time together unpleasant."

As the landscape outside their train car changed, Tom began asking questions about where they were going and what might happen to them. Sarah's inability to answer only increased his curiosity. The uncertainty of their future began to take its toll on her patience just as Mr. Tice leaned over the seat to peer out the window beside Tom. Mr. Tice laughed good-naturedly at Tom's questions and spent nearly an hour listening to and answering the youngster. Finally worn out, Tom leaned his head against the window until the rhythm of the rails lulled him to sleep and Sarah pulled him into her lap.

As the grime of the city gave way to rolling hills and meadows dotted with grazing cows, Sarah dared to think that perhaps a new life out west would be a good thing. She dozed for a while but woke with a start when the train lurched on a steep uphill grade. Looking out the window, she saw a newborn foal taking its first steps. Its spindly legs trembled and shook as the foal approached its mother and nuzzled to nurse. The sight reminded Sarah of Emma. She turned away from the window, stroking Tom's shank of blond hair and concentrating on breathing as smoothly as possible while she fought off tears.

Sarah's growling stomach woke Tom. He yawned sleepily and leaned against his sister's shoulder. Mrs. Granwich waddled to the back of the train car and had several children stand in the aisle while she covered their seat with a tablecloth. From a huge picnic basket she produced bread and red jelly. Just as she finished the last sandwich, the train came to a halt at a small station from which Mr. Tice was able to procure a jug of water. No second helpings were offered the hungry children. Instead, they disembarked the train for a brief walk through town escorted by Mr. Tice while Mrs. Granwich returned bread and jelly to the oversized basket.

As night fell the children nodded off. By morning they were less interested in the passing landscape. Mr. Tice introduced games to entertain them and encouraged them to walk whenever the train stopped. As they wandered along the streets of each new city, the older children soon realized that the townspeople watched them carefully and often whispered comments to one another as the children passed by.

At one stopover that lasted several hours, Mr. Tice organized a baseball game for boys while the girls walked along Main Street, peering in shopwindows at wonderful hats and dresses. Several of the girls were from Italian or German parents, and their thick accents filled the air with a chorus of admiring comments.

"I want a home where I can wear things like that," declared Milly Wats.

Ethel Tisdale was unimpressed. "Don't care much about the clothes," she countered. "But I'd be good for anybody who would buy me some of that candy."

Hettie Parson was older and more cynical. "I don't care what they buy me. If they hit me I won't stay."

"Mrs. Granwich said we don't have to stay with folks we don't like," Ethel reminded her.

Hettie tossed her head. "Mrs. Granwich just wants to get rid of us and get off that train. I heard her tell Mr. Tice that if she had to eat one more jelly sandwich she would just go hungry."

Milly giggled. "Do her good to go without a few meals, I'd say. But I'm sick of jelly and bread, too."

"I'll never eat jelly again as long as I live," agreed Ethel.

The girls made their way along the street, peering in shopwindows and whispering until a dumpy woman hustled out one door and barked, "You get away from my store and back on that train. We don't want your kind in here! Now, go on! Foreigners! Shoulda stayed where you belonged!"

With sheepish glances at one another, the girls skittered away. Sarah had stayed to watch Tom try to play ball with the other boys and Mr. Tice, but she saw the woman shake her finger at the girls and imagined what was being said. They hurried back to the train where Mrs. Granwich clucked and shook her head. "Might as well get used to it, girls. Not everyone cares about the children from the Society as much as we'd like. You'll meet all kinds. But in Nebraska, there will be good folks waiting for you. Now don't carry on like that, Milly. Brace up and get on the train. Next stop you girls had best stay near the train unless Mr. Tice or I can walk with you."

The ride west soon lost its glamorous appeal to even the most adventurous of the children. They ate bread and jelly at every meal, having milk to drink only once when they arrived at a station located near a small farm. Mr. Tice took two of the older boys with him and, with the help of the kindhearted farmer's wife, convinced the farmer to sell a churn full of fresh milk.

It was noon of the third day when Mrs. Granwich rose and announced that at the next stop the children would go into the train station, clean up, and don their change of clothes. "This evening we'll arive at the first stop where we'll meet people interested in adopting children. You will all want to look your best."

The very air in the train car felt tense as the children anticipated that first meeting. Sarah donned her new dress of lavender calico with shaking hands. Some thoughtful woman back in New York had included a wide matching ribbon, which Sarah decided to wrap around the brim of her hat. Coming out of the station in her new clothes, she met Tom, dressed in a little wool suit with a wide white collar and tie. He looked adorable, and Sarah felt a surge of love followed immediately by pain at Emma's absence. Tom limped toward Sarah; she bent down and hugged him fiercely.

When the train pulled into the station where they were to meet the first group of prospective families, the children were immediately silent. They filed off the train, following Mr. Tice and Mrs. Granwich down the street and through the doors of a whitewashed church.

Sarah paused at the door of the church to glance over the broadside that had been posted. Large letters proclaimed, WANTED: HOMES FOR CHILDREN. Mrs. Granwich called out from the front of the church, and Sarah hurried onto the stage.

"Folks will begin arriving to meet you soon. You must remember that they are looking for good children who will work hard. This is your opportunity to have a better life. Remember what it was like for you in New York. Remember and behave in such a way that you can earn a better life."

Next, Mr. Tice stood before them and said simply, "Remember, children, you are not to go with anyone you do not like. There will be other cities, other families, and you do not have to stay here if you do not wish to."

The children had been arranged on the stage of the church in two rows. Sarah stood behind Tom, her hand on his shoulder. As Mr. Tice looked into each young face, Sarah thought that he seemed to be fighting back tears. Suddenly, he bowed his head, and without any warning began to pray. "Dear Father in Heaven, You have promised to be Father to the fatherless. You have said that the orphan and the stranger are especially dear to You. Hear us as we pray for these children. Bring them into homes where they will be loved. Bring them into homes where they will learn of You." Mr. Tice's voice broke. He cleared his throat and ended the prayer quickly. "These things we ask of You, our God, in the name of Your Son, our Savior, Jesus Christ. Amen."

Sarah looked up from the prayer to see that folks had begun filing quietly into the church. She felt a moment of panic as she surveyed the group of strangers. Just then Mr. Tice caught her eye. He smiled and nodded encouragement. Sarah leaned over and whispered to Tom, "Don't be scared, Tom. We'll go together or we won't go. And Mr. Tice said we don't have to go with nobody we don't like."

What followed was a ritual that Tom and Sarah would witness many times. The head of the local committee rose and made a speech. No matter the town, the speech always included reference to "Christian charity," "responsibility to provide for the children," and "providing religious training." Following the speech, during which the children looked over the crowd that was inspecting them, Mrs. Granwich rose and read the handbill.

"We have brought you children of various ages and of both sexes, having been thrown friendless upon the world. They come under the auspices of the Children's Aid Society of New York. They are well disciplined. The citizens of this community are asked to assist the agent in finding good homes for them. Persons taking these children must be recommended by the local committee. They must treat the children in every way as a member of the family, sending them to school, church, and Sabbath school and properly clothing them until they are seventeen years old. Your applications must have been completed and endorsed by the local committee and should be presented to either Mr. Tice or myself before you converse with the children. Distribution will take place only after you have presented the appropriate papers. If you take a child home with you this evening, be advised that the children have been assured they do not have to stay if they do not wish to. They may return to the train station of their own free will any time before the train departs at ten o'clock tomorrow morning. Families accepting a child into their home will be visited within the next month by a Visiting Agent, at which time unsatisfactory situations will be ameliorated. Children are encouraged to correspond with the Society regularly about their new situation. It is expected that their new families will assist them in this duty."

Sarah tried to listen to Mrs. Granwich while she kept Mr. Tice in view out of the corner of her eye. She finally gave up trying to listen and stared openly at the crowd. A knot grew in her stomach as her gaze went from face to face. There was an older couple who looked kind. Sarah saw the woman point—was it at Milly?—and whisper something to her husband. He nodded and patted his wife's hand. A young couple with five young boys in tow sat in the front row. The woman looked stern. She eyed Sarah carefully. Sarah wondered at the number of lone men strung out across the back of the room. One of them in filthy overalls leaned against the wall chewing tobacco. During Mrs. Granwich's speech he put his head out an open window and spit a stream of tobacco juice.

Sarah felt a moment of panic when Mrs. Granwich stopped speaking and the stern-faced woman on the first row approached her. Her husband stayed back with the boys gathered around him.

The woman reached past Tom and grabbed Sarah's arm. "Are you healthy, dear? Do you know how to care for children?"

Sarah nodded and somehow found her voice. Out of the corner of her eye she noticed with longing that the older couple had taken Milly by the hand and led her to the front pew where they talked in low tones. Milly was smiling and nodding happily.

"Yes, ma'am. I cared for my brother, Tom, here. And my baby sister, Emma."

The woman looked at Tom. "Well, we don't need any more boys . . . but if you'll come and help me with my own boys, we'll give you a home."

Sarah shook her head. "Tom and me stay together."

The woman looked down at Tom doubtfully. He smiled at her, and she looked back at the group of boys flocked around their father. "Well, suppose you go over there and talk to my husband, young Tom. We'll see what we can work out."

Tom climbed down from the stage awkwardly and limped over to the stranger. The woman frowned and turned back to Sarah. "Your brother's leg—"

"He got run over by a wagon. His leg never healed right."

The woman shook her head. "I can't care for a crippled boy—"

"Then you don't want us." Sarah said it with relief. The woman backed away with an expression of disgust and moved on to Hettie.

Hettie looked at the woman with a touch of defiance and blurted out, "I ain't afraid to work hard, ma'am. But you hit me and I won't stay."

The woman smiled. "Of course I won't hit you. I need help with my boys, that's all. You work hard and we'll treat you fair."

Hettie stood down from the platform. "Then I'll try you out."

Sarah smiled to herself as Hettie strode out of the church behind her new family, pondering the surprises in store for the woman if she tried to push Hettie too far.

Milly was going, too. Sarah watched as she left, not sure who was happier, the gentleman and the lady who held the child by each hand or Millie skipping along between them.

The youngest of the group, a three-year-old boy, fairly threw himself into the arms of a middle-aged woman who bent to talk to him. When they started out the door he turned to yell for his "brubbers," but the boys had been parceled out to different families. Their new "parents" assured Mrs. Granwich that they would keep the boys in touch with one another. Sarah again thought of Emma and looked away.

It took only a short time for children to be selected and the meeting to conclude. Making their way back to the train, the "unchosen" were silent. They shuffled along wearily, wordless, wondering. As soon as they had boarded the train, Mr. Tice spoke up. "Those of you who will travel with us a bit longer, take heart. The Lord has homes for each of you. He always gives His best. Remember that the perfect home for you was not in this town, and that is why you were not selected tonight. Take heart, children. Rest well, confident in God's love."

With Tom nestled against her, Sarah took solace in Mr. Tice's words. Perhaps he was right—the best home for them lay ahead. That was why they had not been selected.

Just as the train pulled out the next morning, Hettie came running, pulled herself up onto the car platform, and burst through the door declaring to Mrs. Granwich, "I may have 'bad blood,' Mrs. Granwich, but I'll not be a slave to a sour-faced old thing like that Mrs. Bridges. I told her if she hit me I wouldn't stay. Well, she didn't hit me—but she tried. I took that wooden spoon out of her hand and threw it in the fire." With that, Hettie plopped herself in a seat and burst into tears.

Five towns later, Mr. Tice's words of comfort to The Unchosen had worn thin. Time after time, women and men approached Sarah, seemed interested in giving her a home—until Tom. When she insisted on keeping her brother with her, when they saw Tom's crippled leg, they moved on to other children.

Once an old man chewing tobacco, his mouth all stained brown, asked Sarah to open her mouth and then pushed his dirty finger in to check her teeth. Sarah wanted to bite him, but she resisted. The taste of dirt and tobacco in her mouth made her sick. As soon as the man walked away from her, she pulled Tom after her and went to Mr. Tice, fighting back tears. Mr. Tice patted her shoulder and had her sit next to him.

At another stop, a farmer came up to her to feel her muscles. "You'd make a good hand in the kitchen."

Tom blurted out, "You smell bad. We don't want to go with you."

He took Tom by the arm. Tom struggled.

"You let go of my brother!" Sarah almost shouted, kicking him. The scene labeled them both "incorrigible." No one else came to talk with them.

At the second to the last stop, Hettie found a home. A tall, stern-looking woman approached her. "I'm Isabella Gardner. I teach school here in Schuyler." There was a challenge in her voice as she continued. "Do you think you could be happy with a spinster schoolteacher, young lady?"

Hettie looked her over. Being happy wasn't a concept the girl had contemplated very much.

Isabella misread Hettie's hesitancy. Stepping closer, she bent down. She looked about her before saying quietly, "If you come to live with me, I shall buy you a pony. I shall teach you to read and cipher."

Hettie offered, "I been working in the kitchen at the Society. I cook good."

Isabella stood up stright, looking down her rather long nose. She adjusted her glasses before answering. "Cooking is not something we will have to concern ourselves with, child. I cook perfectly adequately. I am not looking for a servant. Lacking a husband, and lacking any prospects, I have concluded that I shall never have a family in the normally accepted manner. Hence, when I read the handbill I came to see what was available."

Hettie stared up into Isabella's face for a long time. The woman did not gaze away, and whatever Hettie saw there satisfied her. She dropped her guard long enough to say wistfully, "I'd like a pony."

"A pony . . . and perhaps a kitten would be good as well," Isabella added.

At the mention of the kitten, the woman won Hettie over. She reached out to take Isabella's hand. Isabella looked surprised. She cleared her throat nervously. But then something happened inside that broke through the impersonal shell she had constructed about her maidenhood. Looking down at Hettie, Isabella smiled. She seemed to be fighting back tears as she whispered just loudly enough for Sarah to hear, "You may call me Bessie."

Sarah waved good-bye to Hettie, happy for her friend. But in seconds her happiness was replaced by overwhelming sadness and despair. Now there were only five Unchosen. *What if no one takes Tom and me? What if we have to go back?* Sarah didn't think she could bear another train ride and another series of rejections. Mr. Tice said the Lord had the best waiting, but perhaps Mr. Tice was wrong. Perhaps the Lord did not really concern Himself with orphans. What if no one wanted them at the last stop? What if no one wanted them *ever*?

It happened. At the last stop a small group came, looked them over, and selected three of the five remaining children. But no one wanted Sarah and Tom. Walking back to the train, Sarah pulled her hand away from Mr. Tice's. Mrs. Granwich walked behind them, her lips pursed in consternation. The trip she had planned to see her brother in Denver was now impossible. She would have to help Mr. Tice escort The Unchosen back to New York.

Miserable and tired, Sarah helped Tom struggle aboard the train. She plopped herself in the seat, fighting back angry tears. When Mr. Tice settled opposite them, she looked up only briefly. He opened his mouth to offer encouragement, but shut it again when Sarah closed her eyes and leaned back in her seat. Just before she fell asleep, Sarah felt along the edge of the bench to where Tom sat. She collected the corner of his jacket in her hand and held on. Even when she finally dozed off, her hand stayed in position, ready to grab hold.

CHAPTER 4

Turkey Red

----

*"Use hospitality one to another
without grudging."*
1 Peter 4:9

Sarah dozed fitfully as the train chugged east. Each stop where children had been taken into homes seemed more difficult to face than the last. In an attempt to comfort The Unchosen, Mr. Tice bought a fancy meal in a hotel during a stopover. Yet the ache in Sarah's heart did not go away. The dress she had worn for several days began to itch. Every few moments she drew a long, deep breath, trying to get her midsection to relax.

Tom sensed Sarah's mounting tension. He walked up and down the aisle of the train, out onto the platform, back to sit by Sarah in a nervous dance that ended only when Mrs. Granwich grabbed him by both shoulders, pushed him into his seat, and ordered him to stay put.

Sarah lashed out at her. "You leave him alone. He didn't do nothin' to you. He's just tired. Sick and tired of this train. Sick and tired of being paraded up in front of a bunch of strangers. Sick and tired of *everything*."

Mrs. Granwich and Mr. Tice exchanged glances but said nothing.

Sarah hugged Tom to her and turned to look out the window. The landscape outside was flat and uninteresting.

No trees dotted the countryside. She muttered, "Why would anybody want to live in this place anyways? It's ugly. Not like the green hills back ho—" The word *home* caught in her throat. *I don't have any home.*

By the time the train stopped again, Sarah had made up her mind: she and Tom had ridden their last train, had been rejected for the last time. Mr. Tice was not feeling well and stayed on the train. Sarah looked innocently at Mrs. Granwich. "Tom might be able to settle down a little if we could walk a bit, Mrs. Granwich."

"Come along then." Mrs. Granwich hurried them down the aisle of the train. Descending to the platform, she reached up for Tom, surprised when Sarah handed him down. The instant Sarah's feet touched the platform, she grabbed Tom from Mrs. Granwich's arms, shot into the train station, and headed toward the main street of town.

Mrs. Granwich forced her considerable weight to hurry after the fleeing girl, calling out, "Stop her! Stop her! Help! Sarah Biddle, you come back here at once!"

They caused quite a scene in Lincoln, Nebraska—a young woman dressed in lavender, a child in her arms, running for all she was worth from a portly matron who chugged after them screeching at the top of her lungs.

Sarah rounded a corner and nearly bowled over an old woman coming out of an office. Ahead of her she saw her way of escape. A huge, ancient barn identified itself as the town livery in faded letters over the doorway. Sarah plunged through the opening, nearly falling over a bale of hay. Squinting in the half-light, she saw a ladder at the far end of the livery's wide center aisle.

"This way, Tom, come on—*hurry!*" They scampered past mostly empty stalls to the ladder.

"I can't carry you up, Tom, you got to climb—fast!" Sarah urged.

Tom pulled himself up the ladder with Sarah right behind him. The hem of her lavender dress had just disappeared into the loft when Mrs. Granwich lumbered by the livery door calling for the police. Sarah pulled Tom to the far corner of the loft and then stacked up bales of hay, leaving just enough space for the two of them to squeeze between the wall of hay and the wall of the barn.

Peering through a hole in one of the boards, Sarah looked down to the yard below. Two wagons and a fine carriage were parked under a long shed just across from the livery. A white-haired black man was carefully shining the front panel of the carriage. Beyond the shed someone had erected a series of clotheslines, which were laden with what appeared to be dozens of linen towels. Mrs. Granwich, accompanied by someone Sarah assumed to be a police officer, approached the black man. Sarah saw him shake his head back and forth. Mrs. Granwich motioned toward the train station and the man nodded. Sarah sat back, her heart pounding, and clutched Tom to her.

It seemed like hours before Tom and Sarah finally heard the train whistle its departure. Tom's stomach growled. He mouthed *I'm hungry* at his sister and rubbed his stomach. Sarah nodded and leaned over and whispered, "You stay here. I'll see what I can figure out. Just stay put."

Sarah climbed out from behind the bales of hay at the same moment that Joseph Freeman left off shining the carriage and walked through the livery to close the front door. He heard rustling overhead and saw bits of hay filter through the cracks in the loft floor. He closed the livery door, ran to the back of the barn, and shot up the ladder of the loft. As he reached the top, a flash of lavender disappeared behind a stack of hay bales against the far wall.

"Well, I'll be—didn't know those stable rats could stack hay so good. Seems I remember just tossin' them bales up here ever' which way." Joseph bent over to pick up a pitchfork. He addressed the wall of hay bales. "Now, you listen. My name's Joseph Freeman. I own this here livery—along with Miz Augusta Hathaway. Don't take to folks sneakin' around my horses. You might as well come out, 'cause there's only one way outta this here loft, and I'm not leavin' without whoever is behind those bales."

Sarah peeked over the wall. Her heart lurched as she surveyed the massive forearm holding the pitchfork. She ducked back down behind her wall of hay. She was about to give up, but then Tom whimpered. Reminded of her role as Tom's protector, Sarah retorted, "We'll *starve* then, 'cause we ain't comin' out to be sent back to New York!"

"Yeah, we ain't comin' out!" Tom repeated, trying to sound as adult as possible.

Sarah peered between two bales of hay and watched the man. Tossing the pitchfork aside, he sat on a lone hay bale near the ladder. Scratching the back of his neck, he wondered aloud. "There an echo in here?" After a long moment of silence, the man stood up and stretched, arching his back and sighing. "Well, I was just fixin' to head over to Hathaway House for supper. They fixin' fried chicken tonight. Heaps of it. Mashed potatoes too. And pie. *Oo-ee* that Miz King, she makes good pie! Too bad you two visitors can't come and have some."

Sarah was defiant. "Miss King ain't givin' away free meals, is she? We got no money, so we ain't gittin' no fried chicken. 'Sides, 'Granny Grump' Granwich is probably just waitin' outside with the police to haul us off." Sarah hunkered down next to Tom, fighting back tears of frustration and hunger. Visions of fried chicken, mashed potatoes, and pie were almost too much to bear.

The man answered back, his voice big but gentle. "Well, the way I heard tell it was that Miz Ophelia Granwich left word with the police that if one Sarah Biddle and her brother, Tom, was found, they was to be returned to New York on the next train. Said if somebody wanted Sarah and Tom, somethin' called 'The Lincoln Committee' could take care of it. Left train fare with the police. Said she had to get back to some feller on the train who was feelin' poorly."

Sarah answered bitterly, "Ain't nobody wanted us yet."

"Well now, this Miz King I was talking about—the one what makes the good pie—she and Miz Hathaway run the hotel here, and I jus' happen to know they been needin' help. If a person was to work for them, they'd get good meals, I know that."

"Ain't no Miss King gonna want us. My brother's crippled. He can't work hard. Nobody wants us *both*—and I ain't leavin' Tom. I *ain't!*"

The desperation in the young voice sounded a note with Joseph. He had worked very hard to forget that sound, but Sarah's voice brought it back to him—his own children screaming for someone to help them as their new master hauled them off the auction block and away to another plantation.

Joseph wiped his hand over his face to clear his mind. His voice was gentle and convincing as he said, "Well, look at it this way, then. Train don't come back 'til tomorrow. You got to spend the night here anyway. And Lincoln has this rule. The first night in town, every visitor gets a free meal at Hathaway House. The city pays for it. It's a way to get folks to stay on and try us out. So, since you two got to spend the night, how about you come down out of this loft and go over to the hotel with me? Could be you'll like it. Could be Miz King and Miz Hathaway will like you."

Just when Joseph had despaired of a way to win the trust of the two youngsters, they stepped out from behind their wall of hay. Sarah clutched Tom's hand. Joseph started down the ladder. "Here, Miz Biddle—hand your brother to me—I'll help him—"

"No!" Sarah said adamantly. "You stay back. I'll do it."

Joseph backed down the ladder and kept his distance while Sarah struggled to help her brother down the ladder. As they descended, Joseph noticed the deep scar that began at the boy's ankle and ran up as far as he could see.

He led the children toward the back of the livery, across the yard, past the lines where the linen towels still hung, and in the back door of the hotel.

They stepped into the kitchen and were immediately surrounded by aromas—frying chicken, boiling potatoes, thickening gravy, baking apples—so wonderful that Sarah felt weak. Tom gripped her hand tightly and stared about him with the wonder of a child seeing his first Christmas tree ablaze with candles.

Two women were there. One about the size of Mrs. Granwich surveyed the children carefully, looking pointedly at her redheaded partner but saying nothing. The second woman was frying chicken in great iron pans atop a wood-burning stove. As she looked at Tom and Sarah, her face seemed to light up with friendliness. She wiped her hands on her apron and absentmindedly pushed at the tufts of curly red hair that had escaped her hairdo to fringe her face. She didn't say anything; she just stood quietly, smiling at the children as Joseph spoke.

"Miz Hathaway, Miz King, this here is Sarah Biddle and her brother, Tom. They's just visitin' Lincoln . . . come off the train. I told 'em about the free meal we offer every newcomer. I remembered to tell 'em it's only *one* free meal. Since they don't know if they'll be stayin' in town, or not, they came to get their free meal tonight."

Augusta Hathaway winked at her friend Jesse King. "Why, of course, Joseph. That'll be just fine." Turning to Sarah, she said politely, "Would you two like to wash up before supper?"

Sarah nodded.

The woman with the red hair and the beautiful smile finally spoke. Her voice was gentle. "I am Mrs. Jesse King. Please, come this way."

Sarah followed Mrs. King down a narrow hall and to the doorway of the most beautiful room she had ever seen. In the room there was a bed and a small table with a pitcher and bowl. Clean linen towels hung on a rung above the pitcher. But the bed was what astounded Sarah. The mattress was up off the floor, and at each corner of the mattress there was beautiful wood, like the spindles on a staircase, that reached up and up until they nearly touched the ceiling of the room. They didn't *do* anything—they just stood at the corners of the mattress being beautiful. And on the bed there was a red and white quilt. It looked new. And there were pillows, big, plump pillows with red and white covers over them.

"This used to be my daughter's room," Mrs. King explained. "But LisBeth is married now." She sighed. "Her husband, MacKenzie, is in the cavalry. They are together out west somewhere." As she talked, Mrs. King poured water from the pitcher into a huge bowl.

Sarah let go of Tom's hand, and he reached out to touch the quilt on the bed. "Don't touch it, Tom. You might get it dirty."

Mrs. King's smile lit up the room. "Oh, it's all right, dear. My quilts are made to be used. I do hope you'll see fit to stay with us tonight. That one's my Turkey Red, and it hasn't been properly broken in yet. A quilt's not a quilt until someone has slept under it." Jesse made her way to the door. "Supper's ready whenever you are, children. Just come to the kitchen."

She left the children alone. Sarah tried to guard herself from a feeling of hope, but Tom was exuberant. He climbed onto the bed and bounced happily. "I like it here!"

Sarah scrubbed herself and Tom, wetting her hands and trying to push Tom's stubborn hair into place. Tom looked past his sister to the dresser across the room. "There's a comb, Sarah."

Sarah shook her head. "It don't belong to us, Tom."

"Aren't we stayin', Sarah?"

She shook her head. "Don't think so, Tom. Just eatin' the free meal. If we help Mr. Freeman feed his horses tonight, he'll probably let us sleep in the loft. Then we'll go to the police and get the train tickets."

Tom whimpered, "I don't want to go back on the train, Sarah. I hate trains!"

"I hate trains, too, Tom. But we got no choice." Miserable, she snapped, "Quit whinin', Tom. We're gittin' a decent meal. That's enough. Let's go eat!"

Back in the kitchen, Sarah tried and failed to evidence the manners she had been taught in the Society dining room back in New York. Taking a small bite of chicken, she soon found herself eating ravenously. Between gargantuan bites of chicken, Tom talked enough for both of them. He directed his chatter to Joseph while Mrs. King and Mrs. Hathaway busied themselves going back and forth between the kitchen and the adjoining dining room. "Them two ladies own this hotel? Are they nice? How come those people out there don't eat all their food?"

Sarah concentrated on her meal, letting Tom prattle on. "You folks eat like this every night? When's the train come tomorrow? If we help you feed your horses tonight, would you let us sleep in your loft? We'd like to stay here. You folks eat good!"

When at last they had eaten their fill, the two children sat at the table growing sleepier by the minute. Sarah knew she should force herself to offer to help the two women as they washed dishes, but such a great weariness had settled over her that she simply could not make the effort.

Mrs. King noticed Tom's nodding head. "Miss Biddle, you're welcome to stay in the room you saw—"

Sarah shook her head. "Can't. We got no money." She turned to Joseph. "Tom here's too tired, but if I help you feed and water the horses in that livery, could we maybe sleep up in the loft?"

At Joseph's questioning look, Mrs. Hathaway spoke up. "Well now, Miss Biddle, as a matter of fact, I am a partner with Mr. Freeman in that livery. And if you would want to help him feed and water those horses, I'd say you certainly would earn a night here in the hotel—as long as you don't mind the room down the hall. The rest of the rooms are all filled up tonight."

Tired as she was, Sarah hopped up. "Be glad to. Come on, Tom."

Tom jerked himself awake. "It's all right, Miss Biddle," Mrs. King said. "Tom can stay here with us. He can go right to bed."

Sarah clutched at her brother. "No! Tom stays with me!"

The two women exchanged glances with Joseph. Mrs. King spoke up. "Well, what if you put him to bed yourself? Then you can help Mr. Freeman."

Sarah considered. "In there?" She pointed down the hall.

"Yes."

"And you won't take him nowhere while I'm gone?"

Mrs. King knelt down by Tom. Looking up at Sarah she said, "You're a very good sister to care so much for Tom, Miss Biddle. You take him in and put him to bed under that quilt of mine. I'll give him this bell to ring if anyone bothers him. The window of that room is just a few feet from the back door of the livery. Joseph can leave the door open, and if anyone bothers Tom, you'll know."

Somehow this woman understood Sarah's desperate need to be certain that no one was going to take Tom away from her. Sarah felt something inside let go—not enough to let her cry all the tears she'd been storing up over the last year, but enough for her to feel that perhaps, just perhaps, there were people in the world you could trust, after all.

When a ray of sunlight fell across Sarah's face early the next morning, she sat up abruptly, looking about her in amazement before she remembered where she was. Then she sank back onto her pillow, pulling the bedcovers to her face and inhaling their freshness. *Heaven must smell just like this.* She looked at Tom asleep next to her. *I wonder if Emma has a room this nice. . . .*

Someone had washed and pressed their clothing and laid it at the foot of the bed. Sarah slipped on her lavender dress, noting that a missing button had been replaced. A tear in Tom's jacket had been mended. Just as she was wondering if it would be all right to use the brush on the dresser, Mrs. King appeared at the door.

"Good morning, Miss Biddle. When you're ready, Mrs. Hathaway and I would like to speak with you in the kitchen. The train doesn't come through for another two hours, so take your time—" She turned to go before adding casually, "And of course you may use the dresser set. You have lovely blonde hair. Take all the time you need."

Sarah left Tom snoring softly and went to the kitchen. As soon as she entered, Mrs. King made a proposal too marvelous for Sarah to believe.

"Mrs. Hathaway and I own this hotel together, Sarah— may I call you Sarah? Until recently, my daughter lived here. But she's married now. With her gone, Augusta and I need help. Cooking, cleaning, gardening—running a hotel is a lot of work, and we're both too old to keep up like we should." Mrs. King hurried ahead. "Now, mind you, we're not looking for someone to work to death. We may have to get more than one person to work, but if you—"

Sarah had begun to feel hopeful again, but at the mention of a need for more than one worker, the hope vanished. She interrupted. "Tom's crippled. He can't work much."

"Oh, we'd never expect a little boy to work. We'll hire someone else to help if need be. We thought you might want Tom to go to school. We have a good teacher here in Lincoln."

Sarah looked suspicious. Mrs. King set down the glass she had been drying. "Sarah, when I was very young, I lost a little boy about Tom's age. His name was Jacob. He fell under the wheels of a wagon." She closed her eyes a moment before continuing. "It occurred to me last night that if you and Tom would stay with us, it would be like God giving me another chance to have a little boy."

Sarah's eyes widened with amazement. "Tom got runned over by a wagon too. Only he didn't die. It hurt his leg real bad. He ain't walked right since."

Mrs. King blinked back tears. Augusta Hathaway spoke. "Sarah, I'm not so gentle talking as Jesse. But, fact is I'd like to have you too. You and Tom."

Sarah surveyed the kitchen. She looked wistfully down the hall. "Can we stay in that room back there?"

"Of course."

"Will you leave the bed in it—and the quilts and things?"

Mrs. King fought back a smile. "Of course, Sarah. It would be *your* bed. Your room and Tom's. We could ask Joseph to build a trundle to slide underneath for Tom. That way you could each have your own bed."

And so, early in 1876, at the age of fourteen, Sarah Biddle came to realize that what Mr. Tice had said was true, after all. She and Tom had not been chosen from the orphan train for a *good* home because God had the *best* home waiting somewhere else. It was not in New York, or in Omaha, or in Schuyler. It was not with a couple or a family. It was in Lincoln, Nebraska, at a hotel owned by two old women. It was the best place for them because the two women opened more than just their home to the orphans. They opened their hearts.

CHAPTER 5

Saffron Yellow

"Suffer the little children to come unto me."
Mark 10:14b

"Emma!" Sarah screamed. "Emma!" She bounded out of the bed onto the cold floor, bumping into Tom's trundle bed as she blindly groped for the door. In the thick darkness she stumbled and fell against the door. Her heart pounding wildly, she pulled open the door and felt along the hallway toward the dim glow in the distance. She must get to Emma—she must—

Sarah stood at the end of the hallway staring into the dimly lit kitchen. She looked about her stupidly, rubbing her eyes.

Jesse King sat with her back to Sarah. A huge quilting frame had been lowered from the ceiling, and Jesse was so intent upon her stitching that for a moment she was unaware of Sarah's presence. The quilt was composed of long strips that ran from top to bottom. One row was pieced with large triangles that Jesse had called "Flying Geese." Each row of "geese" was separated by a long strip of saffron yellow. In the dim light of the kitchen, the saffron yellow fabric glowed with warmth.

Sarah took a deep breath, looking around the kitchen to reassure herself that Emma's crying had, indeed, been part of another dream.

At the sound of Sarah's sigh, Jesse started. She turned in her chair and held out her hand. "Come over here, dear. Have you had another dream?"

Sarah nodded and crossed the room, where she accepted Jesse's offered hand and sank into a chair beside her.

"I wish you could tell me about it, Sarah," Jesse urged. "Sometimes, if you can only put the dream into words, it goes away." At Sarah's doubtful look Jesse nodded. "I know it seems impossible, but sometimes it works. Can't you tell me about it, Sarah?"

It had been several weeks since the morning Sarah and Tom Biddle had come to live at the hotel. Tom had accepted his new home easily. Augusta Hathaway had enrolled him at Miss Griswall's school, and he was proving himself a good student. He had taken to hugging both Augusta and Jesse every day when he came home from school; in fact, he had even begun to call the two women "Aunt." Sarah, however, was not so easily won.

Jesse's gentle voice brought Sarah back to the present. Jesse had turned back to her quilting, and she was careful not to look at Sarah as she said again, "There's no one here but us two, Sarah."

"Think I could learn to do that?" Sarah asked suddenly.

Jesse looked up, pleased. "Why, anyone can learn to quilt, dear. I'd love to teach you." Jesse reached for a needle, threaded it. "You just follow the line I've drawn on the fabric with the needle and thread. Let's put the needle in here." Jesse demonstrated. "Just slide the needle between the layers—you don't go all the way through. There. Then we bring the needle back up over here right on this line . . . and pull just hard enough to pull the knot between the two layers of our fabric sandwich." Jesse reached for an extra thimble before handing the needle to

Sarah. "Put this on your middle finger. Now you just push the tip of the needle against the top of the thimble, rocking back and forth, back and forth until you've collected a few stitches on the needle." Jesse demonstrated with her own needle and thread. "And then you pull it through to make a little row of stitches. That's all there is to it."

Sarah inspected the tiny stitches Jesse had just put into the quilt. Stabbing the needle into the fabric, she did her best to imitate Jesse, but whereas Jesse had collected six stitches onto her needle, Sarah could get only two. Sarah shook her head. "It don't look right."

Jesse nodded encouragement. "It looks fine, Sarah. It takes practice. If you're not too tired, you can sit up with me now and try for a little while. You'll be surprised at how quickly those stitches get smaller and more even." Jesse returned to her own stitching with a smile. "I can't sing or write, and I'm only an adequate cook. But I can quilt, and when I see something beautiful and know I made it—" She looked at Sarah. "You'll see what I mean."

Sarah persevered through the frustration of knotted thread and pricked fingers until she managed to do an entire row of stitches that she thought looked almost nice. Leaning back in her chair she yawned sleepily, but when Jesse didn't stop quilting, Sarah decided to try some more.

The two had quilted for nearly half an hour when Sarah blurted out, "It's Emma. I always dream about Emma." She looked sideways at Jesse. Jesse continued to quilt, but the tilt of her head told Sarah she was listening. "That's my baby sister." She corrected herself. "*Was* my baby sister." Sarah stopped quilting, took a deep breath, and recited the details of Emma's loss. At some point in the telling, Jesse King stopped quilting and gathered Sarah into her arms so that at the end of the story, Sarah was sobbing on Jesse's shoulder, being rocked in much the same manner that she had rocked Emma.

When Sarah's sobbing finally quieted, Jesse said softly, "Thank you for telling me about Emma. Let's pray for her right now." Before Sarah could say a word, Jesse was praying. "Lord, thank You that You know where Emma is right this minute. Thank You for showing us while You were here upon the earth that You love children, that You care about them. Help Sarah, Lord. She is feeling terribly guilty about letting Emma go. Help her to know that You care for her, and that You love Emma more than any human ever could. Give her the peace that passes understanding." Jesse paused for just a moment before adding, "Help me to know just how to help Sarah and Tom, Lord. Thank You for bringing them to us. Help them to believe and to know how much we love them. But most of all, Lord, help them to know You and Your eternal love."

Jesse finished praying, expecting Sarah to push away, to once again establish the distance between them that she had so carefully maintained for weeks. But Sarah didn't push away. Instead, she leaned her head on Jesse's shoulder as the older woman led her down the hall and tucked her into bed. She sighed happily after Jesse had bent down to kiss her on the cheek.

"Sleep well, Sarah," Jesse said from the doorway.

Sarah nodded sleepily. And she never again dreamed that Emma was screaming and she could not find her.

The morning after her first quilting lesson, Sarah lingered in bed long after 5 A.M., savoring a strange sense of contentment. "All I'm saying, Jesse," Augusta's voice sounded in the hall, "is you'll be ripping out stitches and working twice as hard."

As the two voices retreated down the hall toward the kitchen, Sarah bounded out of bed. She hurried to dress and entered the kitchen where Augusta and Jesse were already at work preparing breakfast for their boarders. Looking up at the quilt overhead, she sought out her stitches. Her heart fell. Over the entire surface of the quilt, Jesse's quilting created a beautiful design. But along one edge, Sarah's stitches were so long that barely any pattern at all was discernible.

Sarah turned to Jesse. "Aunt Jesse, you'll be wantin' to rip out those stitches of mine." She hung her head. "I don't want to ruin your quilt."

Jesse King looked up from where she stood kneading bread dough. "Whatever are you talking about, Sarah Biddle? I wouldn't rip out those stitches if it meant losing a thousand-dollar prize." Jesse punched the dough for emphasis. "Those stitches are going to be in that quilt long after I am gone, and I don't want to hear another word about it." She picked up the huge mound of dough and slapped it against the breadboard to push out any air bubbles. "But I do expect one thing," she said, smiling. "I expect you to get better. So I'll be setting up two chairs at the quilting frame tonight."

All through the spring of 1876 Jesse King and Sarah Biddle quilted while Tom studied. Augusta threaded needles for the quilters and corrected lessons for Tom. When letters arrived from Jesse's daughter, LisBeth, Augusta read them aloud. LisBeth took time to describe every aspect of the life of a military officer's wife. She made light of the hardships and praised her young husband with unbounded pride. LisBeth also spoke highly of MacKenzie's commanding officer, General George Custer.

Sarah wrote a letter to Mr. Tice of the Children's Aid Society:

> *I been working hard at the hotel. When Mrs. Hathaway learned I wanted to pay the Society back, she said I could make bread to sell in the general store down the street. Mrs. Hathaway checked with the local committee and they said it cost about fifteen dol-*

*lars to bring a child out here. So as soon as I have
thirty dollars, I will be sending it. I know I should be
telling you I am sorry for running away, but I ain't
sorry and I won't lie about it. Mrs. King and Mrs.
Hathaway sent Tom to school and they are good to
us. I'm glad I ran off. If Pa—Mason Biddle—ever
comes to ask about us, tell him we are in Lincoln,
Nebraska, at the Hathaway House Hotel and we are
doing good. I was mad at him for a while, but I guess
he didn't have no choice but to send us away or we
would of starved. He done the best he could. Thank
you for being so nice to Tom and me on the train.*

Any doubts that might have lurked in Sarah's mind
about her newfound home were laid to rest one day when
Tom came limping home from school. Stepping inside the
back door, he turned to set his schoolbooks on a stool,
cried out in pain, and nearly fell.

Augusta came running from the dining room. "What is
it, Tom? What is it?"

Sarah helped Tom up. "Must be going to rain, Aunt
Augusta. Tom's leg gits worse just before a storm."

Tom sat on a chair, grimacing and rubbing his leg.

Augusta didn't hesitate. She bustled to the back door.
"Jesse's over at the church sewing society. You stay with
Tom, Sarah. I'm going to get Dr. Gilbert."

Sarah looked at the bubbling kettles on the stove.
"But—what about supper for the boarders, Aunt
Augusta?"

"The boarders can wait if they have to. Tom's more
important." Augusta let the door slam behind her.

Sarah massaged her brother's leg. "Does it hurt awful,
Tom?"

The boy nodded and bit his lip.

"Did you fall and not tell me?"

Tom ducked his head, didn't answer.

"Tom Biddle," Sarah scolded, "you climbed that ladder over at the livery. And after I told you not to."

Tom nodded guiltily. "Well, the kittens are up in the loft. How was I going to see the kittens if I didn't climb the ladder?"

"I told you I'd help you get up the ladder. You just had to wait a little. But you couldn't wait, could you? You fell and didn't tell me," Sarah said accusingly.

Tom was repentant. "I'm sorry, Sarah. I should have waited. But you're always so busy."

"Oh, it's all right, Tom." Sarah's voice was gentle. "I just wish you didn't have to hurt, that's all."

"It's not so bad, now. Feels good, you rubbin' on it." Tom bit his lip again.

"You're tryin' to be brave, Tom, and I'm proud of you. But I know it hurts awful. Come on. I'll help you into the bed. Maybe if we prop it up with some pillows it'll feel better."

Tom limped down the hall to his trundle bed. He had just gotten settled when Sarah heard the kitchen door open.

Augusta's concerned voice filtered down the hallway. "He's gone to bed, poor thing."

Footsteps came briskly down the hall.

"Sarah," Augusta said from the doorway, "let's give Dr. Gilbert a chance to examine Tom. He's the best doctor for miles around."

Sarah looked up. Dr. Gilbert was standing in the doorway. In spite of the scorching heat, he was dressed in a dark suit and tie. He carried a rather large black leather bag and entered the room with a quiet authority that instantly put Sarah at ease.

He extended his hand and shook Sarah's hand solemnly. "What can you tell me about your brother's injury, Miss Biddle?"

Sarah shrugged. "It was when Tom was only about two. We used to play along the street sometimes. Tom tumbled into the street and got run over by a big carriage. He bled somethin' awful. Pa grabbed him up and ran to the hospital. They cleaned him up."

"Did he have a splint or a cast on his leg?"

Sarah shook her head. "No. They just sewed up the cut and wrapped it real tight. Said he shouldn't walk on it. Said if there was trouble to come back, they might have to cut it off."

Dr. Gilbert frowned. "And no doctor suggested a splint or a cast?" He looked at the ugly scar that ran down Tom's leg. "It appears someone has operated."

"Ma did that."

At the doctor's look of disbelief, Sarah repeated, "Ma did. Tom's leg puffed up. She said she wasn't sendin' her baby back to that hospital to have his leg cut off." Sarah hesitated. "She knew things. Plants and things to make it better. When it swelled up, she used a knife and cut it open. She washed it out and kept at it for a long time." Sarah's voice was apologetic. "I don't know exactly what she done, Dr. Gilbert, but she saved Tom's leg. We didn't take him back to the hospital and he kept his leg."

Dr. Gilbert whistled low in amazement. "I'd say Tom had the best nursing possible under the circumstances." While Sarah looked on, he completed his examination. "We're going to put some hot packs on your leg, Tom," he explained. "I think it will help the inflammation in the tissues, maybe relieve some of the pain. And—" He reached into his bag and pulled out a bottle. "I'll be leaving some of this with Mrs. Hathaway. When your leg hurts, you tell her and she'll mix you up something to help."

Dr. Gilbert patted Tom on the shoulder and headed for the hotel kitchen, motioning for Sarah to follow him. Once in the kitchen, he reported to Augusta. "It's a simple case of botched medicine, Mrs. Hathaway. Unfortunately,

I don't have the skill to repair the damage. It's a miracle he kept the leg at all. The bones have healed well—but orthopedically the leg is a mess. I'll wire back east for advice. Perhaps there's a specialist who can offer suggestions." Dr. Gilbert held up the bottle of powders. "In the meantime, when he's suffering, mix one teaspoon of this in a cup of tea and let the little fellow rest. I hate to curtail his activities, but he really must be kept from climbing. Another fall, another break, and he may not be so fortunate as to keep his leg."

Augusta looked at Sarah and shook her head. "We've both told him, Dr. Gilbert, but ladders and lofts are terrible temptations for little boys."

"Especially when there's a litter of kittens at the top of the ladder," Sarah added.

Augusta looked at Sarah. "Is that it? Is it the kittens that have him climbing ladders, then?" Augusta looked guiltily at Dr. Gilbert. "I told Tom that there'd be no cats hanging about my kitchen."

While Dr. Gilbert retreated down the hallway to talk to Tom about the dangers of ladder-climbing, Sarah and Augusta busied themselves with completing the evening meal for the boarders, who were beginning to complain about the lateness of dinner.

Sarah was so busy in the dining room that evening that she had no time to check back on Tom. When she finally did, what she saw brought tears to her eyes and swelled her heart with love for Augusta Hathaway. Tom lay sound asleep, his arm curled around a purring yellow kitten.

CHAPTER 6

White Linen

---

*"Charge them that are rich in this world, that
they be not highminded, nor trust in uncertain
riches, but in the living God, who giveth us richly
all things to enjoy; that they do good, that they be
rich in good works."*
1 Timothy 6:17–18

Aunt Jesse died less than a year after Sarah and Tom
arrived in Lincoln. Dr. Gilbert had warned her to slow
down, told her that her heart was weak and she needed
more rest. But Jesse King was not one to "coddle herself."
She had allowed Sarah and Tom and Augusta to wheedle
her into seeing the doctor. But she had ignored his instructions, managing to hide most of her "spells." She had continued to drive herself, working in the hotel kitchen long
hours each day, serving on various charitable committees
about town, and often stealing out long after dark to some
poor home in the growing city to provide secret assistance.

Sarah had sensed Jesse's growing concern for LisBeth
and MacKenzie Baird, so far to the west, so near the war-
ring tribes of Sioux. Mrs. King had combed every newspaper for information about where MacKenzie's company
might go next. Sarah believed it was shock that killed Aunt
Jesse. When news came of the Battle of the Little Big Horn,
horrific descriptions detailed the annihilation of an entire

company of men. MacKenzie's company. Jesse had listened as Augusta read the account in the newspaper, stumbling off to her own room to pray. She had died that very night. But Jesse had been granted just enough time with Sarah and Tom. Enough time for Sarah to begin to believe that God had, indeed, given His best when He kept them among The Unchosen on the orphan train. Enough for Sarah to see past Aunt Augusta's "prickles and quills" to the kindness and generosity she tried to hide. Enough for Tom to receive much needed therapy in the form of hugs and encouragement—and a yellow kitten.

Shortly after Aunt Jesse was laid to rest in Wyuka Cemetery, MacKenzie Baird's widow returned from the west. Learning that her mother had died only days before her return, LisBeth was overwhelmed with grief. Sarah followed Jesse's example of gentle love, and a friendship was born between LisBeth and her that made the few years' difference in their ages irrelevant.

Sarah's days were filled with growing responsibility. Augusta Hathaway soon realized she had taken in a capable and hardworking young woman. Delighted by the revelation, she began to teach Sarah every aspect of running a hotel. Soon, Sarah was managing the kitchen alone while Augusta served her boarders. When Augusta convinced a grieving LisBeth to accompany her to the great Centennial Exposition in Philadelphia, Sarah managed the hotel in their absence. Upon their return, she accepted Augusta's praise and her first salary, beaming with pride.

Sarah listened with interest to Augusta and LisBeth's tales of the Exposition, expressing special interest in the new inventions that might impact the hotel business. When Augusta spoke of expanding the hotel, Sarah began to hope that expansion meant more responsibility for her, more promise for Tom's future.

Seeing Sarah busily drawing at the kitchen table one evening, Augusta peered over her shoulder to see sketches of a hotel called "Biddle House." Sarah was embarrassed, but Augusta encouraged her. "I think it's wonderful. You *should* be ambitious about your future, Sarah. Most girls your age are dreaming nonsense about knights on white horses whisking them off to fairyland."

"Not me. I'm goin' to make a future for Tom and me. I'm an orphan, but I'm not stupid and I can work hard." With a little laugh, Sarah blushed. "I'm too thin, my mouth is too wide, my hair is too straight, and my eyes are too pale. LisBeth is the beautiful one. She'll get another white knight. I'll do much better to trust myself to take care of Tom and me. I don't think any white knight is goin' to be interested in me."

"Sarah, you'll do much better in life with a practical outlook like that," Augusta answered honestly. "Now if only I can get LisBeth grounded in sensible plans like you, I'll be happy. No woman should build her life waiting for a man to come along and save her. It's a tragic waste of brains and talent."

Sarah nodded her agreement. She went back to sketching her future hotel, humming to herself to shut out the faint glimmer of feeling that threatened to ruin her resolve for her future. *A home and a family just aren't going to happen for you, Sarah Biddle. Face it. You're not the same as everybody else. What man is going to come around wanting you? Not a one. You work hard and take care of Tom and don't let any foolish notion of romance get in the way.*

Besides, there was hardly anyone to give rise to such notions. Sarah's life revolved around the hotel kitchen, her brother, Tom, and weekly attendance at Aunt Augusta's church. Except for the cursory nods she received from passersby and an occasional visit from Jim Callaway, whom LisBeth had hired to work MacKenzie's family farm just south of Lincoln, no young men crossed Sarah's path. She convinced herself that she was content the way things were. As the weeks went by, however, Sarah developed a distinct liking for Jim Callaway. His frequent trips to Lincoln to buy supplies and to report to LisBeth—not to mention the fact that he was quite handsome—had caught Sarah's eye. But though he was always polite to Sarah, Jim remained distant.

As Sarah suspected, LisBeth's prospects for romance were a little better. One day when Sarah was sorting mail, she noticed a letter postmarked from Philadelphia addressed to *Mrs. LisBeth King Baird.* Sarah recognized the handwriting. Several such letters had come to LisBeth since she and Augusta had attended the Exposition. When LisBeth opened the letter, she blushed. "Aunt Augusta," she announced, "Mr. Braddock and his mother are planning a visit to Lincoln." Something in LisBeth's voice made Sarah suspect that Mr. Braddock was more than a casual acquaintance.

Deep snows and bitter cold during the winter of 1876 resulted in fewer hotel guests and less labor for the three women. They gathered each evening in the hotel kitchen, in which one corner had been set up to resemble a parlor. One evening when a fresh snowstorm began to rage against the kitchen door, Augusta sighed and leaned back in her rocker, glancing up toward the bare beams over the dining table. With an exclamation, she went to a pulley in the corner and lowered Jesse's quilting frame.

"For weeks I didn't have the heart to even look at it, and then I forgot about it. I bet Jesse's been wondering just how long we were going to let her quilt languish up there in the rafters." Augusta fought back tears as she winked at LisBeth. "I bet she's finished at least a dozen quilts up in glory."

Looking up toward heaven, Aunt Augusta said, "I'm sorry, Jesse. I didn't mean to forget about it. But you know me, old girl. I'm not much when it comes to handwork!"

LisBeth pulled away a dust-covered protective sheet to reveal an elaborate green and red appliqué quilt. Her mother's fine stitches covered only about a third of the surface. LisBeth murmured, "It's the same colors as the 'Princess Feather' Mama made for me and Mac."

Augusta cleared her throat before explaining, "She called it the 'Whig Rose,' LisBeth." Looking across the quilt at Sarah, who was running one hand lovingly over its surface, Augusta added, "Jesse said it was going to be for Sarah's hope chest."

Sarah looked up, wide-eyed. Then she tucked her chin to her chest and said with wonder, "For me? Oh, I never dreamed—"

LisBeth reminisced, "Mama helped me make a little nine-patch quilt when I was a child. I can still hear her saying, 'Fifteen stitches to the inch, LisBeth. That's the goal. When you can do fifteen, then you're a good quilter.'" LisBeth paused before continuing. "Well, I certainly can't do fifteen stitches to the inch, but I think we must finish it—and just do the best we can." Looking across at Sarah she added, "'Every girl needs a special quilt just for company.' That's something else Mama always said. This will be your company quilt, Sarah."

Augusta did more threading of needles than actual quilting that winter, but the fellowship around Jesse King's last quilt brought Augusta, LisBeth, and Sarah immeasurable blessing. They stitched and drank tea, unconscious of the fact that they were sewing more than a quilt—they were mending the grief in their own souls, stitching their hearts and lives together.

The evening after the quilt was bound, Sarah laid it carefully in the trunk Aunt Augusta had had brought over from Miller's Store. She closed the lid gently and looked up at LisBeth and Aunt Augusta, her eyes sparkling with joy. "I never had hope of any kind of future before Tom and I came here." She meant to say more but could not find the words to describe what had taken place in her heart since her arrival at Hathaway House. She remained silent, and the silence said more than words ever could.

In the spring of 1877, David Braddock and his mother, Abigail, arrived in Lincoln, ostensibly to investigate investment opportunities in the city. They were housed at the Hathaway House Hotel, and from her vantage point in the various aspects of helping manage the hotel, Sarah soon concluded that while Mr. Braddock might invest in some Lincoln businesses, he was most interested in the business of marriage with LisBeth King Baird.

LisBeth expressed consternation over the situation. "He said that he was visiting Lincoln to investigate the growth opportunities that Aunt Augusta talked about. Mrs. Braddock has encouraged him to buy several lots here in Lincoln. I believe they've even bought a farm. I've been careful to be friendly, but not to encourage him—and yet—"

Sarah was unsympathetic. "LisBeth, he's so *fine*-looking. He always smells so good. And he's such a *gentleman*. Just think of it—living in a mansion in Philadelphia—" Sarah could not believe LisBeth was unmoved by David's attention. "You'd be one of the leading citizens." She sat back in her chair and said wistfully, "And you'd have Mrs. Braddock for a mother."

"I don't *need* a mother, Sarah," LisBeth said impatiently. "And I most certainly do not need another husband. All the Bay Rum cologne in the world isn't going to change my mind, either. If only David Braddock would accept that."

Sarah had just taken a flatiron off the stove and begun to iron the first of two dozen linen hand towels when a mellow voice called from the doorway to the dining room. "Miss Biddle, might I have a moment of your time?"

Sarah looked up to see Abigail Braddock. Glancing down at her soiled apron, Sarah hesitated. Abigail turned to go. "I'm sorry. I've come at a bad time. You're obviously busy."

"No, Mrs. Braddock, no," Sarah protested. "It isn't that—" She replaced the flatiron on the woodstove, rushed to a hook by the back door, and quickly changed into a clean apron. Reaching up in a nervous attempt to tidy her hair, she smiled primly. "Please, what can I do to help you?"

Abigail Braddock crossed the room gracefully and leaned against the tall stool where Tom usually sat watching through the kitchen window for Joseph Freeman to emerge from the back of the livery. "Miss Biddle," she began, "I have something to ask you. I have discussed it with Augusta, and I have her permission to make my proposal." Pausing briefly, Abigail said, "David and I have decided that we wish to build a second home here in Lincoln. We will need a housekeeper. If you are interested, I should like to offer you the position."

Sarah stood in openmouthed amazement as Abigail rushed on. "My own housekeeper in Philadelphia will train you." Abigail chuckled. "Even though I have been her employer for nearly thirty years, I would not dare to ask Mrs. Titus if she would contemplate heading west. She made no secret of her opinion of our trip here. I believe her exact words were, 'the most dismal folly ever.'"

When Sarah remained speechless, Abigail continued. "The house here will be more modest, of course." She was almost apologetic. "I think it should require only one housekeeper. You will occasionally need help for special receptions and the like. But that should not be a problem with your connections gained here at the Hathaway House."

Still, Sarah was silent. Abigail went on. "We would give you a sizable increase in salary. Now, mind you," Abigail said earnestly, "I'm not trying to hire you away with a tall salary. I told Augusta the same. But the responsibility involved merits a good wage."

Sarah finally managed to stammer, "Mrs. Braddock— I—I wouldn't know the first thing—"

Abigail waved her hand in the air. "Oh, yes, I know. You don't know the first thing about keeping a private house. But, dear, Augusta has raved about your intelligence and hard work so much, I'm certain you'll learn quickly. Mrs. Titus knows *everything* about keeping a house. She'll teach you. And," Abigail added with a wink, "when we are here in Lincoln, I can offer assistance. You see, the senior Mr. Braddock married quite far *down* the social ladder when he chose little Abigail Sutton as his bride." Abigail raised a finger to her lips. "Now, don't you tell a soul, dear. It's our little secret."

"But what would Aunt Augusta—"

"I believe Augusta went over to the Immigrant House this morning to 'look things over,' as she put it. I think that meant she was going to look for a prospective new employee or two. She insists it will probably take two to replace you."

At the compliment, Sarah blushed. She looked down at her hands, each one full of a wad of apron. She let go of the apron she had nervously gathered up and tried to smooth it. Without looking up she murmured, "Tom—"

Mrs. Braddock said happily, "Of course I want Tom to come with you. The house in Philadelphia has been bereft of childish laughter for so many years. It seems that grandchildren are yet a few years off for me." She added with a sigh, "And from what I've seen of young Thomas Biddle, he would benefit from the challenge of a private tutor. I know Miss Griswall is a fine teacher, but I have a tutor in mind who could really advance Tom in the time you'd spend in Philadelphia."

"Philadelphia," Sarah said doubtfully. "I don't care much for big cities like that."

Abigail's voice was gentle. "And no wonder. Not much good ever happened in the big city for you or Tom, did it, dear?" She reached over to pat Sarah's hand. "Well, we'll work on replacing the old memories with better ones. There are many fascinating things to see and do in

Philadelphia. We'll make certain Tom takes advantage of them, and we'll also make certain that you have a day off now and then to accompany him."

Sarah was overwhelmed. She looked up at Abigail. *Beautiful*, she thought. *How can someone that old be so beautiful?* And those eyes—they were the kind of eyes a girl could trust. The image of Mrs. Hurd, weeping openly for Sarah and Tom when it was revealed that Emma was gone, receded. Sarah shook her head slightly. "I . . . I'd have to talk it over with Aunt Augusta." She looked up a little fearfully. "You don't mind, do you?"

"Of course I don't mind, Sarah. I'd expect it. This is a big change for you to contemplate. David and I plan to leave next Tuesday. If you can let us know by Sunday, we'll have time to have a trunk delivered and pack your things."

"We don't need a trunk, Mrs. Braddock," Sarah blurted out. "Me and Tom's things together wouldn't fill a trunk. Just a little case is all we need. We travel light."

Abigail suppressed a smile and stood up. She extended her hand to Sarah, who took it. "You remind me of someone, Sarah. She was an orphan, working in a hotel kitchen one day when someone very kind and very wonderful took notice of her. His name was William Braddock. I'm not nearly so kind or wonderful as William was, but I hope you'll let me help you and Tom. It would mean so much to me, dear." Abigail dropped Sarah's hand and went to the door. She turned to say finally, "I think you and I could get on, Sarah."

Sarah absentmindedly removed her clean apron and retrieved the stained one. She pumped a bowl of water, which she set on her ironing board. Unrolling a linen towel, she sprinkled it with water, then retrieved the flat-iron from the woodstove. As she watched the wrinkles disappear from the linen, she wondered aloud if Mrs. Titus of Philadelphia would know how to get elderberry stains out of white linen.

CHAPTER 7

Satin and Velvet Scraps

"She openeth her mouth with wisdom;
and in her tongue is the law of kindness."
Proverbs 31:26

Mrs. Titus knew not only how to get elderberry stains out of white linen, but also how to polish silver, make cut glass sparkle, and create the smoothest of sugar creams for candy fondants and pastils. She knew how to clean brass and bronze, ivory and mother-of-pearl, cherrywood clocks and crystal stoppers. She knew the proper way to care for point lace and battenberg, colored silks and woolens, calicoes and satins. She knew how to prevent rust on iron and mildew on canvas. What she did not know, she considered not worth knowing. What she did know, she insisted Sarah write down. "I won't have you ruining the linens and silks."

Mrs. Titus's wisdom was not limited to the details of running a well-appointed house. Mrs. Titus knew much more than that. She knew what it was like to be the student of an older woman far more skilled in every detail of living. She knew the feeling of being overwhelmed and terrified at the prospect of caring for even one small part of a huge house. She knew just when Sarah Biddle had absorbed as much knowledge as she could for one day.

She knew these things because even though she was middle-aged, Mrs. Titus remembered standing in the vast entryway of the Braddock manse when William Braddock was only a boy and she was but a girl. She remembered, and in her remembering was Sarah Biddle's salvation. Just when Sarah was ready to give up, just when she thought she would never learn, Mrs. Titus approved of her pastils. "Mr. David loves candy. He will enjoy these immensely, Miss Biddle. They are very good."

Sarah had just begun to believe that she could, indeed, master the more important facets of running a small house in Nebraska when Abigail Braddock presented yet another challenge. "Mrs. Titus says that you are learning quickly, Sarah. You can still work with her in the mornings and evenings, but in the afternoons I'd like it very much if you would sit in with Tom."

Sarah protested. "I can read a little. I can write my name. I got no need for more education."

Abigail disagreed. "Sarah," she said gently, "we both share great ambition for Tom. He's very bright, and I've no doubt he will go far. But *I'm* paying the tutor, Sarah, and I'd like it very much if you would sit in on the lessons. It would motivate Tom to do better, and you might be surprised. You might like it." Abigail's gentle prodding convinced Sarah. For the rest of her stay in Philadelphia, Sarah Biddle was instructed by Tom's private tutor.

Tom and Sarah settled into a routine. Sarah rose at 4:30 every morning and made her way down the back stairs to the kitchen, where she built a fire in the stove and joined other servants in preparing breakfast for "Mr. David and Mrs. Braddock." Tom came down by six o'clock, dining in the kitchen with Sarah while the breakfast room maid served the Braddocks.

Sarah spent her mornings with Mrs. Titus while Tom roamed the mansion and the grounds. He inevitably ended up in the stable where an aged driver allowed him to help groom carriage horses and oil tack. By noon, he tumbled back into the kitchen ravenously hungry. He and Sarah ate hastily, helping to clean the kitchen before the arrival of Mr. Dubois, the tutor. For the afternoon, Tom, Sarah, and Mr. Dubois sequestered thelmselves in the library. Mr. Dubois departed by four o'clock each afternoon, whereupon Sarah served tea to Mrs. Braddock and a variety of the grand dames of Philadelphia society. Sarah's evenings were spent alongside Mrs. Titus again, serving elaborate meals, preparing cakes and puddings, mending and sewing.

"I shouldn't bother with the mending and sewing," Mrs. Titus sighed, "except that you'll likely be the only servant in the house in Nebraska." Mrs. Titus looked at Sarah critically. "I certainly hope you can manage, Miss Biddle. It will require a great deal of effort to keep things in hand. Of course, I realize standards in the West are not what they are here. Still, you'll be very busy."

Mrs. Titus scoffed at Sarah's fondness for quilting. "You'll have no time for that kind of thing, Miss Biddle. The days of poverty that required recycling old garments into quilts and old suits into rag rugs have long since departed the Braddocks, thank heaven. Quilting is a rather lowly occupation, Miss Biddle. Keep your mind on more useful things. Small decorative pieces for the parlor and boudoir are always welcome, of course. Lacking daughters, Mrs. Braddock would surely appreciate your making an antimacassar to protect the back of her new chair. Better yet, you could crochet a set so that the arms and the back could all be covered with the same pattern. Here—refer to this for ideas if you want to occupy your hands." Mrs. Titus produced a bound edition of *Godey's Ladies Book*. "The upstairs maid, Millicent, is excellent at the decorative arts. She can help you if you find you have spare time. But the Braddocks need your hands engaged in useful activity. Don't waste your time with old-fashioned and outdated skills."

Sarah perused the *Godey's* book one evening, delighting in the fashion plates and the many needlework projects. Still, she secretly continued work on a miniature piece of patchwork that would serve as a pincushion for Mrs. Braddock's workbasket. She worked diligently, cutting and piecing one-inch triangles of satins and velvets together to make tiny squares. Stitching sixteen of the squares together, she backed them with a piece of velvet, then made a running stitch along the edge and drew the piece into a tiny puff that she filled with sawdust. A piece of braid along the edge finished the pincushion, which Sarah hoped would just fit into one corner of Mrs. Braddock's workbasket.

The next afternoon, Sarah tucked the completed pincushion into her apron pocket. She had difficulty listening to Mr. Dubois that afternoon. She kept reaching into her pocket, running her finger along the braid, feeling the texture of the patchwork pattern. When at last it was time to serve Mrs. Braddock's tea, Sarah mounted the servants' stairs to Mrs. Braddock's private parlor, her heart pounding. Mrs. Braddock was to have tea alone today. Sarah paused just outside the door. She set the elaborate tea service on the floor and withdrew the pincushion from her pocket, placing it first here, then there on the tray. At last she decided to balance it against the small vase of rosebuds near the teapot. Satisfied with the arrangement, Sarah knocked at the door.

But it was not Abigail Braddock who opened the door. It was Mr. David. Sarah blushed, stammered a greeting, and set the tray down hastily, trying to grab the pincushion and secret it once again in her pocket.

"Sarah, what are you hiding there?" Abigail asked.

"Oh, it's nothing, ma'am." Sarah backed toward the door. "I'll leave you and Mr. Braddock alone now."

"Come here, Sarah, please," David called out. He settled himself comfortably in a huge chair beside his mother, helping himself to a plateful of sandwiches.

Sarah paused at the door. Seeing Abigail smile encouragement, she stepped back into the room, absentmindedly putting her hand in her pocket to grasp the pincushion.

Abigail encouraged her. "Goodness, Sarah, there's no need to be shy. David was just saying that he feels guilty for having ignored Tom. He's been terribly busy, but things have quieted down now, and he wondered if you and Tom would enjoy an outing on Saturday. You've seen nothing of the city since your arrival. We'd like to take you both for a drive. Would you like that?"

Having finished his plate of sandwiches, David stood up. He was not a tall man, but his powerful build, combined with flashing dark eyes and a bold, deep voice, were intimidating. Sarah answered uncertainly, "Tom loves new things, Mr. Braddock. It's kind of you to be so interested in him—"

"But, Sarah," Abigail interjected, "we mean to take you both. Don't you want to see Philadelphia?"

Sarah shook her head.

David boomed enthusiastically, "That's nonsense, Sarah, pure nonsense. It's a beautiful city. We'll show you where the Exposition was held last year. LisBeth loved it. Every bit of it. You will too. I'll have the carriage brought round at nine o'clock." David bent to kiss his mother on the cheek. "I'll see you at dinner, Mother." With a nod to Sarah, he was out the door, inwardly pleased that he was pleasing his mother by showing some interest in her two protégés.

David was gone only a few seconds when Mrs. Braddock began kindly, "Now, Sarah, David is gone. Are you going to show me what you are hiding in that pocket?"

Sarah blushed, stuttered, then finally withdrew the pincushion and placed it on Mrs. Braddock's tray. "It's just something I made, Mrs. Braddock. I thought you could use it in your workbasket. Mrs. Titus says patchwork is a waste of time. . . ." Sarah looked out the window. "But Aunt Jesse taught me how to do it. I always kind of liked it." Sarah looked doubtfully at Abigail. "You don't have to keep it. I just wanted to do something—something to thank you for bringing Tom and me here." Sarah swallowed hard.

Abigail fingered the small pincushion lovingly. "Oh, Sarah, thank you. It's lovely." She turned and opened her workbasket. "See? You were exactly right. It fits perfectly, right here in the corner." Closing the lid gently, Mrs. Braddock added, "And, Sarah, Mrs. Titus was wrong. *Nothing* is a waste of time when it is done with love and gratitude. I will treasure your gift always."

Abigail reached for a book that lay beside her workbasket. "Sarah, would you mind reading aloud to me today? My eyes are a bit tired, but this story has captured my interest. Please, dear, sit down."

And so began a ritual that was to continue as long as Sarah worked for Abigail Braddock. Each day Sarah served Mrs. Braddock afternoon tea. When there were visitors, Sarah left the room without a word, returning at the ring of Mrs. Braddock's bell to clear the tea service. But on the days when there were no visitors, Sarah stayed on, reading aloud to Mrs. Braddock. At first she read novels. But gradually, Mrs. Braddock's reading tastes seemed to evolve. Sarah began reading philosophy, poetry, and literary classics that opened her to a new world of ideas. The sessions with Mr. Dubois continued, but it was in the private parlor of Abigail Braddock that Sarah Biddle received the greatest knowledge, for in Mrs. Braddock's private parlor Sarah Biddle learned not only to read books, but also to love them.

At 9 A.M. on Saturday, Tom Biddle bounded up into the open backseat of the Braddocks' phaeton, chattering excitedly. Sarah joined her brother in one seat, facing Abigail and David, who sat with their backs to the driver so that Sarah and Tom could have the best view from the carriage. As the phaeton moved down the curving drive and out onto the busy street, Sarah looked back longingly at the mansion. Absentmindedly, she pressed one palm against her chest. She could feel the outline of the small pouch that hung around her neck. Riding along the busy streets of Philadelphia, Sarah pressed her hand against her chest again and again, making sure the pouch was there.

Tom reveled in the sights of the great city. At first they drove past one mansion after another. As Abigail told who owned the beautiful houses, Sarah recognized the names of many of the women who had joined Abigail for tea. When they descended into the city, Tom took over the conversation, chattering incessantly. Sarah, however, grew more and more quiet. Tom saw fine horses and elaborate carriages. Sarah saw peddlers and vagrant children. Tom saw bankers and merchants. Sarah saw men who had grown old before they were old, standing in small groups or sitting on curbs. Tom saw the Braddock Hotel. Sarah saw a hapless woman picking her way through the hotel trash. Tom saw the railway station. Sarah saw Mason Biddle.

She was never certain, but in the years to come she always wondered. Just as they rounded a corner near the station, the sight of a faded plaid shirt made her heart leap. Her mouth fell open, she raised her hand to her mouth. Her mind cried out, *Pa—Pa—is it you—is it really you?* She almost stood up in the carriage, but the hunched figure disappeared into the crowd.

Abigail Braddock saw Sarah's face go white, saw her staring down the street. "Sarah, dear, what is it? Sarah? Are you ill?"

David turned toward Sarah. He frowned. His voice was unusually gentle. "What is it, Sarah? Are you tired? We can go back—"

"But, Mr. David, I don't wanna go back yet," Tom protested. "We haven't seen the Exposition."

Sarah wiped her hands across her eyes and said hoarsely, "It's nothing." She blinked back tears, pasted on a smile, and turned to Tom. "Of course we're going to see the Exposition, Tom."

Abigail reached out to pat Sarah's hand. David reached for Tom. "Come on, Tom, let's get up with the driver. We can see much better from there." With no regard for his undignified behavior in a city where everyone recognized David Braddock, he climbed up beside the amazed driver, pulling Tom to sit beside him. The two rode with their backs to the ladies.

When the carriage had entered the Exposition grounds, David had the driver stop and lifted Tom down. Together they went off toward the vast central building that had housed many of the Exposition's most lauded displays.

The ladies remained in the carriage. "What is it, Sarah?" Abigail asked. When Sarah didn't answer, Abigail insisted. "I know you were reluctant to come, and now something has frightened you. I mean to know what it is, Sarah. And I mean to fix it if I can."

Choking back tears, Sarah began talking. "I'm not ungrateful, Mrs. Braddock. Really, I'm not. Philadelphia is a beautiful city . . . when you see it through Mr. Braddock's eyes. But—"

Abigail looked about her, seeing only beautifully manicured grounds and a magnificent building. But then she followed Sarah's gaze toward the Girard Street Bridge. Beneath the bridge, a group of ragged boys had gathered.

Neither Abigail nor Sarah could hear their words, but as they watched, a fight broke out. One of the boys, younger than the rest, was thrown to the ground. An older boy grabbed something from his hand and danced about in victory, shoving whatever he had taken into his mouth, rubbing his stomach with pleasure. He ran toward a girl who sat near the water's edge sorting rags. Suddenly, Abigail understood. The small boy on the ground could easily have been Tom Biddle. The girl selling rags just across the bridge could have been Sarah. Abigail reached for one of Sarah's hands. "Sarah, that part of your life is over. Philadelphia is not New York. Neither you nor Tom will ever again need a Children's Aid Society. You are no longer orphans. You have a family in Augusta Hathaway and LisBeth Baird. You have a home. You don't need that pouch about your neck any longer, Sarah."

At Sarah's look of amazement, Abigail nodded. "I know about it. LisBeth told me. You keep enough money in that pouch to make certain that you and Tom can make it back to Lincoln. Sarah—" Abigail lifted her chin until their eyes met. "I understand, dear. I *do* see the children and the poverty and the hopelessness. I see it and I hate it. I cannot change it for everyone. But I can change it for *you*. And for Tom. You have had a good home at the Hathaway House. Augusta and LisBeth have become your family. I don't want to change any of that, Sarah. But I would like to add to it. I can help with Tom's education. I can give you a secure position. But I want it to be more than just a position, Sarah." Abigail's blue eyes gleamed as she said quietly, "For as long as I live, Sarah, if you want it, you and Tom have a home with me."

When David and Tom returned to the carriage, Sarah declined David's invitation to inspect the Exposition grounds. On the drive back to the Braddock mansion, Tom grew quiet, sleepily leaning his head against Sarah's shoulder. David Braddock was also quiet, entertaining the notion that having a son just might be a wonderful thing. Abigail Braddock said nothing, seeing her "city of brotherly love" through the eyes of a homeless orphan. And Sarah Biddle rode in silence, thinking through Mrs. Braddock's impassioned promise.

The next afternoon, Mrs. Abigail Braddock entertained the mayor's wife at tea. Sarah brought in the tray, set it down before Abigail, curtsied, and left. It was some time before Abigail noticed it, but when she did, she startled the mayor's wife with an unexpected exclamation of joy. There on the tray lay a small silk purse. Sarah had attached a carefully written note to the purse. It read, "We don't need train fare home anymore. We *are* home."

CHAPTER 8

Madder Plaid

"Exhort servants to be obedient unto their own masters, and to please them well in all things."
Titus 2:9

The Sarah Biddle who descended from the train at Lincoln, Nebraska, in the fall of 1877 was a markedly different girl from the desperate orphan who had once darted through the train station and down a busy street, carrying her brother in her arms. That Sarah Biddle had been running from the train into the unknown. This Sarah Biddle walked with a confidence that belied her fifteen years. She wore a well-tailored dress of madder plaid, spoke with flawless grammar, and was to surprise Augusta Hathaway and LisBeth Baird not only with the scope of her skills in housekeeping, but also with her newfound love of literature.

But when, at LisBeth's request, Jim Callaway drove Sarah to see the house she would be in charge of, she momentarily lost her composure. The "small property" David and Abigail had acquired on which to build what Abigail had called an "unimposing house" consisted of an entire city block surrounded by an ornate wrought-iron fence. The fence was divided into fifteen-foot-long sections by brick pillars, each one topped with a gas coach light.

When Jim Callaway jumped down from his wagon to unlock the gate, swinging it wide to allow his wagon through, their first view of the manse brought a small gasp from Sarah and a whistle of admiration from Jim. "I knew the Braddocks had money, but I sure never thought they had *this* much money."

Sarah sat still, her heart thumping, her blue eyes blinking in disbelief. The Braddock mansion was a massive, three-story conglomeration of porches, gingerbread, and gables. Above the first-floor porch, across the fasciae of the house and along the roofline, trailed a carved border of realistically painted leaves and flowers. Scalloped siding and the trim around ornate windows had been painted in several shades of green. The house itself was a deep red. Accents of pink and cream highlighted the more delicate architectural details. A wide porch wrapped around the left side of the house to a double-wide portico where guests could be let out of their carriages in inclement weather. Stained and beveled glass adorned the top portion of every window on the main floor. A stained-glass *B* was set into a small round window in the peak of the massive roof.

While Sarah stared, Jim led his team through the gate, closed it, and proceeded up the bricked path, under the portico, and to the back of the house to what he assumed was the kitchen door. Nearby a small gazebo was tucked under what would be a grape arbor. Curving flower beds and seedling trees had been planted along the entire length of the wall. A large carriage house with an apartment above dominated the back third of the property. Opposite the carriage house a small picket fence hid the fresh-turned earth that was obviously going to be a garden.

"Go on in the front door, Sarah," Jim urged. "You can't tell me you wouldn't enjoy pretending it all belongs to you—just once. I'll start unloading these boxes and wait for you to open the back door."

Sarah stared wistfully toward the front of the house.

Jim encouraged her. "Mrs. Braddock is trusting you to set the place up for her. You're not doing anything wrong. Go in now, and get the same view Mrs. Braddock's company will get when they come to visit."

"I guess that would help me know how to arrange the furniture," Sarah reasoned. Still, she hesitated. "Would you go in with me?"

Sarah located the key to the main door, and Jim unlocked it and swung it open. Inside, a massive walnut staircase led up to a landing where more stained glass sent brilliant colors scattering across the walls. At the back of the downstairs hall a narrow door led into what Sarah knew would be the kitchen. To their right was a small formal parlor with high windows and polished floors. Sarah walked to the left into a larger room where the walls were papered in deep red silk and heavy velvet draperies hung at the windows. A Persian carpet in the middle of the room awaited the arrival of furniture to fill the empty space around it. The door that led out to the portico was along the opposite wall, and past that door, French doors with etched-glass panels showed the room where Sarah would spend much of her free time—the library. There specially built shelves lined the walls, every shelf boasting a glass door that would lift up and slide in above the rows of books.

Jim wandered into the library and surveyed the empty shelves. "They have enough books to fill this room?" he said in amazement. "I never seen that many books in one place."

Sarah nodded. "Mr. Braddock is bringing the books. He's hired a special car on the train just for his personal things. He has some fine editions of Milton and Johnson that he won't trust to any hands but his own. I'm surprised he's having them sent here, but he insisted."

After a rather awkward silence, Sarah said, "I'm setting up the kitchen today. Mrs. Braddock said that as soon as Tom's and my furniture arrives, we should move in. We have only a month before the Braddocks arrive." Sarah finished her sentence as she opened the swinging door that led from the library into the kitchen. At sight of the massive cookstove, the huge center workstation, and the spotless white tile floor, Sarah exclaimed, "Oh, my!" and sat down abruptly at a small table in one corner.

Jim stared around the room with appreciation. "Well, Sarah, it looks like you're going to be cooking some good-sized meals. LisBeth and Mrs. Hathaway will be taking notes when they see this and ordering up changes at the hotel."

Sarah smiled. "They've already been doing that. Augusta has been sketching and drawing and talking to builders for months. I think Mr. Braddock convinced her to give up on improving the present hotel and building a new one closer to the railroad station. He's going to invest in it."

Jim frowned. "That Mr. Braddock sure gets around, doesn't he?"

"I get the impression he plans to make Lincoln more than just a temporary residence. He seems quite intent on making it a second home. I think he's fond of LisBeth."

Jim turned his back and headed for the kitchen door. "Guess I'd better get to unloading the wagon. You've a lot of work to do here." Jim propped open the door and clomped noisily down the steps, grabbing a crate and hauling it in.

Sarah was prying open a crate when a carriage rattled up the drive. She heard Tom's voice exclaiming, "Great granny, Aunt Augusta. Look at the yard! Look at the porch! I wonder where my room is! This place is so big! I bet they could keep six horses in that carriage house! Do you think Sarah and me will live over the carriage house?"

Tom exploded through the back door, followed by LisBeth and Augusta.

Sarah laughed. "Tom, settle down. You'll have plenty of time to explore. It's going to take us most of the afternoon to unpack all these crates. You might start by going upstairs to find our rooms. The driver will live over the carriage house, Tom, not us." Turning to LisBeth and Augusta she asked, "Are you sure you can spare the time away from the hotel to help me?"

Augusta countered, "Just try to get rid of us, Sarah. I can't wait to see what's in all these crates—" She winked at LisBeth— "and to inspect the rest of the house when I can really *look* instead of showing polite disinterest!"

Tom had already swooped upstairs and returned to the kitchen. He sat down at the table in the corner, but popped up again as soon as Jim Callaway entered the kitchen. "Hey, Jim, let's go look at the carriage house, OK?" He grabbed Jim by the hand and pulled him out the door. While the two were gone, LisBeth and Augusta toured the house, amazed at the wealth displayed in its polished railings and floors, its Persian carpets and lavish drapes.

Upstairs they discovered Sarah's room, just across the hall from Abigail Braddock's. Small in comparison to the other rooms in the manse, it was still larger than what Sarah had expected. To the left a large window looked out over the roof of the porch below and toward the yet-to-be-planted vegetable garden. Opposite the door from the hall was the jewel of Sarah's room. A small door opened out onto a private second-story porch.

Back in the kitchen, LisBeth and Augusta began to help Sarah unpack. Jim took his leave, and Tom made his way upstairs to his own room on the third floor. It had no private porch, but it was larger than Sarah's room. Tom slid down the banister to the main floor, declared his room grand, and shot out the back door to explore the grounds more thoroughly, leaving the three women to exclaim over the contents of every crate.

By the time they had unpacked the Braddocks' everyday dishes, crystal, linens, and utensils and arranged them in their respective cupboards, Sarah had begun to doubt the wisdom of Abigail Braddock's faith in her.

"Now Sarah," Augusta ordered, "don't sell yourself short. You learned everything you need to know from Mrs. Braddock's head housekeeper in Philadelphia. Abigail did nothing but brag on you in her letters. You'll do fine."

Sarah did better than fine. She directed the arranging of furniture in the mansion and planted a fall garden. She set Tom to weeding the garden and planted bulbs that would promise early blooms the next spring. She unpacked more linens and crystal and filled the butler's pantry with enough fine china to feed a small army. She arranged Mrs. Braddock's room with loving care, but solicited LisBeth's help with Mr. Braddock's room. "You've been married, LisBeth," she said. "You'll know what a gentleman would like."

When the Braddocks finally arrived to take up residence in Lincoln, the occasion was marked by an article in the *Nebraska State Journal* and a reception engineered by a capable head housekeeper who anyone would have been astonished to learn was only fifteen years old.

The morning after the reception, Abigail Braddock showered Sarah with such praise that the young woman blushed with pleasure. David Braddock echoed his mother's satisfaction, with special mention of the fine arrangement of his private quarters. When Sarah informed him that LisBeth had provided assistance in those details, he gulped his remaining coffee and took his leave, hurrying to the Hathaway House Hotel where he could extend his personal thanks.

In the weeks that followed the reception, Tom Biddle returned to Miss Griswall's school. Sarah managed her duties as housekeeper with an ease that would have impressed even Mrs. Titus. She visited LisBeth and Augusta often and began work on a new quilt for her room at the manse. She listened with unbounded pride as Tom recounted Miss Griswall's pleasure at his recitation from *Marcus Aurelius*, and developed a growing admiration for David Braddock, who seemed to have taken new interest in life generally, and in Tom specifically. Tom began expounding "Mr. David's" opinions about everything from political candidates to crop rotation. It became clear that "Mr. David's" opinions were challenging the place of holy Writ in young Tom Biddle's mind.

Sarah watched with pleasure as David's interest in LisBeth Baird became more and more obvious. She pored over every new edition of *Godey's* for bridal supper recipes and secretly began another patchwork project when she found a pattern for a wedding quilt. She grew to love Abigail Braddock without reservation and looked to the future with renewed interest, for in the not-too-distant future, Sarah envisioned LisBeth and David Braddock occupying the manse, served by Sarah and Jim Callaway, residing in the apartment over the carriage house.

CHAPTER 9

Moire and Satin

"Look not every man on his own things, but every man also on the things of others."
Philippians 2:4

Early in December, Sarah and Abigail closed the house in Lincoln and she and Tom accompanied the Braddocks to Philadelphia for the winter. LisBeth and Augusta came to Philadelphia for Christmas, and Sarah and Tom were included in the celebration. Sarah watched happily as David Braddock courted LisBeth, and watching them inspired her own dream of having a husband and perhaps even a family of her own.

At Christmas Jim Callaway sent a package for LisBeth, which she opened and set aside quickly. At the time, Sarah failed to understand the significance of the red calico, but it became clear when she received a letter from LisBeth in late January. One line of LisBeth's letter jolted Sarah to reality. The red calico had been an unspoken invitation to LisBeth to finally conclude the wearing of mourning cloth, to put the death of her husband behind her, to begin a new life—with Jim Callaway instead of David Braddock: *Jim Callaway has asked me to be his wife.*

Sitting in her room in Philadelphia with LisBeth's letter in her lap, Sarah replayed the last few months: Jim enjoying a second piece of pie served up by Sarah in the kitchen at the Hathaway House Hotel. Jim driving Sarah to her first view of the Braddocks' home in Lincoln. Jim alongside her as she walked through the door. Jim delivering crates of supplies, praising her abilities, selecting and training two matched pairs of carriage horses, helping Tom weed the garden. All these things she had interpreted as interest in herself. Sarah's dreams of a husband and family had included Jim for quite some time. LisBeth's letter brought those dreams to an abrupt end:

> *I hope that when you come in the spring you will allow me to tell you all about it. Sarah, can you forgive me? I know this news causes you pain. You have grown to be a woman since you first saw Jim Callaway. I am hoping that what you have felt for him was what we call a "crush." I am also hoping that God will enable you to be happy for us, and that this news will not separate you and me. Please, Sarah, write to me at once. I need to hear from you.*

LisBeth had signed the letter, *Your loving sister.* Sarah read the closing and smiled. She wanted to be angry, to cry out against LisBeth, to somehow convince herself that LisBeth had dishonestly stolen Jim's affections. But she knew it wasn't true.

As was her custom when her mind whirled, Sarah's hands reached for her workbasket. Absentmindedly, she reached for a fragment of cloth. Before she could write LisBeth, she had to sort through her own feelings. She hardly looked down as she began the repetitive in-and-out motion, stitching together two squares of fabric. The rhythm of the needle in her hands settled her emotions. She knew that neither Jim nor LisBeth had acted deceitfully. Still, she was hurt. She tried to feel betrayed, but her hurt gave way to embarrassment when, after replaying her many encounters with Jim Callaway, she finally admitted to herself that he had given no real hint of interest in her.

Sarah was forced to admit that he had been polite and friendly in the way any good man would be polite and friendly. She had been drawn to that kindness and had misinterpreted it. It was *LisBeth* he had watched carefully when he dined at the hotel. For *LisBeth* he had created a little graveyard at her dead husband's homestead, carving the name "Mac" in a rock so that she would have a grave to visit. For *LisBeth* Jim had left his beloved farm, driving far to the north to facilitate a reunion between LisBeth and her Lakota Sioux brother.*

It was always LisBeth. Standing up and moving to the window, Sarah looked out onto the snow-covered lawn. She leaned her head against the window, feeling the exquisite ache of loss. A carriage was coming up the long drive. David Braddock was returning from another late business meeting. Suddenly, Sarah's sorrow faded amid concern for Abigail's son. *Poor Mr. Braddock,* Sarah thought. *He will be devastated. And Mrs. Braddock—she will be so disappointed.*

Sarah began to think of ways she could help Abigail Braddock get past her disappointment. She began to wonder how David Braddock would deal with the news.

Staring into the fire she heard David's footsteps on the stairs. His room was at the far end of the hall, but Sarah heard muffled voices as Hobbes, David's personal servant, exited his employer's room. She heard Hobbes's steps retreat toward his own room, located in another wing of the house. She pictured David taking LisBeth's letter from the silver tray Hobbes would have presented before retiring. She imagined David opening it, reading it, refusing to believe it . . . and rereading it, just as she had her own letter.

---

*LisBeth and Soaring Eagle's story is told in Stephanie Grace Whitson's *Soaring Eagle,* Thomas Nelson Publishers, 1996.

The ache in her heart returned, then grew in intensity, as she sympathized with the man down the hall.

Sarah sat up until long after the fire in her tiny fireplace had died. She reread LisBeth's pleading letter several times, finally retiring with one sentence ringing in her mind. *Jim Callaway has asked me to be his wife.*

It was weeks before Sarah was able to answer LisBeth's letter. It would be months before David Braddock spoke of LisBeth. Business in Philadelphia prevented his accompanying his mother back to Nebraska the spring that LisBeth and Jim Callaway were married. Indeed, business increasingly prevented David's spending much time with his mother over the next few years.

But in David's absence the relationship between Abigail Braddock and Sarah grew closer until Sarah became more a companion than a servant. Tom's status in the household remained ambiguous. Not really a servant, he roamed the great house and its grounds, willingly helping gardeners and coachmen, begging sweets in the kitchen and generally charming everyone except his tutor, Mr. Dubois.

Seeing potential in the child, Mr. Dubois grew more demanding each day and each year. Tom rose to every challenge, mastering Latin and Greek, parsing and declining, philosophy and literature, computing and debating, writing long letters to "Mr. David," which were answered by the benefactor who insisted that, outside of a few brief visits, he could not possibly return to Philadelphia, he must remain in New York.

The thing that finally brought David Braddock home to stay was a letter from Tom.

Dear Mr. David,
    Sarah says that I mustn't bother you with our little worries, but I'm telling you anyway because you said I could write you about anything and I'm scared. Dr.

Braxton came to dinner, and he told Mrs. Braddock he thinks he can fix my leg. The only problem is that I have to go to a hospital, and they must put me to sleep. When I wake up Dr. Braxton said it will hurt something awful, but then he said I'll be able to walk better. Sarah cried and said I must have it done, and I guess I must because it would be nice to be able to run and not limp. But I wonder if maybe you could come home and make sure about the doctor. Mrs. Braddock says he is the best, but you know more about business and things like that. I'd like it better if you were here anyway. But if you can't come, I understand because Sarah says you are a very busy man and you have had a disappointment and we must be very patient with you. So I will be patient. But if you could come it would be good. The operation is in two weeks, but if you don't get this in time then I will understand. Sarah is going to stay in the hospital with me, and Mrs. Braddock says she will come and visit and bring me some candy. The good news is that I won't have to do lessons with Mr. Dubois for a while, so that will make it almost fun I guess.

Your faithful servant,

Thomas Biddle

David Braddock swore at himself as he read the letter. He wondered why he had never thought to have Dr. Braxton examine Tom Biddle's crooked leg. He did not like the answer: *You've convinced yourself that all this business travel is about furthering the family fortune. What you're really doing is wallowing in self-pity.*

David laid aside Tom's letter, threw a few things into a valise, and headed for the train station.

Dr. Emery Braxton had won his reputation in Europe, having traveled there as a young man seeking to escape the conflict between North and South that nearly tore his own country apart. While in Europe, he had charmed himself into the inner circle of Napoleon and Eugenie's confreres, from whom he received obscene amounts of money for palliative care.

But Dr. Braxton had not totally wasted his time in Europe. While there, he had pioneered experimental orthopedic surgery on the hopelessly crippled child of the cousin to the Duc D'Orleans. The successful procedure plunged Dr. Braxton into a new specialty and secured his place among the court.

Eventually, however, Emery Braxton wearied of his self-imposed exile and longed to return home. When he did, he found his former friends less than receptive to their colleague. They saw him as a deserter and resented the wealth he had acquired while many of them had lost everything as a result of the war.

Emery Braxton set about winning his way back. He opened a clinic for the destitute. He practiced medicine quietly and efficiently, occasionally working an orthopedic wonder for a hopeless case. When one such patient, belonging to a prominent family in Philadelphia, walked for the first time, Braxton was once again accepted, once again sought-after, once again part of the society he had left as a young man.

The total acceptance of the Braxtons by Philadelphia society was assured with the arrival of an invitation to one of Abigail Braddock's receptions. Reading their engraved invitation, the three Braxton girls squealed with excitement. Their mother ordered new dresses. Their father hoped that David Braddock would be present and find at least one of his daughters attractive.

Rumor had it that David Braddock had once been rejected by the object of his affections. Rebecca Braxton sniffed, "Oh, I know about *her*. Elizabeth, I think her name was. Pretty in an unrefined sort of way. But really just a country bumpkin. She was very attractive in her little widow's garb, though. And she was so perfectly *careful* to *seem* disinterested." Rebecca smiled at her sisters. "But now she's gone, and poor David will need someone to help him get over her."

Belinda shook her head. "He's much too old for me, Rebecca. You can have him. Although," she mused, "I wouldn't mind a dance or two with him. He's a fine dancer, and if Zachary Winters thought I were interested in David Braddock, it might bring him to his senses."

Grace said quietly, "You two go right ahead and fight over him. I'm not going to the reception. Mother refused me that silk moire for a new gown. I simply won't go if I can't have it."

The talk turned to moire and satin, and the Braxton ladies momentarily forgot about David Braddock, basking in the knowledge that they had, at last, been looked upon favorably by Mrs. Abigail Braddock. Having been included on just one of Abigail Braddock's guest lists would win them innumerable invitations for the upcoming season. Yes, indeed, 1882 was going to be a very good year.

David Braddock arrived in Philadelphia too late.

"His surgery was yesterday, dear," Abigail said, holding David's hand as they sat together in her parlor. "Dr. Braxton said that everything went very well. He expects that Tom will walk without a limp and be nearly free of pain. It's wonderful!" Abigail frowned slightly. "Now, if I can only get Sarah to come home and get some rest. . . ."

"You're always worrying about someone or something, Mother."

"Well, dear, you've assured me I no longer have to worry about *you*, so I guess I must have someone new to worry about. And dear Sarah has been nearly beside herself with worry. I suggested she come home to rest, and she was almost angry in her refusal." Abigail sighed. "I'd thought that after all this time, she finally had learned to trust me."

David put his arm around his mother. "Well, Mother, you'll just have to keep assuring her. In the meantime, I think I can help. Tom wrote that he would feel much better if I could be here, although why he still thinks good of me I'll never know. I hate it that I wasn't here before the surgery, but I can be here for him now." He stood up. "I'm going to the hospital. Perhaps I can convince Sarah to come back here for a few hours. I'll stay with Tom."

When David entered the children's ward he could hear a young voice crying, "Sarah—Sarah, please—please make him stop hurting me. Sarah—please!" At the far end of the children's ward, Sarah Biddle bent over the bed where her brother muttered and cried and tossed about. She lay her hand on Tom's forehead, whispering comfort. Her voice was gentle, but her hand shook and tears coursed down her cheeks as she tried to comfort him.

"It's all right, Tommy boy. Sarah's here. It's all right, dear. It will be better soon. The doctor says you'll walk again, Tommy. No more limping. Please, Tommy, just lie still. Think of home . . . think of your room . . . think. . . ." When her comfort had little effect, Sarah slumped in the chair next to the bed.

The doctor had tried to prepare Sarah for Tom's convalescence, but the reality proved much worse than she expected. Seeing her brother's suffering plunged her back to a time when she had been helpless to comfort another sibling. Exhausted by her vigil, she lost her composure and leaned over to rest her head on the edge of the bed. "Oh, Tommy boy, I'm so sorry . . . I didn't know they would hurt you so. I'm sorry, baby . . . so sorry . . ."

A hand on her shoulder made her jump. She looked up into David Braddock's compassionate dark brown eyes.

Wiping away her tears, Sarah looked toward Tom. He was still thrashing about. David put a hand on Tom's shoulder and spoke in a gentle tone Sarah had never heard before. "Tommy boy, it's Mr. David. I didn't get your letter in time to come for the surgery, but I'm here now.

"I can tell you, Tom, that Dr. Braxton is definitely all right. He's fixed your leg, and you're going to be running about the place soon. As soon as you get well we're going on a hunting trip, you and I. We'll hike into the preserve, and we won't come back until you've shot your first deer. Now what do you think of that, Tom Biddle?"

Tom didn't respond, but he grew still, stopped thrashing, quit muttering for Sarah. Sarah sat back in her chair, relieved. "Thank you," she said quietly. "I'm sorry he bothered you, Mr. Braddock. He really shouldn't have."

"And why shouldn't he have written me?" David asked, settling on the edge of Tom's bed.

"I told him not to bother you with—"

David interrupted Sarah. "Yes, I know. You told him that I have had 'a disappointment' and that everyone must be 'patient with me.'"

Sarah blushed and looked away. David concluded, "Well, I believe the time has come that you may all stop being patient with me and begin being honest. I've spent quite enough time feeling sorry for myself. That's done now. What do you hear from LisBeth? Is she happy?"

Sarah looked up at him and nodded. "Yes, Mr. Braddock. I believe she's extremely happy. She and Jim are on the homestead. Things are going well for them."

"Good." David said it sincerely. "That's good. Now, Miss Biddle, shall we turn our interests to getting this young man up and running? It will be a fine day, the day our Tommy boy runs."

"Tommy boy" ran for the first time without a limp a few months after his surgery. It wasn't a true run, but it was the harbinger of better things to come. When the better things came, there were times when the staff at the Braddock estate actually wondered if it had not been easier when Tom Biddle had to move a little more slowly.

CHAPTER 10

Indigo Silk

"God is no respecter of persons."
Acts 10:34

"But, *Mother* . . ." David groaned.

"The Braxtons have generously supported every charitable venture I have initiated," Abigail said firmly. "More
important, we have Dr. Braxton to thank for young Tom
Biddle's new life. It's the perfect time of year for a ball—
the beginning of the winter season. And it would be rude
if you didn't attend." She offered a compromise. "It's only
one evening, dear—a few dances. You can make your
escape early."

From where she sat across the room at Mrs. Braddock's
desk addressing invitations, Sarah could not help but hear
the conversation. But Sarah had long since learned the art
of being privy to the Braddocks' private conversations
without giving any evidence that she heard what was said.
In spite of herself, she realized that she was straining to
hear what David Braddock thought of the Braxtons.

To Sarah's surprise, David called her to his defense.
"Sarah, help me out. What does a man do with a mother
who's constantly pushing him at the eligible women in
town?"

Abigail snorted. "Pushing you, indeed! I've begun to despair of ever having grandchildren at all, David."

David held up his hand. "Then you admit it. You *are* pushing me at the Braxtons." He turned to Sarah. "Tell her, Sarah. Tell her what you've observed about the Braxton women."

Sarah hedged. "Dr. Braxton effected a near miracle in Tom's life, Mr. Braddock. I'll never be able to thank him appropriately, and I'm in your mother's debt—as always —for thinking of the dinner and ball in his honor. It's a wonderful idea." Sarah turned back to addressing her invitations.

David leaned back in his chair, defeated. "I see I'll get no support from you, Miss Biddle. Loyal to Mother to the end."

With a sigh of resignation, David said, "You're both right, of course. When Emery refused to accept his usual fee for the surgery, I knew we would have to do something highly public to thank him." Putting his hands on his knees, David pushed himself to a standing position. "Saturday evening. Seven o'clock. I'll host the dinner. I'll escort Rebecca Braxton to the ballroom and dance at least one waltz with her. No, I'll do better than that. I'll dance one waltz with *each* of the Braxton women." His dark eyes flashed as he concluded, "But *then* I'll be joining the gentlemen in the library for the remainder of the evening. The only member of that family with any sense at all is Emery. For his sake, I'll be charming to his vacuous daughters."

David left the room and Sarah returned to her work. Just as she addressed the final invitation, Mrs. Braddock suggested, "Sarah, dear, why don't you take these to the post and then stop by Hoffman's and select a new gown for the ball?" When Sarah didn't respond, Abigail went on. "I know, Sarah. You didn't have a thought of attending. But I'd like it if you would. In fact," Abigail said, rising as she spoke, "let's call Tom and we'll all go shopping. We'll have a new suit for Tom and a gown for you. I saw a beautiful indigo silk just a few days ago. You'll look lovely in it, and they'll be able to have the alterations completed well in time for the ball."

When Sarah still hesitated, Abigail prodded, "Yes, I know, Sarah. You expected you would be serving the dinner, and retiring early with the rest of the servants. Let's get over this little hump in our relationship, dear. I have plenty of servants. What I've been missing is a couple of young people about like you and Tom.

"Well, now I have you and you must realize that you are so much more than a servant. You are my companion, my friend. Goodness, dear, how many times a day do you anticipate what I'm about to say? And just now I knew exactly what you were thinking. I want you to attend the ball as a guest." Abigail smiled mischievously. "And I'm paying your salary, so you must comply." Once again, she beckoned, "Now, come along. Let's round up that little brother of yours and be off to Hoffman's. Everyone at the ball will be delighted to meet you both."

Everyone was *not* delighted to meet Sarah and Tom Biddle. Rebecca Braxton, in fact, was decidedly *against* their presence at the dinner in her father's honor. The only saving grace about the entire affair, as far as Rebecca was concerned, was that Mrs. Braddock dictated that the two servants be seated at the opposite end of the table from her. They sat near *Mrs.* Braddock. Rebecca, on the other hand, sat next to her mother who sat next to *David*.

Rebecca had eyes for nothing and no one else but David throughout the several courses of the elegant meal. She was fashionably certain to eat very little, claiming she had no appetite at all and was watching her waistline. Much to her disappointment, David Braddock did not respond with the expected gallant remark complimenting her tiny waist.

As the dinner wore on, Rebecca became increasingly frustrated by her inability to dominate David's conversation and attention. Indeed, David seemed more interested in quiet little Grace.

But Rebecca had her moment of triumph when the meal was concluded and David asked to escort her to the ballroom. Heart pounding, she extended her gloved hand to take his proffered arm. When David failed to make the obligatory small talk, Rebecca tried to fill the silence between them. As they passed by the library she exclaimed, "Oh, what lovely carpeting! It's the latest fashion."

David responded in a tone of voice he might have used with a bothersome child. "Actually, Miss Braxton, that carpet was ordered by my father about thirty years ago."

"Oh," Rebecca faltered. "Well, it's classic. Stunning." Looking about her, she tried again. Her voice dripped with an unwelcome familiarity as she said, "We're so happy you've returned home again, David. Not a single ball has been quite right this season without you."

David stared blankly ahead. Rebecca's cheeks took on more color. The moment the party reached the arched doorway leading to the ballroom, David disengaged his arm and stepped away. Turning to Grace and Belinda, who were walking behind them, David said, "You'll forgive me if I desert you here. I hope you enjoy the evening, ladies. I shall look forward to a waltz with each of you, if you would be kind enough to add my name to your dance cards." He was gone before any of the three young women could reply.

Sarah and Tom had been walking behind Mrs. Braddock and Mrs. Braxton. When they reached the ballroom, they hesitated uncertainly. They had seldom been in this wing of the house. The ballroom was generally closed up, the furniture covered with sheets. This evening, it was glorious, its glass chandeliers sparkling, its inlaid floors gleaming. At the far end of the dance floor a small orchestra was already seated, tuning their instruments for the evening's entertainment.

Abigail reached for Tom's hand. "Now, Tom, that's my chair over there." She pointed across the dance floor to an atrium where a couch and a group of chairs had been arranged in a gardenlike setting replete with potted plants and freshly cut flowers. "I want you and Sarah to help me welcome our guests, but once the ball begins I'll be just over there." Abigail bent down and winked at Tom. "You'll notice that I've arranged it so I sit near the food. You may have as many of the dainties as you like, and when you've eaten your fill, you may take your leave."

Abigail turned to Sarah and said quietly, "Sarah, dear, please relax. There's nothing to be nervous about. Just smile and say hello. You'll recognize many of the women. Most have come to call at least once since you've been with us."

Having danced the promised waltzes with the female members of the Braxton tribe, David made his escape to the library. He relaxed, totally engrossed in a heated discussion with Emery Braxton over the political fate of a mutual friend. He was unaware that in spite of his concentrated efforts to resist her control, Rebecca Braxton would succeed in changing his life that very evening.

It began when Hobbes entered the room, approached his employer, and whispered, "There's a bit of a problem in the kitchen, sir."

David followed Hobbes into the hall. "It's one of the coachmen, sir. He's imbibed a bit too freely and gone on to behave a bit too freely with two of the upstairs maids." He led David to the wine cellar where the offending party had been closeted by several other more trustworthy coachmen.

David had the drunken coachman hauled back up to the kitchen and poured several cups of hot coffee down him. When the man appeared to be sobering, David leaned down, peered into his face, and delivered a warning. "As I recall, Chambers, we had a similar altercation the last time you drove to one of my mother's soirees. If you cause any further trouble, I'll see to it that you're demoted to stable hand by your employer. Now, you get a grip on yourself."

Fully sober and fully terrified at the prospect of losing his position, Chambers sputtered promises and hurried out of the kitchen while the two maids he had "insulted" tittered in the corner. David glared at them and left. He decided to avoid most of the crowd in general and Rebecca Braxton in particular by skirting through the garden. He was still quite some distance from the house, walking along a tall hedge, when he heard Tom Biddle talking.

"Aw, don't cry, Sarah. She didn't mean it."

There was a slight snuffling sound, and then the clearing of a throat before Sarah's voice responded. "It's all right, Tom. She *did* mean it. But she's right. We *don't* belong. We *are* just like two children playing dress-up. Or, at least I am—was." Sarah's voice grew wistful. "Just for a moment I felt as though I *were* part of the Braddock family. As if the ball and the dinner and—" David heard the silken rustle of Sarah's gown— "and this gown were normal parts of my life." Sarah paused. "I know that Rebecca meant to hurt me when she said those things, Tom, but, in a way, I should thank her. She brought me back to reality. I'm a common girl with common parents, and I'd best cultivate common dreams."

Sarah's gown rustled again as she turned toward Tom and said softly, "Being Tom and Sarah Biddle is nothing to be ashamed of, although Rebecca Braxton surely meant for us to be ashamed. Mason and Ivy Biddle were good, hard-working people, Tom. Biddle is an honest name. But Rebecca was right. We don't really belong. We are here because Abigail Braddock took on one more charity case."

"Then why were you crying, Sarah?"

"I was *not* crying."

"You were."

Sarah groaned softly, waiting before answering. "I was sad and angry and embarrassed and frustrated all at once; angry with Rebecca Braxton for being such a snob; embarrassed that Mrs. Braddock insisted we come; angry at David Braddock for being so handsome and kind and very nearly perfect." Sarah laughed sadly. "Most of all, though, I think I was angry and disappointed in myself. I've been a fool this evening, thinking that I could pretend my way into being treated like everyone else. Why, for a while I was even thinking perhaps someone would ask me to dance. Now, isn't that ridiculous?"

Tom sounded surprised. "I didn't know you could dance."

Sarah explained. "You couldn't remember, Tom, but when I was very little—before Ma got sick, before times got so very bad, we had some good times. Pa used to sing and waltz Ma and me around the room. Hearing the beautiful music tonight, watching all the dancers whirling about . . . I remembered . . . and I thought it would be fun to have one waltz in that beautiful ballroom." Sarah paused briefly before concluding in a matter-of-fact voice, "Of course none of the men in there are going to want to dance with Sarah Biddle."

"Why not? They aren't all like the Braxtons, are they?"

"Probably not, Tom. But, still, I am a servant. And gentry do not dance with servants."

"Well, even if I was gen-uh-tree I'd dance with you. You're pretty and you're nice and I wouldn't care about the servant part."

Sarah chuckled and David heard her noisily kiss Tom's cheek. "God bless you, Tom. Now, let's go tell Mrs. Braddock good evening."

From his place on the opposite side of the hedge, David Braddock had listened, his anger rising. As the sound of Sarah's and Tom's footsteps retreated toward the house, he became more and more angry. He replayed the scene that had probably ensued between Sarah and Rebecca, pacing along the hedge.

I wonder what would have become of Rebecca Braxton if her father had deserted her in an orphanage. I wonder if she would have refused home after home so she could keep her little brother with her. I wonder if she would have had the pluck to make a run for it. David thought through every detail he knew of Sarah's story. *Sarah Biddle has more character, more drive, more ability than a hundred Rebecca Braxtons,* he concluded. *How dare that little snob come into my home and insult her! She actually told Sarah to her face that she doesn't belong? Why, I ought to—* Suddenly, David knew what he ought to do.

Going inside the house, he paused in the back hall, looking into a full-length mirror. He practiced a charming smile, showing his perfect white teeth. Reaching up with both hands, he raked his fingers through his beard and mustache. He straightened his silk cravat, grateful that in his self-indulgence over LisBeth's rejection he had not indulged himself to the point of ruining his athletic figure. He hurried into the ballroom, looking for Rebecca Braxton.

Rebecca caught David's eye from across the ballroom. She blushed crimson as he made his way toward her. Her rib cage swelled against the whalebone stays in her corset as she attempted to take a deep breath to calm herself. As David came closer she bit her lips to redden them. He smiled warmly and Rebecca Braxton extended her hand toward him expectantly. But then, the awful *thing* happened. David Braddock walked *past* her, right up to where Sarah Biddle stood, her back to them, speaking to Mrs. Braddock.

"Miss Biddle, may I have the honor of a waltz this evening?"

For Sarah, things after that seemed to happen in slow motion. She turned around, unable to believe that David Braddock's voice had said the words. Abigail patted her hand and held on while looking up at her son. "Well. It's about time, David. I feared you and Emery had buried yourselves in the library for the remainder of the evening."

Sarah nodded her head slowly. It wasn't a dream, after all. David's deep voice was actually speaking to her, asking again, "Miss Biddle, may I tempt you to remain with us a little longer? I haven't had the privilege of dancing with you this evening." Without waiting for Sarah's reply, David took her hand, wrapped her arm through his, and escorted her to the dance floor.

The orchestra began playing, and Sarah felt a moment of panic. David leaned close. "I'm a very good dancer, Sarah. Just follow me. It will come back."

Only a few measures had been played before Sarah and David were moving gracefully across the ballroom floor. Sarah could see Mrs. Braddock nodding approvingly. But she could also see feminine eyes staring over opened fans as their owners whispered to one another. She could see Rebecca Braxton's olive-toned skin growing darker and darker as the enraged debutante fought to control her temper.

But everything suddenly faded in the realization that David Braddock, the most sought-after bachelor in Philadelphia, had lowered himself to dance with his mother's companion. Sarah wondered why. "I didn't think you were very interested in dancing, Mr. Braddock."

"I wasn't. Never have been."

"But you're very good."

David tightened his grip on her waist. "As good as Mason Biddle?"

Mason Biddle! So that was it. Somehow he had overheard Tom and her in the garden. Sarah blushed crimson. David's face blurred as she struggled to keep back a flood of tears. She managed to finish the dance, to thank David, to make her way to the hall before the flow of tears came. Tom had already gone to bed. Trying not to run, Sarah barely made it to the staircase leading up to Mrs. Braddock's quarters and her own tiny room. Halfway up the grand staircase, her emotions finally found voice. She ran down the hall and into her room, where she fell on her knees beside her bed, buried her face in her hands, and wept.

It took David Braddock only a few moments to decipher the meaning of Sarah's hasty departure from the ballroom. He retraced his steps to where Abigail sat. As he recounted the events of the evening to Abigail, he saw his mother begin to shake her head. "Oh, really, David . . . how could you be so insensitive?"

"Insensitive? But, Mother," David protested. "I wasn't being insensitive. I was trying to put Rebecca Braxton in her place—"

"And in doing that, David, you reminded Sarah—more cruelly than Rebecca Braxton ever could—of her place. You actually told her that the only reason you were dancing with her was to hurt Rebecca Braxton. Oh, David," Abigail said sadly, "you proved that Rebecca was *right*."

Abigail saw understanding dawn in her son's eyes. She continued, "All Sarah wanted this evening was for one person to overlook her position in life, to appreciate her as a young woman. But she couldn't have even that, could she? Not one solitary friend of ours could look past all the artificial trappings of Philadelphia society and just give a sweet, lovely young girl an evening to remember. Not even you, David. Even you couldn't let Sarah be just a young woman attending her first ball."

Abigail put her hand on David's shoulder. "You know, David, if you had really looked at Sarah Biddle, you might have been surprised to see a very attractive young woman. I hoped you would. But I couldn't suggest it, because then I would have been doing the same thing you did. I would have been making her into a 'cause to be championed' rather than a young woman to be accepted and enjoyed on her own merits—which are, I might add, considerable." Abigail gave her words time to sink in before concluding, "Is it really so surprising that she retired after that dance, David?"

David Braddock spent the remainder of the ball walking in the garden, his fists thrust into his pockets. He took no joy in the knowledge that the Braxton women had left early, clustered about Rebecca, who had had some sort of emotional crisis.

Sarah was sitting on her bed staring out the window when someone knocked at her door. Reaching up to smooth her hair, she crossed the room calling softly, "I'm coming, Mrs. Braddock. What can I do—"

It was not Mrs. Braddock. Instead, David stood in the hall. The moment Sarah opened her door, he began to talk. "Sarah. I'm so sorry. Can you forgive me? I didn't mean to hurt you. I'd been to the kitchen to deal with that Chambers fellow again—" David digressed, "You know, that redheaded oaf the Carletons hired to drive their carriage. He causes trouble every time—" He stopped abruptly.

Clearing his throat, David continued. "Anyway, I settled things with Chambers and decided to return to the library through the garden. I wanted to avoid—" Looking at Sarah, David took the plunge into total honesty. "I wanted to avoid Rebecca Braxton. All the Braxton women. I never could abide those women." He grinned, but Sarah did not return his smile. She just stood there, her hand on her door, listening.

David continued. "I was walking along the tall hedge when I overheard you and Tom. The more I heard, the more I wanted to teach Rebecca Braxton—and everyone else—a lesson."

Sarah nodded her head. "It's all right, Mr. Braddock. I know you meant well." She was remote, having pulled down the curtain that separated employer from employee.

Frustrated, David raked one hand through his hair. "But I *didn't* mean well at all, Sarah," he admitted sadly. "I see that now. All I meant was to hurt Rebecca Braxton. And I succeeded. But in hurting Rebecca Braxton, I've hurt you." David placed one hand on the door frame, then leaned forward. "Sarah, can you forgive me? Can you believe me? I honestly didn't mean to hurt you."

"I know you didn't mean to hurt me, Mr. Braddock." Sarah looked at David, clasped both hands tightly in front of her, resisted the urge to push an unruly curl of his hair back in place. His intensity disarmed her. Disturbed her. She stood motionless, looked away, waited for him to dismiss her.

But instead of dismissing Sarah, David studied her. When had her voice taken on that mellow, musical quality? What had happened, he wondered, to the skinny orphan girl his mother had taken in? Why hadn't he noticed her blue eyes before? Had her blonde hair always had that glow, or was it just the lighting in the hall that made it shine so?

Impulsively, David grabbed Sarah's hand. "I've come to make it up to you, Sarah. Come with me." He pulled her gently out of her room, closed the door behind them, hushed her protests. When she finally realized where he was headed, Sarah tried to disengage her hand. "Really, Mr. Braddock, there's no need—"

"Hush. And call me David."

The idea of calling Mr. Braddock "David" kept Sarah quiet until they had reached the ballroom. But the ballroom was not quite empty. At the far end, the orchestra waited. David led Sarah across the polished floor to the center of the room. Bowing, he asked, "Miss Biddle—Sarah—may I have the honor of the last waltz?" He didn't wait for Sarah to answer. Instead, he pulled her close, whirling her about the huge, empty ballroom while the orchestra played.

At some point during the last waltz of the evening, David Braddock did what his mother had suggested. He lifted the curtain that Sarah hid behind. There he found the very thing he had always wanted—a quiet and gentle spirit, a truly generous heart, a kind concern for others that all the money in her father's bank account would never buy Rebecca Braxton.

When the music ended, David did not take his hand from Sarah's waist. He continued holding her at arm's length. She returned his gaze calmly until he leaned toward her and whispered, "And now, Sarah, I really must insist that you call me David." He stepped away from her, crossed the ballroom to dismiss the orchestra, and turned back, intending to suggest that they walk in the garden. But Sarah Biddle had once again fled to her room, where she spent the rest of the night trying unsuccessfully to pull down the curtain that must separate the worlds of employer and employee, master and servant, Braddock and Biddle.

CHAPTER 11

Old Rose Calico

----

*"He healeth the broken in heart,
and bindeth up their wounds."*
Psalm 147:3

In the weeks and months that followed the ball, David Braddock found fewer reasons to travel and less need to attend evening meetings. He spent more time at home, took Tom Biddle on more outings, joined his mother and Sarah for more afternoon teas.

Abigail Braddock met with Mrs. Titus, who agreed with her employer that the household ran quite smoothly without Sarah Biddle and that she could certainly be spared to attend to Mrs. Braddock's personal needs. Sarah became a full-time companion to Mrs. Braddock.

In spite of David Braddock's friendly interest, Sarah continued to hide behind the curtain of rank that, according to Philadelphia society, was permanently drawn between her world and the Braddocks'. Rebecca Braxton's spiteful words were never far from her mind.

When David planned an outing for Tom and invited Sarah to join them, she steadfastly refused unless Mrs. Braddock was going as well. When David came for tea and asked her to join him and his mother, Sarah found that she had pressing duties elsewhere. When David asked her to walk in the garden, she agreed, but she chose her words carefully and refused to discuss anything remotely personal.

Sarah began to look forward to the family's return to Lincoln, where she would be busy running a house, where Tom would be occupied at Miss Griswall's school, and where David Braddock would be absent, remaining back east to conduct his business.

Abigail and Sarah and Tom arrived in Lincoln on the first day of April. Determined to forget the nonsensical thoughts she had begun to entertain about David Braddock, Sarah concentrated on reestablishing old friendships and familiar routines. She grew to love Nebraska, where there were no Braxtons to remind her of her station in life, where she was among friends who accepted her on her own merits and rejoiced in her small successes, where she could visit LisBeth Callaway and Augusta Hathaway, where she could rejoin the quilting group at the Congregational Church.

Two weeks after her arrival in Lincoln, Abigail Braddock had an early appointment at Dr. Gilbert's office "to see to a small matter." Sarah was sitting on her private porch reading when she heard a carriage drive in. It was too soon for Mrs. Braddock's return, and Sarah was somewhat disgruntled to think that the driver had forgotten to lock the gate after Abigail's departure. Descending the back staircase, she hurried through the butler's pantry and into the kitchen, intending to walk up the long bricked drive and attend to the lock herself. But in the doorway she collided with David Braddock.

David held her in his arms until she backed away stammering, "Oh—Mr. Braddock—what are you—" Self-consciously she raised both hands to smooth her hair. "Mrs. Braddock is gone until the afternoon—" Sarah walked across the kitchen toward the stove. "Can I make you some coffee? I'll bring it into the library—"

David followed her across the kitchen, ran his index finger along her jawline, and dropped his hand to his side before saying quietly, "You have no idea how much I have missed hearing your voice these last few weeks."

Sarah looked away nervously, groped for the coffeepot, and then went to the sink to pump water.

David leaned against the workstation that dominated the center of the kitchen. Folding his arms, he stood quietly looking at Sarah. "Aren't you even a little glad to see me, Sarah?"

Sarah looked out the window over the sink. She answered without turning around. "Of course I am. Mrs. Braddock will be thrilled that you've come to Lincoln."

"Don't put Mother between us, Sarah. I asked if *you* were glad to see me."

David retreated to sit down at the small table in the corner where Tom and Sarah usually ate breakfast. Leaning back, he began to rock his chair. It creaked in rhythm with his fingers rapping the tabletop. Finally he raised his fine brown eyes to look piercingly at Sarah. "Last Sunday the Reverend used First Corinthians, chapter thirteen, as his text. 'Charity suffereth long, and is kind; charity envieth not; charity vaunteth not itself, is not puffed up, doth not behave itself unseemly, seeketh not her own, is not easily provoked, thinketh no evil . . .' I was sitting in the Braddock family pew, and it suddenly dawned on me that a young woman who resides under my own roof exhibits those qualities."

David stopped rocking his chair, got up, and began to pace about the kitchen. "A young woman whose personality suits me, who daily proves her devotion to my family, who possesses the added blessing of a younger brother who provides rollicking entertainment every hour of the day."

Sarah had not moved from her place by the sink throughout David's speech. She had, at some point, put one hand out to steady herself.

David continued. "So, I have concluded that there is within my reach a woman who could be my heart's companion. Except there is a problem. The woman in question withdraws from me. Every time I am in her presence she pulls down a curtain between us. Now, I've been thinking about that curtain. I've decided that on her side of the curtain it must say, 'Sarah Biddle, charity case.' That seems to be the role she insists on playing in spite of my efforts to draw her out."

David stopped pacing, leaned on the work island that separated Sarah from him, and asked, "Tell me, Sarah, what does it say on *my* side of the curtain? What is it about the two of us that dictates that we remain apart?"

Sarah looked at him honestly and then answered quietly, "Your side says, 'David Braddock, wealthy benefactor, son of my mistress, kind friend.'"

David shook his head sadly. "I expected better of you, Sarah. You of all people, who have been hurt by those who judge others based on their social rank. You should know better."

"I'm not sure what you mean."

"I mean that if I were the butler, or the coach driver, or anyone else except the owner of the house, you would *respond* differently to me. Unless, of course, you find me unattractive. I am a few years older than you are. Is that it? Am I so totally conceited that I've merely assumed you feel some attraction for me?"

Sarah pleaded, "Please, David—Mr. Braddock. Whether or not I find you attractive is beside the point. I'm a *maid*." She looked down at her apron. "I wear old rose calico and white cotton aprons. A man in your position deserves a woman accustomed to white lawn and silk."

To Sarah's surprise, David went to the kitchen door and prepared to leave. "I've taken the suite at the Hathaway House, Sarah. Please tell Mother I'd be pleased if she'd dine with me this evening." He turned to go, then looked back. "I've come to Lincoln with one purpose in mind, Sarah. I mean to court you. I mean to tear down that curtain that divides us, and I don't care what people think or say."

Sarah poured herself a glass of water and raised it to her lips with trembling hands. She felt his gaze on her back and turned toward him, steadying herself with one hand on the rim of the porcelain sink.

"I love you, Sarah Biddle. Not with some passionate boyish attachment, but with respect for who you are, with delight in your inner beauty—and," he added quickly, "with no small amount of pleasure in your blue eyes, your slim figure, and your classic nose. Get accustomed to the idea that one day very soon you're going to be the mistress of this house, not the maid in the kitchen."

David retreated down the back stairs to his carriage, made his way down the drive and out onto J Street. Sarah slid to the floor, buried her face in her hands, and cried tears that washed out the bitterness she had felt against Rebecca Braxton, the grief she had felt over past emptiness and loss. And then something happened. The tears washed away the curtain that separated Sarah from what she had wanted most.

Sarah Biddle was granted only a few days of untarnished joy before David was called away on business. The week after he left found Sarah sitting beside Mrs. Braddock in Dr. Gilbert's office, her mind reeling with the horrible reality that confronted her.

Dr. Gilbert was adamant. "Almost every imaginable form of treatment has been adopted, Mrs. Braddock, but modern medical science is still completely baffled so far as a radical cure is concerned. Little is known of the cause. Had you consulted your surgeon in Philadelphia at the beginning—"

Sarah was amazed to hear Abigail snap back at the doctor. "Well, I didn't. I ignored it. I thought it was nothing. Unfortunately, I can't go back and change that." Abigail stood up. "I think we can conclude this appointment now, Dr. Gilbert."

Abigail and Sarah rode back to the manse in silence. Immediately after their arrival, Abigail went to her room. Sarah spent the afternoon wandering aimlessly about the house, finally settling into David's oversized chair in the library with an unopened book in her lap. *Aunt Jesse would tell me to pray*, Sarah thought. *Aunt Jesse would say, "Read God's Word, Sarah. It always brings comfort."* In spite of the persistent thought, Sarah did not pray, nor did she pull a Bible from the library shelves. She sat quietly, listening to the silence in the great house.

Later, when Sarah delivered the customary tray for afternoon tea, she found Abigail sitting at her dressing table brushing her long white hair.

Sarah put the tea tray on a small table by the door and had turned to go when Abigail called out, "Sarah, please, stay with me a while."

Instead of sitting down Sarah crossed the room and put her hand on Abigail's shoulder. The touch of the younger woman resulted in an uncharacteristic show of emotion. Abigail began to cry softly.

"It will be all right," Sarah soothed. "David and I are with you. We love you. We'll care for you."

"Oh, Sarah," Abigail sighed. "It's not that. I'm just so completely grieved that I've brought this upon you. I needed you to go with me to Dr. Gilbert's so that he could tell you. I knew I couldn't hide it any longer, and I need your help. But I'm so very sorry, Sarah. How will I ever make it up to you?"

Sarah looked at Mrs. Braddock's reflection in her dressing mirror. "Don't think that. Please, don't ever think that you have anything to make up for. Not after all you've done for Tom and me. Not after you've welcomed me like a daughter."

"I wouldn't blame you at all if you wanted to leave right now—just pack up Tom and leave. I would understand completely."

Sarah looked amazed. "How could you think I would ever do such a thing? Of course we're not going anywhere. We're going to take care of you. We're going to pray for God to heal you. David will wire every specialist in the country until we find—"

"No." Abigail interrupted her. "No. I don't want David to know. Not yet. I needed someone to know—to help me—but, Sarah, you must promise me that you won't breathe a word of this to David. Not until—" Abigail took in a sharp breath and reached up to lay her hand over her left breast. "Not until it can't be helped. The business he's attending to in Virginia is vital to the future of his new company—vital to your future together. I won't have him distracted by concern for me. Promise me."

Caught between loyalty to Mrs. Braddock and her love for David, Sarah hesitated. Abigail argued, "I'm not asking you to lie to David, Sarah. I will tell him. But this kind of thing must be done in person. I want to do it myself, in my own time, in my own way. Please, dear, grant me this one favor."

Reluctantly, Sarah agreed. "Whatever you wish. But you *will* tell him?"

"Of course. But not yet. We have time yet before—" Abigail didn't finish the sentence.

Sarah took the brush from Abigail's hand and began to brush her long hair. The two women were silent for a few moments. Sarah braided Abigail's hair, wrapped it about her head, pinned it in place. She poured tea, sitting down to discuss plans for the grand dinner that was to welcome David home in a few weeks, and then reported that Miss Griswall had selected Tom to give an address at the Tartaraxx Pageant planned in Lincoln the next month.

Just when Sarah had almost succeeded in forgetting about the disease that had imposed its presence upon them, Abigail asked, "Didn't Dr. Gilbert recommend iced compresses—"

"You're in pain," Sarah said, leaping to her feet. "Why didn't you say something?" She was out the door instantly. Downstairs in the kitchen she opened *Kellogg's Ladies Guide in Health and Disease*. The recently published leather-bound book presented the latest findings medical science offered, stated in plain language for the layman. Turning to page 582, Sarah read quickly what Dr. Gilbert had underlined, "Frequent freezing of the diseased parts by means of a mixture of salt and pounded ice, in proportion of one part of the former to two of the latter, applied by means of a muslin bag, has been very highly recommended for holding in check the progress of this terrible malady."

Running upstairs to her room, Sarah rummaged through a pile of fabric scraps by her rocker, retrieved a square of muslin, quickly ran a basting stitch around the edges, and drew the square up into a bag. Returning to the kitchen and Dr. Kellogg's printed instructions, she concocted his remedy and returned to Mrs. Braddock's side.

When her pain subsided, Abigail said gently, "You know, dear, all this 'Mrs. Braddock' nonsense seems ridiculous in light of recent developments." She smiled and patted Sarah's hand. "I should like it very much if you would call me 'Mother Braddock.'"

CHAPTER 12

Cadet Blue

"Moreover it is required in stewards,
that a man be found faithful."
1 Corinthians 4:2

Try as she might, Abigail Braddock found herself totally unable to inform her son that, short of miracle, she would likely die before the year was out. She could not write it while he was away, and when he returned she could not say it. Ridiculing her own cowardice, she sent David to see Dr. Gilbert with a note in hand asking that the doctor discuss her case with her son, answer his questions, then send him home.

So it was that one afternoon David Braddock entered his mansion with a huge weight on his shoulders. Instead of going to his mother, David went to Sarah. He pulled out one of the two chairs at the small white table in the corner of the kitchen and sat, waiting.

Sarah and Tom had been in the garden, and when they came in the back door and Sarah saw the expression on David's face, she sent Tom upstairs to Mrs. Braddock. "See if she needs help coming down, Tom. I'll begin to dish up supper."

Tom left and Sarah stood motionless, waiting for David to speak. His voice was strained as he said, "I saw Dr.

Gilbert. He told me." Anguish filled his eyes, and he bowed his head and covered his face with his hands.

Sarah crossed the spotless white kitchen floor and laid a hand on the broad shoulders. At her touch, David took a deep breath, wrapped both his arms around her, and held on so tightly she could barely breathe. She stroked his hair.

When David finally let go he looked up at her, his eyes shining with unspilled tears. "You knew."

"Yes."

"Why didn't you tell me?"

"I promised I wouldn't. Not until she was ready. She wanted to tell you herself, in her own way, in her own time."

David stood up. "I have to complete the details of the business in Virginia. I'll need some time with my attorneys in Philadelphia. If I wire my uncle Ira, he can get things going. It shouldn't take long."

Sarah nodded. "You should go as soon as possible. Then come back home so that you'll be here when—" Sarah was unable to finish the sentence.

Impulsively, David sat back down and pulled Sarah into his lap. "When I come back, we'll be married. Mother will be able to attend."

Sarah bit her lip and didn't reply. Gently she pushed herself away, went to the stove, and began slicing turkey.

David ran his hands through his hair again. "That wasn't a proper proposal, Sarah. It was miserable. Please, forgive me." Crossing to where she stood, he kissed her on the cheek, turned her face toward his, and cradled it in his hands. "I love you, Sarah. Will you be my wife?"

Hearing David Braddock propose was something Sarah had dreamed of. Now that it had happened, she was overwhelmed with the reality of it. She tried to picture herself presiding over his dinner parties, seated at the head of the massive banquet table in Philadelphia. The absurdity of an orphan-become-housekeeper-become-companion playing such a role made her pull away from him.

David read her thoughts. "Don't look at the *house*, Sarah. Look at *me*. Don't look at Philadelphia society. Look at *me*."

Sarah glanced about the kitchen doubtfully. "I'm a *maid*, David. I've benefited from the education your mother provided, I speak with good grammar, I know everything required to run a fine house. But the fact remains that I am a domestic servant. Think of it, David. What will your friends say?"

"If they say anything other than a polite welcome, then they will no longer be my friends."

"Don't be immature, David. You're not considering—"

"I've done little else *but* consider every aspect of this situation for the past few months, Sarah." David's eyes flashed. "Perhaps *you* are the one who's immature. Too immature to take on a challenge. Is that it? You don't really have what's required to overcome a few obstacles?"

Sarah's cheeks grew crimson. Eyes blazing, she pulled off her apron, picked up a platter of turkey, and headed for the dining room. "I think I've proven my mettle, David. And I think you are proving my point." With an unusual display of anger, Sarah swept out of the room.

It was only a moment before David wandered sheepishly into the dining room. He kissed his mother on the cheek and took his place at the head of the table, snapping his napkin angrily and shoving it into his lap.

Abigail Braddock's eyes sparkled with mischief as she commented, "Sarah, you have a new dress. That color of blue makes your eyes just glow." Abigail chuckled. "My, my, children, such a lot of fuss over a simple engagement."

Tom plunked down his water glass and let out a loud *"What?"*

David emptied his wine glass and speared a huge piece of turkey, casting a glance not unlike that of a hurt child in Sarah's direction.

Abigail went on. "Children, of all the things that could have happened to me today, this is the very happiest. I'll have Elsie Thornburn in this week and we'll discuss Sarah's gown—something elegant, but simple. David, you must announce the engagement in all the Philadelphia papers. I'll call in a decorator to redo my rooms for you. Oh, dear," she worried, "I hope there will be time. When did you say you wanted to have the ceremony?"

David looked at Sarah. Sarah looked at David. For once in his young life, Tom looked on speechless.

"Well, children—when?"

David reached under the table to take Sarah's hand. He squeezed it gently, refused to let go. "Mother wants to know when the ceremony is to take place, Sarah."

Sarah Biddle looked into Abigail's shining blue eyes. The love and happiness there overshadowed every doubt. Looking at David, Sarah smiled and said, "Whenever you say, David."

Try as he might, David Braddock was not able to complete the complicated transfer of significant amounts of real estate to the Braddock name quickly. Legal entanglements and complications arose again and again. Summer waned and the seedling trees along the high brick wall dropped their leaves. David managed one quick return to Nebraska for a brief visit, and then was called away again. Shortly after he left the second time, Abigail wrote that she had improved a little. David was unable to get back to Lincoln to enjoy his mother's last good days.

When the downturn came, it happened so quickly that Sarah was totally unprepared. Standing on the landing just outside Abigail's door, Dr. Gilbert tried to prepare Sarah for the next few weeks. Speaking in the voice he had learned to use when telling the thing he hated most to people he admired, the doctor slowly and distinctly tried to comfort, even as he outlined what Abigail—and Sarah—would face.

"Toward the end it could get—" The doctor paused. "Difficult for her. I'll do what I can. I'll teach you to administer morphine. We must pray that God takes her before she suffers unduly."

Over the doctor's shoulder, Sarah could see the door to Mrs. Braddock's room, the door that had always been open to her, welcoming her in as a daughter, not a housemaid. Sarah stared at the door for only a moment before she fixed her eyes on Dr. Gilbert's and said calmly, "I'll do whatever you say, Doctor. And I'll send for David—for Mr. Braddock—immediately."

"Be certain he knows that he is not to delay." Dr. Gilbert walked beside Sarah as they descended to the kitchen. "You'll likely need help toward the end. It's a pity we don't have trained nurses in Lincoln as yet, but—"

Sarah interrupted him with a shake of the head. "No. I'll get someone to help with the house if necessary, but I'll take care of Mother Braddock myself." She added hopefully, "David will come at once, and he'll take care of the details."

Withdrawing a note from his medical bag, Dr. Gilbert wrote on it and handed it to Sarah. *Chloral hydrate, gr. 5, Vaseline, oz. 1. to correct fetor and allay pain.* "If you have any questions, don't hesitate to ask. Have Tom go to the druggist today and get those items. You'll want to get it mixed right away. You'll likely need it soon."

Dr. Gilbert turned to go, pausing at the door to say gently, "You are not alone in this, Miss Biddle. My office is only a short distance away. I'm available day or night. Just send Tom to the back door. My living quarters are at the rear of the clinic."

Sarah thanked the doctor, set the script he had written on the table, and went back upstairs. She hesitated for a moment just outside the closed door that separated her from Abigail Braddock and the unavoidable. Then, with a bright smile on her face she went through the door to Mother Braddock's side.

In only a few days, Sarah was forced to send Tom for Dr. Gilbert. "I've tried the tamarind tea and rice milk you suggested. She can't tolerate anything on her stomach. I've given several injections of pancreas and cream. She's losing weight." Sarah's voice trembled. "And she's still in so much pain. I can sense it, even when I'm out of the room."

"When is Mr. Braddock expected?" the doctor asked.

"He wasn't in Philadelphia when we first tried to contact him. It seems his uncle put off furthering the message a few days. When David finally got the wire, he made arrangements immediately. I've just had another wire this morning. He should be home tomorrow."

Dr. Gilbert's face was somber. "Good." He picked up his bag. When Sarah started up the stairs, he stopped her. "I'm certain you've done everything you can at the moment, Miss Biddle. You are nearly exhausted. While I am with Mrs. Braddock, I want you to get some rest. I'm going to give her an injection that will make her sleep all afternoon." Dr. Gilbert looked at Sarah sternly. "You are going to need every ounce of strength in you during the next few days—or hours. We must pray for a miracle, but we must also prepare for the usual sequence of events. You must be rested for the battle, Miss Biddle."

Dr. Gilbert proceeded up the stairs. Sarah went into the parlor and collapsed into a chair. The blinds had been drawn. Sarah welcomed the dark, giving way to the tears she had held for so long.

"David!" Abigail moaned. "When are you coming, David? I've waited so long. I'm tired." Abigail turned her face away from Sarah and began to thrash about.

Sarah laid a cool hand on Abigail's forehead. At Sarah's touch, Abigail grew still. "David's coming, Mother Braddock. He'll be here soon. Only yesterday he sent a telegram that said he was taking the very next train out of Philadelphia." Sarah added lovingly, "I'm sorry you have to suffer so, Mother Braddock."

Abigail opened her eyes. The fog of pain cleared momentarily and she smiled weakly. With effort she whispered, "Yes, dear Sarah. I remember. David is coming." She closed her eyes again and muttered, "I'll wait for David before—" She flinched again and gripped Sarah's hand. "I'll wait for David, then I'm going."

Sarah raised Abigail's head gently, coaxing her to sip some tea. It contained only a mild sedative, but combined with an injection it took effect quickly, and Abigail sank into a deep sleep. Even though she slept, she moaned and tossed her head. Sarah sat by her bedside, replacing cool compresses and trying to fluff pillows to cushion Abigail's emaciated limbs.

When it was time to change Abigail's dressing, Sarah's hands shook. Somehow she made her way through it. When it was done, Sarah sat motionless in a chair, her clothing drenched with her own sweat, her face pale. She watched Abigail struggling to live until David arrived and wondered at the spirit that could survive so long when the body was so near death.

Halfway through the night it became apparent to Sarah that Abigail was going to lose her battle to see David one last time. Tom ran for Dr. Gilbert, and he came momentarily, his shirttails not quite tucked into his waist, his black hair rumpled.

Abigail's moaning had increased until she let out a shriek that sent a chill down Sarah's spine. Dr. Gilbert pulled out a blue-tinted bottle. "This will take the pain. Unfortunately it will also keep her unconscious. She may not know when Mr. Braddock comes."

From the bed, a remarkably lucid voice said, "No. I won't have it. I must be awake when David comes."

Sarah and Dr. Gilbert turned to look at the frail body that was Abigail Braddock. Sarah looked beyond the shrunken, ashen face and into sparkling eyes that were bright and smiling.

At the look of amazement on Sarah's face, Abigail said, "I'm about to die, Sarah dear. I know that. But I really do want to be awake for David. When do you think he will come?"

"By morning, I think, Mother Braddock."

"Then I shall wait until morning. This thing in my body and I have done battle for a long time, and it is about to win. But I will win one more battle first." Without turning her head, Abigail said softly, "Dr. Gilbert, I'd like it if you'd stay in case I can't bear it. But, please, I feel better now. Don't do anything unless, unless—"

"I'll stay as long as I'm needed, Mrs. Braddock. And I won't administer any more sedatives unless you request them."

Abigail nodded, sighed, seeming to relax a little. "Sarah," she called, patting the bed beside her. "Come here, dear, where I can see you."

Sarah obeyed, and Abigail began to talk. "I have been so blessed to know you, Sarah. You've been a dear daughter. Sarah, I'm so happy that David will have you when I am gone. You must take very good care of him. And don't let anyone make you think that you don't deserve the name Braddock. We love you, Sarah, and I'm proud to know that you will be the mother of the future generation of Braddocks." Abigail took a breath. "Now, I'd like to see Tom, please."

Sarah fetched her brother, who entered the room with the reluctance of any child who fears the changes illness brings to beloved elders. But when Tom stood by the bed and looked into the blue eyes, he saw Mrs. Braddock. The illness and the odd smells in the room melted away.

Mrs. Braddock smiled lovingly. "Tom, dear," she said, reaching feebly for his hand, "I've great plans for you. Now you study hard, and make me proud. I shall be watching you, young man. I'm leaving you enough money to finish school and go on to the university. Someday, when you are a great lawyer, you remember me and do something good to share your success with others. Remember, Tom, that when God blesses us, He expects us to pass that blessing on to others." Abigail paused again, received Tom's kiss on her cheek, and sent him away. "You're a good boy, Tom Biddle. Now run along."

When Tom had gone, Abigail Braddock began to ramble. "You know, Sarah, I resent it highly that I'll not be around to be a proper doting grandmother. . . . Don't let David brood, Sarah. Remind him that I'm looking forward to seeing his father. . . . There are some in the family who aren't too kind, Sarah. They may be a bit rude to you. You just remember that Abigail and David Braddock love you. . . ." Finally, Abigail drew a sharp breath and said between clenched teeth. "I think I'll have to take another rest, Sarah. Is it near morning yet?"

Sarah looked through the window at the black sky and lied. "Yes, Mother Braddock. I think dawn will be here soon."

"Dawn . . . David . . ." Abigail sighed, sinking away from consciousness.

Sarah held Abigail's hand tightly and sank onto the floor, resting her head on the edge of the mattress. When she could stay awake no longer, she dragged a rocking chair to the side of the bed, then took Abigail's hand once again. Night wore on, and Abigail's enemy raised its wicked head and began to pound at her body. Pain seared through her, and the sound of it escaped her pale lips. Dr. Gilbert was forced to administer morphine. Abigail sank into unconsciousness, her mind no longer aware of the agonies of her body.

When dawn really arrived, someone pounded at the front door. Sarah dragged herself from her rocker and went out into the hall. At the top of the stairs, she stopped and looked down at Tom, who was closing the door, a telegram in his hand.

"From Iowa, Sarah."

Sarah opened the telegram and read it, then sank down onto the stairs. In disbelief she read it again and again. Her head sank onto her knees and she began to cry. Then, from behind her, came the sound of Abigail's voice screeching her son's name and calling for Sarah.

Sarah ran back into the room. Kneeling by the bed, she called out, "It's Sarah, Mother Braddock."

Abigail could no longer wait for David. Her body had fought against the pain as long as it could. She was being called across the pain and into eternity. To Sarah's amazement, as she took her last breath, Abigail opened her eyes, called out David's name. She died with an odd look of contentment on her translucent face.

Sarah fell into the rocker at the bedside, trembling, clutching the telegram. Dr. Gilbert sat beside his patient, closed her eyes, and folded her emaciated hands across her waist.

Sarah Biddle began to weep, rocking back and forth, patting Mrs. Braddock's hands. She handed Dr. Gilbert the telegram, where he read that Mr. David Braddock had been on a train that had left the tracks in Iowa. The telegram offered condolences to his family, as Mr. Braddock was among the deceased.

"Oh, my dear. My poor, poor, dear." Dr. Gilbert rummaged in his medical bag for smelling salts.

Tom Biddle came to the door, went to his sister's side, read the telegram. He was hopeful. "Maybe they're wrong, Sarah. Maybe they mistook him for someone else. He could be all right—"

Sarah shook her head wearily. "No, Tom. I can feel it. He's gone." She sat quietly for a few moments before asking Dr. Gilbert, "Do you think it's possible that Mother Braddock actually saw David, Dr. Gilbert? Do you think he came for her after all? Could that be why she called out his name so happily?"

Dr. Miles Gilbert was a man of science. And as such, he was not given to nonsensical presuppositions about the afterlife. But he was also a religious man, and as such he was given to kindness and a humble belief that in matters concerning the afterlife there were many things that only God knew. Thus, Dr. Gilbert put a caring hand on Sarah Biddle's trembling shoulder and said softly, "I think that must have been it, Miss Biddle. The good Lord let David come for his mother. They are together, God rest their souls."

Throughout the rest of that night and into the next day, while Augusta Hathaway managed funeral arrangements, while acquaintances came and went, Sarah Biddle pondered the thought that perhaps God had allowed David to escort his mother across the river of pain and into eternity.

In the days that followed, Sarah began to feel aged. In the mirror she saw the evidence of her grief. Tom stayed nearby, spoke softly, tried not to disturb his sister. He answered the door and prepared lunch, weeded the garden and swept the floor. Sarah waited for word from Philadelphia regarding the disposition of the Braddock estate.

Augusta Hathaway offered what comfort she could, urging Sarah and Tom to move back to the hotel immediately. Sarah declined. "I owe it to the Braddocks to take care of their things until I hear from David's uncle Ira. David said that Ira is very efficient, and it surely will not be long before he sends instructions."

CHAPTER 13

Shaker Gray

----

*"He that loveth silver shall not be satisfied with
silver; nor he that loveth abundance with
increase: this is also vanity."*
Ecclesiastes 5:10

Ira Braddock believed in the gospel of efficiency and
expediency, particularly in matters involving large sums of
money to which he felt entitled. Hence, when, as trustee
of the Braddock estate, he was informed of the deaths of
both David and Abigail Braddock, Ira booked himself on
the first train west. He arrived in Lincoln, Nebraska, with
a preconceived notion of what he would find. Expecting a
small town full of "country bumpkins," he discovered a
rapidly growing city where the best homes had gaslights
and indoor plumbing. Expecting to meet rough and uneducated westerners, he found literate professionals. Expecting
to find an overwrought and uneducated housemaid, he
found Sarah Biddle.

Ira arrived unannounced, a move calculated to prevent
any hiding of silver or selling of valuables. Standing at the
door of the Braddock manse, he introduced himself and
stepped across the threshold, almost pushing Sarah aside
before she could step out of his way.

Sarah stifled a smile, thinking that this was, indeed, the
first human she had seen who closely resembled a banty

rooster. She closed the door. "Please don't be offended, sir, but we've not had the pleasure of meeting, and I wonder if you have any identification?"

Ira had already strode into the front parlor and was surveying the room for any obviously empty spaces. At Sarah's question, he looked at her sharply over his pincenez spectacles. "I beg your pardon?"

Sarah repeated her question. "Well, sir, I'm sure the Braddock family would want to know that their interests have been looked after. Mr. Braddock had nothing but the highest regard for Ira Braddock. I'm certain the latter would never approve of my disposing of Braddock property until I was certain it was, indeed, Ira Braddock who was guiding me."

Braddock smoothed his ruffled feathers, preened, cleared his throat. "Of course, Miss Biddle, of course." He reached inside his coat and produced a document that authorized him to "transact in the best interest of the estate of Mr. David and Mrs. Abigail Braddock."

Sarah nodded. "Thank you."

Braddock was shown through the entire manse room by room. "I'll need an inventory," he ordered.

"I've been working on that for you, Mr. Braddock." Sarah walked back into the library and emerged with a few sheets of paper in hand. "It's nearly complete, except for Mr. Braddock's quarters." Sarah swallowed hard. "I haven't been in those rooms since the telegram came." As Ira looked at her, a question in his eyes, she answered, "I began in the kitchen. The library alone took a few days. I've just finished Mrs. Braddock's room. Perhaps you would like to complete Mr. Braddock's room yourself."

Sarah was relieved when Ira nodded. "Yes, of course. I've hired a secretary to assist me." He looked down over the lists Sarah had prepared. "We should have these verified and be ready to complete the sale in a few days."

At the mention of a sale, Sarah paled. She had known that it was inevitable, but Ira's saying it aloud somehow brought a fresh sense of loss. Looking about her, she found it difficult to imagine another family occupying the rooms, repainting the walls, perhaps carpeting the inlaid dining room floor David had strode across so energetically.

Sarah spent the remainder of the morning with Ira Braddock. Bristling inwardly at the man's disdain for all things Nebraskan, she managed to be patient when he wondered aloud at David and Abigail's interest in the state. She soon gave up trying to explain what made Lincoln so attractive to immigrants. Ira Braddock had made up his mind and was not to be confused by facts.

Ira was sitting on the veranda enjoying a glass of lemonade when he suggested that Sarah might be more comfortable elsewhere. "After all, Miss Biddle, the house is empty. Now that I have arrived, things will be taken care of quickly. Surely you would like to get on with your life elsewhere."

I have no life elsewhere, Mr. Braddock. My life died two weeks ago. It's somewhere in Iowa. Sarah stared blankly at Braddock. When the import of his words became clear, she nodded graciously. "Of course. Tom and I will pack our things this evening. I'll bring you the keys in the morning."

"Oh, that won't be necessary, Miss Biddle," Ira said with forced friendliness. "I'll be happy to stay out here on the porch until you've packed. It's quite pleasant."

I'm being forced from David's home.

The man's crass insensitivity, his obvious greed, overcame Sarah's usually gentle nature. Desperately wanting to "heap burning coals" on Ira Braddock's head, she thought of only one gesture that could best him. She reached down to remove the sterling silver chatelaine that hung from her waist. "You'll be wanting this. All the door and cabinet keys are right here. I have the only complete set, so be certain not to misplace these. Tom will be home from school in about an hour. We'll be packed and gone twenty minutes after he gets home." Sarah turned angrily and walked into the house.

Exactly twenty minutes after Tom Biddle came home from school, he and Sarah exited the mansion by the front door. Out of the corner of her eye, Sarah could see Ira Braddock fumbling with the keys she had given him, trying to unlock an ancient door at the back of the carriage house. She placed one hand on Tom's shoulder and guided him straight out the main gate. "Don't even look at him, Tom," she ordered through half-closed lips.

The two walked the half-mile to Hathaway House, arriving at the kitchen door just as Augusta Hathaway returned from a drive to visit LisBeth Callaway. Earlier in the day, Augusta had witnessed the arrival of Ira Braddock as he checked in with Silas Kellum at the Hathaway House. She had personally served him coffee, offering her condolences at the death of his nephew and sister-in-law. A generous woman who honestly tried to give every man a fair chance, Augusta had done her best to suppress her immediate dislike for the pompous little man. But as she came around the corner from the livery, as she saw Sarah and Tom Biddle, saw their valises, Augusta Hathaway threw caution to the winds and allowed her intense dislike for Ira Braddock to flourish. Without a word, Augusta went to Sarah and Tom, took the suitcases from their hands, and enveloped them both in her ample arms.

In spite of herself, Sarah began to cry. Tom followed suit.

"It's all right, children, it's all right. You're back home with Aunt Augusta." Augusta kissed Sarah on the cheek and chucked Tom under the chin. "And I'm so *glad* to have you."

The morning after Sarah and Tom had been summarily thrown out of their home, Dr. Miles Gilbert dined at the Hathaway House, requesting an interview with Miss Biddle.

"I went by the manse earlier this morning and Ira Braddock informed me that the 'servants' had been dismissed." Dr. Gilbert took a gulp of coffee before continuing. "As the Braddock family physician, I was privy to much information about the Braddocks' holdings here in Nebraska, Miss Biddle, and I want to offer my services to you. You must arrange a meeting with an attorney as soon as possible."

Sarah stared at the doctor blankly. "Whatever for? David trusted Ira Braddock. He'll certainly handle things efficiently."

"And as selfishly as possible. Unless you are mentioned in Abigail's will, you are obviously going to be left with nothing, Miss Biddle. It's an outrage. I know of your relationship to David Braddock and I know he would want you to have your fair portion of his estate. His mother said she had provided for Tom. She most certainly would have done the same for you, had she ever dreamed that David would predecease your marriage."

Sarah was adamant. "Dr. Gilbert. No one knew of our engagement because I wanted it that way. You are bound by your oath as a physician not to reveal what ensues between a patient and her doctor." Sarah leaned forward and said intensely, "I remind you of that promise, Dr. Gilbert, even as I beg you to keep what you know forever to yourself. I've already told Tom not to say anything. He doesn't understand, either, but he's proud that I've trusted him to keep a secret. He won't tell anyone."

Sarah took her elbows off the table, dropped a sugar cube in her cold coffee, and stirred it before continuing. "I have absolutely no 'right' that the surviving Braddocks wouldn't take into a court. I won't have that. I won't have David's name dragged into a court over *things*, Dr. Gilbert. I don't want any trouble. I intend to do my duty by David and Mother Braddock. I'll assist Ira in any way possible to see that the estate is properly executed."

Dr. Gilbert snorted. "That man's idea of 'proper' will no doubt include leaving you with nothing. Nothing for all the years of service you gave that family. Nothing despite the relationship that existed between you and David Braddock. It's unconscionable."

Sarah's eyes softened. "Oh, no, Dr. Gilbert. It's not like that at all. I may have no *things* to show for my years with the Braddocks, but I've the memory of Mother Braddock's smile—her belief in me. I've proper grammar and knowledge of housekeeping. I'll be able to get a good position soon. I may even look for a little house for Tom and me. We'll be all right."

Leaning back in his chair, Dr. Gilbert inspected Sarah's tired face as he stirred his coffee. Finally, he said with admiration, "I hope David Braddock knew what a fine young woman he planned to marry."

Sarah didn't respond to his comment. She had spent the night folding away the love between her and David Braddock, storing it behind a facade of calm where it could not hurt her.

Dr. Gilbert shook his head. "I totally disagree with your compliance, Miss Biddle. I believe David Braddock would want more for you. However, I will respect your decision."

"Thank you, Dr. Gilbert." Sarah rose to go. "Now, if you'll excuse me, there's a matter of the reading of the will this morning at the attorney's office. Mr. Braddock left a note for me late last evening asking me to meet him this morning." She left the dining room through the kitchen door.

In spite of her careful attempt to control her emotions throughout the ordeal, Sarah barely hid her enjoyment of Ira Braddock's reaction to the reading of the will. When the attorney announced that Tom Biddle was the recipient of a generous gift, Ira raised a few pointed questions regarding the legitimacy of the bequest and Mrs. Braddock's mental state when she added that particular addendum to the will. Assured that the bequest was irreversible, Ira regained control of himself. He smiled indulgently, commented on his sister-in-law's "idiosyncrasies," and resumed his superior position in the universe.

On Ira Braddock's final day at the manse, he requested that Sarah Biddle be present. Sarah didn't want to go, but her loyalty to the Braddocks required it. Ira had already dismissed the secretary hired to help him. Sarah was disappointed when he personally answered the door. He ushered her inside. "I've just completed arrangements to have the valuable items shipped back east, where there will be an auction." He explained with a sniff that doing so would ensure that the fine glassware and objets d'art would bring "top dollar." "Bidders back east," he added, "will have a more refined appreciation for their intrinsic value."

"But before things are packed up, Miss Biddle," Ira said, "I thought it only right to offer you something from the house as a memento." As he spoke, Ira drew himself up to his full stature of five feet, four inches and somehow managed to look down his nose at five-foot-seven Sarah. "Take anything you like, Miss Biddle. Something to remember the Braddocks by."

Sarah looked at him with blue eyes that had darkened to the color of steel. In a voice dripping with sarcasm, she said, "How very thoughtful of you, Mr. Braddock. But I won't require *things* to remember the kindness of the Braddocks—" She paused for an instant before clarifying herself. "Abigail and David, that is."

Turning to go, Sarah opened the door for herself. Her Shaker gray skirt swept down the wide stairs of the front porch and across the lawn as she marched through the front gate empty-handed. Heartily hoping that Ira Braddock was watching, she forced herself to walk north on Seventeenth Street without a backward glance.

CHAPTER 14

Claret Silk

"Therefore I hated life;
because the work that is wrought under the
sun is grievous unto me:
for all is vanity and vexation of spirit."
Ecclesiastes 2:17

Sarah managed a few weeks with no outward evidence of the weight of grief she carried. Tom returned to his routine at Miss Griswall's school while his sister filled in for various absent hotel employees. Augusta made certain Sarah had ample time to renew her friendship with LisBeth Callaway. LisBeth was expecting a child, and Sarah often drove to the Callaway homestead south of Lincoln. LisBeth was the proud owner of a new treadle sewing machine, which enabled her to stitch infant sacques and diapers with impressive speed. Sarah preferred to busy herself sewing on tiny buttons, hand-stitching hems, beginning a crib quilt.

David's body had been buried in a small cemetery in Iowa, near the site of the tragedy. From her meager funds, Sarah secretly paid to have a headstone placed beside Abigail's. Everyone in Lincoln assumed the appearance of the headstone resulted from some heretofore unnoticed family loyalty on the part of Ira Braddock. Just when Sarah thought she had begun to look toward her future, the railroad delivered a trunk that ripped open her past and plunged her headlong into fresh grief.

"Frank Reynolds over at the station sent a note here," Augusta explained. "He knew you were living here, and didn't quite know what he should do with this. I told him the house is empty and locked up, that you would take care of it." Augusta unfolded a sheet of paper. "He sent this along with the trunk. It's an apology from the railroad for taking so long to deliver it. Apparently David had the trunk with him when—"

Sarah's face paled and she sat down. Her voice was shaky as she said, "Mrs. Braddock's brother-in-law didn't leave any instructions with me, Augusta. Maybe the real estate people will know what we should do."

"It's *David's*, Sarah," Augusta urged. "His name is on the plate right there by the lock. Somehow it seems wrong to just deliver it to an empty house. And frankly, dear, I don't want Ira Braddock to have the satisfaction of getting his hands on anything else. As the Braddocks' housekeeper, you should have been the one to close up the house and dispose of their things. I know Abigail and David would have wanted it that way. You knew their hearts much better than that *little* man. I know they would want you to at least inspect the contents before deciding what to do about the trunk."

Sarah ran her fingers over the brass plate that bore David's name. She didn't really want to think in legalities and proprieties at the moment. Inside that trunk lay some tangible connection with David. "All right, Augusta . . . but there's no key."

"Not a problem, dear." With a glint of mischief in her eyes, Augusta removed one of her hairpins and knelt by the trunk. In only a moment she had it open. While Sarah looked on, Augusta lifted out the top tray and set it on a small table beside her. The faint aroma of roses filled the room. Augusta let out an exclamation of surprise.

Sarah paled. She sat motionless, glancing at Augusta. Finally, with trembling hands, she reached out to touch the most exquisite gown she had ever seen. Only the bodice showed, but as she pulled it toward her, fold upon fold of heavy wine-colored silk cascaded to the floor, showering the carpet with the dried rose petals that had been tucked in the folds. Sarah clutched the gown to her, watching as Augusta carefully unpacked layer after layer of exquisite clothing.

"It's an entire trousseau, Sarah. David must have finally fallen in love." Augusta shook her head sadly. "Poor, poor, boy. What a shame . . ." Realizing that Sarah had said nothing for quite a few moments, Augusta studied her.

Sarah sat on the edge of Augusta's couch. She had folded the wedding gown at the waist and smoothed the bodice so that it lay neatly across her lap, the sleeves stretching out on each side of her, the train pooling on the floor about her feet. Slowly, she bent to pick up a pair of lace gloves that had dropped on the floor. With extreme care, she pulled on one glove, then the other. She held her hands in front of her, stretching out her fingers, inspecting the exquisite pattern of the lace. She ran her index finger along the gown's high collar, down the rows of tiny pin tucks, to a cluster of soft pink ribbon roses at the waist of the dress.

"Oh, my dear," Augusta said softly. "My dear, dear, Sarah." Augusta sat down next to her. "Why didn't you tell anyone?"

Sarah shrugged. "It took a long time for David to convince me that it could work—Mother Braddock's illness hurried things along."

Holding Sarah while she cried, Augusta gazed at the finery spread about them. All at once Augusta realized something. "Sarah," she insisted, "you are entitled to that house—or at least a portion of the estate. Ira Braddock had no right to turn you out the way he did. Something has to be done."

"There's nothing to be done, Aunt Augusta. Who would believe it anyway," Sarah asked. "Mr. David Braddock of Philadelphia marrying an orphaned housekeeper." Sarah looked solemn. "I told David that people would disapprove. And now that it's over, I won't have it brought out where strangers can discuss it and doubt it and laugh at it." Tenderly Sarah pulled the wedding gown toward her. "It was good and true and beautiful . . . and I won't let people turn it into something else."

Augusta frowned, looked about the room. "All right, Sarah. I will never agree with you, but I will respect your wishes. As to this trunk, it's obvious that it was intended for you, and on that I will not compromise. This trunk stays here in Lincoln with you. Ira Braddock has no right to it. He will never know about it, and that is the end of that."

Sarah acquiesced.

"I'm going to leave you alone for a while, dear," Augusta said gently. "Grieving takes time, and it's not to be rushed. I'll be back in a little while with some tea." As Augusta rose to go, something caught her eye. "Sarah, there's an envelope tucked into the lid—" She pulled it out. "It has your name written on it." Augusta laid it in Sarah's lap and left the room, softly closing the door.

Sarah held the envelope for a long time. She traced the letters that had been written by David Braddock with her finger, caressed the silk gown that covered her lap, inspected the lace gloves. Finally, she opened the envelope.

My own Sarah,
In all my years of schooling I was never given words for the most important transaction I should ever initiate—and now I am proving it again, as I refer to our engagement as a "transaction." Alas, I fear that

you will have to finally accept that I am totally inept when it comes to romance.

I said I had come to Lincoln to court you. Now I realize that while I know very well how to court new business partners, I have almost no talent for courting the woman I wish to marry. There have been so many times when I wanted to express the deepest of emotions. But words have failed me just when words are most important. Having failed in words, perhaps I shall succeed in deeds.

One of the reasons I tarried so long before returning home is contained in this trunk. My hope is that in these things you will see the love that I have been so inept at expressing. Of course I enlisted Mother's assistance in the selection. I hope you find the result of our conspiracy pleasing.

Knowing you as I do, I think you will take most delight in the very last items you will unpack. You have often mentioned your lack of a proper "heritage." These things will ensure that you never again feel that you lack in the matter of family heirlooms and connections to the past. They were made by Cordelia Braddock, the wife of Captain Flint Braddock, who emigrated to a very new country known as the United States in 1782. Mother was adamant that you should have these things in addition to her wedding ring, which you will find inside the purple velvet box in this tray.

Sarah stopped reading. Yes, there it was. She reached for the box, opened it, gasped in amazement. She set the open box aside to finish David's letter.

Once you inspect what we have included in this trunk, I think that you will realize that there are/were more Braddocks than just Abigail and David with whom you may enjoy a very real connection of the heart and mind. Mother can tell you the complete history of the Captain and his wife. She can also tell you a wonderful story about the ring.

You have said over and over that you fear you cannot fill the role as mistress of a great house. I beg you to believe me when I say again that we do not need a great house, Sarah. We only need a great love, the beginnings of which I believe we have been granted by our great God.

You are the mistress of my heart, dear Sarah. That is enough for me. Will you let it be enough for you?

Yours,

David

When Sarah had spent her emotions, she refolded the letter, knelt by the trunk, and pulled out the last items to which David had referred. One was a stunning chintz quilt. Sarah opened it carefully, spread it out on the floor, reached out to touch the pieced star that formed the quilt's center. Swagged borders, appliquéd wreath borders, and a border of pieced stars had been added in breathtaking hues of blue, red, and green. For the next to the last border, Cordelia had cut urns of flowers from a stunning floral fabric. Sarah counted twenty-one urns, cut out and affixed to plain muslin with the finest stitches she had ever seen. She guessed that the quilting alone must have taken Cordelia months, perhaps years. She could picture herself seated with Cordelia at a giant quilting frame. *You're right, David. Cordelia Braddock and I would have gotten on. What a wonderful experience it would have been to create such a masterpiece.*

Sarah unfolded the last item, a small sampler that had been folded with the quilt. Minute *x*s stitched onto a piece of linen created an ornate urn of flowers below which Cordelia had stitched a verse. Sarah shivered as she read,

> *Cordelia Braddock is My Name New York is My*
> *Station Heaven is my Dwelling Place and Chri*
> *St is My Salvation When I am Dead and in my Gr*
> *ave and all my Bones are Rotten When This you*
> *see Remember me That I be not Forgotten 1807*

Laying aside the sampler, Sarah refolded the quilt and returned it to the bottom of the trunk. She repacked her trousseau, set the tray in place on top of everything, and sat down once again to contemplate the sampler.

> *Sarah Biddle is My Name*
> *Lincoln is My Station*
> *Heaven is my Dwelling Place—*

Sarah stopped, wondered, *Is it indeed? Is heaven my dwelling place?* She wasn't sure.

The sampler went on . . . *and Christ is my salvation.*

And who is my salvation? Sarah asked herself. *Aunt Jesse saved me from homelessness, but then she died. Augusta saved me next. I thought Jim Callaway would save me from being lonely, but he loved LisBeth instead. Then there was Mother Braddock . . . and David . . . bent on saving me to be their own. But now,* Sarah thought bitterly, *they are dead, just like Cordelia Braddock. Dead with only me to remember them, to make certain they are not forgotten.*

"Christ is my salvation." What did Cordelia Braddock mean by that? Christ certainly had not saved her from dying. Christ hadn't saved Aunt Jesse either. In spite of the fact that Sarah Biddle had done her best to be a good person, had read her Bible, prayed, and talked quite a bit about God, Christ had saved neither her nor Tom from many, many hardships. He had done nothing to prevent David Braddock from dying, nothing to prevent Mother

Braddock from suffering horribly. What did the phrase "Christ is my salvation" really mean?

Sarah decided that Cordelia Braddock's sampler might reflect a nice little rhyme, but that the words were not relevant to her own life, to the almost unbearable weight of loneliness and grief that had settled over her. Yet when she folded away the contents of the trunk, she kept Cordelia Braddock's sampler out. It lay on the top of the trunk for a few days before Sarah made her way to Miller's Department Store, where she purchased a frame and hung the sampler in her room.

Well, Cordelia, Sarah thought as she stood back from hanging the sampler, *your wish has been granted. I didn't know you, but I'll see your work every day, and I'll think of you.* Sarah pondered the grim realities of rotten bones, graves, and citizenship in heaven. The phrase "Christ is my salvation" haunted her. She knew that all the people she had truly loved and respected believed that phrase. She also knew that, try as she might to be like those she loved, to believe what they believed, Sarah Biddle did not.

CHAPTER 15

Calcutta Blue

---

*"Who comforteth us in all our tribulation, that
we may be able to comfort them which are in any
trouble, by the comfort wherewith we ourselves
are comforted of God."*
2 Corinthians 1:4

Augusta Hathaway peered over her newspaper at Sarah
Biddle. The two women had retired to Augusta's apartment, Augusta to read her newspaper and Sarah to add to
the ever-increasing pile of crib-quilt blocks in her sewing
basket. Sarah worked slowly, painstakingly cutting and
piecing one-inch blue squares into a myriad of nine-patch
blocks, each one less than three inches square. She paused
often to lean back in her chair. She seemed half asleep, but
Augusta knew that Sarah's weariness was the kind that
more often prevented, rather than resulted in, sleep.

"You haven't been sleeping well, Sarah," Augusta said
quietly.

Sarah started at the sound of Augusta's voice. "I'm
sorry, Aunt Augusta. Has my midnight prowl to the
kitchen been waking you?"

"Of course not," Augusta said as she folded her newspaper. "But Cora says you're in the kitchen most every
morning when she comes in. That you've already built a

fire, that your sewing is usually laid out—but that you're rarely sewing." Augusta paused before adding gently, "I'm worried about you, dear. Can't I do something to help?"

Sarah looked down at the patchwork in her lap and smiled halfheartedly, shaking her head.

"That trunk in your room, Sarah. We should store it somewhere out of sight. It's not good for you to see it day after day."

Sarah looked piercingly at Augusta. "I don't want that trunk moved."

Augusta unfolded her newspaper and began to read again. After a few moments she asked, "Sarah, would you drive out tomorrow and check on LisBeth? She insisted that Jim make that trip north without her, but her confinement is nearing, and I know she'd welcome some company."

"Oh, Aunt Augusta," Sarah protested, "I'm not fit company for LisBeth. Not now."

Augusta looked over her newspaper. "Maybe not, Sarah, but she'll certainly be good company for you. Have you forgotten that LisBeth knows what it's like to lose the man she loves? She and MacKenzie had been married less than a year when he was killed. She would understand. It will only be the two of you out there on the farm. No one else would ever know what the two of you discuss. You can trust LisBeth."

"I know I can trust LisBeth, Aunt Augusta," Sarah said. "But I don't want to *talk* about it. I want to *forget* about it."

Augusta said firmly, "Forget the pain, Sarah. But don't forget the fine things about David and Abigail and your life with them. Remember it, celebrate it. See evidence of God's love for you in their love."

At the mention of God's love, Sarah became newly engrossed in her patchwork. Augusta tried another tactic.

"LisBeth has come to expect me on Sundays, but after the Red Ribbon Club this week we've scheduled a board meeting for the Home for the Friendless. We've simply got to do something about getting better funding for those children."

Sarah looked up from her sewing. "That's not fair, Aunt Augusta. You know I can't refuse when you mention the Home for the Friendless." She sighed. "All right, I'll go out to LisBeth's. But don't expect me to bare my soul to her."

"You do what you think best, Sarah," Augusta agreed. Sarah rose to retire and Augusta called out to her, "If LisBeth wants you to stay over, don't feel you need to rush back."

Sarah forfeited attending church the next morning in favor of an early drive to the Callaway farm. The old mare hitched to her carriage plodded patiently along, and Sarah did nothing to hurry her. In spite of herself, she began to enjoy the view of the greening countryside, the smell of the warm earth, the songs of the birds that were just returning from the South to nest in the shrubs along the dirt road.

At some point along the road Sarah began talking to God. *You know, God, what hurts the most is that You let me have those expectations, and then took them away. When I was a homeless orphan, I never expected to be loved or cared about. When Aunt Jesse and Aunt Augusta took me in, I never expected to be anything at all. But then I went to work for Mrs. Braddock, and a whole new world opened. I learned so much . . . and then there was David. He made me almost believe I could actually be a good wife to him—me, a homeless orphan, the wife of a leading citizen. If You weren't going to let that happen, they why did You let me build that dream? Why did You let me believe in it, and then destroy it? That sampler hanging in my room says that Christ is my salvation. Well,*

I don't feel like You're very interested in saving Sarah Biddle.

Sarah drove into the Callaway farmyard no less depressed than when she had left Lincoln. LisBeth waved to her from behind the picket fence that Jim had erected around the tiny burial plot just across the road from the house. "Sarah! It's wonderful to see you." LisBeth pressed a hand against the small of her back. "Think you could help a very indisposed friend finish weeding over here?"

Sarah climbed down from the carriage and joined LisBeth inside the picket fence where three rocks had been crudely engraved, *Ma*, *Pa*, and *Mac*. "Augusta told me about this little plot, LisBeth, but I didn't realize Jim had put so much work into it."

LisBeth leaned against the fence. "The first thing he did when he stumbled on this place was to clean up Ma and Pa Baird's graves. Then after he bought the homestead from me, he added the stone for MacKenzie. Of course, MacKenzie is really out west at the Little Big Horn . . . but it meant a lot to me when he first died to have a place to visit."

Sarah nodded. "I know. I've felt the same way—" She interrupted herself, finishing her sentence with a vague reference to David Braddock's tombstone up at Lincoln.

"I'm so sorry about Mrs. Braddock and David, Sarah. I wish I could have at least come to the service."

From where she knelt by the fence pulling weeds, Sarah managed a faint "Thank you." Looking up, she could see LisBeth's bulging profile. "Let me finish, LisBeth. You must be worn out."

LisBeth answered, "I *am* worn out, Sarah. Worn out with waiting. But I guess it'll be worth it when the baby finally comes."

"You just settle there in the shade. There's not much left to do. I'll take care of it." Sarah reached to pull away the tall grasses that had grown around the three headstones.

"I hope you can stay the night, Sarah," LisBeth said.

"Well, Aunt Augusta encouraged just that—if you're sure you want the company. I need to unhitch Sadie and then I'll be in."

LisBeth headed for the house while Sarah tended to her horse. Moments later, she joined LisBeth, who was still rubbing her back while she heated water for coffee.

"It won't be long now, LisBeth," Sarah reassured her. "I've almost got your baby quilt finished. I brought it along." She grinned. "It had better be a boy. I used all Calcutta blue prints. Maybe I can even finish it while I'm here."

LisBeth sat down at the kitchen table with a groan. "I've just got to lie down for a few minutes, Sarah. My back is killing me." Without waiting for Sarah to answer, LisBeth made her way through the parlor and into her bedroom.

Sarah went to retrieve her satchel from the carriage. She had just started for the house when she heard a wagon coming up the road. Peering down the road, Sarah saw a rangy team of bays and a redheaded driver. She ran into the house calling out, "LisBeth, Jim's back!"

No answer came from the bedroom. Sarah smiled to herself. *She's fallen asleep.* But when Sarah looked inside the room, she realized that LisBeth was not asleep. She was curled up in bed, holding her back with both hands. She looked up at Sarah, fear shining in her eyes. "I think—" LisBeth squeezed her eyes shut and grunted. When the contraction had passed, she panted. "I think the baby's coming. Tell Jim—"

Sarah didn't wait for LisBeth to finish. Instead, she ran out to meet Jim, who was just getting down from the wagon. One look at Sarah's face sent Jim bounding into the house. He planted a kiss on LisBeth's cheek. "I'm on my way to get Dr. Gilbert, LisBeth. The team's worn out. I'll ride Buck. It'll be faster."

LisBeth grabbed her back and groaned again. "Hurry, Jim. Please hurry."

Sarah followed Jim to the back door. "Jim, it's the first baby," she said calmly. "It will take a while. It always does—at least that's what Dr. Gilbert says. He often came by to check on Mrs. Braddock when he was waiting on someone's confinement. Just stay calm and don't break your neck between here and Lincoln. We'll be fine."

Sarah spoke with far more confidence than she felt. The moment the two separated, the calming effect they had had on one another was gone. Jim tore out of the farmyard on Buck, and Sarah rushed into the kitchen to heat water and ready clean linen.

Before the water was even lukewarm, LisBeth staggered into the kitchen. Her dark eyes were wide with terror. She blurted out, "No time, Sarah. No time for the doc—" She was overcome by a contraction that left her pale and breathless, her knuckles whitening as she leaned over, gasping.

As soon as LisBeth's grip on the chair relaxed, Sarah helped her to bed. She barely had the quilts pulled up before LisBeth was struggling against another contraction. LisBeth fought the labor. Sarah ran back to the kitchen for a knife and the kettle of warm water.

LisBeth was calling for her, and Sarah hurried back to her side. Setting the kettle on the floor she dampened a cloth. "LisBeth," she called out. Sarah nearly shouted, turning LisBeth's face toward her and looking into her terrified eyes. "LisBeth, listen to me. There's nothing to be afraid of. I know what to do. I helped my mother birth my baby sister. There's nothing to be afraid of. Do you hear me?"

LisBeth stopped moaning and a glimmer of hope came into her eyes.

"Listen to me, LisBeth. We can do this." Sarah paused and consciously forced confidence into her voice. "You're young and healthy. There's nothing to birthing a baby. Just stay calm and hold my hand, LisBeth. I'm right here. I'm not going anywhere." Even as she spoke, Sarah was shouting at God, *Please let it be true. Let this baby come easy. Help me know what to do. If You really are our salvation, then save LisBeth and her baby for Jim.*

There was no time for Sarah to contemplate why she prayed to a God she really did not trust, for another contraction came quickly, thrusting LisBeth and Sarah into the world where birth and the valley of the shadow of death were very often the same place.

In the years that followed, LisBeth Callaway was often to tease Sarah Biddle for saying, "There's nothing to birthing a baby." Both women discovered in the next two hours that there was, indeed, a great deal to the process. LisBeth strained against it, clasping Sarah's hands until Sarah thought they would break. Between contractions, LisBeth grunted and moaned against her terrible backache, which Sarah tried in vain to relieve.

When the moment came to actually birth the baby, instinct took over. LisBeth strained and pushed and yelled with every ounce of strength while Sarah waited with outstretched hands to receive a miracle. That miracle arrived screaming lustily at his new surroundings. Sarah cut the umbilical cord with trembling hands, tied it off with a string, and wrapped the baby in a yard of hastily procured flannel.

LisBeth's eyes shone with tears as she took her miracle from Sarah. She stared down into his face, fingering the cleft in his chin and murmuring her love while the baby flailed his tiny arms in the air. When he gave another yell, LisBeth looked at Sarah and grinned. Mimicking Sarah's voice she said, "There's nothing to it . . ." and put the baby to her breast.

When Jim Callaway and Dr. Gilbert rode into the farmyard some time later, Dr. Gilbert was saying to Jim, "I know you're anxious, Mr. Callaway, but really, Sarah Biddle is a capable nurse and, as I said, this is your wife's first child. It will no doubt be some time this evening before—"

Dr. Gilbert's discourse was interrupted by something that sounded suspiciously like the cry of a newborn. Jim jumped down from the doctor's still-moving carriage and ran into the house. Dr. Gilbert took time to pull his horse up. He entered the house just as Sarah Biddle began heating water for coffee.

"I think they're all right, Dr. Gilbert—"

Dr. Gilbert proceeded into the bedroom. After a thorough examination of both mother and child, he reassured Sarah, surprising her by adding, "Miss Biddle, I don't know what your plans are for the future, but you would make a very good nurse. Lincoln is growing rapidly, and I often wish for someone reliable to help care for my patients. Until we have a proper hospital, home care will continue to be necessary. The right care given in a doctor's absence can often make the difference between death and life. Think about it, Miss Biddle. If you are in the least interested, please come by the office when you return to Lincoln."

Sarah remained on the Callaway farm for several days, caring for LisBeth and the baby, cooking and cleaning. She did not realize what her service to her friend was accomplishing in her own life until she returned to Lincoln. Driving Sadie east and then north along a familiar street where a pair of massive iron gates were set into a high brick wall, Sarah lingered for a moment, pondering the reality of losing access to the mansion on the other side of the wall. It struck her that, while her sadness lingered, the sharpness of the pain had receded. In its place was the awe-inspiring knowledge that in recent weeks she had participated in two wondrous events—helping one eternal soul leave the earth, and helping another enter it.

Nursing Mother Braddock had been exhausting and difficult beyond words, but Sarah finally admitted to herself that she had done it well. She had done everything in her power to give comfort and relieve pain. That knowledge was finally beginning to assuage her own pain.

Assisting in J.W. Callaway's birth had been just as exhausting as nursing Mrs. Braddock. In its own way it had been just as difficult. But the wonderful difference was that the event sang in Sarah's memory, unblemished by sorrow. Sarah remembered receiving the newborn in her hands, the overwhelming wonder and joy.

Slapping the reins across Sadie's back, Sarah continued along the route to the livery and the Hathaway House Hotel. The next morning she paid a visit to Dr. Miles Gilbert.

CHAPTER 16

A Paisley Print

"My soul fainteth for thy salvation. . . .
When wilt thou comfort me?"
Psalm 119:81–82

Sarah walked up and down the boardwalk that fronted
Dr. Gilbert's office for over an hour before summoning the
courage to go in. When she finally did, she was relieved to
see that the office was empty. Its furnishings were spartan.
A row of worn but sturdy stairs strung out along the wall
next to the door. Across from the door was the doctor's
walnut secretary. Only a few papers occupied one of the
myriad cubbyholes in the secretary. The doctor's ledger
book lay closed, an inkwell at its side.

When no one responded to the sound of the office door
closing, Sarah walked to the doorway behind the secretary.
From there she could see that the entire main floor of the
building was divided into three rooms of equal size. The
second room was furnished with only three pieces of furniture, an examining table, a cabinet that Sarah assumed
contained the doctor's instruments, and a third table that
held Dr. Gilbert's medical library, seven volumes with titles
like *Materia Medica, Gray's Anatomy, Flint's Practice.*
Absorbed in reading the titles of the books, Sarah jumped
when Dr. Gilbert called from the back room, "I'll be right
out." She quickly retreated to the waiting room.

Dr. Gilbert emerged from the back of the building, wiping his hands on a linen towel. Sarah half turned to flee out the door. "Perhaps it's not convenient for you to see me now."

"No, no it's fine. In fact, I was just thinking about you, hoping you would come by." Dr. Gilbert finished drying his hands, reached into his pocket for his watch, and checked the time. "I'm lecturing at the university this afternoon, but we have plenty of time." Dr. Gilbert brought one of the waiting-room chairs nearer, motioned for Sarah to sit down, then leaned against the edge of his secretary. "You have come because of what I said at the Callaway farm?"

"I had a speech all prepared," Sarah said nervously, "but now I can't remember what I was going to say. Perhaps I should just say that if you can use me, I think I'd like to try to be of some help."

"Good," Dr. Gilbert said. He sat down and leaned forward eagerly, his blue eyes sparkling. "I am often torn between the bedsides of more than one critically ill patient. At times like that, constant trained care could mean the difference between life and death. Even when a life is not in danger, the presence of a nurse can be invaluable. For example, I try to call on new mothers daily for ten days after their confinement. It would be a great help to have a nurse to help with those calls."

Sarah asked, "But would your patients accept me? I don't have any formal training."

Dr. Gilbert smiled. "All the training in the world cannot provide the most basic qualities necessary for good nursing. Were I to put an advertisement today in the *State Democrat* for this position, I would include as requirements the patience of Job, the wisdom of Solomon, and the kindness of the good Samaritan—all three of which are far more important to my patients than clinical knowledge. Your care of both Mrs. Braddock and Mrs. Callaway demonstrated aspects of all three of these attributes. You are cheerful and willing to learn. You respond calmly in crisis and are able to reassure those in your care. These qualities cannot be taught, Miss Biddle. They are gifts from God. At the moment I have a much greater need for someone with these gifts than for someone with a knowledge of the *Materia Medica*. Really, the only limitations I see would be those presented by your current responsibilities with your brother, Tom, and your work at the hotel."

Sarah answered quickly. "I've discussed this possibility with Augusta, and she is very supportive. As for Tom, he's eleven now and well able to look after himself a good deal of the time. He and Augusta are very close. Of course if I'm required to stay with a patient for an extended time, I'd like it if Tom could be with me."

"I'm certain that can be worked out on a case-by-case basis," Dr. Gilbert said briskly. "When can you begin?"

"As soon as you need me, I should think."

"Can I call for you at the hotel at three o'clock today? I have a patient who would benefit greatly from your care—and your cooking."

Thus Sarah Biddle was quickly thrust into the world of medicine. Her first patient was Widow Langley, who made no secret of the fact that she attributed her recovery from mastoid disease almost entirely to Nurse Biddle. Sarah's popularity spread further when she ably assisted the convalescence of an amputee. Soon she began to work in Dr. Gilbert's office receiving patients, and keeping the doctor's ledger book. Dr. Gilbert taught her to dress wounds and remove sutures so that when he was called out, patients could still receive minimal care. Dr. Gilbert's practice began to grow, especially in the area of women's ailments.

"They like having a feminine ear to listen to their complaints," he told Sarah, teasing. "I'll be losing you to some *seminary* if you hear many more emotional complaints."

Sarah shook her head. "I've little to offer in the way of explaining life's greater meaning, Dr. Gilbert. I just listen. More often than not, that seems to be all they need."

"See, what did I tell you? The patience of Job, the wisdom of Solomon, the kindness of the good Samaritan—and minimal medical knowledge—can often effect a complete 'cure.'"

Sarah smiled. "I try to have the patience and the kindness, Dr. Gilbert. But I most sincerely defer to your wisdom."

Sarah thought she saw Dr. Gilbert wink at her. "Wise nurse."

It was not long before Sarah began keeping a notebook, writing down things that the doctor advised in specific cases. She listed symptoms, diagnoses, treatment, results. When Dr. Gilbert was away on calls outside the city, Sarah often spent the afternoon at the small table in his examining room, poring over textbooks, struggling with the medical terminology, determined to decipher the texts. She began to believe that in learning, in keeping busy, she had at last found a way to overcome the loss of David Braddock. Still, there were moments when something seemingly innocuous sent her reeling backward.

One evening when Dr. Gilbert was on a "country call," Sarah determined to remain in the office and read. She had read only a small portion of *Lusk's Midwifery* when a sentence leaped out at her. "*Quickening* is the term used to designate the earliest movements of the foetus perceived by the mother. They are at first slight, and have been compared 'to the tremulous emotion of a little bird held in the hand' (Montgomery)." The clinical description struck Sarah hard. *I will never experience that wondrous moment. David is dead and there is little hope that I will ever marry.* Amazed at her emotional response to a clinical text, Sarah impatiently wiped away tears, closed the textbook, and went back to the hotel. Tom had already gone to bed, leaving his assignment for the day on the kitchen table where Sarah could review it. She read only a few sentences before retreating down the hall to her room.

For a long time Sarah sat in her little room staring at Cordelia Braddock's sampler in the waning light. The simple phrase "Christ is my salvation" stirred something in her, something she could not verbalize. Nursing had opened new possibilities and filled her life with useful, rewarding work. Still, Sarah was not at peace. Increasingly, she had begun to wonder if in all her years of churchgoing she had somehow failed to grasp something that Cordelia Braddock understood—something about Christ, about salvation, something that might enable her to declare that while Lincoln might be her "station," heaven was her home.

Home. Sarah contemplated the word. It brought to mind the now-empty mansion just a few blocks away. No matter how fond she was of Augusta Hathaway, the Hathaway House Hotel no longer felt like home. Sarah turned down her lamp and went to bed, turning her back to the sampler. *It's all well and good for Cordelia Braddock to intone spiritual concepts about salvation and heaven being her home. She was a Braddock. She obviously didn't have to spend every waking moment trying to keep life and limb together. She could well afford to contemplate eternity. Biddles have to be more concerned with realities.*

Sarah turned over, looked through the dark at where the trunk stood across the room, an ever-present reminder of her most painful reality. She closed her eyes, trying to envision a different reality—herself back home at the Braddock mansion. She was dressed in a fashionable paisley print, seated in the parlor with children playing at her feet. They were waiting for David to come home. There it was again. That word *home*.

Sarah sat up, fluffed her pillow, then lay back down. She lay with her eyes open, staring through the dark at where the sampler hung on the wall. *I should just take that thing down and pack it away.*

But she did not.

CHAPTER 17

White Petticoats

"O death, where is thy sting?"
1 Corinthians 15:55

"Is it malignant?" Anna Dowd asked the question in a hoarse whisper. She was standing in the hallway outside eight-year-old Billy's room, nervously twisting the edge of her apron. Her eyes pleaded with Dr. Gilbert. Sarah looked on, her heart swelling with compassion for the terrified mother.

Dr. Gilbert shook his head. "Now, Mrs. Dowd. Don't be too distressed. It's true that scarlet fever has run rampant for the last few weeks, but I don't think Billy's case merits the term 'malignant.'" He turned to Sarah and explained, "The settlers seem to think if it's 'malignant' anything, it's a worse form. Its an incorrect terminology, of course, but it's ingrained in the population."

"But what can be done, Doctor?" Anna was growing impatient.

"Just what you've been doing, Mrs. Dowd," Dr. Gilbert answered. "Relieve the dryness and the burning sensation in Billy's skin. Soothe his throat, manage the fever." He nodded toward Sarah. "I've taught Nurse Biddle some remedies that may prove even more effective than what you've been doing." Dr. Gilbert wisely refrained from criticizing Anna's having applied bacon rind to Billy's skin. "Carbolized vaseline should give Billy some relief. I don't want him eating anything for the next couple of days. Give him milk if he's hungry."

While Dr. Gilbert continued to explain his treatments, Sarah slipped past him and Mrs. Dowd into Billy's room. Billy lay on his bed, his eyes bright with fever. He opened his mouth to talk, but Sarah interrupted him. "Don't talk, Billy. I know it hurts." Gathering up Dr. Gilbert's instruments, Sarah packed his bag and turned to go. She smiled at Billy. "I'll be back in just a little while with some medicine to make you feel better. I'm going to stay with you while your mother gets some rest tonight." She winked. "And soon you'll feel well enough that we can play a game or two. Does that sound all right?" Billy nodded.

Sarah carried Dr. Gilbert's bag out to him just as he said, "I realize that the idea of full-time nursing is new, Mrs. Dowd. But it is nearly 1884, and we must move into more modern medical practices. That includes the use of specially trained nurses. The next few hours are going to be critical for Billy. So many people have come down with this fever in the past few days, I simply can't stay myself. Nurse Biddle has been with me for over a year now. She is well trained, and she'll know exactly what to do."

Mrs. Dowd still looked doubtful.

"*I* pay Nurse Biddle, Mrs. Dowd. Her presence will increase only Billy's comfort—not my bill." Dr. Gilbert saw that this last assurance broke through Mrs. Dowd's concerns. He nodded. "Good. Now, Nurse Biddle will be back in a little while with the preparations Billy needs. I want her to sit up with him tonight so you can get some rest. I'll be by in the morning—unless I'm needed before then."

Mrs. Dowd expressed her thanks and ushered Sarah and Dr. Gilbert to the door. As soon as they were outside, Sarah said, "I don't want to force myself on the Dowds, Dr. Gilbert. If they don't want a nurse—" Dr. Gilbert interrupted her. "Mrs. Dowd was worried about the money, Nurse Biddle. The family has had a few setbacks. I'm certain that at heart she is relieved to know that you will be there to care for Billy." The two had barely climbed into his carriage before Dr. Gilbert launched into a lengthy explanation of the management of scarlet fever. "It ranks right up there with diphtheria as one of the most fatal of diseases. Unfortunately, it spreads even more rapidly than the latter. I've had cases where the glands of the neck became so swollen it was almost impossible for the patient to swallow. Cases that survive the initial fever and eruption often suffer a breakdown of the glands of the neck. I have actually seen the glands entirely sloughed out, leaving a crater down which I could see the pulsating carotid artery." He paused before adding sadly. "Of course, such cases rarely survive."

They had arrived at Dr. Gilbert's clinic. He smiled and said, "But I don't think Billy Dowd is going to be one of those. He's had incredible resiliency to every disease he's encountered thus far in his short life. He was exposed to scarlet fever last year at school. For some reason, he didn't come down with it. I think he may have some sort of natural immunity." Dr. Gilbert sighed. "If only we could come to understand what gives some people that immunity and make it available to everyone." He climbed down from his carriage to hitch up the horse.

Inside the clinic, Dr. Gilbert instructed Sarah as to the administration of small doses of calomel "to stimulate the secretions," aconite to control fever, and a special gargle for Billy's throat. She hurried back to the Dowd residence and settled in for the night. True to Doctor Gilbert's prediction, Billy suffered only a mild case of scarlet fever. When Dr. Gilbert explained the idea of a natural immunity to Anna Dowd, she listened respectfully but held on to her firm belief that her son's quick recovery was due almost completely to the presence of Nurse Biddle in her home.

One crisp fall day two weeks after Billy's recovery, Sarah arrived back at the hotel after her day at Dr. Gilbert's clinic to find a note lying on the table beside her bed. Pulling off her shoes, she settled on the edge of her bed and read, *I wasn't much for nurses when you first came, Nurse Biddle. But you saved my boy and you won me over. If you ever have a need and I can help it, you can count on Anna Dowd.*

Smiling faintly, Sarah tucked the note inside her Bible. She sighed, scolding herself. *What exactly is it that you want, Sarah Biddle? You're giving real help to people with real needs. You're associated with one of the most respected physicians in town. There are thousands of other twenty-two year olds much less fortunate than you.*

Sarah finally managed to argue herself into agreeing with herself that she *should* be happy. It was not the same thing as *being* happy, but for the moment it would have to do.

The night had been a particularly difficult one, a night in which the contents of David's trunk entered Sarah's dreams and stole her rest. She saw herself in the bridal gown, but always in ridiculous places and incongruous situations. The dreams began as simply nonsense, but they took on garish details, becoming more and more frightening until Sarah woke with a start, sitting bolt upright in her bed. She had been crying in her sleep. Quickly, she slipped out of bed, wrapped herself in a shawl, and slipped down the hall to the hotel kitchen. Passing by their room, she could hear soft snoring that assured her Cora and Odessa, the cooks for Hathaway House, had not been disturbed by the sound of her footsteps.

It was warm enough to need no fire in the kitchen stove. The kitchen was pitch-black. Sarah felt along the wall toward the shelf in the corner for an oil lamp and matches. In the half-light, the lamp's amber-colored base gave off a warm glow. Once lit, the lamp was set back on the shelf, where its light would shine down on the surface of the quilt Sarah lowered slowly from the rafters. She bent over the fabric, quilting furiously, a dark silhouette in an amber sphere of soft light.

After only a few moments, she shivered, looking about her into the dark shadows in the room. She leaned back in her chair and sighed. *Keeping busy has its advantages, but it doesn't always keep one's thoughts where they should be.*

An insistent knock at the kitchen door startled her. She noticed that tiny ice crystals had begun to form in the raindrops that pounded against the kitchen window. She opened the door to a young man barely older than herself. He stood, the giant brim of his hat shedding water in tiny rivulets about his shoulders. He did not remove his hat, but shifted his weight from one foot to the other nervously, speaking in a pleading tone. "You Nurse Biddle?" When Sarah answered yes, he rushed on. "Thought so. I been sent by Doc Gilbert. He said you could maybe help with my Loula. She's in a bad way. Having our first. Things aren't going too good. Loula, she's about wore out, but the baby still ain't come."

He choked back emotion. "Please, ma'am—could we hurry?" Without a word, he turned and stepped out into the yard, where a wagon waited.

Sarah hurried to her room to change. She didn't bother to put up her hair, simply tucked her long braid inside her coat. At the kitchen door she simultaneously clamped a huge hat on her head and grabbed a small bag of supplies. She opened the kitchen door to run to the wagon. Two steps later she remembered the oil lamp in the kitchen and ran back in to turn it down. She bumped the quilt frame against the wall on her way out.

On the other side of the wall, Cora Schlegelmilch woke up. She heard a wagon retreating toward the west. It seemed that the storm outside had grown worse. A draft of cold air told her that the back door had been left ajar. Shuffling out to the kitchen, Cora bumped against the quilt frame. Instantly she understood what had happened. She closed the kitchen door. In the dark, she felt for where Sarah had rolled back the corner of the cover sheet to quilt. Pulling it back across the surface of the quilt, Cora raised the quilt back up to the rafters, frowning and mumbling to herself as she returned to bed.

Odessa stirred, mumbled a question.

"Sleep, Odessa, sleep. Is only the doctor sending for Sarah again. Sleep. We'll have fresh biscuits and hot coffee ready when she gets back. Now, we sleep." Cora tumbled into bed and was snoring again in moments.

Sarah did her best to reassure the frightened young man driving his half-lame horse almost to exhaustion. "Dr. Gilbert will take good care of your wife. He's an excellent physician."

The answer was doubtful. "It's been since yesterday, and my Loula still ain't birthed that baby." He lashed at his horse again, who responded more to the loud clap of thunder that crashed across the open fields than to the whip. In the distance, lightning struck a giant cottonwood tree. It blazed bright on the horizon, finally sputtering out when the rain became a downpour. Sarah hunkered down in her raincoat and hat, grateful that the air had warmed and the great drops of rain no longer contained crystals of ice to pelt them.

They rode west for many miles in darkness so thick that Sarah wondered at the young man's ability to find his way. Only an occasional flicker of lightning helped show the way. There was no road, only two wagon-wheel ruts carved into the earth. Sarah's back and hips had begun to ache, and she was nearly soaked through when she saw a flicker of light in the distance. She wondered if the light was just a lamp set in the window of a soddy—or, worse yet, a dugout. But this farmer had erected a large cabin. Hurrying inside, Sarah was further surprised that she walked not on packed earth but rather on a clean puncheon floor. To the left of the door was a huge fireplace made of rough stone plastered with mud. An obviously new stove was sitting in the far corner of the cabin, tucked beside the fireplace. It was at this stove that Dr. Gilbert stood, pouring water from an oak bucket into a pot atop the stove.

He turned just as Sarah stepped inside. "Thank God you're here. Come with me."

Sarah removed her dripping coat and hat, laid them on a crate near the fireplace, and followed Dr. Gilbert into a room created by quilts hanging from the exposed ceiling joists. Her first sight of the woman lying on the bed sent a chill through Sarah. It was apparent that trouble lay ahead for this couple who had worked so hard to build a good cabin. Loula lay as still as death on a lumpy mattress. As Sarah approached the bed, a contraction gripped the young woman and she began thrashing about, struggling pitifully to bring her child into the world.

Dr. Gilbert sat at her side, placing his hand on her shoulder. He leaned forward, speaking in low tones, trying to encourage her, but when he looked up at Sarah, his face was ashen. Sarah's heart fell.

"Still no baby?" the young man asked in disbelief.

Dr. Gilbert shook his head. "I'm afraid not, Sam."

"She's worn out, Doc. How can she birth a baby so worn out?" The young man's voice was forlorn. His eyes asked what he could not: *Am I going to lose her?*

Sarah laid a hand on Sam's arm. "Sam—" She used his first name, speaking it with familiarity, hoping to instill trust. "Do you think you could find dry wood or straw and rekindle the fire in the stove?" Sarah nodded toward the corner she assumed served as Loula's kitchen.

"I got a little lean-to out back. I been keepin' some wood back. I'll get it."

"Are there any clean things for Loula—for the baby?"

Sam shook his head. "We only got what we got on, ma'am." He hesitated for a moment; then, seeing Sarah's expression of pity, he added, "Loula sent back to her ma for some things. I was supposed to check at the depot in Lincoln next week and see if the barrel come, but the baby come early."

Sarah nodded. "Well, then, we'll make do with what we have. That kettle on the stove already has warm water in it. But now you'll need to get the biggest pail or pan you have and heat more water. I'll think of something to do about the clothing. Don't worry."

Grateful for something to do, Sam hurried out to retrieve the dry firewood. While he was gone, Dr. Gilbert explained the situation to Sarah. When he proposed a solution, Sarah stared at him in disbelief. "But, Dr. Gilbert," she stammered, "I've—I've never—I can't."

"Nurse Biddle—" Dr. Gilbert's eyes were cold, his voice firm. "I think Loula has about another hour left in her. We must attempt to turn the baby. The physical reality is, this mother is too small to deliver this baby in the breech position. I cannot perform the podalic version. My hands are too large."

Sarah shook her head, almost backed away. Dr. Gilbert persisted. His voice lowered, lost its insistent tone. "Nurse Biddle, when I attended my first confinement, the husband of the young woman actually expected me to deliver his child while his wife was fully clothed and covered with sheets and blankets to ensure modesty. He sat against the wall with his rifle in his hands to make certain I did nothing he could interpret as improper. That man's notion of propriety resulted in the death of his child, because he refused to allow me to perform the very procedure required here."

Dr. Gilbert shook his head, grimaced, continued. "I have no patience with false modesty and pretense when the lives of my patients are at stake, Nurse Biddle. I must be able to give you clear direction, to have frank discussion of medical condition and treatment. If we cannot agree on this, then you are of no help to me." His tone softened. "If you refuse your assistance tonight, Sam is going to lose both his wife and his first child. I have full confidence in your ability to accomplish this, Nurse Biddle. Can we agree to dispense with the ridiculous notions of our age in the interest of the life of these two patients?"

Sarah's face paled. Loula moaned. With a frightened look in Loula's direction, Sarah nodded and whispered, "Yes—yes—I'm sorry. I'll try."

Immediately Dr. Gilbert began giving orders. "Get over there to that kettle of water. Roll up your sleeves. Wash your hands—your forearms all the way up to the elbows. Do it twice. Pay special attention to the nails. I am of the opinion that Mother's Sickness is caused more by doctors and nurses than anything else." Dr. Gilbert sighed and shook his head. "The bed linens should have been cleaner, and I wish we had clean clothing for the mother and baby, but we shall do our best."

Sam came in with his arms full of wood. He set the heated pot of water aside and wrestled a full pail of well water onto the woodstove. Sarah rolled up her sleeves and washed, twice, giving special attention to her already clean fingernails, while Dr. Gilbert talked Loula through another fruitless contraction.

Sarah approached the bedside, trembling with fear. She was surprised to find herself praying. *God, I don't think I can do this.* The moment the words came to her mind, an unearthly peace washed over her. She seemed to be watching herself perform as Dr. Gilbert directed her. Later she would realize that the moment the prayer was uttered, it was as if someone literally took hold of her hands and guided them in response to Dr. Gilbert's direction.

Dr. Gilbert spoke softly and clearly. "Reach up very slowly, very deliberately. Not too fast. Just tiny increments. There. You should feel the breech presentation. Yes. Now, in even smaller increments, slide your hands alongside—"

Loula flinched, bit her lips, but did not complain.

Sam turned his back on the whole affair, inwardly vowing to never cause his wife this agony again.

"Now, you will feel the cranium. Gently, very gently, bring one hand back down to the infant's buttocks. Yes, that's it. Now guide the cranium toward the birth canal—Loula, try to relax."

Try to relax. Sarah took the words to her own heart and felt some tension go out of her body. Somehow Loula managed to obey Dr. Gilbert. Sarah felt the baby's head come into position. A mighty contraction followed, and Loula responded with all of her remaining strength. Things happened so quickly that Sarah had no time to give way to Dr. Gilbert. Instead, she received into her hands a slimy blue creature.

With a little cry of fear, Sarah looked up, supposing the baby was dead. But as quickly as she pushed the baby toward Dr. Gilbert, a pink glow washed over the little body. With a deft finger Dr. Gilbert cleared mucus from the baby's throat and was rewarded by gasping and gurgling. Seconds later, infant cries were joined by cries of joy from his parents—and cries of relief from Sarah.

Dr. Gilbert gave out his own cry of joy. "Praise be!" Sarah looked at him, surprised at his show of emotion. He said nothing more but went back to work with his two patients while Sarah washed up.

It was dawn before Dr. Gilbert told Sarah to prepare for their return to Lincoln. He and Sam went outside to hitch up his horse and buggy. The moment the two men left the room, Sarah turned to Loula. "Mrs.—"

Loula looked up, tired but smiling, her infant nestled against her. "Kemp. Loula Kemp. But you call me Loula, Nurse Biddle."

"Loula, Sam mentioned last night that you were expecting a barrel of things from your mother next week."

Loula looked surprised. She slowly shook her head. "Don't know what he was meanin', Nurse Biddle. Sam and me got no one but each other." Her voice grew wistful. "Sure wish that was true about a barrel from my ma, but the fact is my ma's been gone since I was ten."

Sarah's look of compassion brought a response that amazed her. "Oh, it's all right, Nurse Biddle. The Lord will surely take care of us. He always has. He gave us this child, and our homestead. He just keeps on savin' us from trouble—one after t'other. Don't you fret for us. We'll get by."

Impulsively Sarah said, "Loula, please don't take offense, but you and I are about the same size. If you'd allow me, I'll just slip this dress off—" Sarah kept one eye on the door as she slipped out of her dress so quickly Loula had no time to react. She had laid her dress at the foot of the bed and pulled on her coat before Loula could protest. "It's all right, Loula. I want to. I'll be back yet today with more things, but you need something now. In fact—" Sarah reached under her coat and pulled off her petticoats. "Use these to wrap the baby. I'll be back soon." Sarah squeezed Loula's hand. Hearing Dr. Gilbert's carriage pull up to the door, she hurried out.

Hoping to prevent Dr. Gilbert's taking notice of the two inches of stocking that now showed between the top of her boots and the bottom of her coat, Sarah began to talk with uncharacteristic animation. "I promised Loula I'd be back later today with some things for the baby. It's going to be a lovely day. Clouds disappearing, the sun will no doubt dry things up in a hurry. What a fine baby boy!"

She rattled on for nearly a mile before she realized Dr. Gilbert hadn't said a word. In fact, he wasn't really driving the carriage. Instead, he had leaned back against his seat and seemed to be half asleep. There was a contented smile on his tired face. Studying him, Sarah realized the man Tom had once called "old Doc Gilbert" was not really old. His black hair showed flecks of gray at the temples, but gray was not evident in either his drooping mustache or the night's growth of beard.

When Sarah's prattle ceased, he opened his eyes and said, "These are the moments that make up for every interrupted dinner, every hour of lost sleep—the moments when I can say I have looked death in the face and wrested victory from its jaws." He smiled happily. "You performed admirably, Nurse Biddle. Sam Kemp owes the lives of his wife and son to you. Think about that for a moment. Is that not a feeling you would like to savor again?"

Sarah nodded. "But it's a little overwhelming. The responsibility."

Dr. Gilbert turned to look her square in the face. "But without the overwhelming responsibility, one would never experience the overwhelming joy." He laughed, snapped the reins smartly. "Get along there, Patty. It's been a hard night, but we've won and I'm famished. I need some of Cora Schlegelmilch's biscuits and gravy!"

Sarah remained quiet, suddenly too exhausted to join in his banter. The sound of a swiftly running creek darting through the grass alongside the wagon trail threatened to lull her to sleep. Dr. Gilbert's little mare trotted smartly along. Dawn broke, flooding the drenched earth with light. Drops of water held on to leaves and grass sparkled as if someone in the night had cast a handful of diamonds across the earth. Sarah closed her eyes, only to be jolted awake when the doctor's carriage halted in the yard at Freeman's Livery.

Dr. Gilbert jumped down and made his way to Sarah's side of the carriage. Lifting Sarah down, he suddenly noticed the change in Sarah's dress—or lack thereof. He guessed the reason, stifled laughter. His eyes sparkled merrily as he spoke. "Nurse Biddle, I hope you will join me in the hotel dining room for a well-deserved breakfast. Of course, you will want to change first." He winked at her.

Sarah blushed, nodded, then walked toward the hotel. Unknown to her, Dr. Gilbert watched her until she had disappeared inside.

Joseph Freeman emerged from the livery to take Dr. Gilbert's horse. But Dr. Gilbert was distracted. *Fine ankles. Very fine ankles, Nurse Biddle.*

CHAPTER 18

Madder Brown

----

*"Withhold not good from them to whom it is
due, when it is in the power of thine
hand to do it."*
Proverbs 3:27

Sarah slept only a few hours before rising to share Sam and Loula Kemp's need with Augusta Hathaway. "Anna Dowd will surely help with a few things. I have about twenty dollars saved up. That will buy quite a few groceries, but I wish I could do more."

"Well, God be praised, Sarah," Augusta exclaimed, "the means to doing a great deal more is expected in my dining room in about an hour. There's a board meeting for the Home for the Friendless. The women will be delighted to help."

Whether the women were truly delighted or Augusta Hathaway coerced them, Sarah never knew. It didn't really matter. While the ladies of the Committee for the Home for the Friendless were meeting in the Hathaway House Hotel dining room, Joseph Freeman was moving one of his supply wagons into position by the kitchen door at the back of the hotel. By lunchtime, a barrel of baby clothes had appeared in the back of the wagon. Soon thereafter, when Sarah went outside to hang out freshly washed linen, she saw that a large piece of folded cloth and two entire bolts of calico had been added. About an hour later a basketful of sewing supplies appeared, followed by a pair of overalls and some women's clothing. By the time Joseph Freeman hitched up his team to drive Sarah out to the Kemps' home, two comforters and a soft used baby quilt had been laid atop the supplies.

"I don't know what you said at that meeting," Sarah said as she hugged Augusta, "but it must have been convincing. Thank you."

Augusta would not be praised. "Oh, posh, Sarah. Any woman in my position would have done as much. It's a joy to help others—especially young people. We were all glad to help."

Sarah picked up her bag and prepared to climb up into the wagon beside Joseph Freeman. Augusta called from the kitchen door, "Dr. Gilbert said you must come by his office before you leave town, Sarah. He has a prescription he wants filled for Loula." Sarah frowned as the wagon rumbled out onto O Street and toward Dr. Gilbert's office. *I thought he said everything went well . . .*

Dr. Gilbert was watching for the wagon when it pulled up to the clinic door. He stepped outside and handed the script up to Sarah. "Just head on over to Miller's and they'll be able to fill this."

Sarah looked down at the script, even more perplexed than before. Miller's had never carried powders or ointments. In fact, Miller's was little more than a general store.

The moment Sarah looked down at the prescription written in Dr. Gilbert's beautiful script, she understood. Her heart swelled with admiration as she read, *Beans, Onions, Apples, Rice, Cheese. One peck each available Vegetables and Fruit. Canning supplies. Charge to account of Dr. Miles Gilbert by special arrangement with the patient.*

Sarah and Joseph drove into the Kemps' farmyard at sundown. A thin line of smoke curled heavenward from the chimney. At the sound of the wagon, Loula appeared in the doorway of the cabin. Her hair was freshly washed and braided, and she was wearing Sarah's dress. When Sarah climbed down from the wagon and came near, expressing concern that perhaps she had overdone, Loula smiled softly. "Oh, now, Nurse Biddle. I'm just fine. Sam brung in the water and washed my hair for me. He combed it and braided it." Loula blushed. "Sam kinda likes it when I let down my hair."

Just then Sam came around the corner of the cabin. He and Loula walked to the wagon together. Sarah introduced Joseph, and Sam reached up to shake his hand as he said, "Don't get to town much, but I know your livery. You got some fine horses in that stable." Sam looked down at Loula affectionately. "I promised Loula a little mare of her own soon as we get on our feet. Then she can visit all she wants, maybe go into town without having to wait for me to come out of the field."

Joseph nodded. "When you're ready, you let me know, Mr. Kemp. I'll keep my eye out for something just right for the missus."

When Sarah pulled back the comforter that hid the supplies, Sam shook his head. "We sure appreciate your working so hard, Nurse Biddle. But we can't take it all." Sam nodded toward the cabin. "'Course we need a few things for Davey. Maybe that calico for Loula." Sam laid the overalls aside. "I'm fine with what I got. Patches don't bother me none."

Loula followed Sam's lead. Choosing a piece of madder brown cotton, she nodded and said, "Sam's right, Nurse Biddle. We can't take it all, but we sure appreciate what you brought." With a longing glance at two bolts of indigo calico, Loula stepped away from the wagon. "You just make a list of what we took, and I'll keep account.

We'll sign whatever you want. Sam's promised the neighbors to break sod this spring. They'll pay four dollars an acre. We can pay as soon as the job's done."

Sam nodded. "I figure I'll do about five acres before I have to plant my wheat. So that's twenty dollars. . . ." He turned to Loula. "Now, Loula, I think you could have one of them bolts of calico—that blue'd look real pretty with your eyes. Can't be much for that bolt."

Loula shook her head and patted the piece of cloth folded over her arm. "This is plenty for me, Sam. I can probably get a little baby quilt out of the scraps. I'll fill it with the rest of that red flannel, and Davey'll be warm as a bug all next winter."

The bounty of groceries piled in the wagon was almost too much for the Kemps to believe. They didn't open any of the burlap bags, but stood away from the wagon as Loula said, "We're doing fine, Nurse Biddle. We can get by. Won't be long 'til spring and gardenin'. Sam's going to plant three acres of corn and a half-acre of potatoes. For now we got plenty of cornmeal for corn bread, and we got wheat enough to roast and make coffee. My Sam works hard. Come spring he'll break enough sod that we can pay for what we took today, maybe even a cow before next winter." Loula lifted her chin, threw back her head, and gazed at Sarah with such pride in her husband that Sarah wanted to cry.

But Sarah insisted, "Loula, you have a baby to feed now. You can't take good care of him if you're poorly fed. You need vegetables and fruit. That's why Dr. Gilbert wrote the script and had me bring these things out."

Sam's mouth was set in a stubborn line. "We don't go into debt, Nurse Biddle. Loula and Davey need a few things, but as long as I can hunt and Loula has cornmeal, we'll get by. We don't want to owe any more."

Sarah reached into her pocket and produced Dr. Gilbert's prescription. "It's in the doctor's own handwriting,

Sam. It's as necessary as if Davey were sick. Both he and Loula need those groceries." Seeing stubbornness growing in Sam's eyes, Sarah surprised herself by saying, "Dr. Gilbert said he provided it *by special arrangement with his patient*. That means Miller's doesn't think it's charity—and neither does Dr. Gilbert." Sarah had an idea, paused, then plunged ahead. "Didn't Loula tell me you were a carpenter before you came out here, Sam?"

Sam shook his head. "Not exactly. My pa was. I worked alongside him—learned plenty. Never done carpenter work on my own, though, not until I built this cabin."

"Well, Dr. Gilbert saw something that impressed him when he was here. He wants your help at his clinic in town." Sarah continued. "He bought a small cottage a few blocks from the clinic. He plans on moving out of the back of the office so it can be changed over to a small hospital. There's a storeroom upstairs to be renovated into a small apartment. Dr. Gilbert wants a full-time nurse to staff his new hospital." She smiled shyly. "He's asked if Tom and I would come." She looked beseechingly at Sam. "But he needs a good carpenter to do some work. If you'd be willing to do it before fieldwork begins, you'd earn enough to pay for this food and more. Maybe even that cow Loula mentioned."

Sam looked doubtful. Joseph Freeman subtly shook the reins. His team stepped forward, reminding Sarah that dark was fast approaching and it was time they headed back to Lincoln.

Sarah took the cue. Her voice was almost stern as she said, "Now you look here, Sam Kemp. Augusta Hathaway and her friends worked nearly all day collecting these things. They will be highly insulted if you refuse them. You seem to be a religious man. Doesn't the Bible say that folks are supposed to help one another? Well, for that to happen, *someone* has to be willing to *accept* help." Sarah nodded toward the house. "From the looks of the start you and Loula have made here, Sam, I'd guess that someday you will be in a position to help others. How will you feel if some young man is unwilling to accept things his family needs because he is too proud? Isn't pride a sin, too, Sam?"

Sam grinned. "All right, Nurse Biddle. When you bring God's Word into the discussion, you've beat me. But you tell Dr. Gilbert he'd better have plenty of work for me, because the Good Book also says a man should pay his debts. And I want to pay for everything Dr. Gilbert sent out, no matter what it takes."

Sarah nodded. "I'll tell him. Now let's get these things unloaded. Joseph and I need to get back to town."

"Loula," Sam said quietly, "you best be getting inside and resting. Mr. Freeman and I can unload these things." Sam looked to Sarah. "And I'm sure Nurse Biddle would like to see how well Davey is doing."

Sarah and Loula went inside the cabin where Davey lay on the bed, fast asleep in a cloud of red flannel and white petticoat.

Loula settled beside her sleeping baby. "After Sam brought in water for a bath and washed my hair, I felt so much better I got inspiration to sew a bit. Between your white petticoats and my red flannel, Davey's dressed as fine as any baby. 'Course I still got to hem everything, but I ran out of thread just on the seams for that little gown."

"Well, there are three new spools of thread in that sewing basket the men are about to bring in, Loula," Sarah said, adding, "You put your feet up, too. I'm glad you're feeling so strong, but you need to rest when you get the chance. Don't overdo."

Loula chuckled. "You sound just like Sam. He was madder'n anything when I got up this morning and made hotcakes." She smiled softly. "But he ate 'em. Said they was real good too." Loula's eyes sparkled. "He's real proud of his new son. Real proud. Held him already and took him out to see the barn. Talks to him just like he could understand."

Sarah reached out to touch the sleeping baby's tiny fist. "I'm so glad everything has turned out for you."

Loula smiled. "We been praisin' the Lord all day long, Nurse Biddle." She leaned back against the rough-hewn headboard, closed her eyes, and began to reminisce. "The first time I saw Sam Kemp he was standing in the door of his folks' cabin with a whip in his hand. My ma and pa had just come into the territory and heard Sam's pa knew all the best homesteads. While Pa and Mr. Kemp—that's Sam's pa—was talkin', Sam come in from the barn. I looked up and there he was. He saw me and got the funniest little smile on his face." Loula blushed. "He was sure good to look at." She opened her eyes, looked over at her sleeping baby. "Maybe I didn't fall in love with Sam right then, but I did soon after."

While Loula talked, Joseph and Sam carried in supplies. Soon the crates that formed Loula's kitchen cupboard were filled with bags of supplies. Loula gazed upon her filled larder with amazement. Sam brought her the sewing basket, laid it in her lap, and kissed her on the cheek. Loula opened it, exclaiming at the beauty of the silver thimble that lay atop a small pile of fabric squares.

"I hope it fits," Sarah offered. "I like having a pretty thimble—" She looked about at the quilts that formed the bedroom they were sitting in. "I assumed you like to sew, Loula. These are beautiful."

Loula nodded. "That's my New York Beauty," she said, pointing to a red and blue masterpiece with slivers of fabric less than half an inch wide forming incredible patterns across the surface.

"My grandma made that one when she was a bride," Loula said, pointing to the largest quilt Sarah had ever seen. Twenty huge stars in red, blue, and yellow calico marched across the top of the quilt to create a beautiful pattern Loula called Feathered Star. "I don't think I'll ever have a bed that big, but it sure came in handy when we wanted to hang all the quilts to make the bedroom."

Sarah was looking at the walls of the cabin with a puzzled expression. "In the dark last night I thought you had quilts insulating the cabin walls, as well, but—" Someone had papered the inside of the walls with newspapers. Where the corners of the paper met, a one inch square of red flannel was held in place with a tack.

Loula turned to look at the wall. "Had to cut up my favorite petticoat to get those squares. But it makes it more cheerful. The way I look at it, if God took seven days to put all the colors in the world so's it'd be beautiful, then I should do what I can to make my world look pretty, too. Quilts is one way. But I didn't have enough quilts to hang over all the walls and still cover the bed."

Loula continued. "The folks was surprised we wanted to come all the way out here, but Sam and me wanted a home of our own. I worked alongside him all summer last. He cut cottonwoods down at the creek a mile from here for the timbers for the cabin. Drug them up here one at a time. I helped peel the bark off. Neighbors helped Sam all they could. We got good neighbors."

Sarah nodded. "I expected to come to a soddy—or, worse, a dugout—last night."

Loula shook her head. "Sam said he wouldn't have his family living in no cave. We made a tent alongside the wagon last summer. Sam could've broke more sod, made more money, but he spent so much time on the house . . ." Loula looked about her. "But it's a mighty fine house." Her voice lowered, she said tenderly, "We're gonna be real happy here. I wish the folks would have lived to see it." Loula smiled brightly before going on. "Soon as we get money, Sam's gonna put some cottonwood shingles on the roof. Said he'd make me some shutters for the windows, and a real front door too. Not just that slab of wood."

Joseph and Sam finished unloading supplies. Sarah reluctantly gave the sleeping infant back to Loula and turned to go. "Dr. Gilbert will be back in a couple of days to check on you." She added with a grin, "And you'd better have eaten some of those vegetables the men just unloaded!"

As she went out the door, Sarah turned to survey the interior of the cabin. What last night appeared to her as little more than a well-constructed hovel had been transformed. Knowing the Kemps, seeing their love, Sarah now looked on the cabin as a work in progress, the beginning of a dream, the physical reality of emotional ties.

Joseph had clucked to his team and turned the wagon around when Sarah laid a hand on his arm. "Wait a minute, Joseph. I forgot something." Reaching under her seat she pulled out a small basket and called back to Sam, who was standing in the doorway of his cabin watching them go. "Sam—there's one more thing." Sarah handed Sam a small basket holding an amber-colored quart jar nestled in fabric scraps.

Sarah laughed. "This is one precious quart of last year's peaches canned by Mrs. H. A. Tuttle herself, who everyone knows is the best cook in the county." As Sam unwrapped the jar, Sarah explained, "She told me herself what to say when I presented those peaches." Sarah added, "She's not very humble, but she's truthful. She probably *is* the best cook in the county. The men almost fight to get a piece of her pie at every church social."

Loula appeared behind Sam, accepted the quart of peaches with shining eyes, and called out over Sam's shoulder, "When Dr. Gilbert comes out you come too, Nurse Biddle. I'll make us a pie with these peaches."

Sam spoke up proudly. "And after you eat Loula's peach pie, I expect you'll be telling that Mrs. Tuttle she has some serious competition out west of town."

"I'm afraid I've spoken out of hand, Dr. Gilbert." It was the morning after Sarah had visited the Kemps. She and Dr. Gilbert were preparing to open the clinic. Sarah reached behind her to tie her apron on as she continued nervously, "And you may be very unhappy with me when I tell you about it."

Dr. Gilbert looked up from where he sat at his library table, his copy of *Flint's Practice* open before him. Trying to imagine what quiet, unassuming Sarah Biddle could possibly do to displease him, he asked, "Well, what is it?"

"Sam Kemp is intolerably proud. The only way I was able to convince him to accept the things Joseph and I took out yesterday was to promise him a way to repay you." She walked to the front of the office, hoping that some patients had already arrived, but the waiting room was empty. She took a deep breath and continued. "I told him about your buying the cottage, about your plans to move out and convert your living quarters here into a small hospital. I even mentioned your wanting to remodel the storeroom upstairs into an apartment for a resident nurse. Then I said he could work off his debt by doing the carpentry work for you."

"I see." Dr. Gilbert closed the medical book, stood up, walked to the doorway that separated his living quarters from the clinic. He opened the door and looked in. Without turning around he said, "The only difficulty, Nurse Biddle, is that the ten dollars I usually charge for a confinement call in the country, coupled with the cost of the food I sent out, doesn't begin to cover what I would have to pay a carpenter for the remodeling." He turned around to look at her.

Sarah avoided his gaze. "I was afraid you'd say that." She hesitated before continuing. "But I've been thinking, Dr. Gilbert—Aunt Augusta won't hear of me paying room and board for Tom and me. The last time I raised the topic she really got angry. And, as you know, Mrs. Braddock provided for Tom." She offered, "As a result, we have few needs." She finally looked Dr. Gilbert in the eyes. "I think I could get by on half my salary. If that would help."

Dr. Gilbert shook his head. "No. Absolutely not."

"But why not, Dr. Gilbert? You've said it yourself. It's totally unacceptable for a city the size of Lincoln, growing at the rate we are, to be sending patients to the Omaha hospitals. Granted, four beds at the back of the clinic isn't much of a start, but it *is* a beginning." She added almost shyly, "And I like to be part of new beginnings."

"I appreciate your enthusiasm, Nurse Biddle," he said, "but I cannot have my nurse paying for a project I should be able to fund."

Sarah argued, "Dr. Gilbert, you have made yourself available to every citizen in the surrounding area, every hour of day and night, regardless of their ability to pay." With a rare reference to her life with the Braddocks, she added, "I have observed the wealthy physicians who practice back east." She hesitated before saying quietly, "You have nothing to apologize for. Some chose to pursue wealth. You chose to serve your fellow man."

Dr. Gilbert held up his hand. "Don't praise me too highly, Nurse Biddle. I still like to be paid for my services. It just doesn't always work out. And I despise talking about money with my patients. It seems inappropriate, somehow." He grinned. "Especially when I really *like* the idea of them thinking of me as the noble servant you have just so beautifully described."

"Perhaps you could present the matter to Aunt Augusta. She's had fairly good success collecting past due accounts, in spite of the fact that women in business encounter unique challenges. She might have some very helpful suggestions. You know how she is when it comes to anything she connects with progress. The idea of a hospital for Lincoln would definitely interest her."

Dr. Gilbert appeared to be coming around to her viewpoint just when the front door opened and the first patient of the day arrived. He and Sarah were drawn into a busy morning, but the moment Sarah pulled down the window shade that read, THE DOCTOR IS OUT, Dr. Gilbert suggested, "Let's drive out to the Kemps' place this afternoon. I should check on Loula and the baby, and while we're there I can talk to Sam Kemp about the specifics of this remodeling project."

"Perhaps I should stay and keep the clinic open—" Sarah began.

"No." Dr. Gilbert was adamant. "No, I want you there. I have an idea that just might make this whole plan of a small hospital really work." At the question in Sarah's eyes, he smiled. "But I need the time driving out to the Kemps' to think it through."

They were halfway to the Kemps', and Dr. Gilbert had been deep in thought when he suddenly asked, "Did Harriet Tuttle really contribute a quart of her prized peaches to the Kemps?"

Sarah laughed aloud. "Yes, Dr. Gilbert, she did. And from what I saw of Loula yesterday, you have a very good chance of comparing Loula's cooking to Mrs. Tuttle's this very day."

Dr. Gilbert nodded with satisfaction. "Good. Glad to hear it." He glanced sideways, winked at Sarah. "Even selfless servants enjoy a bit of self-indulgence from time to time, Nurse Biddle. In fact," he said as he leaned back, "at the moment I am entirely open to the notion of trading one confinement fee for one peach pie."

A Garibaldi Print

Sam and Loula Kemp were part of a dramatic influx of people arriving in Nebraska in the 1880s. Immigrants flooded Lincoln, staying only long enough to fill wagons and flow out onto the prairie, trickling into valleys and gorges, setting up homesteads, praying for a better future. Nature smiled on them all. Rainfall was above average and food production tripled. The state teemed with activity, and Lincoln teemed with it, fast overtaking the once remote Wyuka Cemetery.

The Lincoln Railway Company was granted a right-of-way and built lines connecting all parts of the city. The City Water Works and a Telephone Exchange were founded. Businessmen dared to talk of paving the streets in the center of the city. Five new full-time firemen and a two-horse, four-wheel carriage assured the safety of residents. Even though Lincoln's police force numbered only seventeen men, it was boasted that "fewer cities in the United States are better policed owing to the high grade of the citizenship." Near the outskirts of Lincoln, the villages of Havelock and College View sprung up.

While the *Nebraska State Journal* reported the comings and goings of waves of immigrants, it bemoaned the fate of farmers who realized no profit from bumper crops because of the exorbitant rates the railroads were charging to transport crops to market. The *Journal* railed against the railroads and did its best to take note of every event of significance to the growing state. However, it failed to report the arrival of one new citizen who was to have a significant impact on the health and well-being of hundreds of its inhabitants.

She arrived one July day when the temperature had soared and the air was so thick with dust and humidity that everyone and everything wilted. Passengers descending from the train were hit by a relentless blast of heat reflected from the platform. Gentlemen took one breath of the superheated air and hastened to the nearest saloon to quench their thirst. Ladies whose corsets had been cinched to effect stylish twenty-inch waistlines regretted their inability to gasp for air. More than one felt faint. Smelling salts tucked daintily inside their sleeves enabled most to navigate the maze of luggage and passengers.

Nellie Spomer was not so fortunate. Early that morning she had donned her new black-and-red Garibaldi print dress, insisting that her maid help cinch her corset "not a smidgen over eighteen inches. I simply will not allow myself out in public looking like that sow at the cotillion last night. Goodness, her waist was twenty-three inches at least. If I must, I'll have Dr. Carter remove a couple of ribs. Eliza Osborne had it done last winter and her gown fit so beautifully I wanted to slap her."

That afternoon Nebraska's heat and Nellie Spomer's corset did battle, and Nebraska won. Nellie Spomer went down in a heap on the railroad platform.

Two gentlemen had just leaned over to rescue the maiden when a voice from above commanded, "Carry her into the station." Both men looked up at once, at the angular six-foot frame and into the piercing hazel eyes of the woman who gave the order. "She needs shade. And water," the woman said impatiently. A third gentleman lifted Nellie's still form from the ground. The woman surveyed Nellie's waistline and added in a disgusted tone of voice, "And some common sense."

Nellie Spomer returned to consciousness, sputtering as someone sprinkled cold water on her face. Her eyes opened and she saw an unfamiliar woman glowering at her. "Young lady," she lectured, "you are committing fashionable suicide."

Nellie blinked stupidly and struggled to sit up. The woman went on. "You can't possibly expand your lungs properly. The lungs, young lady, move air to purify the blood. If the blood is not purified, the entire body suffers. The tone of your skin indicates poisoning of the nerve tissues. You are risking consumption, heart disease, perhaps fissure of the liver." The woman shook her finger in Nellie's face. "More than one case is on record of young ladies who have applied the corset so tightly that a blood vessel has ruptured. Death ensues almost instantly when that happens, young lady!"

"Who *are* you?" Nellie sputtered. She was beginning to recover, and amazement was quickly metamorphosing into resentment of this tall stranger, imperiously delivering a lecture with clinical passion and no regard for the fact that bystanders could hear her every word.

The woman stood back with a satisfied air. Drawing a card from her small handbag, she extended it to Nellie, who read, *Dr. Maude Allbright, Obstetrics and Diseases of Women.* Nellie held out the card to return it, but Dr. Allbright shook her head. "No, you keep it. I shall have opened an office within two weeks. If you continue this ridiculous and totally unnatural constriction, you will soon suffer from some ailment requiring medical attention. When you do, you will be wanting that card."

Nellie Spomer doubted that she would ever want to see this woman again. Still, she obeyed her, tucking the card inside her own bag. She stood up slowly, fighting the urge to slump back onto the bench.

Dr. Allbright scooped something up from beside Nellie and turned to go. She walked back toward the train, absentmindedly stroking the fur of the black spaniel puppy cradled in her arms. She did not see one of the gentlemen who had assisted Nellie inside the train station approach and offer the girl his arm.

Most of the train's passengers had disembarked, collected their luggage, and headed for home or a nearby hotel. Dr. Allbright exited the station. Shading her eyes, she spotted two round hatboxes at the far end of the platform. Not a porter was in sight.

Two ragged boys were playing along the train tracks. She called out to them. "Here, boys, come help me and I'll pay you well."

"*Nous ne parlons pas anglais,*" one boy shouted back. He said it in a pleasant tone of voice, moving toward the doctor.

"*Ça ne fait rien,*" Dr. Allbright replied in perfect French. "*J'ai etudié à Paris. Prenez les valises là bas—*" she motioned toward her hatboxes. "*Je vais à l'hôtel Hathaway House. Vous connaissez cet hôtel?*"

The boys nodded. Each one grabbed a hatbox. Expecting them to be light, they were surprised when they had to struggle to lift them. Nevertheless, they valiantly heaved them, managing to wrestle the boxes out of the train station and across the street to the Hathaway House, where they deposited them in the lobby.

Dr. Allbright smiled. *"Bien. Merci bien. Voilà."* She tipped the young men generously, warning them to spend only a small portion on candy before giving the rest to their mother. *"Votre mère est ici, non?"*

The boys nodded. "Yes, madame. Our mother is here. She waits at the Immigrant House for Papa to find land. Then we will go west to build a house."

"So you do speak English, after all." Dr. Allbright chuckled.

The boys blushed and ducked their heads. "Only a little."

"Well, see to it that you learn to speak it well. You must learn English and then nothing will keep you from success. America welcomes boys who will work hard."

"May I pet your puppy?" the younger boy asked.

Dr. Allbright knelt down. "Of course. His name is Jet. When I first chose him from the litter, his sparkling eyes reminded me of jet buttons."

"You should have named him Buttons," one boy suggested shyly. "I like the name Buttons."

Dr. Allbright shook her head. "Buttons. A banal name suggesting an adorable but brainless animal." She patted Jet on the head. "This is a fine little animal. Bred for brains. He deserves a far better name than Buttons."

Dr. Allbright realized that the boys had long since given up trying to understand her English. In the manner of boys they were lost in their enjoyment of Jet, who was doing his best to prove himself both adorable and brainless in his joy over their attention.

The boys were still petting Jet when Silas Kellum arrived at the desk to register Dr. Allbright. The doctor stood up abruptly, waved the boys away, and barked her demands. "I shall require a small room. Modest. I am due at the university in two hours to lecture. Can someone take my bags up right away? Good.

"I also need a boy to help with Jet. A boy with sense and kindness. I'll not have my puppy teased or mistreated.

But I'll pay well for a boy who will see that Jet is exercised and attended to while I am gone."

Dr. Allbright signed the register book with a flourish and turned toward the door. "I shall make arrangements at the livery for Jet to occupy a stall there. He's not fully housebroken as yet. I shall have him in my room only when I am present to see that he behaves himself. You may be assured that I'll allow no damage to hotel property." Dr. Allbright paused at the door to ask, "Do you know a boy who might care to help?"

Silas replied, "Yes, ma'am. Tom Biddle will do it."

"Tom Biddle." Dr. Allbright said the name carefully, as if the sound of it would reveal some clue as to the boy's qualifications. She looked sharply at Silas Kellum. "Well then, have Tom Biddle found and sent up to my room. I'll interview him at once." Dr. Allbright swept out the door. Silas had just taken her bags up to her room and was descending the stairs to the hotel lobby when Dr. Allbright returned. She looked about the lobby carefully. Silas watched, amused, as she ran her gloved hands along the edge of some molding and inspected her gloves for dust. Apparently satisfied, she turned toward the stairs, nodding briefly to Silas, accepting his direction and her room key without a word.

She descended a half hour later, scribbled a note for the housekeeper that read, *Kindly attend to the dust beneath the bed*, and went next door to the livery, where she confronted Joseph Freeman, saying abruptly, "I need a carriage for the afternoon."

Joseph Freeman was an aged former slave with an inordinate love for his horses and an uncanny ability to judge people. In Joseph's estimation, any woman who rented an entire stall to ensure the comfort of a puppy was worthy of one of the better carriage horses. But before letting Blizzard go, he had to be certain the woman could handle him.

"You had much experience at drivin', ma'am?" Joseph inquired.

Dr. Allbright bristled. "I've driven for years, sir. Dozens of horses in dozens of cities. I've never had a problem, and I've never met a horse I was afraid to drive—if that is what you are inferring."

Joseph nodded his head apologetically. "Didn't mean nothin' by it, ma'am. I try to match the driver with the horse, that's all."

Dr. Allbright looked past Joseph at a huge white horse standing in the stall next to the one she had rented for Jet. "He wasn't in here only half an hour ago. Is he available?"

"That's Blizzard, ma'am. Friend of mine just brought him back. I gave him a little time off out on the farm. He's well broke, but he takes a mite of handling. He's a mind that tests who's holding the reins, if you know what I mean."

"Excellent. I've a mind that likes to be tested. Hitch him up. I haven't any time to spare."

Joseph noted Dr. Allbright's large hands. "I can see you can handle a horse, ma'am," Joseph intoned. "But with Blizzard—well, ma'am, he don't need a lot of pulling. Just a firm hand."

Dr. Allbright's voice softened as she replied, "I've never owned my own horse, Mr. Freeman, but I have no use for anyone who mistreats animals, and I can promise you that I won't mistreat Blizzard." Dr. Allbright walked over to Blizzard's stall. The tall horse looked her over, whickered softly. Maude Allbright removed a glove and reached up to scratch behind Blizzard's ears. Blizzard lowered his head and stood entranced by the unusual attention.

Joseph looked on, satisfied with the match of Blizzard and Dr. Maude Allbright, unaware that he was about to create a partnership between horse and driver that would span years. Decades later, even folks who had never been cared for by Dr. Allbright would remember her as "the one who always drove that big white horse—the one that gave fits to anyone else, but was gentle as could be when Dr. Allbright held the reins."

CHAPTER 20

Black Cashmere

"The wisdom of the prudent is to
understand his way:
but the folly of fools is deceit."
Proverbs 14:8

When George McCann descended from the train he had unwittingly shared with Maude Allbright, he swore against the heat. Intending to hurry to the nearest saloon for a cold draft of beer, he was distracted by the commotion at the opposite end of the platform. The sight of a beautiful young woman crumpled in a cloud of red-and-black calico made him forget his plans for beer. He joined two other men in a rush to the young woman's aid. George almost single-handedly carried her into the station at the bidding of another woman he assumed was the beauty's mother.

However, standing back with a few other passengers, George soon learned he was mistaken, for the older woman commenced a diatribe regarding corsets and various other torturous inventions of fashion that left bystanders smiling with a combination of amazement and amusement. When the woman, who had identified herself as Dr. Maude Allbright left, George stepped forward, offering Nellie his arm. En route to the Cadman House Hotel, Nellie revealed (with just the appropriate amount of shyness) that, while she much preferred a more cosmopolitan city, she had agreed to accompany her guardian and uncle to Lincoln to settle some business.

"Uncle wants me to consider the university here," Nellie sniffed. "But I can't imagine attending classes in a building where if one steps off the boardwalk one might step into cow—" Nellie hid behind her fan. "Oh, dear. Please excuse me. How indelicate of me."

George smiled solicitously. "Not at all, Miss Spomer. I understand completely. As it happens, however, I've decided to endure the hardships and attend the university. Perhaps we shall see each other again." The carriage had arrived at the Cadman House and George leaped to the ground. "Are you feeling quite recovered, Miss Spomer?"

Nellie nodded and extended her hand, but George had already turned his back and was making his way hastily up the boardwalk, leaving Nellie to fend for herself. She tried to be angry, but George's auburn hair, green eyes, and square jawline made it difficult. Instead of getting angry, Nellie determined to humor her uncle and investigate the university's offerings. Perhaps Uncle was right, after all. Perhaps there were advantages to attending a small university. Of course, Uncle had been referring to the excellent staff and the attention they could give individual students because of small class size. Nellie had in mind another advantage involving the possibility of "chance" encounters with a certain gentleman.

George McCann made his way down the boardwalk completely aware of the fact that Nellie Spomer was watching his retreat. He assumed that she was simpering like a spoiled child. He had no doubt of his ability to pacify her hurt feelings when they met again, and he would be certain they did meet again. He filed the name Nellie Spomer in a mental drawer marked "Girls to Have Fun With" and cleared his mind for his next challenge: Dr. Miles Gilbert.

THE DOCTOR IS IN proclaimed a sign hanging on Dr. Gilbert's office door. George opened the door, stepped inside, and frowned slightly when he saw that Dr. Gilbert had patients waiting. He prepared to take a seat as a blonde nurse stepped into the room. "May I help you?"

"Oh, I'm not here as a patient," George said. "Please tell Dr. Gilbert that George McCann requests an interview."

Sarah wrote the name George McCann on the patient list. Whoever he was, she thought, George McCann had the greenest eyes she had ever seen. At least six feet tall, with an athletic build, he sported unfashionably long but impeccably groomed auburn hair that fairly glowed against his black cashmere suit. Yes, George McCann was a beautiful man.

Dr. Gilbert called for her, and Sarah retreated at once into the examining room where she helped convince ten-year-old Billy Dowd to cooperate while Dr. Gilbert cleansed and stitched a wicked-looking cut across the top of his foot.

Dr. Gilbert had just tied off Billy's last stitch when Sarah saw him look up. His face immediately flushed red, and Sarah realized with amazement that Miles Gilbert had become angrier than she had ever seen him—in about two seconds. Looking around, Sarah saw George McCann standing in the doorway. She busied herself dressing Billy's wound, but not before she noted, blushing, that those beautiful green eyes had turned their gaze upon her.

Dr. Gilbert said coldly, "If you'll please be seated in the waiting room, I'll be with you when I can." The visitor shrugged and disappeared from the doorway.

George McCann. Sarah thought back. No, she had never heard Dr. Gilbert speak of a George McCann. And Dr. Gilbert was certainly not speaking of him now. He worked so methodically that Sarah began to wonder if he was postponing his meeting with the visitor.

As Sarah went back and forth between examining room and waiting room summoning patients, she noticed that George McCann appeared undisturbed by Dr. Gilbert's reluctance to see him. After the first hour he withdrew a small book from the inner pocket of his jacket and, leaning his chair back against the wall, began to read.

When the last patient had been seen, Sarah washed her hands, removed her apron, and turned to leave.

"I wish you wouldn't, Nurse Biddle," Dr. Gilbert said.

"What, Dr. Gilbert?"

"I wish you wouldn't go." Dr. Gilbert was standing in the doorway between the examining room and his living quarters. "I've got to deal with George McCann, and I'd like it if you'd stay here in the clinic. Perhaps you could read over one of the cases from last week, balance the ledger book, roll bandages . . ." He smiled weakly. "I don't have a lot of patience with that fellow. If you're in the room, I'll be forced to exercise some self-control."

Sarah agreed to stay, her curiosity growing.

"Thank you." Dr. Gilbert walked past her and to the doorway. He made no attempt to hide his displeasure at the man's presence. "All right, George, come in." When the two were facing one another, Dr. Gilbert motioned for George to sit on his examining table. Leaning against the table that held his medical books, Dr. Gilbert said, "Please get right to the point. What is it you want?"

"A moment with you in private would be nice," George said, pointedly looking at Sarah.

"I've asked Nurse Biddle to remain and prepare the office for tomorrow. Either say what you have to say now or leave. It's of no concern to me either way."

George stood up, rubbed the back of his neck. "Is it always so insufferably hot here in July? Can a man at least have a glass of water?"

Sarah started for the door to get some water, but Dr. Gilbert stopped her. "You'll get plenty to drink at your next stop, I expect, George. The nearest saloon is just around the corner. Get on with it. Why did you come to Lincoln? What do you want?"

McCann pursed his lips, hooked his thumbs in the pockets of his jacket, and thought a moment before answering. "All right, Cousin Miles. I deserved that. And any other insults you want to throw my way. But I've changed since you last saw me. For good. I'm not frequenting saloons anymore. I've reformed. I've even given up women—and I apologize to the lady present for even touching on that topic."

"Get on with it, George. What do you want?"

"I need a recommendation so that I can get accepted to the medical college."

From the look on Dr. Gilbert's face, Sarah knew he would not have been more surprised if George McCann had come to the doctor for medical care to treat a pregnancy—his. Without hesitation Dr. Gilbert said tersely, "No. Now, if that is all, Nurse Biddle and I have had a long day."

George McCann had apparently steeled himself for a lengthy discussion. Being dismissed with a simple "no," he rubbed the back of his neck again, laughed oddly, looked at the floor. Finally, he said quietly, "I expected you to doubt my sincerity, Cousin Miles. But I thought you might give me a chance to—"

"No."

Sarah had finished washing the medical instruments. Pulling open a drawer, she drew out a white sheet and began cutting it into strips and rolling bandages. Dr. Gilbert pushed a chair at her. "Sit down, Nurse Biddle. I'll escort my cousin to the door and then we can lock up."

From where she sat, Sarah could hear perfectly. It was obvious that George was not going to give up so easily. "I've been profligate. Totally. But I have sincerely repented. I want to make something of myself."

Miles retorted, "Medicine is a worthy calling for honest men who don't mind giving up their own lives for the sake of others—who don't mind riding miles in blinding rain or snow to hopeless cases that likely won't pay their fee. Now, let's see, George, how does your résumé compare with that list of qualifications? *Honest*. Hmm, unfortunately there's the matter of that little business dealing with the Philbricks back in St. Louis. Sorry to say, George, you don't have a reputation for being honest. Ah well, let's try the next one— *willing to give up one's life for others*. I seem to recall a little incident where you were willing to ruin someone else's life because of your own desires. But for Nurse Biddle's sake, we shall venture no further into that incident. *Willing to ride miles in blinding rain and snow* . . . Dear me, George, you're not doing very well, are you? Wasn't that you I found sitting at home drinking hot coffee the day we were all out in the freezing weather trying to keep the flood-waters from destroying the neighbor's livestock?"

George protested, "All right, Cousin Miles, all right. You've made your point. I can't argue about the past. But I'm telling you that I am finished with that life. I want to be a success. I want to be a doctor."

"Contrary to popular belief, George," Dr. Gilbert said sarcastically, "medicine is not always the way to wealth and fame. Since wealth and fame would, of course, be an inherent part of your definition of success, you have chosen poorly. What I said about people often not paying their physicians is true. George McCann would never want to care for people unable to pay him. Word would get around, George. You'd fail. So why trouble yourself with the amusing idea that perhaps medical school would be entertaining? We have a serious college here, with serious students who sincerely want to serve others. I will not have my reputation linked to your name. *Now get out of my office*."

Sarah heard Dr. Gilbert open the door. But George McCann did not give up.

"All right, don't believe me. Don't write the recommendation. Let me work for you for a while. Test me out. See if I haven't changed. I'll do anything you say, from driving your buggy on every midnight call to cleaning your horses hooves to sweeping out the office. Just let me prove myself to you. Prove that I've changed. Miles, you know I'm bright. I can do anything I set my mind to."

"Yes, I know that, George. Unfortunately, you never set your mind to accomplish anything worthwhile."

"Well I'm doing so now." George's voice was pleading. "Please, Cousin Miles. I have nowhere else to go."

Dr. Gilbert took a deep breath. He closed the door. Quietly he said, "Are you running from another unfortunate encounter with a sheriff somewhere?"

"No."

"Is there a woman involved?"

When George didn't answer, Miles said abruptly, "I see."

George spoke up. "But I've promised to help her, Cousin Miles. Here. This is her address. Write and ask her. I've promised to send her whatever I can for at least a year. And I mean to do it. But I've got to make a start. If you don't help me, Priscilla and her child will have to go without. Really, Miles. I have nowhere else to turn." He sounded near tears. "God knows I've made a mess of things."

Dr. Gilbert took a deep breath. He closed the door. "Where are you staying, George?"

A very contrite voice said, "I was hoping to stay with you." His voice actually broke before he admitted, "Aunt Lucy wouldn't even see me. Mother and Father are abroad. The servants have orders to shut me out."

Dr. Gilbert called for Sarah. She went to the doorway of the waiting room and saw George McCann slumped in a chair, his head bowed, his beautiful auburn hair falling down to hide his clenched fists, upon which he had rested his forehead.

Miles said quietly, "Thank you for staying, Nurse Biddle. You may go now."

Sarah nodded, retreated to the examining room, and removed her apron. She called out a good night and left through the rear entrance.

The next morning when Sarah opened the office door, she was startled to see George McCann cheerfully sweeping the waiting-room floor. "Good morning, Nurse Biddle," George said. "Cousin Miles said that I could stay for a few days if I earn my keep." He smiled sheepishly. "He left a list of things that he thought I could do to help get the upstairs ready for the carpenter. Said I should have you read it over and see if there's anything to be added."

George McCann spent the next two weeks acquiring blisters on his hands from scrubbing, sweeping, and cleaning. Much to his cousin's amazement, he performed every task well and without complaint. He requested that Miles send his entire salary to one Priscilla Bates of Akron, Ohio.

Things seemed to be going well between George and his cousin Miles until the afternoon when Dr. Gilbert returned from lecturing at the university to find George leaning over Sarah Biddle as she studied *Gray's Anatomy*.

"I asked you to get the last of Nurse Biddle's furniture today, George." Dr. Gilbert's voice was icy.

George looked up, dropped his hand from the back of Sarah's chair. He smiled good-naturedly. "And I have done so, Cousin Miles. Miller's loaded it up for me before they opened this morning. Everything is out back, just waiting for Sam to arrive. Then we can haul it all upstairs and Sarah can tell us how she wants things arranged." He put his hand back on Sarah's chair.

"Nurse Biddle would do well to keep to the agreed-upon schedule for her office hours," Dr. Gilbert said crisply. Turning to Sarah he said, "I believe we discussed your reporting to the office about 1 P.M. today, Miss Biddle."

Sarah looked at him, amazed. Then with a slight frown on her face, she shut the book, returned it to its place, and stood up. "Should I have returned to the hotel when you were late, Doctor?" she asked sweetly.

Dr. Gilbert looked down at his watch. It was 1:30. "No, no—of course not." He shoved his watch back into its pocket with a vague reference to being delayed at the university by a Dr. Allbright. He turned abruptly to George. "George, I need to discuss something with Nurse Biddle. Would you excuse us?"

George went outside to watch for Sam, and Sarah began to pack Dr. Gilbert's medical bag.

Dr. Gilbert cleared his throat nervously, then said, "Nurse Biddle, would you mind very much calling me Miles? While I admit to being a few years older than my charming cousin, I hardly qualify as a senior member of our citizenry. I think we have established the kind of relationship that might benefit from a relaxing of the formalities." He hastened to clarify himself. "What I mean is, there are times when your calling me Dr. Gilbert seems ridiculously formal."

Sarah looked up at him, smiled, nodded. "As long as you agree to call me Sarah." She laughed softly. "I've never quite gotten used to 'Nurse Biddle.' It makes me sound like a sour old spinster."

From outside they heard George call a hello to Sam.

"Well, I guess it's officially moving day for Tom and Sarah Biddle," Sarah said, heading for the back door.

Miles reached out to touch her arm. "Sarah. There's something else."

Sarah turned to look at him, suddenly serious. "What is it, Miles? What's wrong?"

Miles looked toward the back door, then said earnestly, "I know it appears that he's really trying—and I hope he is, but—and I say this sincerely—watch out for George." Before Sarah could reply, he repeated, "I mean it. Watch out for him."

CHAPTER 21

Indigo Blues and Shirting

"As we have therefore opportunity, let us do good unto all men, especially unto them who are of the household of faith."
Galatians 6:10

The summer of 1884 was miserably hot. Not long after Sarah and Tom Biddle settled into their tiny apartment over Dr. Gilbert's clinic, Augusta Hathaway called on Sarah to inform her that Sam Kemp would be arriving within the week to give them a housewarming gift. "He's going to cut a door where that small window by the stove is, Sarah, and then you and Tom will have your own private upstairs porch. And I'm having it screened in."

Before Sarah could say a word, Augusta waved her hand in the air. "I know, I know. 'Aunt Augusta, it's too much. You shouldn't be doing this.' Well, Sarah, I don't want to hear it. Your little apartment needs the ventilation, Miles will benefit from the roof over his hospital entrance, your firewood will stay dry no matter what the weather, and Sam Kemp needs the work. It's going to be drier than last year, and I'm not certain crops are going to be what they should be."

Augusta sighed. "Even with a bumper crop, if the railroad keeps up their nonsensical shipping charges, Sam won't be able to get one bit ahead. I declare, when it costs

186

a man more to ship his crop to market than he gets for the crop, things have come to a bad pass. I've told Sam that he should consider moving into Lincoln and concentrating on carpentry."

When Sam Kemp's wagon rumbled up to the clinic's back door later in the week, Sarah was delighted to see that Loula had accompanied her husband to town. Dr. Gilbert declared Davey "the healthiest baby I've seen all week," making Loula blush with pleasure.

With a glance in Sarah's direction, Dr. Gilbert quickly determined that it was going to be a very slow day at the clinic and suggested Sarah and Loula inspect the new dry goods at Miller's.

Taking Sarah aside, he explained, "Sam paid back what he owed me long ago, and now the tables are turned. Because of the hospital renovation, I find myself short of cash to pay Sam for his wonderful transformation upstairs. Hence, Sam and I have made rather creative arrangements. Thanks to your making out regular bills for our patients, Mr. Miller has finally proposed a solution to the rather large sum of money he owes me. He has agreed to open an account in my name with that amount showing as a credit. I've arranged for Sam to draw against that credit for the amount of money I owe him." He smiled sheepishly. "It's a rather circuitous route, but everyone seems satisfied."

Sarah nodded just as Loula came up and said happily, "Sam told me I can go pick out enough calico for *two* new dresses."

The two women were headed out the door for Miller's when the new female doctor in town made her entrance into the waiting room of the clinic. Sarah had heard about Dr. Allbright through several different sources. Augusta had attended one of her lectures on women's health issues. A few of Dr. Gilbert's more neurotic female patients had consulted with her. She had also been the topic of conversation at the most recent quilting bee.

Sarah had formed a mental image of a large, rather masculine woman. She was surprised to see that Dr. Allbright was dressed in a very fashionable gown and a very stylish hat—the largest hat, in fact, Sarah had ever seen. Other women would have looked ridiculous in it, but Dr. Allbright had the regal bearing to carry it off successfully.

Not waiting for Sarah to speak, Dr. Allbright crossed the waiting room and extended her hand. "You must be Nurse Biddle," she said abruptly. "I've heard about you."

Sarah shook Dr. Allbright's hand, surprised by the woman's firm grip. *She shakes hands like a man.* Indeed, many of Dr. Allbright's brusque mannerisms created quite a contrast with her stylish dress.

Before Sarah could say anything, Miles brushed by her, hurrying to put on his coat, hastily grabbing his hat from his desk in the waiting room. "Maude," he said warmly, "I see you've met Sar—Nurse Biddle."

"Yes. Just now. Doesn't look a thing like I expected. Rather attractive, actually."

Miles looked at Sarah, then back at Maude. "Yes. Well. Shall we go?"

He offered Maude his arm, but she had already opened the door for him and was waiting for him to precede her into the street. Somewhat flustered, he moved forward, then turned back toward Sarah. "Nurse Biddle, Dr. Allbright and I are walking up to the Hathaway House for a meeting. If I'm needed—" Miles suddenly remembered that Loula was there. "Oh, yes, Loula. You two were going to shop, weren't you?"

"It's all right, Miles," Sarah said. "I'll post a note on the door in case there's an emergency. What time should I say the doctor will return?"

Maude answered for him. "It shouldn't be more than an hour."

Sarah looked to Miles, who nodded in agreement. "Yes, an hour I think."

The two left abruptly. Sarah scribbled a note and tacked it to the door. As she and Loula closed the door behind them, they looked up the street in the direction of the Hathaway House. Dr. Allbright and Dr. Gilbert were walking along together, and every person they passed on the boardwalk turned back to watch them.

Loula laughed. "They're causin' quite a stir." She turned toward Sarah. "It'd be awful not to be able to even walk down the street without folks watchin' and makin' comment."

Sarah agreed. She and Loula headed in the opposite direction. When they reached the end of the block where they were to turn north, Sarah could not resist looking back up the street. She could not deny it. Dr. Maude Allbright and Dr. Miles Gilbert made quite a handsome couple.

Miles was visibly uneasy as he entered the dining room of the hotel with Dr. Allbright on his arm. Every pair of eyes looked their way, and more than one head nodded as its owner whispered about the two physicians being together.

Under her breath Maude muttered, "We're causing quite a sensation, Miles. Let's have fun with it, shall we?" She squeezed his arm affectionately, then announced to the dining room, "Yes, ladies and gentlemen, Dr. Miles Gilbert and Dr. Maude Allbright are dining together. However, Dr. Allbright hastens to inform you that Dr. Gilbert is *not* a candidate to be her husband. He is much too good a Christian to consider marrying a divorced woman, and Dr. Allbright is much too sensible a woman to ever wish to marry again." Maude sat down, her back to the room, and then turned around in her chair to add, "Now, if you will all please return to your breakfasts, Dr. Gilbert and I can enjoy our coffee. Thank you."

Miles sat down opposite Maude, barely controlling his laughter. "You never cease to amaze me, Maude Allbright."

Maude winked. "Well, a woman doctor must have both nerve and initiative if she wants to succeed. I believe I have a good supply of both." She took her napkin, snapped it smartly, and then spread it across her lap before continuing. "And yes, I am divorced. Almost. Actually, I was unable to locate my husband to finalize the legalities. Still, I consider myself divorced. Since I am adamantly opposed to any future union, I haven't concerned myself with discovering whether my dear husband ever appeared to actually sign his name to the document." Maude held out her cup to the waitress who had just approached the table, coffeepot in hand. "Now, let's get on with breakfast. I'm suddenly very hungry."

Maude ordered a breakfast large enough to satisfy two men. Miles followed suit, and the two were soon chatting comfortably while they ate.

"I want to thank you for your referrals these past few weeks, Miles," she said warmly. "It has done a great deal to help establish my practice." Maude chuckled. "If I had to depend on my natural warmth and overflowing gentility, I would be in desperate straits by now. Thankfully, the fact that I am a woman brings me patients of the fairer sex who find it difficult to discuss their condition with men."

"And that is a perfect segue into one of the reasons for this breakfast," Miles began. "As you know, the medical college here in Lincoln has been struggling. The community is very uneasy about the more critical aspects of our studies—"

"I don't suppose the CASH FOR STIFFS banner across the roof of University Hall helped that situation," Maude said, smiling.

"Oh, you heard about that, did you?"

"I believe it's safe to say that everyone in the state heard about that, Miles. It was quite a stunt. Actually, the custodian told me. He said you had been keeping specimens for study in the basement of University Hall, but that the banner incident necessitated a move."

Dr. Gilbert nodded. "Yes, that's true. The medical students do their dissecting in another location now. We try to be discreet."

"Do you think the medical school is going to survive here in Lincoln?"

Reluctantly, Dr. Gilbert replied, "No. I fear not. The medical college in Omaha is already larger, and community support is much stronger there."

"And Omaha does not suffer from what I consider to be the crucial weakness of your program—no hospital to provide clinical training."

"Yes," Miles agreed. "My little four-bed clinic is rarely full. People still prefer Omaha when a hospital stay is imminent. I hope that someday soon that can be changed. But in the meantime, the college is severely limited."

Dr. Gilbert poured them each another cup of coffee. "The faculty would like you to know that we are grateful for your presence in our community. There is much to be done in the area of women's health care, and we are hoping that we can enlist your help in serving our women students. They need instruction in proper dress, food chemistry, posture—all the aspects of feminine development that will ensure their personal health long after they have graduated and married. Would you consider staying at the university regardless of the future of the medical college? You would be in charge of the women students' dispensary and health work, teaching sex hygiene and nutrition. Unlike the medical college faculty, you would be paid a regular salary. And you would, of course, be free to continue your private practice. Will you consider the position?"

Dr. Allbright considered only briefly. "I would insist that women's physical education classes be required."

"Why not draw up a complete proposal, Maude. I'll get it on the agenda at our next meeting with the chancellor. It should be rather simple to garner the support of the Medical Society." Miles sipped his coffee. "If only garnering support for a hospital were that easy."

"Perhaps what's needed is a special feature, something unique to set us apart from Omaha." She smiled brightly. "I know I'm being terribly forward, but what about a concentration in women's diseases?"

Miles nodded. "Exactly what I've been thinking." He looked at her expectantly. "Would you be able to carry the workload and still help the university?"

Maude was thrilled. "Miles Gilbert, are you actually inviting me to join you in a practice—to build a hospital—to work *together*?"

"If you are interested."

"Sounds delightful. I accept."

Dr. Gilbert could not hide his surprise. "Do you not wish to consider—"

"Consider what, Miles? Lincoln needs a hospital. Together we can provide it. You already have an excellent nurse in your employ. I have money. Did I mention that? I am an only child. Mother and Father were very well off. You select a site, order up the carpenter and the materials. I'll pay the bills. Of course we need to get this all down in writing, but I see no reason to put it off."

"I cannot ask you to invest personal funds—"

"You didn't ask, Miles. I offered. The fact is, I've been contemplating building a clinic of my own. I'm not overly taken with spiritualizing events, but I think this is meant to happen, Miles. Why else would you have timed this breakfast so well? You had no way of knowing I have the funds to realize the plan." Maude second-guessed Dr. Gilbert. "I know, I know. It doesn't sound like something I would care about, does it? But I am pragmatic, Miles. Our fair community is probably not quite ready to support a hospital conceived and run by a woman. Of course, we both know that no matter what the public thinks there will be a woman in charge. But the community doesn't need to know that Nurse Biddle has so much power."

Dr. Gilbert asked, "Do you think we can have the plans ready to present at the next Society meeting?"

Maude stood up. "I don't know why not. Do you know a good architect? Of course you do. Have you selected a site? We mustn't be too far from the university. After all, the medical college may surprise us and survive. When you have the plans drawn up, please contact me. I shall see you Tuesday evening." She hesitated only briefly. "Miles, there is one thing. I won't give up my suffrage work."

Miles didn't hesitate to answer. "I can't imagine you would need to do so. In fact, I would hope that we might attract other physicians by emphasizing that in sharing the workload, we could *all* finally have time to pursue our personal interests. We should be able to work out a schedule providing patient care twenty-four hours a day while providing physicians with time off for their families—or other pursuits."

Maude looked down at her watch. "Excellent. As long as we understand one another. Well, Miles. I have patients to see. So do you." She reached up to adjust her gigantic hat with a chuckle. "For all my lectures on the excesses of fashion, I can't seem to give up my own fascination with hats." Without waiting for Dr. Gilbert to reply, she was gone.

While Dr. Miles Gilbert was enjoying breakfast with Dr. Maude Allbright, Loula and Sarah were admiring bolt after bolt of mourning prints and cretonnes, madders and cinnamon pinks, indigos and greens all neatly arranged just inside the front door of Miller's Store. Loula had no trouble at all selecting the two bolts she wanted.

"Sam says blue makes my eyes look pretty," Loula said shyly, and Mr. Miller himself wrapped up two different bolts of fabric with brown paper and string.

Sarah purchased enough shirting to outfit Tom for school. "If that boy grows any faster, I'm going to burn out the belt on my sewing machine making clothes for him."

Loula looked at Sarah with envy. "You got a *machine*?"

Sarah nodded. "I saved for nearly six months, but I finally got enough money." They had finally reached the clinic, and Sarah invited Loula upstairs. "Come up and see it. Tom set it up for me by a window, and in summer I can get quite a bit done by natural light." Sarah shook her head. "I don't know how you keep up, Loula, doing it all by hand."

The two women mounted the stairs to Sarah's apartment for Loula to see Sarah's treadle machine. But before Sarah had opened the machine, Loula was exclaiming in wonder over the sampler that hung over David Braddock's trunk. She stood in front of the sampler, fascinated, reading the verse. "Oh, Sarah," she said, "what a wonderful, wonderful treasure." She paused only briefly before saying, "Cordelia was my grandma's name. I was kind of hoping that little Davey might be a girl so I could honor Grandma."

Wanting to avoid further discussion of Cordelia Braddock, Sarah didn't comment. "Loula," she offered, "I don't sew every day. What if you were to ride into Lincoln with Sam once a week? You could come up here and sew all day long."

"You mean it, Sarah? You wouldn't mind?"

"I work in the clinic all morning. Why, you could have the entire apartment to yourself."

To Sarah's amazement, Loula began to cry. "Oh, Sarah, you just been so kind to me. Thank you for lettin' God love me through you. Some might not be so willin' to serve Him."

Not knowing what to say, Sarah said nothing. But Loula began coming every Monday to sew, and when Sam had finished building Sarah's porch, he insisted that Loula still spend Mondays in Lincoln where she could sew miles of seams with little effort on that wonderful invention so expertly perfected and marketed by Mr. Isaac Singer.

CHAPTER 22

A Linen Sampler

---

*"For God so loved the world, that he gave his
only begotten Son, that whosoever believeth in
him should not perish, but have
everlasting life."*
John 3:16

Loula Kemp stood in the doorway of her cabin looking
down in disbelief at Cordelia Braddock's 1807 sampler.
Her eyes filled with tears as she said, "Oh, Sarah, I never
had anything so beautiful to hang on my walls. . . ." She
looked up doubtfully. "But you shouldn't be parting with
this just for me."

"Don't you want it?"

Loula touched the fine stitches gently. "Why, who
wouldn't want it? It's a treasure. But—"

Baby sounds from behind the quilts that formed the
bedroom in the cabin interrupted the two women. Loula
went inside, laid the sampler on her makeshift table, and
emerged with Davey in her arms. Sarah reached for him.
"I'm so glad Dr. Gilbert invited me to ride out."

Loula smiled and nodded. "I didn't know you and the
doc was courtin'."

Sarah shook her head. "Oh, no—it's nothing like that.
But he knows I miss your coming every Monday to sew."

"I miss it too, Sarah. But the gardening's just got to be done. Things is comin' on so fast I can barely keep up with the cannin' and preservin'."

Sarah nodded understanding. "When Dr. Gilbert said he was driving right by your place on the way to check on the Portsche baby, he invited me to ride this far." She grinned. "Truth be told, I think he's hoping for another piece of pie." Sarah hugged the baby. "I miss your coming into town every week, Loula—but I understand." She stroked Davey's cheek. "This little man is obviously doing just fine." Sarah looked up at Loula. "And so are you, Loula. You look fit as a fiddle."

Loula blushed. "Well, bein' a mama agrees with me. At least that's what Sam says." She turned toward her stove. "And speakin' of Sam, I better get some supper on. He'll be in from the fields soon—and mighty glad to see we have company." Loula pulled a rustic chair away from the table. "I can have a pie ready in no time. Sam brought in a bucket of chokecherries just this mornin'. You just sit down with Davey and I'll get my pie crust started. Then you and Dr. Gilbert can see for yourselves if I can't make chokecherries taste just as good as Mrs. Tuttle's peaches."

Loula set to work in the tiny space of the cabin allotted for a kitchen. She nodded toward the sampler, then asked, "Who was Cordelia Braddock?"

"An ancestor of some friends of mine. They left me the sampler." Sarah paused before adding, "You probably don't remember, but the day Davey was born you said something very near the words that are in that sampler. 'Christ is my salvation.'"

Loula paused in her work, crossed to where the sampler lay on the table, and read again, "'Cordelia Braddock is my name, New York is my station, Heaven is my home, and Christ is my salvation.'" She murmured, "Well, when I meet Cordelia Braddock in heaven, I'll just have to tell her how much I enjoyed her work."

Sarah laughed, but Loula was serious. "If she really believed what she put on this sampler, then we'll all be in heaven together, and I'll meet her." When Sarah didn't respond, Loula returned to her work. A few moments passed before she asked softly, "Don't you believe that, Sarah? Isn't Christ *your* salvation?"

The question hit Sarah hard. She looked up at Loula with a little frown, then answered, "I'm not really certain what that means, Loula. I've had that sampler hanging on my wall for a long time, and I've pondered it a lot. You know, I've gone to church and read the Bible all my life, but no one ever asked me until just now if Christ is *my* salvation. I don't know, Loula. Is Christ my salvation from *what*?"

Sam Kemp had always told his wife that if God was ever wanting to use her, she would be given words. On this day in 1884, Loula Kemp was given words written nearly two thousand years before, living words supernaturally able to breathe eternal life into Sarah Biddle's lonely soul.

Loula was crimping the edges of her pie when Sarah asked the question. She hurried to finish, wiped off her hands, went through the quilts into her bedroom, and came back to the little table with a huge Bible in her hands. She set the Bible on the little table near Sarah, then slipped the pie into the oven. "Sam and me read the Bible every night after supper, Sarah. Sam's a right good preacher when he's called on."

Loula sat down next to Sarah and reached over to stroke her baby's cheek as she said, "Time was we thought Sam might be preachin' for a livin'. But God called us out here to Nebraska to farm instead." Loula opened the two silver hinges along the side of the Bible, then turned the pages carefully.

"Now, you was askin' me about bein' saved. Sam teaches it this way: first, we got to be saved from the penalty of sin." Loula pointed to a verse. "It says right here that the wages of sin is death. And there's another verse that says that we're all sinners."

Sarah smiled. "You'll get no argument from me on that count, Loula. I've done my share of sinning."

"Everybody has," Loula agreed. "God says there's a penalty for sin and that's death. Somebody's got to pay the penalty of death." Loula smiled. "But we don't. That's the wonderful part. Jesus paid the penalty by dyin' on the cross for us. Once we accept His death for us, then another part of salvation comes in. That's bein' saved from the power of sin. Listen, Sarah." Loula turned the pages of the Bible and read, "'There hath no temptation taken you but such as is common to man: but God is faithful, who will not suffer you to be tempted above that ye are able; but will with the temptation also make a way to escape, that ye may be able to bear it.'

"You see, Sarah," Loula explained, "everybody has things happen to them that look bad. But when we belong to God, we can bear it. Sin causes all kinds of awful things to happen, but it don't have no real power over those that are saved, because they belong to God and God promises that He causes all things to work together for good to those that love Him."

Loula fumbled for another passage of Scripture. "Now, here's the best part of all this salvation business," she said. "Someday we won't even have to be around sin at all. Sam calls it being saved from the presence of sin. Forever." She turned to another verse of Scripture and read, "'And the devil that deceived them was cast into the lake of fire and brimstone . . . and shall be tormented day and night for ever and ever.'"

Loula reached across the little orange-crate table to take Sarah's hand. "Sam could explain it better. But this is how I remember it. There's three *P*s. We're saved from the *penalty* of sin because Jesus died for each one of us. We're saved from the *power* of sin because we can choose to praise the Lord no matter what happens. And when we're in heaven we'll be saved from the *presence* of sin."

Loula squeezed Sarah's hand, then said softly, "See, Sarah, it's not salvation from hard times. Hard times are here to stay, 'cause we aren't in heaven yet. But hard times can't take your peace away when you know you got salvation for your soul."

Sarah looked at Loula Kemp and saw such joy and peace in her eyes that she had to look away. Even as she looked away, she drew closer to Loula by sharing her heart. "Loula, the truth is, I've felt sort of lost for most of my life. Things just never seem to work out for me. I've been in an orphanage, worked at a hotel, been a house-keeper . . ." Shyly she added, "I even thought I was going to marry once, but that didn't work out either." Sarah shivered. "Even now, as much as I love nursing, I can't help wondering when something is going to happen to end it. To end my working with Miles." Hastily she added, "I don't mean to sound ungrateful. Some good things have happened—it's just that no matter what, I always seem to feel—"

Loula interrupted. "Lost?" When Sarah nodded, Loula added gently, "Maybe it's because you *are* lost, Sarah. Lost from God. 'He satisfieth the longing soul, and filleth the hungry soul with goodness.' No one can feel truly at peace until they get across the sin that is keeping them from God. He wants you to belong to Him, Sarah."

It was with great difficulty that Sarah admitted aloud, "It would be wonderful to feel that I belonged to God. To know the kind of peace you seem to have, Loula. I'd like to believe that He cares about me. I've had lots of people tell me that's true. I've just never really felt it—inside."

"Oh, Sarah," Loula whispered, "you got to know God cares for you. Look at the cross, Sarah. The only way to get you and me into heaven was for Jesus to die and take our sins onto Himself. He did it. Herein is love . . . while

Sarah was yet a sinner, Christ died for her. . . . For God so loved *Sarah Biddle*, that He gave His only begotten Son, that *Sarah* might believe in Him, and not perish, but have everlasting life."

Sarah swallowed hard, then asked, "What do I have to do to know the kind of peace you have, Loula?"

"That's the best part," Loula said happily. You don't have to *do* anything. 'The gift of God is eternal life through Jesus Christ our Lord.' That's what God says. All you have to do is accept the gift. You already know you need salvation from sin. Just thank Jesus that He done what He done. Throw your sins up to Him. Throw that lost feelin' you got inside up to Him. He'll fill you up so full you'll never feel lost again."

"Now where's that chokecherry pie?"

Both women started at the sound of a male voice booming the question from the cabin door. Sarah turned around to see Sam coming in through the doorway, Miles close behind. Sam looked at Loula, saw the open Bible, and blanched.

After an awkward silence, Loula managed to say, "Come on in, Sam, Dr. Gilbert." She handed the baby to Sam, closed the Bible, and cradled it in her arms as she said, "Sarah and me just been havin' us a good talk." Even as she spoke, Loula grieved. The moment for the "good talk" was past, and the opportunity for Sarah Biddle to join Cordelia Braddock in being able to say, "Christ is my salvation," had been lost.

"Loula and Sam Kemp seem to have a brand of religion I haven't run across since Aunt Jesse died." Sarah and Dr. Gilbert were on their way back to Lincoln, having declared Loula's pie a serious threat to Mrs. Tuttle's reputation in the county.

"You seemed to be having quite a deep discussion with her. I was sorry we interrupted you, especially with such an unspiritual topic as chokecherry pie. Although indulging in Loula's scrumptious pie was very nearly a spiritual experience." Miles rubbed his stomach.

"Don't let Harriet Tuttle hear you say that. She'll find a new doctor."

"And wouldn't that be tragic." He rolled his eyes.

After a brief silence between them, Sarah said, "I'm beginning to wonder if I've known any true Christians besides Jesse King and the Kemps. There's something unique about their faith . . . and something very attractive about it. It seems to give such peace."

Miles teased, "Well, I must admit that it's rather disheartening to think that after all the time you have spent in my employ, you think me a profligate."

"Oh, Miles—I didn't mean that. I just—"

"It's all right, Sarah. I've come to accept your quiet nature. Actually, I've grown rather fond of it. Although it's sometimes rather trying to keep to the accepted subjects of the weather and the condition of our patients."

Sarah turned to look at him, trying to interpret his expression. But Miles was studying the horizon, waiting for her to guide the conversation. Sarah decided to plunge into the unknown waters of Miles Gilbert. "You know more about me than anyone else in Lincoln, Miles. You know how I came to Lincoln, why I'm no longer a housekeeper—you know everything." She added, "In fact, it is I who know almost nothing about you."

She asked quietly, "For example, how did you come to choose medicine as a profession?"

He leaned back in his seat, let the reins go slack, and began to reminisce. "When I was a boy, we lost our schoolmaster to diphtheria. He was boarding in our home the night he died. I remember watching him struggle to breathe. My father had gone for the doctor, but he arrived too late to save him." He went on. "In those days, the basics of contagion were largely unknown. The doctor went home, but before dawn my baby sister was struggling to breathe. I shall never forget the awful sound—and the panic in my mother's eyes as she tried to relieve Liza's discomfort. When I thought she would surely die, the old doctor arrived, pulled out his penknife, and performed a tracheotomy. He asked Mother for a needle and coarse thread. He attached a thread to each side of the wound, tied it behind my sister's neck to hold the wound open, and then rode like everything back to his office to retrieve the tracheotomy tube he had left out of his bag. It was the most amazing thing I'd ever seen. When I saw the look on my mother's face as Liza drew a full breath, I determined I should never be anything but a doctor."

"Loula would say that was the night God called you."

Miles nodded. "Yes, she probably would. And if I had been introduced to the fundamentals of the Christian faith by someone like Sam and Loula Kemp, I would probably agree. Unfortunately, my earliest memory of a so-called Christian is of the new minister who came to dinner soon after my sister recovered. I'll never forget him. He was probably the ugliest man I've ever seen. Wild hair, eyes that looked in different directions, craggy features. He got down from his horse, bent to pat me on the head, asked if Christ was my salvation . . . and at that very moment kicked my little dog who had come up to say hello. Someone has said that there's no better way to alienate a boy than to kick his dog. It was all I could do to sit at the table that day and pass the potatoes to that no-account.

"Now, the doctor who had saved my baby sister's life was not a religious man at all. I remember my parents being scandalized when they learned that he was a firm believer in Charles Darwin's newly publicized theory of evolution. He never went to church, and he could swear better than anyone I'd ever heard. To this day I am amazed by the man's unfaltering vocabulary of profanity. He once said to me, 'The only creed worth anything is the

Hypocratic oath, boy. That's the one I live by.' Of course, I've edited the phrase out of consideration for the present company, but given the choice between the religion that gave a man freedom to kick my dog and the religion that said, 'Relieve suffering whenever possible,' I chose the latter. I still went to church with my parents, but the moment I left home I began spending the Sabbath fishing. I didn't go back to church voluntarily until I was out of medical school."

"What made you go back at all?"

Miles smiled. "The desire to impress a certain young lady. But that didn't last long. I failed to impress the young lady, and her minister failed to impress me." He turned toward Sarah. "I thought I had my own philosophy of life fairly well determined. The intricacy of the human body convinces me that there is a Creator. Yet I look about me and see so much evil performed by those who claim religion—"

"Like kicking dogs?"

Miles nodded. "The evil makes me think that the Creator has stepped back from direct involvement with the pathetic results of His efforts." He shrugged. "I thought I could live with the tension between what I think I believe and what I cannot understand. And I have. But then George McCann arrived in town."

At Sarah's look of surprise, Miles shook his head. "Yes, good old George. You wouldn't expect George to encourage a weighty examination of life's deeper meaning, would you?" He chuckled. "I know this graying hair makes me look much older than George, but the truth is I'm only five years his senior. While George was putting frogs in our minister's pulpit and generally raising you-know-what, I was sitting quietly in Sunday school being a good boy. Lately I've been thinking a good deal about George." Miles shook his head. "He's had a hard life. He seemed to be at the end of his rope when he came to the clinic that day. But one thing about George is he always recovers quickly. And he's also had a great deal more fun than I ever did. Sometimes I wonder if I made the right choice, just being the good boy and doing what was expected of me."

Sarah spoke up. "Miles. How can you even think of regretting what you've become? I don't know what I would have done without you during that awful year with Abigail Braddock."

Miles nodded gratefully. "Thank you, Sarah. But in the end the remedies I could offer Abigail were pathetically ineffective. What really helped her was that someone else cared about her pain. In that sense, *you* gave much more effective care than I."

He looked at her with a warm light in his eyes. "You don't seem to realize it, but you have a gift in that area, Sarah. I must admit I hadn't realized it—until Maude Allbright brought it to my attention. And she's right. You are able to enter into the world of the patient, to truly empathize with their suffering. They can feel it."

Uncomfortable with his praise, Sarah smoothed her dress, reached up to nervously push at her hair. "Dr. Allbright said that about me?"

Miles nodded. "You know as well as I do that the doctors in our fair city are often tried and sentenced at the quilting bees. It seems that word has it that some of the patients I've referred to Maude have returned to us because—and I quote Maude—'She may be a woman but she don't hold nothing to Nurse Biddle when it comes to understanding, and I'll take Nurse Biddle's understanding and a male doctor's examining any day over that Dr. Allbright and her uppity ways.'" Miles laughed softly. "You can imagine how hard that was for Maude to hear. But she wanted to make certain I knew what a good nurse you are."

He changed the subject. "Underneath Dr. Allbright's rather overbearing manner there is a superb mind. Which is another reason I've been pondering the deeper things of the universe of late. She challenges everything I've been taught about the roles of men and women. And she is a disciple of Darwin." He chuckled. "Medical Society meetings have been rather uproarious since Maude's arrival."

For some unknown reason, Sarah became aware that she was growing rather tired of hearing Dr. Gilbert expound on the brilliance of Maude Allbright. She returned the conversation to Sam and Loula. "Well, I doubt Dr. Allbright would think much of Sam and Loula Kemp's simple faith. But I certainly found what Loula had to say both interesting and challenging. And I admit to envying their simple acceptance of what the Bible says. They both firmly believe the Bible has the answers to all of life's problems. And from what I've seen they wouldn't care what Darwin or anyone else said about the origin of the world. I can just see Loula turning to Genesis chapter one and reading it aloud. She'd simply say, 'In the beginning God created the heavens and the earth, and it don't matter what Charles Darwin thinks.'"

Together, Miles and Sarah shook their heads and said, "If only life were that simple."

CHAPTER 23

A Paisley Shawl

"The LORD gave, and the LORD hath taken away;
blessed be the name of the LORD."
Job 1:21

Only a week after her talk with Loula Kemp, Sarah was closing the clinic for the day when someone beat on the back door of the clinic so hard he nearly broke it down. Sarah opened the door and was met by a picture that would be forever seared in her memory—Sam Kemp, his face blackened with soot, his eyes wide with fear, staggering under the load of Loula, her dress nearly burned off, her exposed skin blistered.

Sam burst in the door, sobbing. "I was breaking sod—fire jumped the creek—couldn't get there in time—" He staggered across the room to lay Loula on a cot, then turned and rubbed his eyes.

Dr. Gilbert stood over Loula with his stethoscope. "It's all right, Sam, her heart's beating strong. We'll get her cleaned up, she'll be fine."

"She was trying to get through the fire to—"

Sarah couldn't believe it. "Davey?"

Sam looked up toward the ceiling, blinked rapidly, and shook his head. "Couldn't get in."

Loula began to moan softly. Sam bent over her. "Loula, my Loula. It's all right, Loula. I love you, Loula. We'll be

207

all right, sweetheart—" He looked up at Dr. Gilbert, imploring, "Can you keep her from hurting too bad, Doc?"

Dr. Gilbert spoke lowly. "I'll administer morphine right away, Sam. These burns are serious, but not life-threatening. You did the right thing bringing her here. It's critical that we keep the dressings clean, avoid infection. But she'll be fine."

"I'll stay with her Sam, you go get cleaned up. There's a well out back. When she wakes up, she'll want to see you first." Sarah spoke mechanically, giving the orders through her own numbed senses. She simply could not believe that God would have allowed such a horrific thing to happen to Sam and Loula Kemp, who loved Him so.

Sarah and Dr. Gilbert worked on Loula for nearly two hours. When they had finished, her arms and legs were covered with strips of clean cloth. Sarah washed and combed her hair, braiding it neatly.

"That's my angel," Sam crooned, leaning over his wife. "You rest now, Loula." His voice broke. "I got to go back and see to Davey."

"No." Dr. Gilbert spoke firmly. "No, Sam, I think not. You need to be here when Loula awakens. I will see that Davey is taken care of. You just take care of your wife."

Sam nodded gratefully.

Dr. Gilbert added, "I'll be back with clean clothes for you both in a few hours. In the meantime, you try to get some rest. Just stretch out on that cot right there. We'll make other arrangements later." Dr. Gilbert motioned to Sarah to follow him to the front of the office.

"I'd prefer they not be left alone. Can you stay downstairs until I get back?"

"Of course. I wouldn't have it any other way."

"When Loula regains consciousness, someone will have to tell her."

Sarah took a deep breath. "I'll do it."

Miles nodded. "Good. Thank you, Sarah. I'll ride out and see what can be done about Davey. I'll be back as soon as possible."

"Miles, wait—" Sarah ran up the stairs to her apartment. When she returned she held out her paisley shawl. "You can wrap—" She couldn't bring herself to say it. Miles reached for the shawl, touched her hand. "God bless you, Sarah."

Sarah went back to the clinic to tell Sam that she would stay, but Sam had already fallen into a deep sleep. Sarah looked from one cot to the other, wondering what could possibly be said that would bring comfort in the face of such a loss.

When Loula Kemp regained consciousness, Sarah was sitting by her bedside. Loula opened her eyes, looked at Sarah, looked about herself, realized where she was.

"Sam?" she said weakly.

Sam woke up with a start. "I'm right here, Loula. Right here." He fairly leaped off his own cot and moved to her side. Loula looked up at Sam with a question in her eyes. Sam shook his head, bent over to embrace her. The couple clung to one another, weeping freely. Sarah left the room as quietly as possible, busying herself in the examining room, cutting sheets for more bandages. From where she worked, she could hear what the Kemps said.

"You don't think he suffered, do you, Sam?" Loula asked, her voice wavering.

Sarah's own eyes smarted with tears as Sam answered tenderly, "'Course not, Loula. I just know God carried that little lamb home on the wings of an angel."

"I wish I could have got through that fire, Sam," Loula said through her tears.

"I'm thankful you didn't, Loula. I would have lost you both. Then where would I be?"

"You'd be all right, Sam. You know it. God would pull you through."

"I know it, Loula. But I'm glad it's us that has to pull through. Together."

"Sam?" The voice was already tired. "Sam, could you pray?"

Sarah stopped rolling bandages and listened, amazed, at Sam Kemp's simple prayer. Having lost his firstborn child, having lost his home, Sam Kemp began by thanking God for His goodness. "Thank You, Lord, for saving my Loula. Thank You that we still got the team and the plow. Thank You that Dr. Gilbert and Sarah were here to take care of us." Sam's voice broke as he added, "And thank You, God, for giving us Davey. We wish we could of kept him longer, Lord. You tell him his Ma and Pa love him, and we'll be looking for him just inside the gate when we get up there." Sam's voice cracked, and Sarah could hear him weeping quietly. Just as Sarah rose to go to them, she heard Loula's voice add, "And please, Lord, use this trial for Jesus' glory. Amen."

Sarah Biddle was unable to go to the Kemps immediately. She stood by Dr. Gilbert's library table with a half-rolled bandage in her hand, tears rolling down her cheeks. *I want to know You that way. Please, God, give me the faith Sam and Loula have. They've just lost their child, and they are declaring victory. How can it be, God? God,* she cried out in her mind, *God, where are You?*

Sam Kemp stood at the head of his baby's grave, hat in hand. On his left stood Dr. Miles Gilbert and Nurse Sarah Biddle. Augusta Hathaway stood beside Sarah. A few of the women who had helped gather things for the Kemps had insisted their husbands join them to lend support to the hardworking couple whose lives seemed so fraught with tragedy.

Augusta's minister arrived last. Reaching into his pocket he withdrew a small Testament, read through a few preselected verses, led the group in two verses of "Amazing Grace," and prepared to close in prayer. But Sam Kemp stepped forward, cleared his throat, and said, "I'd like to offer a few words, if I could, Reverend."

When the surprised minister nodded, Sam continued. "My Loula couldn't be here. That's a grief to her. But she said I should say a few words for the both of us." Clear-eyed, Sam looked at each person standing around the grave. He spoke in an unwavering voice. "Folks, you all know that Loula and me, we've had some hard times. There's two ways to look at hard times. The first way is like the Israelites. They wandered around the desert, and they just figured God had forgotten them. In Numbers chapter eleven it says that God's people got tired of not knowing what the next day was bringing. And they started to complain." Sam paused, and then quoted, "'And when the people complained, it displeased the LORD: and the LORD heard it; and his anger was kindled.'" Sam paused, letting the words sink in before he continued. "The way I read that, it don't matter what God lets happen to us all, we got no right to complain, 'cause God is God, and we're not. I got no right to tell God what to do. Just looking at the cross I know God loves me. Whatever happens, He cares about it. Now, I don't always understand it. That's for sure. But I don't want to be like the Israelites and complain. I don't want to displease the Lord, to make Him angry. No.

"I want to be like Job. You all here are churchgoing folks. You remember Job, how God let Satan take away all he owned. Job had seven sons and three daughters and God let Satan take them all. And how did Job act when that come to pass." Sam recited, "'Then Job arose, and rent his mantle, and shaved his head, and fell down upon the ground, and worshipped, and said, "Naked came I out of my mother's womb, and naked shall I return thither: the LORD gave, and the LORD hath taken away; blessed be the name of the LORD." In all this Job sinned not, nor charged God foolishly.'

"Loula and me are doing our best to follow the example of Job. It hurts worse than I can say to be standing by this little grave today. We don't understand. We are grieving. But, folks, we don't charge God. 'The LORD gave, and the LORD hath taken away; blessed be the name of the LORD.'"

Sarah Biddle and Miles Gilbert were not at all surprised to hear Sam giving glory to his God even as he buried his child, but they were not prepared for the challenge Sam gave as he closed his brief message.

"The Lord is blessed. The Lord has a reason. The same Lord who has taken our baby home to be with Him will some day take us home, too. And then we will see our Davey.

"What about you, folks? If God took all your family, could you stand by the graves knowing you would see them again? Believe in Jesus. He died for your sins and mine. He can forgive your sins. He can take you to heaven. Then you can say, with Loula and me, that someday we will see the one we love again. That's how we can stand with Job and say 'Blessed be the name of the LORD.'"

Sam looked around the small group of people. "That's all I got to say, folks. Blessed be the name of the LORD."

Stooping down, he took a handful of earth, then watched it sift over the little casket. As he stood up, Sarah thought she could almost see the supernatural mantle of peace settle over him. Stepping away from the grave, Sam drew back his shoulders, put on his hat, and said with solemn dignity, "Loula and I want to thank you for coming." Turning to Miles, Sam said quietly, "I'll be walking back, Dr. Gilbert. I'd like some time with the Lord."

Miles drove Sarah and Augusta home. They passed Sam walking along the road. He was deep in thought and did not acknowledge their presence. There was no conversation as the carriage made its way down O Street. Augusta climbed down from the carriage, said a simple "Thank you" to Dr. Gilbert, and went inside.

At the clinic, Sarah climbed down. "Would you like to come in for some coffee?"

Miles shook his head. "No, Sarah. Thank you. I promised Maude I would check in on a couple of her patients this afternoon."

Loula was sleeping. Sarah retreated to her little apartment over the clinic alone. Heating water for tea, she laid out her patchwork and settled into her rocker. The rocker was near the window that looked out on the street below. Sarah finished one small row of featherstitching along a seam of her crazy quilt before she laid the work in her lap. It was early afternoon.

Laying aside her patchwork, Sarah went to the opposite side of the room. She hadn't opened David Braddock's trunk in months, but something made her open it now. Deliberately, she pulled out layer after layer of its contents, spread them on her bed, on the floor. Then she sat in her rocker, surveying the display of beautiful things.

Sarah ran her hand across the surface of Cordelia Braddock's quilt. She looked back across the room at the growing stack of squares she was assembling. *I wonder if my crazy quilt will be stored in a trunk like this someday . . . when I am gone.* Sarah turned toward the small mirror that hung on her wall. She looked at herself, tried to imagine her hair white, her face wrinkled. *But there is no guarantee that I will even live that long . . . no guarantee at all.* She remembered a verse of Scripture Loula had quoted. "It gives me comfort, Sarah," she had said. "Because it says that Davey's life wasn't cut short. I don't

213

have to bear the blame that I failed to save my baby. God had it all worked out. It says so right here in Psalm—" *Psalm what?* Sarah looked around the room for her Bible. She finally found it under a stack of medical books. She perused Psalms, looking for the verse Loula had quoted. Along the way, she read:

> The LORD *looked down from heaven upon the children of men, to see if there were any that did understand, and seek God. They are all gone aside, they are all together become filthy: there is none that doeth good, no, not one. . . . Blessed is he whose transgression is forgiven, whose sin is covered. . . . Have mercy upon me, O God, according to thy lovingkindness: according unto the multitude of thy tender mercies blot out my transgressions. . . . Truly my soul waiteth upon God: from him cometh my salvation. . . . O God, thou art my God; early will I seek thee: my soul thirsteth for thee, my flesh longeth for thee in a dry and thirsty land, where no water is.*

Sarah never found the verse Loula had said brought her such comfort, for somewhere along her journey through the Psalms, Sarah began to cry. It seemed that every word she read spoke directly to her longing. Somehow, Loula's words from long ago came back to her. *The gift of God is eternal life through Jesus Christ our Lord. That's what God says. All you have to do is accept the gift. You already know you need salvation from sin. Just thank Jesus that He done what He done. Throw your sins up to Him. Throw that lost feeling you got inside up to Him. He'll fill you up so full you'll never feel lost again, Sarah.*

Sarah stood up. She held her hands out, palms up, and made a little motion as if tossing something up toward the ceiling. Nothing visible happened. But in that moment, mortality in the form of Sarah Biddle put on immortality.

Sitting back down in her rocker, Sarah returned to the Psalms. She read with delight:

> *In thee, O LORD, do I put my trust: let me never be put to confusion. . . . Be thou my strong habitation, whereunto I may continually resort: thou hast given commandment to save me; for thou art my rock and my fortress. . . . Thou art my hope, O Lord God . . . by thee have I been holden up from the womb: thou art he that took me out of my mother's bowels: my praise shall be continually of thee. I am as a wonder unto many; but thou art my strong refuge. . . . Let my mouth be filled with thy praise and with thy honour all the day. . . .*

When Sarah looked up from her reading, she saw the things spread about her room with new eyes. She put Cordelia Braddock's exquisite quilt on her bed, smiling as she echoed Loula's words: *Someday when I meet you in heaven, Cordelia, I'll have to tell you how I admired your handwork.* She packed away her trousseau without bitter regret. When Sarah laid the tray back in the top of the trunk, her hand moved to take out David's letter. But she didn't. Newly confident of God's love for her, she found that she no longer needed a reminder of David Braddock's love.

CHAPTER 24

Gossamer
Satin

----

*"Let favour be shewed to the wicked, yet will he
not learn righteousness; in the land of uprightness
will he deal unjustly, and will not behold the
majesty of the LORD."*
Isaiah 26:10

The moment Nellie Spomer lay back on the table, a
prominence of her abdomen gave Dr. Gilbert the proper
diagnosis for her "missing catamenia."

"Have you been true to yourself, Miss Spomer?" he
asked gently, helping her to sit up.

Nellie blushed deeply. She thrust out her lower lip. It
began to quiver.

Dr. Gilbert repeated the question.

A tear slid down Nellie's cheek.

"I would estimate that you may expect confinement
next spring, Miss Spomer."

Nellie looked at the doctor, her eyes wide with terror.
"Isn't there—can't you—can't something be done?"

Dr. Gilbert patted Nellie's hand. "Is marriage out of the
question, my dear?"

Nellie laughed bitterly. "*Marriage?* I'm not *marrying*,
Dr. Gilbert. There must be some other way." Nellie
hopped down from the examining table, began to walk
back and forth across the room. "There *must* be some

other way." She stopped pacing, looked at Sarah, then Dr. Gilbert. Her face a mask of innocence she said, "I've heard there are things—things you can do to bring on the catamenia."

Dr. Gilbert put his hand on Nellie's shoulder. "You cannot mean what you are saying, Miss Spomer. This is a shock, of course, but in due time—"

Nellie's blue eyes flashed. "I most certainly *do* mean it, Dr. Gilbert. In due time I shall be married, but not to the bummer who did this. Never." She pounded the examining table angrily. "Next spring, Dr. Gilbert, I am invited to the Veiled Prophet Ball in St. Louis. I've already ordered the gossamer satin for my gown. And I intend to be at the ball *without entanglements*." With just a hint of desperation in her voice she said, "If you refuse to help me, I'll find someone who will. Wherever I have to go. Whatever I have to do."

When Miles and Sarah exchanged glances, Nellie added pitifully, "I thought I could come to you . . ."

Dr. Gilbert spoke carefully. "Miss Spomer, I *will* help you. But if you know about these matters, you have made inquiry. And thus you also know that I would never—"

"I thought you would make an exception."

"Why would you expect—"

"Because your cousin George McCann is to blame for this mess I'm in!" Nellie blurted out. Miles took a step backward, bumped into his library table, leaned against it.

"There," Nellie said defiantly. "I've said it. Your cousin George McCann is responsible. And if you care for your reputation in this community, you will see to it—"

Standing near Nellie, Sarah barely resisted the urge to slap her. She had actually raised her hand when Dr. Gilbert spoke. "Miss Spomer, I will do everything in my power to help you in this difficult time. If what you say is true—if George McCann is responsible for your predicament—I shall see to it that he performs his duty."

Nellie stamped her foot. "I don't want to *marry* George McCann! I told you that." Nellie hid her face in her hands, began to cry. "I cannot tell my uncle. He'll turn me out."

Miles disagreed. "He will be very disappointed, Miss Spomer, but I've known your uncle since his first business trip to Lincoln years ago. The moment the telegram arrived telling him that you were joining him in Lincoln, he spoke of little else. He would never turn you out. Now, dry your tears and go home. We shall speak of this again—when I have had the opportunity to confront my cousin. Come to see me tomorrow evening, just when the office closes." Miles spoke convincingly enough that Nellie stopped crying, calmed down, and listened. "I will do everything in my power to help you, Miss Spomer."

Turning to Sarah he said, "Nurse Biddle, send Miss Spomer home with the medication we usually give in these cases. I'll be in the clinic."

Sarah prepared a bromide mixture to ensure Nellie a restful night. Then she escorted her out the front door of the office, locked the door, and pulled down the shades. She went back into the examining room. It was empty. She found Dr. Gilbert seated on a cot in the clinic, his head in his hands. At the sound of Sarah's footsteps, he looked up. Weariness showed in every line of his face. Sarah went to him, laying one hand on his shoulder. He reached up to pat her hand and forced himself to smile. "And now you know why I warned you about Cousin George when he first came to Lincoln." He groaned. "I was a fool to think he could change."

"But, Miles," Sarah began, trying to hold out hope, "George told me he's been sending money back to—"

"Most likely to an address where someone is depositing it for him while he enjoys a few free months at the expense of his gullible cousin Miles."

"Oh, Miles," Sarah objected. "Surely he isn't that far gone."

Miles smiled wearily. "Well, perhaps not. But I'm having difficulty thinking anything but the worst."

"Miles—there isn't really—in Lincoln—I mean, Nellie couldn't really—"

He shook his head. "No. I don't think so. She would have to go outside the city. Which means we have time to deal with George and to talk further with Nellie."

"Can we convince her? Is there any way at all?"

Miles sighed. "I don't know. She's a spoiled, self-centered young woman."

"Perhaps if we pray. Perhaps God would help us know what to do?" When Miles looked up at her, Sarah smiled weakly. "I guess I might as well admit something, Miles. I've accepted—that is, I'm trying to live by the simple creed Loula shared with me. I know there hasn't been much change in me—at least not one people can see." Sarah looked at Miles, her eyes shining. "But there *is* a difference in *here*." She pressed her hand against her heart.

"Well then, Nurse Biddle, you pray."

"I will, Miles. For Nellie and George—and for you."

Miles walked to the door of the clinic. "I believe I can handle George. If I can find him. He has a way of slipping out of town when these things happen." His tone of voice frightened Sarah.

"Perhaps if we offer to help. He must have *some* feelings for Nellie."

Miles looked at Sarah blankly. "Don't let your new-found religion turn you into a fool, Sarah."

The dart of Miles's words went straight to Sarah's heart. She stepped away from him. Seeing the hurt in her eyes before she turned away, Miles put out his hand. "Sarah, I didn't mean—"

Sarah waved her hand at him. "Go on, Miles. Go to George. It's all right."

But it was not all right. As Miles closed the door to the clinic, Sarah slumped in chair. *Don't let your newfound religion turn you into a fool. . . .* The words stung. *But surely, God, no one is beyond Your reach. Surely a few kind words to George McCann would make a difference. . . .*

Sarah retrieved her bonnet and left the clinic. *Let me find him first, Lord. Let me find George and talk to him before Miles does.*

Miles was only a few steps away from his clinic when a buggy rushed up and a wild-eyed young farmer shouted, "Doc! You got to come—Joe Bayard's shot hisself!" Miles turned on his heels, dashed back into his clinic, and shouted for Sarah. When she did not come, he realized her bonnet was missing from the hook by the clinic door. Without noticing Sarah's scribbled note, he grabbed his bag, ran out the front door and was gone.

The moment George opened the door at Miles's cottage, Sarah saw that he was drunk. His beautiful auburn hair was rumpled, his collar unbuttoned, his green eyes dull.

"Thank heavens you're here," Sarah said, laying her hand on the door. "May I come in, George? We need to talk before Miles finds you."

McCann backed up awkwardly, made an attempt to straighten his collar, smooth his hair. He bowed, made a sweeping motion with his hand. "Enter my humble abode, Nurse Biddle. I presume this is more than a social call."

Sarah stepped inside.

George retrieved a half-empty bottle of whiskey from a table before saying, "You are not my first female visitor today." He roared with laughter, taking a drink from the bottle before stumbling across the room and falling into a chair. Belching loudly, he continued, "You are preceded by Miss Spomer." He took another drink of whiskey. "But then, you probably know that." He slumped over.

"Highfalutin Miss Spomer told me everything." He chuckled drunkenly. "And so I guess Cousin Miles will be along directly to kick me out of town. If he can."

"George," Sarah began, trembling inside, "this doesn't have to be the end of everything for you. It can be the beginning. You can start over, right here in Lincoln, with Nellie. I know that Miles will help you, if you are only willing."

George looked at Sarah as if she were speaking Chinese. It seemed an eternity before he reacted at all to what she had said. When he did, it was with an ugly sneer. "You mean *marry* Nellie Spomer?" He roared with laughter. "Now there's a picture. George McCann, family man."

Standing up, he waved the bottle of whiskey in the air at Sarah. "Suppose you just sit down, Nurse Biddle. Let's talk over this little plan of yours." He walked unsteadily toward her and thrust the bottle of liquor in her face. "But first, let's have a little drink together. Get acquainted." He ran his hand along her chin.

Sarah turned her face away from George, aware of a knot that was growing in her stomach, wondering if perhaps she shouldn't have come.

George stepped away from her. "You probably don't drink, do you, Nurse Biddle? Don't drink, don't swear. Why, Nurse Biddle, you positively reek of innocence and light. No wonder Cousin Miles thinks so highly of you."

"George," Sarah begged, "won't you let us help you? We want to help—consider the future, George. If you run out on Nellie, what will you say when you meet God?"

George swore, laughed, shook his head. "I'll say 'Just send me on to hell. That's where all my friends are, anyway.'"

"George, please."

George slammed the bottle of whiskey down on the table beside Sarah. He loomed over her, his long hair falling around his face. "There's no reason on earth my life should be ruined by an empty-headed little flirt like Nellie Spomer. She made it real clear all she wanted was a little fun. She's goin' to St. Louis to trap herself a rich husband at some big ball. Said only to count on her bein' around 'til then." George laughed hoarsely. "Well, we had our fun, and now it's over." He smiled wickedly at Sarah. "An' that's just fine with me. There's always another hen in the henhouse."

Sarah was terrified, but still she felt compelled to try again. "George, it doesn't have to be over for you and Nellie. This could be a beginning for you both. A new life. Think of it, George. Your baby could be raised by you and Nellie. If you'll only let Him, God can work this for good in your life."

At the mention of God, George became enraged. He shouted, "I told you I don't want you meddlin' in my affairs! I don't want your *opinion*, I don't want your *advice*, and I especially don't want your *religion*!" Just as he shouted the word *religion,* George slapped Sarah's cheek hard.

He had raised his hand again when Sarah heard a familiar voice say, "You touch her again and I'll kill you."

George staggered uncertainly, then wheeled about to face Miles, who was standing in the doorway. He repeated with frightening calm. "I said, if you touch her again I'll kill you."

Years of drinking had taught George McCann when to allow the effects of drink to overtake him, and when to fight against it. Looking into Miles's face, George McCann became instantly sober. He backed away from Sarah.

Sarah looked toward Miles and saw that he was holding out his hands to her. He called her name. Somehow she managed to walk across the room to him. He reached up to cup her bruised cheek in his hand and put his arms around her.

Still holding Sarah, Miles said, "A short while ago I was headed here to offer you help, George." Reaching into his pocket, Miles pulled out his money clip, tossed it on the floor. "Get on the next train and go as far as that money will take you. Nellie doesn't need the scandal of trying to force you to own up to your obligations, and it's obvious that even if you did agree to marriage, it would be a sham. Go wallow in another pigsty, George. We shall see that Nellie and your child are well cared for."

Holding onto Sarah, Miles turned away. "I am taking Sarah home. When I get back, George, you had better be gone." As he reached to pull the door closed behind them, he added, "And may God have mercy on your soul."

Sarah began to shiver. Miles wrapped her in his coat, whispering gently, "You're in shock, Sarah. Just hold on to me." He managed to hurry her down secluded byways to the back door of the clinic. Once inside, he half-carried her upstairs to her apartment.

He wanted her to lie down, but she insisted on making her way across the room to her rocker. Sinking gratefully into it, she leaned her head against its high back and tried to reassure him. "I'll be fine, Miles. Really. Just let me sit for a while."

"I'll be right back," Miles said quietly. "I'm going to mix you something to help you sleep." He went downstairs, returning with a cup of hot tea, which he set by the rocker.

Sarah smiled weakly. "You can scold me if you like. I didn't heed your warning about George. I thought that God would protect me."

"And God did. He sent me." Miles leaned over, cupped her bruised cheek in his hand. "Something for which I must remember to thank Him."

At his touch, Sarah leaned toward him. He knelt down, put his arms around her, and drew her close. She did not know how long Miles held her before she was able to stop crying, to push away from him and sit upright.

Instead of moving away, Miles pulled up a small footstool. He perched on it, his elbows on his knees, his chin resting on his hands. His eyes never left Sarah's face as he said quietly, "I really must insist you drink that tea, Sarah."

Sarah looked at the tea and back at Miles. Whatever was happening between them, Sarah knew that drinking the tea would bring it to an end. She shook her head. She took a deep breath and forced herself to smile. Reaching up to feel her swollen cheek, she said quietly, "Thank you for rescuing me."

"It was my great pleasure." Miles finally looked away, stood up. "You're certain you'll be all right?"

Sarah nodded.

"I'll be going, then." He bent over and kissed her lightly before going to the stairs that led down to the clinic. She thought he was going to turn back toward her, but he didn't. Sarah heard the back door of the clinic close, the lock turn. It was quite some time after Miles's departure before Sarah finally drank the tea that would ensure a peaceful rest.

CHAPTER 25

Pastel Silks

----

*"A man's heart deviseth his way: but the LORD
directeth his steps."*
Proverbs 16:9

"Loula and Sam!" Sarah sat bolt upright in bed, saying
the names, wondering why she had not thought of it
before. *It's so obvious.* She hurried to dress and went
downstairs to the clinic where she waited impatiently for
Miles. When he finally arrived, Sarah met him at the door.
"Miles, I can't believe I didn't think of this before, but
what if Sam—"

"—and Loula would take Nellie's baby?" Miles finished the sentence for her as he took off his hat and hung
it by the door.

Sarah laughed. "Now there's frightening evidence that
we may be like-minded."

Miles smiled, reached out to touch her bruised cheek.
"Did you rest well, Sarah? Is it painful? I can mix some
more—"

"No." Sarah shook her head. "It's fine."

Miles frowned. "You're going to have quite a bruise.
When people hear what happened, the sheriff will be looking for George. I've spent the night heartily wishing I
would have called him myself instead of giving George
train fare."

Sarah disagreed. "No. You did the right thing. I wouldn't have wanted the sheriff involved." She reached up to touch the bruise. "Is it very noticeable?"

Miles nodded. "Very."

"Well, I'll simply have to allude to having fallen out of bed or something equally harmless. Thank the Lord He sent you along to be my knight in shining armor." The moment the words were out Sarah wished them back. She glanced at Miles out of the corner of her eye, then hurried to say, "I sincerely hope to learn someday that George has accepted the Lord into his life and changed."

Miles interrupted her. "I sincerely hope to learn some-day that George has been caught and made to pay for his ways."

"Don't be vengeful, Miles. It just wasn't George's season to come to know God."

"And where did this bit of wisdom come from?" Miles asked. "Never mind. I know. Loula Kemp."

"Actually," Sarah said shyly, "it came from the Bible. Although without Loula's example, I doubt I'd have turned to the Scriptures. But Loula has mentioned time and time again that the Bible helps her think more clearly when she's wrestling with a decision. So last night after you left I pulled my Bible down and began to read."

"If you'd followed your doctor's orders, you would have drunk the tea and that would have been the end of it."

"Yes, I know. But I needed to think."

"All right, Sarah. I'll lecture you some other time about following doctor's orders. What's this about the Bible and seasons—and what could it possibly have to do with Nellie and George?"

Sarah took a deep breath. "Well, I've spent most of my adult life being afraid that what I love and care about will be taken away from me. But reading the Scriptures last evening helped me look at my life in a different way. There was a season for me to become closely tied to Tom. That was when we lost our parents. Then God gave us a season to be loved by Aunt Jesse." Sarah smiled. "I never thought I would say it, but I am so *glad* we were never chosen by the folks who took in the orphan train children." Sarah hurried on. "Then there was that season to serve the Braddocks." She blushed and hurried on. "And a season to be in love with David . . . and the season to grieve when he and Abigail died."

Miles leaned against the doorway, his arms folded. "Do go on. What season are you in now, Nurse Biddle?"

Sarah thought for a moment before she answered. "I think it's a time in my life when I have opportunity to serve."

"Then the season of grieving has passed?" He met her gaze directly.

She nodded her head. "Yes. It has."

His voice was gentle as he asked, "Could there perhaps be another version of a season you have already experienced?"

Sarah looked away uncertainly. "I don't—know." She reached for a dust cloth and then moved toward the waiting room. Pausing at the doorway she said, "I'm trying to learn to hold today in an open hand—not to hold on so tightly to the things and people around me."

"And how does this relate to George McCann's abominable behavior?"

Sarah thought hard before answering. "I don't know if I can explain it exactly. I remember telling Loula Kemp that I would give anything to have the kind of inner peace that she and Sam had. I didn't understand that true peace would come only when I opened up both hands and gave everything up. I didn't think it could possibly be that simple, but it is."

"And this newfound peace enables you to forgive George McCann?" Miles wanted to know.

Sarah nodded her head. "Yes. I tried to talk to George. But he wasn't ready. I feel at peace leaving George in God's hands."

The sound of the front door opening interrupted them. Red-eyed from crying, Nellie Spomer waited uncertainly just inside the door. Sarah went to her, put her arm around her. "Come in, Nellie. The doctor is here."

Nellie reached into her reticule for a handkerchief and began to sniffle as Sarah led her through the doorway into the examining room.

"Well, I've just been looking for George. He's gone. No one knows where." She began to cry. "I thought he'd at least have the decency to say good-bye."

Miles came into the examining room from the clinic and explained bluntly. "Nurse Biddle and I both visited with George last night, Nellie." Nellie looked at Sarah, focused on her bruised cheek. Her eyes widened. Miles continued, "When it became clear that he had no intention of doing his duty by you, I provided funds and suggested he quit Lincoln."

"But what am I going to do now, Dr. Gilbert? Uncle is growing suspicious. I haven't been able to eat a thing." She asked innocently, "Does this sick feeling last forever?"

"You're overwrought, Nellie. If we can help settle a few things, you'll feel better."

"Peppermint tea might help, Nellie. I'll make you some." Sarah went to make the tea. When she returned, Miles was assuring Nellie she was perfectly healthy. Nellie was sitting at the library table, fighting back tears.

"Nellie," Dr. Gilbert began, "when did you say you were planning on going to St. Louis?"

"Next Spring. Though that's all ruined now."

"Perhaps not, Nellie. Perhaps not. What if I told you we know someone who might be willing to adopt your baby?"

Nellie looked at Sarah. "Is that true?"

Sarah nodded. "I haven't spoken to them yet, but I feel quite certain they would entertain the idea. How would you feel about that?"

Nellie thought about it but quickly shook her head. "I can't possibly stay in Lincoln and have a baby."

Miles spoke up. "Your uncle could take you to St. Louis early. I know of a secluded location where young women with similar—uh, challenges—have been well cared for."

Nellie looked confused, then her face brightened. "Do you think Uncle would do that for me?"

"I think he would do anything for you, if he thought you were going to become a responsible young woman who would bring him credit."

Nellie sighed. "Well, if you're talking about the likes of George McCann, I don't have any intention of ever associating with his kind again. Uncle was going to introduce me to his old cronies at the ball in St. Louis. Several of them have eligible sons."

The longer Nellie talked, the more Sarah was reminded of Rebecca Braxton. Sarah fought against her own feelings of dislike and forced herself to speak up. "Would you like me to speak with the couple in question, Nellie?"

Nellie was doubtful. "I'd be all alone in St. Louis. There's no one there I know. I'd be terrified."

Sarah spoke up, unaware that what she was about to say would introduce a new season of her life. "Perhaps I could go with you. If you'd feel better. I could be your private nurse." She looked over Nellie's head at Miles, who was staring at her in disbelief. "Ask Dr. Gilbert. I've delivered several babies. I'm a good midwife. I could give you excellent care. Of course, we would call for a physician for the actual birth. Then I could care for the baby and bring it back here to Lincoln."

"Would I get my figure back in time for the ball?"

Sarah turned and walked away from Nellie, barely suppressing her impatience. Dr. Gilbert spoke up. "Not completely," he answered honestly. "But that shouldn't impair your ability to be your charming self, Nellie."

Nellie considered. "All right. I'll do it." She looked up at Sarah. "If you'll come with me. If Uncle agrees. If that couple really wants the baby." She giggled nervously. "Heaven knows *I* wouldn't know what to do with a *baby*."

Yes, heaven does certainly know that, Sarah thought. Nellie left, with Miles promising to follow and speak to her uncle right away.

The moment the door closed behind her, Miles said half angrily, "What on earth were you thinking, Sarah? You can't go to St. Louis for the next few months."

"I was thinking of saving a child for Sam and Loula. And why on earth can't I go to St. Louis?"

"Because I need you here."

"You got along without me before I began nursing, and you'll do fine for a few months."

"What about Tom?"

Sarah hesitated only briefly. "Tom can go with me. There are schools in St. Louis."

"Sarah, the place I have in mind for Nellie is no place for a young boy. It's females only—and most of them are in a family way without the family."

"Well, I'll work that out. Certainly Aunt Augusta wouldn't mind him staying with her. He's already been talking of finding a job for the summer, anyway. He can work at the hotel and Aunt Augusta can keep an eye on him."

"What if he worked here at the clinic with me?" Miles suggested. "I'll need help, especially if I'm really going to have to muddle through the next few months without you. He could still live upstairs."

Sarah shook her head. "Tom's a good boy, but I don't think living alone—"

"Then he can come and stay with me."

"You wouldn't mind?"

"As a matter of fact, I rather like the idea. Tom's becoming a fine young man. He didn't like George at all. I like that about Tom."

"I'll talk to him about it."

"No. Let me do it. Give me a few hours to get the arrangements made with Phineas and Nellie and to think things through a bit. Then I'll talk to him. He'll likely feel more welcome if the idea comes from me instead of his sister."

Miles departed through the front door of his office for the Spomer home. Sarah locked the door behind him, then went out the back on her way to the little cottage Sam and Loula Kemp had been renting from Augusta Hathaway "to keep Loula near the doctor while she heals up and we get back on our feet."

Phineas Spomer blustered and feigned outrage when Dr. Gilbert informed him of Nellie's condition. Once he heard the doctor's plan, which included a private duty nurse for "his Nellie," he calmed down and prepared to wire his cronies in St. Louis that he would be spending the winter in their fair city. Nellie was summoned from her room. When she appeared, the terror in her eyes was soon transformed to relief as Phineas gave up his weak attempt to scold her, instead taking her into his arms and promising his full support "during this unfortunate time."

"Now you will be a good girl, won't you, Nellie?" he asked with all the sternness he could muster.

Nellie nodded. "Yes, Uncle. I've learned my lesson."

Much to Miles's amazement, Nellie seemed sincere when she turned to him and said, "Dr. Gilbert, I've never thanked you for what you are doing. I truly appreciate it. And I meant it just now when I promised Uncle I'll be a good girl. I'll do everything I can to give this baby a good start in life." She asked, "Do you know yet if that couple—will they say yes?"

"Nurse Biddle is there right now, Nellie. Let us hope they say yes."

Loula and Sam Kemp said yes. They said more than yes. Momentary disbelief gave way to incredible joy. Sam departed for work, his face wreathed in smiles.

The moment he left, Loula reached for Sarah and hugged her fiercely. "Sam and me been prayin' and prayin' for another baby. We just never thought God would give us a child this way."

Sarah squeezed Loula's hand. "We have to plan a baby quilt so I have a project to keep me busy while I'm in St. Louis." She chuckled. "Something with a great many very tiny pieces. Perhaps one of those silk honeycomb quilts. It would be so pretty in pastels with a black path."

"It'd be gorgeous, Sarah, but it would take so long."

Sarah nodded. "Exactly. It will take a long time, and it will take my mind off how long I'm away from Mi—" Sarah stopped. "From Lincoln and everyone here." She sighed. "Five *minutes* with Nellie Spomer tries my patience. I'm going to need supernatural help to endure several months."

Loula had been making coffee while they talked. Now she settled across the table from Sarah. "Tom could stay here with us, Sarah. Sam says we'll be a bit longer than he thought here in town. Things is goin' so well with the buildin' that he ain't had time to do much out at the farm." Loula lowered her voice. "Fact is, I don't know as I really want to go back out there to live."

Sarah reached across the table and squeezed Loula's hand. "Thank you, Loula. I really appreciate your offering. But Dr. Gilbert has already offered to keep watch over Tom. He wants him to work in the clinic."

Loula nodded, inspecting Sarah's face carefully. "How'd you get that bruise?"

Sarah reached up to touch her jaw. "Clumsiness. Thought I heard someone at the back door last night. I didn't take time to light the lamp, so I slipped right down the stairs."

"Lyin' is a sin, Sarah Biddle." As Loula spoke, she shook her finger in Sarah's face as if she were a naughty child. "I know the mark of a man's hand on a woman when I see it. And I know only one man of your acquaintance who might do such a thing. So where is George McCann now?"

"I don't know. Miles told him to leave town and he did."

"So it *was* George McCann."

Sarah sighed. "All right, Loula, I'll tell you the entire story." She concluded the telling with the picture of Miles sitting on the footstool looking up at her.

"And then what?"

"Then he got up and left."

"That's all?"

Sarah laughed nervously. "Well, except for one thing. Right before he left he bent down and kissed me."

"Sarah Biddle, I do believe you're blushin'," Loula teased. "From what you said about last night, I'd say our Dr. Gilbert has more than a casual interest in what happens to his clinic nurse. Do you feel the same for him?"

"I don't know." Sarah drummed her fingers on the table. "Honestly, I don't even know if I *want* to know."

"Don't you care for him?"

"I admire him. I respect him. I love working for him. Is that caring?" Sarah looked out the kitchen window as she rested her chin on one hand. "If it is, it certainly isn't the same—"

"The same as what?" Loula asked.

Sarah looked about the kitchen before answering. "It isn't the same as what I felt for David Braddock."

"Braddock." Loula said the name slowly. "Braddock, like Cordelia Braddock—the woman who made that sampler we lost in the fire?"

Sarah nodded, sat back in her chair. "You know that deserted mansion over on Seventeenth Street?"

"Who doesn't? Sam saw it when we were new in town. Said it's a masterpiece. Says it's a shame it's empty."

"Well, I used to live in that house." At Loula's open-mouthed amazement, Sarah hastened to explain. "I was the owner's housekeeper. Their name was Braddock." Sarah nodded. "The sampler was given me because I was supposed to marry David Braddock. It was a gift from David's mother, Abigail."

"Whatever happened?"

"Abigail died of cancer. David was killed in a train accident."

Loula sat back. "Oh, my." She reached across to squeeze Sarah's arm.

Sarah nodded. "I was devastated. Tom and I were sent away. I don't think the trustee ever really tried to see that the house was looked after. He just closed it up, took all the money he could get from the estate, and went back to Philadelphia."

Sarah smiled softly. "It's a wonderful house. I wish you could see it." She described the mansion, detailing every room. "I hate seeing it so overgrown. Abigail had planted every kind of rose you can imagine in her garden. And on the back porch, there was a vine—I don't remember the name—but it ran riot over everything all summer long." Sarah paused before adding, "Someone should be enjoying that house—making it come alive again."

Sarah took her napkin from her lap, folded it, then spread it out again as she talked. "I wallowed in grief for a long, long time. I let the losses in my life control everything. I started keeping part of myself back—away from people. I wasn't going to let them in where they could own part of me. I was too afraid of losing again."

Sarah looked at Loula and smiled. "But then I met you and Sam. I came to know the Lord. And I'm beginning to understand that God really did—and does—have a purpose for every season in my life. I've finally been able to let David go. To move on to—"

"To maybe love someone else?" Loula finished Sarah's sentence.

Sarah blushed. "I wasn't thinking of that, exactly." Sarah looked out the window. "I was thinking more of the coming season in St. Louis. The season where I will either learn patience or contribute to the demise of my patient." She grinned.

Loula shook her head, arched one eyebrow. "Don't be so quick to label all the times in your life, Sarah. And don't be surprised if God decides to repeat one of them seasons you thought was long gone." Loula nodded wisely. "You got to remember, Sarah, God's got His plan—and He only gives the general outline in the Bible. The particulars usually come as quite a surprise to us mortals."

CHAPTER 26

Crazy Work

"Trust in the LORD with all thine heart; and lean
not unto thine own understanding."
Proverbs 3:5

November 30, 1886
Lincoln, Nebraska

Dear Sarah,

Aunt Augusta says that if I don't write you she's
going to quit feeding me. I guess that means you've
been worried. Well, don't. I like it fine at Dr. Gilbert's.
He taught me to drive his mare and so now I go with
him on all the country calls, even the ones that take all
night. It sure is a lot of hard work being a doctor.

We almost got held up. We were crossing the bridge
over Salt Creek when a man came out of the bushes
swinging a lantern and calling for help. Dr. Gilbert
wouldn't stop, though. He grabbed the whip and took
it to Blizzard and he lunged ahead. There was another
man who came out to try to grab the reins, but Dr.
Gilbert kept the whip at Blizzard and we got away.
Lucky we were driving Dr. Allbright's horse. He's big
and strong or we maybe wouldn't have got away.

I helped make a splint. Dr. Gilbert was called out
last week for a broken leg. I went to the barn and

pulled off a piece of the pigpen. Then I held on to the patient while Dr. Gilbert set the leg and we wrapped the splint on. When we got back to town, I thought maybe if I cut some pieces of tin and shears I could make splints. Dr. Gilbert thinks this is a fine idea and says maybe I should think of being a doctor.

I sweep the walk in the front of the clinic every morning and again when we close the office. It's been warm enough I've washed all the windows three times since you left. Yesterday I went upstairs and dusted all the furniture in our apartment, even though we haven't been there and I don't see how it could need it. But Aunt Augusta said I must.

Dr. Gilbert is telling his patients that I am interested in medicine, and some of them have let me stay while he does the examination.

Sometimes I take medicine to patients in town. Sometimes I make our lunch.

For supper we go to Aunt Augusta's. Evenings I usually play with Jet. That's Dr. Allbright's dog. Oh, I forgot to tell you. Dr. Allbright is helping Dr. Gilbert now at the clinic. Things are real busy.

Dr. Gilbert and Dr. Allbright have plans for a real hospital. They are building it the next block west from our old home at the Braddocks.

Kemp Builders is doing the work on the hospital. That is Sam and about five other men who work for him now. I think Sam is probably glad he isn't farming anymore. He's very busy all the time, and Aunt Augusta told me that Sam and Loula are going to buy the house they have been renting from her. I guess they are doing all right.

Well, I guess this is enough to let you know that I am fine. Do you think it would be all right if I doctor instead of read law? Doctoring seems a lot more exciting to me. I know I won't make a lot of money,

*but Dr. Gilbert says that serving other people has its
own rewards that are much greater than money. That
sounded just like something you would say.*

*I miss you and I hope you are getting on fine. Aunt
Augusta says hello and we miss you.*

Your brother,

Thomas Biddle

Tom Biddle would have been surprised to learn that his
letter did not relieve his sister's worries. In fact, several
items in the letter caused Sarah a level of concern that surprised even her. She found herself much more bothered by
Miles driving Dr. Allbright's horse than she was by her
brother's involvement in a near robbery. After all, Sarah
reasoned, Miles responded appropriately and no one was
hurt.

Dr. Allbright certainly had every right to build her private practice, but it rankled Sarah that she was doing so
alongside Miles Gilbert. The additional thought that Dr.
Allbright and Miles were spending many hours together
planning a hospital was "the last straw."

Sarah read and reread Tom's letter. When she realized
how very much it disturbed her, the fact that it disturbed
her disturbed her. No matter how many times a day she
read verses about trusting God, her mind still returned to
the picture of Maude Allbright alongside Miles Gilbert.
Finally, Sarah admitted to herself, *I am truly fond of
Miles.* At the moment she permitted the concept in conscious thought, Sarah held her hand out in front of her,
palm up. *Don't hold on to what you cannot keep.*

At some point in each subsequent day, Sarah was
reminded that Miles and Dr. Allbright had worked alongside one another for another day and had probably
become even closer. *Well, if I am truly fond of Miles, then
that should make me happy.*

But Sarah could not make herself happy in the thought that Miles Gilbert might be courting Maude Allbright. She argued with herself. *It's a perfect match. Two physicians working side by side.* She reasoned with herself. *He kissed me once. Obviously he was only trying to comfort me in a moment of crisis.* She argued with herself. *But he's not the kind of man to show affection so casually.* She reasoned with herself. *What better person to be his companion than Maude. He's already told me she's brilliant. He enjoys her company. I should have realized.* She chastised herself. *I certainly should have realized. And I should have kept a better grip on my own emotions. I should never have let Loula encourage me. She meant well, but I should have kept my own counsel regarding Miles Gilbert.*

Sarah spent days reasoning, arguing, chastising. All the while she was in inner turmoil, she was working on Loula's baby quilt. Her mental state made it impossible for her to concentrate well enough to create a honeycomb quilt. She began a simpler star block. The points on some of the stars were reversed. When the blocks were set together, nothing matched as well as it should. Two weeks after Tom's letter arrived Sarah spread out the baby quilt top and saw her emotional turmoil reflected in her piecework.

"It's lovely," Nellie declared.

"It's a mess," Sarah said. She swept it up off the floor. "A complete mess. I'll have to begin again."

Nellie was amazed. "You're going to take it apart? Every seam?"

Sarah nodded. "Every seam. And while I'm ripping, I want you to read to me, Nellie. Read anything you like, just read and keep my mind busy."

Nellie frowned. "Is there something amiss back in Lincoln, Nurse Biddle? Something with your brother?" She hesitated before adding, "I don't mean to pry, but I'm fine. If you need to go home for a few days, I would understand."

Sarah was unable to hide her amazement.

Nellie smiled. "Yes, I suppose my thinking of someone other than myself would surprise you." Nellie sat down across from Sarah. "I think I've done some growing up, Nurse Biddle. The world really doesn't revolve around me and my problems. Meeting the other girls here, I realize that I've had a pretty easy life. And I've nearly ruined it." She laid her hand over her growing abdomen. "But thanks to you and Dr. Gilbert I'm going to be able to reclaim it. And I'm going to do better."

"I'm so pleased to hear you say that, Nellie. I know your uncle would be very proud of you." Sarah smiled. "You have no idea how happy you are going to make Sam and Loula, Nellie. This baby is going to have the best parents a child could ask for."

Nellie nodded. "I'm glad." She hesitated. "Before I could feel the baby, I didn't care much. It was just an inconvenience. But now it seems so real. I know I'm doing the right thing. But it's not going to be as easy as I thought."

"You don't need to be afraid, Nellie," Sarah encouraged her. "The physician your uncle has engaged has an excellent reputation. You are very healthy, and things will be fine. You'll see."

"Oh, I don't mean the birthing," Nellie said softly. "I mean the giving away part."

Sarah went to Nellie and gave her a hug. "It's terribly difficult, Nellie, but sometimes the most loving thing we can do is to let go."

The words came back to Sarah, challenged her. *And so why are you clinging so to the idea of Miles Gilbert? Why aren't you letting go, trusting God to do what's right?* "Thank you for being concerned, Nellie. Tom is fine. I don't need to go back to Lincoln. I just need to take my own advice."

Sarah repieced the quilt while Nellie read to her. They took long walks along the riverfront beneath towering oak trees. When the weather turned colder, Sarah settled Nellie by the fireplace in her room, propped up her feet, and made herbal teas by the gallon. One day she presented Nellie with a small workbasket filled with swatches of velvet and satin and colored thread. "It's called crazy work, Nellie. It's all the rage—even among the fashionable ladies. If you want to try it, it might help the time pass more quickly. I know it's difficult for you to be so confined."

Nellie took up the needle awkwardly, but once she had executed her first row of decorative stitches, she quipped, "Maybe this crazy work will keep me from going crazy."

The days crept by for both women. Nellie seemed to mature before Sarah's eyes. By early in the new year, Sarah no longer needed supernatural patience to deal with Nellie Spomer. And it was good that she didn't, because every letter that arrived from Tom required a new dose of supernatural patience to keep her off the next train west.

February 25, 1887
Lincoln, Nebraska

Dear Sarah,

I want to be a doctor. I know it now with certainty.

A father came rushing in with his four-year-old boy. He had gotten caught in some farm machinery, and it nearly scalped him. There was a depressed fracture of the skull and a separation at the fronto-parietal suture. Dr. Gilbert was out on a country call, and there was no time to send for him, so Dr. Allbright said I would have to assist. She trephined the skull, elevated the depression, brought the frontal and parietal bones together. Then she brought the scalp forward. It took about thirty-five sutures to close the wound. It was the most amazing thing I have ever seen.

The father stayed in the clinic with the boy to be his nurse. (Don't feel guilty. I think he would have done that even if you were here. He was very insistent that he stay, and he was an excellent nurse.) It was a very stormy time for the next four days and nights. But now the boy is getting better every day and Dr. Allbright thinks she will let him go home in a few days.

Being part of that makes me more sure than ever. I am going to ask Dr. Gilbert if he will be my preceptor when I've finished at Miss Griswall's. I know that Mrs. Braddock left the money intending that I would be a lawyer. Do you think she would mind that I have changed? After this time with the "Two Docs" (that's what folks in town have taken to calling Dr. Gilbert and Dr. Allbright) I can't think of anything worse than being cooped up in a law office with a bunch of musty books.

I've already started studying Gray's Anatomy. *Last night I memorized the names of all the bones in the neck and skull. I recited to Dr. Allbright before the emergency and I think she was fairly impressed. I could even spell the words.*

Really, Sarah, please write to me at once and let me know you will say yes to this endeavor.

Oh—someone is fixing up the Braddocks' house. The vines have been torn down from the back porch and all the overgrowth has been trimmed. There is a crew of workmen there nearly every day. The cobble-stone drive has been repaired, and the house has been painted exactly as it was when we lived there. No one seems to know who bought the place. It is the great mystery that everyone is talking about. I am glad to see that someone is going to enjoy the old place once again. Wouldn't it be fun to see our rooms again? I wonder if anyone will find my stash of rocks under the floorboard in the corner of my old room.

In only a few weeks you will be home. I am ready for your cooking again.

Your brother,

Thomas Biddle, M.D. *

*Just imagine how proud you will be to read that on an office window someday!

CHAPTER 27

A Red Bandana

"Though he slay me, yet will I trust in him."
Job 13:15

COME AT ONCE. TOM VERY ILL. TYPHOID FEVER. Sarah read the telegram and was gripped by fear that almost immobilized her.

Nellie took the wire from her hand, read it, and reached out to her. "I'll go downstairs and see if anyone knows when the next train leaves. You begin packing."

Sarah looked dumbly at Nellie and nodded, but she didn't move. Nellie went to the door. "Nurse Biddle!" she called out. "Get packed!" She started down the stairs.

Sarah went into her room. The initial shock wore off, and she grabbed her carpetbag and began to pack frantically. She was headed out the door to Nellie's and her quarters when Nellie burst through. "Hurry, Nurse Biddle, hurry. There's a train in less than half an hour. It will be close, but perhaps you can make it. They're hitching up the carriage right now—"

Hearing that she could leave at once, Sarah's head cleared. "Oh, Nellie—"

"Don't give it a thought. It's more important that you go to your brother now. I have confidence in the doctor here." She shoved Sarah out the door into the hallway, then stopped at the top of the stairs. "Just go to your brother. He needs you more than I do."

Sarah fairly ran down the stairs. Nellie leaned over and called out, "Wire me as soon as you get there—let me know . . ." Her voice trailed off as Sarah hurried outside to climb into the waiting carriage. The carriage pulled up to Union Station near downtown St. Louis about three minutes before the train west was to leave. Sarah ran as fast as she could and managed to get aboard the train.

She was still clinging to her suitcase when the conductor came through the car collecting tickets. "I haven't got a ticket," Sarah said honestly. "And I haven't money for one." She choked back tears and thrust the telegram in the conductor's face. "But I promise you I'll pay the fare when we get to Lincoln. Just please don't make me get off this train." Her voice was desperate. "If you've an ounce of compassion in you, let me get home to my brother." She stifled a sob. "He's all I've got in this world. Please don't make me get off this train."

As his passenger neared hysteria, the conductor patted her. "There, there, miss. Don't worry. I'll take care of it for you, miss. I'll be on board all the way to Nebraska, and you've nothing to fear. You just calm down and let us get you to your brother. Anyone bothers you, you tell them to talk to George Crenshaw. I'll take care of it."

At the kindness of the stranger, Sarah burst into tears. Crenshaw patted her again, pulled a new red bandana from his breast pocket. "Here, miss."

Sarah sobbed into the bandana for a minute before managing to thank him. With a few more kind words, Crenshaw made his way down the aisle and out of the car. Sarah finished her cry, then turned to stare out the window at the Missouri landscape. Daylight turned to dusk, night wore on. George Crenshaw came by and encouraged Sarah to eat. She shook her head.

"I know you've got no way to buy supper, miss. But just go up into the dining car and tell them George Crenshaw sent you. They'll give you anything you want."

"I'm really not hungry. Thank you."

"Then you get some rest. Your brother will probably be much better by the time you get to Lincoln. He'll need you to be strong to help him convalesce."

Sarah nodded. "Yes. I hope so."

Typhoid fever. Sarah remembered two cases Miles had treated. Lars Christiansen and Emil Gren were friends, young giants who lived on neighboring farms. The boys took ill on about the same day, and Miles was called immediately. He had left Sarah at the Christiansen house and then spent the next ten days driving back and forth between farms. After ten days of high fever and delirium, Emil seemed to grow better, but the improvement lasted only a few hours. Late one evening he developed a severe headache and complained of a stiff neck. He died at dawn. Miles then hurried to the neighboring farm, expecting to find Sarah comforting Lars's family in their hour of grief. Instead he found Sarah taking a well-deserved nap while the family gathered around the kitchen table to watch their seemingly recovered son eat a huge bowl of oatmeal. On the ride back to Lincoln, Miles had said in amazement, "I treated them both exactly the same way."

Sarah replayed the progression of typhoid in Lars Christiansen throughout the night on the train, haunted by the specter of each aspect of the disease. Would Tom be in delirium when she arrived? Would he even know she was there? The question she had kept from her conscious mind broke through. *Will he even be alive?*

On the everlasting train ride to Lincoln Sarah collected her thoughts long enough to plan her arrival. She told George Crenshaw, "When we arrive in Lincoln, go to the Hathaway House Hotel and ask for Augusta Hathaway.

Tell her Sarah Biddle needs her to pay train fare from St. Louis. She'll do it. If there's any reason she can't, you'll just have to follow me to Dr. Gilbert's clinic at Fourteenth and O Street."

George Crenshaw nodded and smiled. "I'm not worried about the fare, Miss Biddle. You just take care of your brother." As the train pulled into the Lincoln station, Crenshaw escorted Sarah off the train ahead of everyone else. He hailed a carriage. As she climbed into the carriage, he patted her on the shoulder. "I'll be praying for young Tom, Miss Biddle."

Sarah had no time to thank him for his kindness. Her heart and mind were intent upon only one thing, and that was getting to Tom. When she finally burst through the front door of the clinic, ran through the examining room, it was to witness a scene that nearly broke her heart. Tom lay tossing and turning, muttering in delirium. But even as the knot in the pit of her stomach grew tighter, Sarah thought, *Alive. Thank You, Lord. Thank You.* Sarah went to Tom, pulled off her gloves, took the cloth from his head and rinsed it in the basin at his bedside.

Miles had been sound asleep, sitting almost upright in a chair next to Tom's bed. The sound of water being wrung into the basin woke him. He turned wearily toward Tom and saw Sarah. He leaned his elbow on Tom's bed, rubbed his forehead. "Thank God." He started to get up, but was so weary he couldn't make himself do it.

"How long have you been sitting in that chair?"

"What day is it?"

"It's Wednesday, Miles."

"Pretty constantly since Sunday, I think."

Sarah reached across Tom to touch Miles's hand. "Then you get yourself to bed. I'm here now and I can do the sponging. He's been like this for how long?"

"His fever was 105 yesterday. We managed to get him into a tub of ice. After a couple of hours it came down to 103."

"Then all we need to do is watch his fever and keep sponging him off. I can do that, Miles. You get some rest."

Miles managed to stand up, staggered to an empty cot in the hospital, and was asleep before he was completely prone.

Sarah felt suddenly energized. Tom was alive, his fever was down, she knew what to do. *Until the end of next week . . . then you'll be watching for the hemorrhage . . . waiting and watching, knowing you can't do a thing.* Sarah forced the thought from her mind as she leaned over her brother. "Tom, it's Sarah. I'm here now, Tom. I'll take care of you. You just get well. Come back to us." She forced her voice to remain calm as she said, "Lincoln needs another doctor, Tom. You'll be a fine doctor. I'm so proud of you, Tom. . . ." She talked until his delirious muttering quieted. Then she sat in the chair Dr. Gilbert had occupied and began the night watch.

Sarah was sitting beside Tom sipping coffee when Miles woke up the next mourning. She smiled at him. "Welcome back to the land of the living, Dr. Gilbert."

Miles pushed himself to a sitting position, ran his fingers through his hair, rubbed his face. Tom muttered, and Miles immediately went to his side.

"He's had a fairly good few hours, Miles. I think—" she broke off, took a deep breath. "He seems to know I'm here. Maybe it's just wishful thinking—but I think he may be all right?" She asked the question, looking up at Miles for confirmation.

Miles's outburst of anguished guilt took Sarah totally by surprise. "Oh, I don't *know*, Sarah. I don't *know*. I totally misdiagnosed him." He turned away from Sarah, went to the window and stared out. "How could I have been so stupid. I thought it was just an inflammation. He complained of a sudden severe pain around the appendix." He paused. "I kept him here at the clinic, stayed with him." Miles laughed hoarsely. "I actually administered Dr. Pierce's Pellets twice—exactly the thing that should not have been done."

"But you didn't *know*, Miles. You didn't know it was typhoid."

He shook his head. "I should have listened to Maude."

"Dr. Allbright?"

Miles nodded. "She knew something wasn't right. 'Miles,' she said, 'I think we might be dealing with something else here. We'd better keep a close watch, and you'd better wire Nurse Biddle and have her come home.'

"She mentioned typhoid. But I insisted. 'No, there aren't any cases now. He couldn't have caught typhoid.' But she was right—*someone* has to be the first case."

He turned toward Sarah. "And Tom is the first case. The rose spots appeared on his abdomen day before yesterday. That's when I wired you." He half-whispered, "I'm so sorry, Sarah. I should have known; I should have listened to Maude. She's quite a woman. She's been taking care of my patients, trying to see her own, and still she spent two nights with Tom."

"Miles," Sarah said gently, "how many times have you told me that typhoid can be very atypical. Didn't you have a pneumonia case once that ended up as typhoid? And you just told me that Tom's case had all the symptoms of an inflammation of the bowels."

He nodded reluctantly.

"Then you have nothing to feel so guilty about, Miles."

"That's what I've been telling him, Nurse Biddle." Maude Allbright was standing in the doorway of the clinic. She looked at Miles, then back at Sarah. "I see you finally got him to get some rest." She directed her next comment at Miles. "Now if we can get him home to breakfast and a change of clothes, he'll perhaps be human again."

When Miles turned around, Maude said, "Miles Gilbert, one of the reasons I became a doctor was for the joy of giving orders to men and seeing them obey. It's a singularly satisfying experience. Now I'm giving you an order and you'd better obey. You get yourself home and we don't want to see you back here until you've shaved and eaten something. Nurse Biddle is here to care for Tom, and if anything develops I'll be in the office for the next few hours."

Like a boy obeying his mother, Miles reached for his hat and coat. "All right, Maude, all right. I'm going." He looked at Sarah. "I'll be gone just a few minutes."

"No, Miles," Maude interrupted, "you'll be gone at least the morning."

Miles looked at Maude, then back at Sarah. He smiled, shrugged his shoulders, and was gone.

Dr. Allbright performed her own examination on Tom, nodding with satisfaction. "He knows you're here, Nurse Biddle. He hasn't rested this quietly for days." The sound of the front door of the office opening interrupted her. "It sounds like patients are already beginning to arrive." Maude bustled to the door of the hospital that led into the clinic's examining room. She opened it and called out, "Dr. Allbright is here. I have to scrub up. I'll be there in a few minutes."

She turned to Sarah. "We're taking extra precautions." She went to the small stove in the corner, poured steaming hot water into a basin, rolled up her sleeves, and began to wash vigorously. Then she reached for a long white coat that hung on a peg next to the sink. "I'll be just on the other side of this door if you need anything." She smiled kindly, her hazel eyes sparkling. "I'm glad you've come, Nurse Biddle. We've a long way to go getting this boy on his feet again. But we will." She stepped into the next room, and Sarah heard her rather imperious voice calling out to whoever had come in the front door.

Sarah gave Tom a sponge bath and tried to get him to sip water. He weakly tried to push the cup away, began to mutter something unintelligible. Sarah leaned over to whisper to him in low tones when someone knocked on the back door. Augusta Hathaway called her name.

"Aunt Augusta!" Sarah almost shouted. "We're in quarantine!"

"I know that, Sarah," Augusta answered through the door. "I'm just bringing you a breakfast tray. I'll set it right here by the door. You have to boil the dishes before I can take them back. Dr. Gilbert has been very insistent about that." She paused briefly before adding an impassioned, "I can't quite stand it not being able to hug you, dear. We're all praying."

The next visitor at the back door was Loula Kemp. "I know, Sarah. Quarantine. I just wanted to let you know Sam and me are prayin' as hard as we can for Tom."

At the sound of Loula's voice, Sarah began to cry quietly. "Oh, Loula, I'm so afraid." She leaned against the back door, choked back tears to say in a half-whisper, "What if—"

"Don't worry about the what-ifs, Sarah. Remember? Hold Tom in an open hand. God loves him a whole lot more than you do. He'll do what's best. For everyone." Loula stood as close to the doorway as she could. "Did you bring your Bible with you, Sarah?"

"Yes," Sarah admitted, "but I haven't read anything."

"The Psalms really comfort me when I'm upset. They aren't hard to understand like some of the other books. Read the Psalms." Loula paused. "You might even read them out loud. The sound of your voice would comfort Tom, and who knows—if anything can get through his delirium, it'd be the Word of God."

Sarah nodded. "Thank you, Loula. I'll try it. Oh, Loula," Sarah whispered, "you're such a good friend. Thank you for coming."

"I brung you some fresh baked bread, Sarah. I'll just put it here by the door. And I'll be back later today. You hang on, Sarah. Just hang on."

Sarah hung on through days of Tom's delirium. She hung on when it seemed that Tom's fever would never come down. She hung on when Dr. Allbright examined Tom, frowned slightly, then feigned a positive expectation. She hung on when Miles sat down next to her, sighed deeply, took her hand in his own, and said nothing. She read the Psalms, talked through the door to Augusta and Loula, and stopped measuring time and measured degrees of fever.

At the end of the week Dr. Allbright suddenly decided to spend the night at the clinic. "Of course we think he's doing better, but I need to mix up some powders anyway, and—"

"It's all right, Dr. Allbright," Sarah said quietly. "I know. Now there's the hemorrhaging to worry about. If that happens," her voice quavered, "then I'll probably lose Tom."

"Well, we're going to do everything in our power to keep that from happening."

Sarah looked up at Maude. She thought, *It isn't in our power, Dr. Allbright. I didn't want Miles to take the blame for a misdiagnosis, and I don't want you taking any blame for whatever happens in the next few hours.* She said, "Tom is in God's hands, Dr. Allbright. Whatever He does is best."

Maude nodded solicitously. Sarah could almost hear her thinking, *Never challenge whatever comforts the sick. Any foolishness they want to believe is fine if it brings comfort.*

"I know you're not of a Christian persuasion, Dr. Allbright," Sarah said quietly, "and I probably haven't been a very good example of Christianity these last few days. I'm new at it and I've a lot of growing to do . . . but I really do believe that God has some reason for allowing Tom to be so ill. And I've resolved not to stand in the way of whatever that purpose is." Her voice wavered. "Even if Tom doesn't survive, Dr. Allbright, God is still God."

Dr. Allbright's expression didn't change. "I'm glad you have your faith to comfort you, Nurse Biddle." Maude did not say what she was really thinking: *Because if this disease takes its usual course, you are going to need something to get you through your brother's funeral.*

But there was no funeral. Three days after Sarah said, "Even if Tom doesn't survive, God is still God," Miles stood up from examining Tom, smiled at Sarah, and said, "It would appear that God agrees that future Lincolnites should have the good fortune of being cared for by Dr. Thomas Biddle." He took off his stethoscope and turned his back on Sarah to fumble in his medical bag.

Sarah was so filled with joy she sat motionless, just staring at Tom, thinking that his even breathing and natural sleep were the most wonderful things she had ever witnessed.

It was a few moments before she realized that Miles was still fumbling with his bag.

Sarah chided, "It would appear that the good doctor needs someone to organize his medical bag." She got up and went to him, but he grabbed the bag, mumbled some excuse, and made for the back door.

"Miles. I haven't thanked you."

He stopped, but didn't turn around. "Don't thank me, Sarah. My bumbling almost killed your brother. Thank the God who answered your prayers."

Sarah reached out to put a hand on his shoulder. "Miles, don't. I don't blame you. Tom won't blame you. Typhoid is a terrible disease. No one knows the exact cause. No one knows the cure." Sarah added, "You relieved so much of Tom's suffering, Miles. So much of mine. If I had to walk through this valley of the shadow of death, Miles, I praise God that you were here to walk with me."

There was such great sorrow in Miles's eyes, that Sarah could not resist the urge to take him in her arms and comfort him. She reached up, put her arms around his neck, and hugged him fiercely. At that moment Dr. Miles Gilbert and Nurse Sarah Biddle set aside their titles and became just a man and a woman clinging to one another, sharing the joy of a victory granted over death. Miles held Sarah closer.

Dr. Allbright's opening the back door of the clinic ended the embrace as she said, "Well, I assume young Thomas is out of danger?"

Miles and Sarah stepped away from one another. Miles reached once again for his medical bag while Sarah smoothed her dress and cleared her throat. "Yes. Dr. Gilbert says that he is."

"Good" was all Maude said. "Then I'll be heading over to the hospital. Sam says they've about finished the interior floors. He wants some decision about the painting of the sign." She turned toward Miles. "Do you want to give your input, Miles?"

Miles shook his head. "No. You do it. I've a few patients to call on."

Maude nodded briskly, then turned to Sarah. "I'm glad your brother is going to be all right, Nurse Biddle. I think," she said, reaching for the quarantine sign, "we can take this down now."

She tossed the sign onto the floor and was gone.

$\mathcal{P}$russian $\mathcal{B}$lue

----

*"The troubles of my heart are enlarged: O bring
thou me out of my distresses."*
Psalm 25:17

"I wish I owned the company that makes carbolic
acid," Sarah quipped to Tom. She was on her knees scrubbing the floor of their apartment. From his bed Tom said
weakly, "I'm sorry I'm causing you so much work,
Sarah."

Sarah hushed him, looking up just in time to see Miles
coming up the stairs.

"Tom," he called out, "when you drove me out to the
Davis farm just before you got sick, did you by any chance
take a drink when you watered Blizzard?"

Tom thought back and nodded. "Sure. I know you said
to be careful about that, but I went down deep and what I
brought up was pretty clear. I didn't drink much—just
enough to take the edge off my thirst."

Dr. Gilbert sat on the edge of the bed. "Well, I think we
have found the cause of your illness. Last year during the
typhoid outbreak William Davis asked me what he could
do to spare his family. I told him typhoid was a water-
borne illness, that he should order his family to boil their
water and plan to fill in that open well by the cattle yard.
He just stopped by to tell me they cleaned out their shallow

well just yesterday and brought up rotten corncobs, a dead rabbit, and two dead rats. He hurried right into town to visit with Cranston Fink about a deep well." Dr. Gilbert patted Tom. "William is a deeply religious man, Tom, and the very soul of honor. When I told him what you had been through, he felt terrible. Wanted to know what he could do."

Tom didn't hesitate. "Tell him a donation to the new hospital would be a perfect way to encourage me." Tom winked at Sarah, looked at Miles. "My ancient preceptor is used to 'bare-bones' medicine. I'm hoping for better things."

Sarah stood up, stretched. "There. I've gone over every square inch of this apartment."

"I thought you were going to scrub clear through the floorboards, Nurse Biddle," Dr. Gilbert teased.

Sarah countered, "You'll notice, Dr. Gilbert, that my brother does not refer to me as 'ancient.' That is because I regularly impress him with my feats of energetic house-keeping." Sarah grew serious. "What's this about dona-tions for the new hospital and 'bare-bones' equipment?"

"Oh, it's nothing. We've hit a bit of a snag, that's all. Sam underestimated a few costs. It will work itself out. Maude has a wonderful idea for raising funds. She wants to form a women's auxiliary to manage fund-raising. She's already talked to Augusta Hathaway, who of course expressed an immediate interest in getting involved."

Miles turned toward Tom. "Undoubtedly in response to the knowledge that Thomas here will one day be practic-ing in that very hospital—if we can get him back from Omaha once his schooling is completed." Miles turned back toward Sarah. "It shouldn't take too long to have things up and running."

"How 'bare bones' is it going to have to be?" Sarah wanted to know.

"Why don't you come over and see?" Miles asked.

"Oh, Miles—" Standing in the foyer of the hospital, Sarah was unable to hide her disappointment. "The building is lovely. But are you really going to have to move your old office furniture into this beautiful place?"

Miles nodded. "For a while, anyway." He led Sarah through a door into the first-floor ward. Sunlight poured through the windows lining both walls. A spotless tile floor stretched away from them toward the back of the building. "We've ordered enough beds for the first floor. The rest will have to wait. Neither Maude nor I anticipated the expense involved." He laughed quietly. "Together Maude and I are a formidable medical team . . . but we're pathetic financiers."

At mention of Maude Allbright, something that Sarah had buried beneath her concern for Tom raised its head and demanded attention. *"Together Maude and I are a formidable medical team," he had said. . . . Miles drives Maude's horse on his calls now. . . . Miles sees Dr. Allbright's patients and she sees his. . . . When Maude orders him around, he doesn't mind a bit; he acts like he's used to it, like he maybe even likes it. . . . He gives her credit for so many things, called her "quite a woman" . . .* Did Sarah only imagine it, or had Dr. Allbright been a bit piqued when she came upon Sarah hugging Miles that day when they knew Tom was going to be all right?

Sarah was still musing quietly when the subject of her imaginations called out from the foyer. Miles's voice echoed a response, and Maude came hurrying into the ward. "Hello, Nurse Biddle," Dr. Allbright said vigorously. Sarah noticed Maude's perfect coiffure, her stylish but sensible dress. *She cuts quite a figure. I'll bet heads turn wherever she goes.* Miles's head certainly did turn. The moment Dr. Allbright entered the ward, he became totally immersed in conversation with her.

Sarah followed Dr. Allbright and Miles back into the foyer of the hospital, and from there she made her way up the winding stairs to a smaller reception area on the second floor. The ward above the first floor remained unfinished. Sarah walked the length of the building on the second floor, went through a pair of doors and down the wide service stairs that lead down to a well-equipped kitchen. A narrow set of stairs led to the subterranean laundry room, serviced by a dumbwaiter.

When Sarah finally made her way back upstairs she found that the doctors had retreated into one of the offices west of the foyer. They were still deep in conversation, bent over the plans for the hospital. Sarah wandered back through the ground floor ward and out the back door. She admired the small garden that had been begun on the grounds, the wide walkways, the hedge that ran directly along the back wall of the Braddock estate.

Tom's letter came back to her. *Someone is fixing up the Braddock's house. The vines have been torn down from the back porch.* Sarah stepped through a break in the hedge, across the narrow alley, and peered through the wrought-iron fretwork that graced the narrow back gate. Yes, someone had pruned back the vine. It barely reached the second-story window of her old room. *There is a crew of workmen there nearly every day.*

Sam Kemp came out the back door.

"Sam!" Sarah called.

When he saw who was calling him, Sam looked around nervously. Two workmen came down the kitchen stairs behind him. He said something to them, then walked along the edge of the rose garden until he reached the back gate.

"Didn't expect to see you here, Sarah."

Sarah put a gloved hand up on the gate. "I thought you were involved in the hospital project, Sam."

He nodded. "I am. Actually, I've got two crews working today. One here and one over at the hospital. Until the two docs make a few decisions, I thought I'd come over here and check up on things."

"It's good to see the manse is going to be used again."

Sam looked at her quizzically, then nodded. "Yep. It's being fixed up just like it was before. Same colors on the outside, same on the inside—or as close to it as we can make it." He shook his head. "Can't figure out how they done it, but somebody got in and did some minor damage in the back hall. Probably just young'uns. Smart though. The doors was all still locked."

"I can tell you how they got in." At Sam's look of surprise, Sarah reminded him, "I lived in that house for a few years, Sam. There's no secrets about it to me. Open this gate and I'll show you the same way they probably took. It had to have been children or somebody really small."

Sam unlocked the gate and followed Sarah around the back of the house. She almost disappeared in some evergreens growing to the right of the kitchen stairs. "Right here, Sam—whoever trimmed the shrubs probably saw it—" Sarah pulled Sam after her and succeeded in parting the greenery enough for him to see a small rectangular door. "Mrs. Braddock had this put in so the iceman could deliver whether or not I was in the kitchen." Sarah pulled on the latch and the small door swung open. "I guess Ira Braddock forgot to have this door locked." She stood back from the door, put her hands on her hips, and looked up at the porch.

"You want to see what we done inside, Sarah?" Sam asked.

"I'd love to—if you're sure the owners won't mind."

Sam shook his head. "Won't mind at all."

Sarah followed him up the back stairs and into the once familiar kitchen. She was surprised by the emotional effect standing in the kitchen had on her. The gleaming tile floor shone like new. The small white table with two chairs still sat in the corner. Memories of dozens of lunches and dinners eaten at that table flooded in, and with the memories came a myriad of emotions. There was the joy of Tom's coming in from school, the warmth of Augusta's friendly visits, the worry when the bell rang summoning her upstairs, the despair of the day David had sat at the table in the corner weeping over his mother's illness.

Leaving the kitchen, Sarah went toward the front of the house. The floors had been polished, the walls repapered. In the library David's bookshelves had been polished. *There*, Sarah thought, looking across the room. *He used to stand right there by the window. He pretended to be reading, but I finally realized he was really watching for Tom to come up the drive from school.*

Feeling her throat tighten, Sarah turned to Sam. "Tom was right. Whoever is doing this obviously wants to preserve it in its original state. Abigail looked everywhere for that Prussian blue silk wall covering. It was an outdated color even then. Almost impossible to locate. Curious. I would think a new owner would want to redecorate."

Sam shook his head. "Nope. We changed one room upstairs. Put in modern plumbing, a telephone. Otherwise my orders were to just fix what needed to be fixed, to make it all like new but keep it as original as I could." He nodded toward the stairs. "Go on up, Sarah. I've still got some time before I got to be getting over to the hospital."

Sarah mounted the stairs, her heart beating a little more rapidly. For some reason, she turned away from what used to be her own little room and went instead toward Abigail's former quarters. The door opened, and she saw the changes Sam had mentioned. Abigail's room had been opened up and connected to David's quarters by a doorway. Whoever would occupy this side of the house would have their own private apartment. Sarah made her way across the empty room, paused at the newly created doorway and looked into David Braddock's world. It retained a masculine feel, but David's favorite colors were no longer evident.

Making her way out of David's room, Sarah went up the narrow stairs to the garret Tom had occupied. It, too, had been masterfully restored. *I wonder* . . . Sarah went to one corner of the room, knelt down. Whoever had done the floor had left the board loose. Sarah lifted it up and let out a little cry of surprise. Tom's rocks were still there, hidden between the joists. Sarah took one, tucked it in a pocket, replaced the board.

Sam was sitting at the bottom of the steps just inside the front door when she came down. She held up the rock. "You really took the idea of keeping things original seriously, didn't you?"

Sam grinned. "We had to ask about that loose board. New owner told us to leave it just like it was—only polish the floor. I guess he likes rocks."

"Who is the new owner, Sam? Is it someone we know? Someone from Lincoln?"

Sam shrugged. "Now, that's the secret everybody—including Loula—keeps asking me. Fact is, I can't say."

Sarah looked at him quizzically. "When are they moving in?"

Before he thought, Sam said, "Oh, about the time the hospital's finished, I expect." He quickly added, "I think of every job I got in terms of when that hospital's going to get finished. It's been a real challenge. But when I get it done, when folks can see the work I do, Kemp Builders should really be a going concern."

Sarah retreated down the back hall. "Well, thank you for the tour, Sam. It's wonderful to see the old place coming back to life. Obviously whoever owns it is going to take good care of it. I'm glad to see that."

And she was glad. Very glad. So glad tears sprung to her eyes as she walked past Abigail's rose garden, past the carriage house. The new owners had fixed that up, too. Sarah could see that the entrance to the apartment over the stable had been improved. *Of course they will probably use that as their office. It will be so convenient. What a good idea.* The good idea elicited a few more tears. Sam opened the back gate and Sarah rushed past him, calling back over her shoulder, "Tell Dr. Gilbert I needed to get back to Tom, won't you, Sam?" She hurried along the narrow lane between the hospital grounds and the Braddock manse and was halfway back to her little apartment over the clinic before she regained her composure.

I wonder if Dr. Allbright will keep her professional name, or will Lincoln have two Dr. Gilberts. Sarah sighed, shook her head. *I wonder if I can find a nursing position in Omaha while Tom is in medical school.*

CHAPTER 29

Purple Velvet

----

*"Thou hast turned for me my mourning into
dancing: thou hast put off my sackcloth, and
girded me with gladness."*
Psalm 30:11

"It's time I got back to Nellie, Tom," Sarah said quietly
one evening. "You're doing very well. If I leave right away
I'll be there in plenty of time to help her prepare for the
baby."

Tom was sitting up in bed poring over *Flint's Practice*.

Sarah chuckled. "Don't tell me Miles has begun to
make assignments only a week after you were at death's
door."

"Not Dr. Gilbert. Dr. Allbright. She said I should begin
reading and memorizing as much as possible. She said it's
a good way to spend my convalescence."

"Well, I certainly agree that we need to keep your mind
occupied, or you'll be sneaking out of bed long before you
really should."

Tom grinned. "It was sure nice of Loula and Sam to say
I could stay with them. I think I'd be a burden to Dr.
Gilbert right now, he's so busy with Dr. Allbright and the
hospital."

Sarah turned away so that Tom couldn't see her face. "Yes. He is." She turned back, smiling brightly. "I'm going to get you settled at the Kemps' in the morning, and then I'll be buying my train ticket. I'm having lunch with Augusta. I'll stop by Sam and Loula's for supper. Then it's back to St. Louis—this time for only a week or two, I imagine."

She shook her finger at Tom. "While I am gone, Master Biddle, you are absolutely forbidden to do *anything* without Miles Gilbert's express permission. He's promised to check in on you every day. You behave yourself, young man. I don't want to get another telegram for the rest of my life."

By mid-morning Tom Biddle was settled in at the Kemps'. Sarah hurried back to the clinic. She opened the back door, was disappointed to see both Miles's and Dr. Allbright's coats hanging by the back door. Through the examining room door she could hear their voices. Maude was laughing about something, and Miles joined in.

Sarah took off her shoes, crept up the stairs, and raised the blinds at the front of the room. Natural light flooded in. Taking off her bonnet, Sarah stood facing the object of her morning's mission. The trunk had not been opened for a long, long time. She knelt by it, removed the clutter that had accumulated on the top, opened the lid. The faint aroma of dried roses still clung to its contents. But Sarah didn't remove the tray. Instead, she reached for the crisp white envelope that lay in the tray alongside a purple velvet ring box.

There was no bitterness in the tears Sarah Biddle shed as she sat in her rocker reading David Braddock's love letter. Bitter disappointment had been replaced by a strange kind of melancholy mingled with excitement. She read slowly, savoring David's words. When she finished reading, she reached for the purple velvet box. Opening it, Sarah removed the ring David had intended as her wedding ring. She slid it onto her finger and held up her hand, admiring the mellow glow of the stone.

Standing up, Sarah moved to the window, stood looking up O Street toward Seventeenth . . . Eighteenth . . . where Dr. Miles Gilbert and Dr. Maude Allbright-soon-to-be-Gilbert were building a hospital. Sarah stepped away from the window, refolded David's letter, tucked it back in its envelope, and laid it in the trunk. She left the ring on while she packed her bag for the next day's trip to St. Louis. When it was time to join Augusta for lunch, Sarah returned the ring to its velvet box and dropped it in her bag.

Sarah had just begun her descent to the clinic below when she heard the back door open. *Miles and Dr. Allbright must be leaving for lunch.*

"It's such a wonderful house, Miles." Dr. Allbright's voice carried up the stairs to stop Sarah in her tracks.

"I'm glad you think so. I wasn't quite sure about the work on the private apartment."

"Who wouldn't love it? Sam Kemp's work on that gorgeous house has been the talk of Lincoln for months. I wonder if anyone has guessed."

"At least Sam has managed to keep it quiet. I'm really pleased with his work."

"The office over the carriage house was an inspired idea. No more midnight runs to the clinic. You'll just have to step out the back gate."

Miles and Dr. Allbright went out the back door of the clinic, never suspecting that their conversation was overheard. They would have been deeply grieved to know that they had just broken Sarah Biddle's heart.

At Augusta's request, her luncheon with Sarah was served in Augusta's private quarters. The two women dined in relative silence, Augusta watching Sarah with curiosity and no small amount of concern. Not until the table service had been removed did Sarah produce the ring box from her reticule.

"I don't know who else to ask, Aunt Augusta," Sarah began. She opened the ring box and held it on her open palm where Augusta could inspect the exquisite ring. "Could you perhaps make inquiries as to the value? What I could expect to get for it?"

Augusta was aghast. "You can't sell David's ring, Sarah!" She went to her secretary, withdrew her checkbook. "Why didn't you come to me? Whatever you need—"

"It's not for me, Aunt Augusta," Sarah said quietly. "I don't need any money. Abigail provided for Tom. Phineas Spomer is paying me very well for taking care of Nellie." Sarah paused to collect her thoughts. "It's Miles. He and Dr. Allbright have hit a snag in the hospital construction."

"I know that," Augusta fairly snapped. "Maude and I discussed it over breakfast yesterday morning. We're forming a ladies' auxiliary to raise funds."

"Then this can be the first donation." Sarah held up one hand. "Please, Aunt Augusta, I want to do this. Why should something this valuable be moldering in a trunk when it can help others? I'm never going to wear it."

"Well, your daughter might."

Sarah looked solemnly at Augusta. "Will you help me sell this ring so the money can go to the hospital, or not? I'm leaving for St. Louis in the morning. Would it be better if I went to Nellie's uncle with it?"

"Is there something wrong, Sarah?" Augusta wanted to know. "You don't seem yourself."

Sarah nodded. "Yes, there is. I've been holding on to false hopes. It's caused me much pain, and it's undoubtedly very displeasing to the Lord. Selling this ring is one way to take the tears of the past and turn them into treasures for tomorrow." She smiled sadly. "It took me half the night to think up that phrase." She looked back at Augusta. "I want to do this."

When Augusta still looked doubtful, Sarah added, "Dr. Gilbert has agreed to be Tom's preceptor. My Tom is going to be practicing medicine in that hospital someday. What better thing to do with my little treasure than to use it for Tom? Abigail and David would agree."

Augusta considered. Finally, she held out her hand. "You're right. They would." She took the ring box and tucked it into a secret compartment in her desk. "I am keeping this ring for two weeks, Sarah. If you change your mind, you wire me—say anything. If I get a wire from you I will know that the real message is that you want to keep the ring."

"Thank you, Aunt Augusta." Sarah sighed with relief. "And now I have to go. I haven't purchased my ticket yet, and it's getting late. Tom and I are eating with Sam and Loula tonight."

"You tell Master Biddle that I'll be by late tomorrow. He promised me a game of chess."

"Aunt Augusta," Sarah teased, "I can't believe you can sit still long enough for a chess game."

Augusta bristled. "Well, young lady, don't be so sure that you know everything there is to know about this old bird." She hugged Sarah, pushed her toward the door, her eyes twinkling. "You'll live to see that Augusta Hathaway has a few surprises left in her."

The night before she left for St. Louis, Sarah took one more thing from her trunk of memories, which she had decided she would transform into a "treasure for tomorrow." Lifting out the wedding gown, she very carefully removed about four yards of lace from the train. She tucked the lace into a pillowcase and lay it atop the contents of her carpetbag. Closing the bag, she set it by the stairs that led down to the clinic, then she turned down her bed and slept a peaceful night underneath Cordelia Braddock's quilt.

Ten days after Sarah arrived back in St. Louis, she assisted in the delivery of Nellie Spomer's daughter. Nellie held the infant close for a few moments before lifting her up to Sarah. Tears welling in her eyes, she said quietly, "Well, Sarah. We did it." She took a deep breath. "Will you come again to see me?"

"Of course I will, Nellie," Sarah said gently. "This little one can't travel quite yet. We'll be here a few days until the doctor says it's safe to leave."

During those few days Sarah stayed near Nellie, helping her recover. She finished the last few stitches of quilting on the baby quilt she had made during their time together.

"It's beautiful, Sarah. No baby could have anything prettier."

"Oh, it's not quite finished," Sarah said. Going into her room, she produced four yards of the most exquisite lace Nellie had ever seen. "I've still got to sew this bit of trim on. *Then* it will be finished."

"Where did you ever find such incredible lace?" Nellie asked, draping it over her lap.

"Oh, I have a little store of heirlooms I like to use in my special projects," Sarah said. She didn't offer further explanation, and for once Nellie didn't press to learn more.

Sarah's first few hours back in Lincoln were filled with joy. She stepped from the train cuddling an infant swathed in a beautiful quilt trimmed with Belgian lace.

"Sam, Loula, here she is," Sarah said, holding out the precious bundle in her arms. "Your daughter."

Loula stared lovingly at Hannah Cordelia Kemp, whispering, "Red hair. She's got red hair just like Ma, Sam. And a dimple in her chin just like your pa." Sam swallowed back his tears and nodded while Sarah looked on, inwardly praising God for giving her one more way to turn her mourning into dancing.

"I've got the carriage right out front," Sam said. He reached for Sarah's bag and followed the two women and his new daughter through the train station.

"I know you want to get to Tom, Sarah," Loula offered. "Dr. Gilbert got him moved home just a little while ago. Said he wanted your homecomin' to be just perfect. So just give me the basics of Hannah's schedule, and you can come over later for coffee and fill in the particulars."

In only a few minutes, Sarah was bounding up the stairs to Tom's and her apartment, hugging her brother, declaring that he looked "fit as a fiddle."

Tom nodded. "I'm feeling stronger every day, Sarah. The two docs have taken real good care of me."

During Tom Biddle's long convalescence he was tutored at home by a faithful Miss Griswall, who dutifully came by twice a week with his assignments. He read from Dr. Gilbert's medical library, recited for Dr. Allbright, and nearly drove Sarah crazy trying to rush his recovery.

Maude insisted that Tom walk every day. "That woman walks far and fast," Tom said one evening as he slowly climbed the stairs to where Sarah sat reading. "But I had her breathing pretty hard keeping up with me tonight." He chuckled, "Those women's fitness classes she has at the university must not be very hard."

Sarah feigned annoyance. "Well, now, Mr. Biddle, the next time you intimate that females aren't athletic, perhaps we shall have you put on shoes with inch-high heels, a corset, three petticoats, and about fifteen yards of calico. Then we'll see who exercises the longest and hardest!"

One evening as Sarah and Tom sat in their apartment, Tom put his schoolwork down and said abruptly, "It will seem very strange when I leave for medical school, Sarah."

Sarah looked up from her stitching. "In what way?"

"Well, I'll be up in Omaha. You'll be here."

Sarah laid down her work. Tom's simple statement hit hard. She nodded. "I hadn't really thought about that, Tom. There are nursing jobs in Omaha, you know."

Tom shook his head. "No. That's asking too much. You've given your entire life to the care and feeding of Tom Biddle. It's time you had a chance to be on your own without a little brother in tow."

And perhaps its time you had a chance to be on your own without a big sister looking over your shoulder. Sarah scolded herself. *Well, Tom's nearly grown up. That's what happens when life works the way it's supposed to. What did you expect, Sarah? To be the spinster sister forever looking out for her little brother?* Sarah smiled to herself. *Yes, that's exactly what I had planned.* She looked up at Tom and smiled brightly. "Dr. Thomas Biddle has *such* a nice ring to it."

"Would you consider being the nurse in my office when I open my own practice?" Tom wanted to know.

Sarah chuckled. "Do you think you could stand having your sister looking over your shoulder again every day? You might change your mind after you've been on your own in Omaha."

He grinned. "No, I won't. But I don't know if Dr. Gilbert will agree to part with you."

Sarah forced a light tone into her voice. "Oh, I don't think Dr. Gilbert will be needing me much longer. He and Dr. Allbright make such a good team. And Dr. Allbright comes from back east. They have real nurses back there. I expect she'll be wanting to hire someone with a degree for their practice."

"Good," Tom said, yawning. "Then it won't cause any hard feelings when you come to work in my office."

"Might I suggest that you first receive your certificate from Miss Griswall before we go looking for an office to rent?" Sarah teased.

"Good idea." He stood up and headed for his room. "Oh—I almost forget to tell you. I stopped by the hospital today. Dr. Gilbert mentioned that he'll be moving his private practice when the hospital opens."

"Did he say when that would be? Do we need to begin looking for rooms?"

Tom shook his head. "No. He said not. Said he has plans."

"What plans?"

Tom shrugged. "Can't say. Don't know. I guess he'll talk to you about it when the time comes."

CHAPTER 30

Chocolate Lane's Net

----

*"In the day of prosperity be joyful, but in the day
of adversity consider: God also hath set the one
over against the other."*
Ecclesiastes 7:14

Sarah's first few weeks back in Lincoln were devoted to
Tom, and the speed of his recovery granted Sarah more
happiness to add to the joy of Hannah Kemp. But under-
lying her happiness there was an uneasiness about her
future and Tom's. And Dr. Miles Gilbert's behavior did
nothing to help alleviate that uncertainty.

"He seems to be avoiding me, Loula," Sarah said one
day as they shared tea. "Tom said that the clinic will be
closing as soon as the hospital is officially open, but when
I suggest we begin to look for rooms elsewhere, Tom just
shrugs and says, 'Wait for Dr. Gilbert. He said he has
plans, said we won't have to worry.' But when I try to talk
to Miles, he suddenly has to go somewhere." Sarah added
miserably, "Usually to a meeting with Dr. Allbright. He's
avoiding giving me some bad news. I just know it."

"Oh, Sarah, don't think that. He's just very busy, that's
all. Why, at quiltin' last Monday the ladies were all sayin'
how many babies Dr. Gilbert has birthed in the past few
weeks. Sam says he spends hours and hours at the house—

er—hospital. He and Dr. Allbright haven't had a moment to themselves in weeks."

Seeing the effect her words had on Sarah, Loula stopped abruptly. "Now, Sarah. You got to remember what we talked about before Tom got sick. God has His plan, and He don't usually reveal the particulars right off. He wants us to walk by faith."

Sarah bit her lower lip. "That's awfully hard to do when all indications are that God's plan is going to once again take you exactly in the opposite direction you thought you wanted to go."

Loula patted her hand. "There's more to things than usually meets the eye, Sarah. You just got to be patient."

Sarah sighed. "Apparently living with Nellie Spomer didn't teach me enough patience. And I'm not very good at the trusting and obeying, either." She stood up. "Well, I promised Dr. Allbright I'd be in to help her pack up some of the things from the clinic this afternoon. Miles has some mysterious errand again."

Sarah walked from the Kemps' to the clinic by a circuitous route that led past the hospital. She told herself that she wanted to see the hospital, but when she left the hospital grounds, she made her way very slowly down the narrow alley that led along the grounds of the Braddock manse. She forced herself not to look in through the gate, but her ears strained to hear if there might be someone out in the garden, perhaps children playing on the lawn. All was silence.

Then she saw it. That explained everything—especially Miles's seeming avoidance of her since her return from St. Louis. A very small brass plaque had been mounted by the back gate. It read, *Dr. & Mrs. Miles Gilbert*. Another plaque just below the first read, *Dr. Maude Allbright*.

Bittersweet emotions swept through her. She had suspected it all along. Miles had certainly hinted at it . . . or, if he had not, he had certainly shown interest in Maude.

She should have known. In spite of the obvious fact that he was avoiding her, there had been that glimmer of hope that perhaps during her absence Miles would miss her, would wish her back. He had protected her from George. And there was that kiss—albeit a little one. Still, Dr. Miles Gilbert was not one to give kisses lightly. She had even allowed herself to feel a bit of anticipation when the mail was delivered in St. Louis, perhaps wondering if a letter would arrive. . . .

Well, Lord, here I am again, Sarah Biddle, trying to take back her own life and plan it all out. Sarah squinted at the brass nameplates, blinked back tears, and hurried on down the alley toward the clinic.

At the clinic, Sarah was met by more news of the union of Miles Gilbert and Maude Allbright. With a flourish, Tom handed his sister an engraved invitation:

Dr. Maude Allbright & Dr. Miles Gilbert
Request the honour of your presence
at a Reception hosted by
The Lincoln Women's Hospital Auxiliary

To announce the opening of
Braddock Memorial Hospital

Thursday evening, June 19, 1887
8 until 11 o'clock in the evening

In support of the hospital,
a charity auction will be held.
All proceeds to go to the Hospital Operating Fund
overseen by the Board of Directors
Mr. W. T. Crawford, Mr. Charles M. Reeves,
Dr. A. L. Queen Mr. Myron Hickox,
Howard W. Veith, Esquire

"The hospital's turned out swell, Sarah," Tom rejoiced. "They didn't have to do 'bare bones' at all. Someone gave a huge sum of money through Aunt Augusta to start things rolling. When word got out that someone had actually donated a treasured family heirloom for the benefit of the hospital, people just started giving.

"It started when a couple of farmers stopped by one day. It was the first day I was back at the clinic doing a little work," Tom said. "This old guy came in and said, 'Five years ago you delivered our first child. You knew I couldn't pay and you never asked. Well, I can pay now,' he said. And he shoved some cash at Dr. Gilbert. The doc wasn't going to take it. Then the other farmer said, 'You sat up day and night for 'most a week when Josie had the fever. I ain't got much, but I sold a cow last week and kept out fifty cents for the hospital.'"

Tom shook his head. "I never saw Dr. Gilbert so at a loss for words. He just nodded and said, 'Thank you.' After they left, he was quiet for a while, then he said that maybe that's what was needed—for folks to feel like it's *their* hospital, not his and Dr. Allbright's. Anyway, he sent me over to Aunt Augusta with the donation, and after that people started coming almost every day. We finally put a sign out front that says, 'Donations to the hospital should be given directly to the chairwoman of the auxiliary, Mrs. Augusta Hathaway. Hathaway House Hotel.' Doc said he didn't want folks thinking he was taking the money and spending it on his house."

"His house?" Sarah asked, hoping Tom didn't notice the waver in her voice.

"Word's out. It's Dr. Gilbert who bought the Braddock place. He won't talk about it much, but I guess he's hoping to move in right after the hospital opens. He and Dr. Allbright fixed up the old apartment over the carriage house for their office."

Sarah swallowed hard, then managed to say, "How nice." She climbed the stairs to the apartment, suddenly aware that she felt very weary. She stared at the trunk that sat in her room. A thought crossed her mind. She dismissed it. *No, Lord, I can't do that. The ring for the hospital, yes. The lace for Sam and Loula's baby—that was a joy. But don't ask me to take something from that trunk and make a wedding gift for Miles Gilbert and Maude Allbright. I can't. I won't. It's too much.*

"*There hath no temptation taken you but such as is common to man. . . . But God . . . will with the temptation also make a way to escape.*"

Sarah pondered. *Tears of the past, treasures for tomorrow . . . a way to escape.* With trembling hands, she opened the trunk. *All right, Lord. I understand. Another season is about to dawn, and You still have plans for Sarah Biddle. But I have to be willing to let go of my own plans.* Sarah checked off a mental inventory of the trunk's contents. *The gloves are too small. Hat? Maude loves hats. No, the ostrich plume is broken. Petticoats? Too personal. Gloves? Too small. A quilt? No time. Pearls? Maude never wears jewelry.* Finally, Sarah found the perfect thing—a long white pincushion with exquisite openwork and the monogram *A* for *Abigail. . . . A could be for Allbright*, Sarah thought. Nodding with satisfaction, Sarah laid the pincushion aside and closed the lid of the trunk. She was still weary, but at peace.

Miles Gilbert had not fallen in love with her, but it didn't mean life was over. It simply meant that God had more living in store for Miss Sarah Biddle. *Who knows*, Sarah thought, *perhaps Tom and I can* both *go to medical school.* She chuckled at the absurdity of the idea and fell asleep almost immediately.

On the evening of June 19, Sarah and Tom met Augusta at the hotel.

"Sarah, you didn't wear the indigo moire." Augusta sounded disappointed.

"No one is going to concern themselves with how Nurse Biddle is dressed this evening, Aunt Augusta," Sarah chided. "Loula and I just finished this dress. The fabric is called Lane's Net, and it's quite popular. I didn't want to overdo. Dr. Allbright and Miles are going to be the center of attention." *I can't believe I'm actually justifying my wardrobe. I sound like a child.*

The trio enjoyed a light supper and then climbed into Joseph Freeman's best carriage for the ride to the newly opened Braddock Memorial Hospital. As the carriage drove up to let them out, Sarah contemplated the building. *I helped build that.* The thought brought a wonderful sense of satisfaction, which was interrupted by Miles's voice saying warmly, "We've been wondering when you would finally arrive." He looked up at Augusta. "Several of our guests are asking to talk to the woman who almost single-handedly furnished both floors of this hospital with the latest equipment."

Augusta replied, "Well, if they think that's me, they are sadly mistaken." Augusta looked at Sarah, who shook her head and frowned at Augusta.

Miles helped Augusta down from the carriage and then turned toward Sarah. She convinced herself that nerves were the cause of her trembling when he looked her over and said, "You look lovely this evening, Sarah." He lifted her down from the carriage, holding her just close enough that she noticed the faint aroma of Bay Rum cologne.

Leaving Sarah to Tom, Miles escorted Augusta inside the hospital. Once inside, Sarah couldn't help but notice how distinguished the white hair at his temples made him look.

From across the room, Sarah watched as Dr. Allbright went to Miles's side, asked him a question. He glanced at Sarah, looked back at Dr. Allbright, and shook his head imperceptibly from side to side. Maude seemed upset, turned away from him.

From that moment, Sarah stayed near Augusta, smiling and making small talk until her face hurt. She had determined to be happy for Miles and Dr. Allbright, and she convinced herself that she was. Still, after more than an hour of smiling, Sarah became aware of the tension in her midsection. She slipped away from the crowd and went to look for the refreshment table.

A cup of punch in hand, Sarah made her way to the back door of the hospital intending to walk around the grounds. Billy Dowd came running up. "Nurse Biddle," he whispered earnestly, "Tanner got caught in a fence and cut his paw somethin' terrible. He needs help. You always been good to me. Ma says I'da died of scarlet fever without you. And you sewed me up real good when I cut my foot. Could you help Tanner?"

Sarah looked down to see that the boy was holding tight to a puppy whose paw was bleeding profusely all over the boy's shirt. Sarah nodded. She glanced back over her shoulder, motioned for Tom, then handed him her half-empty cup of punch. "Tell Augusta that I've been called out on an emergency." She pointed to the puppy. "I'll be back directly, soon as I tend to this."

"What's the trouble?" It was Miles.

The little boy ducked his head. "I didn't mean to bother the *doctor*. Ma'll tan my hide good if'n she finds out I was over here at all . . . but I was goin' down the alley, and I seen Nurse Biddle in the doorway."

Miles knelt down to examine the puppy's paw. "He needs some stitches, young man." He looked up at Sarah with a question in his eyes. "But we can handle it."

"You don't need to concern yourself with this, Miles," Sarah assured him. "I can take care of Tanner. Billy and I can walk over to the clinic. You need to get back to Dr. Allbright and the others." Sarah stepped through the door, her hand on the boy's shoulder.

But Miles insisted. "Maude will understand. And we needn't go all the way over to the clinic. We'll just go over here—" He looked at Sarah. "I was hoping it would be a surprise, but . . ."

"It's all right, Miles. Tom told me." Sarah was grateful she was in front of him and he could not see her face. "I can't think of anyone nicer to have the old manse. It's been wonderfully restored."

"I'm glad you approve. I have an office over the old carriage house. We can take care of the puppy there." They made their way quickly across the hospital grounds and as they approached the back gate, Miles rushed ahead, stood to one side, motioned Sarah and Billy through ahead of him. They went in the former carriage house door, up a newly rebuilt flight of stairs, and into a beautiful office, behind which was a well-equipped examining room.

Sarah was thankful there was no time for Miles to elicit comments about the office. The puppy whimpered, the boy began to cry, and it took all their collective patience to calm both down. Dr. Gilbert finally administered a sedative to the puppy. He had just bent to begin stitching up the cut, which turned out to be quite deep and significantly longer than he had anticipated, when Dr. Allbright appeared at the door.

"Miles!" she almost shouted. "What on *earth* are you doing? Where have you *been*?!"

Miles looked up with the expression of a schoolboy caught playing hooky. "Well, Maude, we've had a little crisis here, and I just thought—"

Maude looked at him imperiously, narrowing her eyes. "You're procrastinating," she chided. She turned to pull down a lab coat and nearly pushed Sarah out of the way. "You have more important matters to take care of this evening." She looked at Miles meaningfully. "I can take over here. Get on with the evening, Miles."

Miles nodded his head. "Yes, Maude. Of course. You're quite right." He turned and retreated toward the stairs.

Maude looked at Sarah. "Miles, I believe you're forgetting someone."

"Oh, yes. I am." Miles took a deep breath. "Sarah, would you join me? I've something to show you. Something to—discuss."

Sarah looked doubtfully at Maude. "You might need help."

"Of course I don't need help. It's a puppy. He'll be stitched up, wrapped up, and healed up before—" Maude shook her head. "Before Miles can manage one sentence of what he has to say, if you two don't get going."

Sarah followed Miles down the stairs. As her foot landed on the bottom step, she looked up at the back of the manse. Someone had lit candles on the second-story landing, and the warm glow illuminated the stained glass in such a way that Sarah let out a low exclamation. "I've never seen it lit up from the inside that way. It's so lovely."

Miles offered his arm. "Well, then, let's go inside where we can talk."

Confused but curious to see the completed manse and its furnishings, Sarah took his arm. He walked her around the side of the house. They went in the front door. Miles's voice was gentle as he said, "Sarah, Sam Kemp told me he showed you around the inside before you went back to St. Louis. He said you were pleased to see the restoration." His voice lowered. "I was so—glad—to hear that. I thought perhaps I was wrong. Perhaps the house would bring back too much pain."

Sarah shook her head. "No." She looked up the stairs toward the landing where candlelight had cast a warm glow against the walls. "No. This house will always be dear to me."

Miles hesitated for a moment. Then, reaching for Sarah's hand, he pulled her gently toward the stairs. "Would you join me on the landing, Miss Biddle?"

Sarah started to reach out her hand, then she stopped. "Miles, it really isn't necessary to go to all this trouble. I know that you and Maude are getting married. I saw the plaques by the back gate earlier today. Obviously you seem to think that I had some notion." She smiled. "And maybe I did. But I've—"

"You did?" he asked gently. "What kind of notion?"

"Please, Miles, don't embarrass me." She felt her cheeks turning red. "I really wish only the best for the both of you."

Miles chuckled. "Come, Sarah. Come upstairs. Indulge me. Please."

Wishing for some way of escape, Sarah reluctantly followed him up the stairs. Halfway up, Miles dropped back behind her. When she reached the top of the stairs, she looked about her in amazement. A small table and two chairs had been set up next to the window seat. On the table, someone had set out an exquisite dessert tray. Not one, but two bottles of wine completed the table setting.

"Two bottles of wine?"

Miles grinned. "One if she says yes. One if she says no. One for friendship. One for love."

Gently, he took her by the shoulders, turned her toward the door that had once led to Abigail Braddock's room. "When Abigail was ill I remember once seeing you stand and look at that door as if the hounds of hell were on the other side." His voice grew quiet, gentle. "But you went through it anyway. I think you're having courage to go through that door was what began it."

"What began—what, Miles?"

"Well," Miles said, walking toward the door. "At first it was admiration. You had so much courage. Then," he said, his hand on the door, "that morning at the hotel when you and I talked, you insisted that giving the key to this door—and all the other doors of this house—to Ira Braddock was just part of your duty to the Braddocks." He shook his head in amazement. "You were so intent upon preserving the aura that existed around the Braddock name. I thought I had never seen such unselfish loyalty in all my life. I began to wonder what it would be like to have someone feel that way about—" He hesitated. "About me."

Suddenly Miles put his arm about her and guided her through the door into Abigail's room. There were no surprises in the room except for one thing. Sarah's eyes immediately went to it. "Dr. Gilbert, that is *my* quilt on the bed."

"Yes, Nurse Biddle it is. Tom brought it over earlier today." He whispered in her ear. "And now you know why I couldn't just up and furnish the hospital with the latest equipment. I wanted you to have your home back."

"But the plaques by the back gate—"

"Maude needs an office until we can renovate the old clinic for her. I didn't think you'd mind."

"But I overheard the two of you talking about the manse—"

"Maude helped plan the restoration."

Sarah shook her head. "You've barely said ten words to me in weeks, Miles. I can't believe—"

Miles stepped in front of her. "It wasn't until you were gone for those weeks that I realized. At first I thought how much I had grown to depend on you. How much I missed your help. But then—" He lifted her chin so that their eyes met. "But then I realized that I didn't just depend on you. I didn't just miss your help. I realized that I love you, Sarah. I need a great deal more than just your help. I need *you*." Reaching down to take Sarah's hand, Miles held it against his heart. "I know about the ring, Sarah. The one you sold for the hospital. Augusta told me." He kissed the palm of her hand. "I wish I could replace it—outdo it."

Sarah looked up at him. The candlelight shining from the hallway was reflected in his eyes, blue eyes that glowed with something that made words unnecessary. Reaching up to caress the gray hair along both his temples, Sarah wrapped her arms around Miles's neck and whispered, "A simple gold band will do nicely, Miles."

After sending Billy Dowd home, Maude Allbright cleaned up after herself, hoping that Nurse Biddle would be much too occupied elsewhere to perform her "nursely duties." She descended the stairs of the new office and turned left at the rose garden, forcing herself not to look toward the house. However, when Maude reached the gate, she could not resist. Turning her head slightly, she allowed herself one glance up at the second-story stained glass windows. There were only shadows on the landing, but the shadows told her what she wanted to know. Smiling happily to herself, Maude went through the gate and back to the reception.

Epilogue

Sarah and Miles Gilbert were blessed with a long and happy marriage. While they never had children of their own, they became surrogate grandparents to many neighborhood children. They supported various children's charities and established a scholarship at the University of Nebraska. After Miles passed away, Sarah began the practice of giving the poorest newborns at Braddock Memorial Hospital a small baby quilt made by her own hands. When an observant nurse at the hospital commented that Mrs. Gilbert's baby quilts always had at least one piece of fine claret satin in the patchwork, Sarah smiled and said, "That's the tears of the past turned into a treasure for tomorrow."

Thomas Mason Biddle graduated from the Omaha Medical College in 1890. He married Edna Vickers shortly after he had returned to Lincoln to practice at Braddock Memorial Hospital. When Tom volunteered to serve in World War I, Edna and her only child, Lorna, went to stay with Sarah. After Tom was killed in the war, Edna and Lorna made their home with Sarah.

Dr. Maude Allbright became the first secretary of the Lincoln Medical Society. In addition to maintaining a successful practice specializing in women's health issues, she was a leader in civic affairs and a moving force behind the movement, which finally won Nebraska women the right to vote.

Nellie Spomer attended the Veiled Prophet Ball in St. Louis, Missouri, one month after the birth of her daughter. She met and married Winston Donovan, a well-to-do businessman who supported his wife's interests. Together, they were able to provide for many unwed mothers.

George McCann served a long sentence in the Oregon State Penitentiary for theft. Once paroled, he drifted from place to place, finally settling on an isolated ranch in the Rocky Mountains. When George died, Miles received word that George had become a "sincere Christian man who was a dependable worker and always spoke highly of his cousin Miles."

Sam and Loula Kemp raised eight children and were active in the First Baptist Church of Lincoln, where Sam served as a deacon for over thirty years. Their descendants own and operate Kemp Builders.

Lorna Biddle's first book secured her future as a writer and enabled her to maintain her home, which was eventually listed on the National Register of Historic Places. Each June, the massive iron gates of the estate are opened to the public when "Sarah's Circle" hosts an outdoor quilt show for the benefit of the Lincoln Crisis Pregnancy Center.

> Oh LORD, thou art my God;
> I will exalt thee, I will praise thy name;
> for thou hast done wonderful things;
> thy counsels of old are faithfulness and truth.
> Isaiah 25:1

Dirt. He expected her to look at dirt and call it home.

Home meant crisp white curtains flapping in the summer breeze and bright flowers growing in window boxes. This house of dirt had one very small, very bare window. There were no curtains, no flowers—nothing but huge slabs of earth piled up like bricks, with dead grass sticking out between the layers.

Home meant a door that opened just off a cobblestone street to welcome visitors onto spotless wooden floors that were scrubbed daily. In place of a door, this soddy had a tattered quilt. Pushing it aside, Karyn pursed her lips in grim realization that she couldn't even scrub this floor, for it, like the walls, was dirt.

Home meant a nightly climb upstairs to a tiny room to laugh and giggle with her sister, Sophie, until Mama shouted, "Girls! Enough!" Stepping inside the sod house, Karyn saw that it was only one cavernous room. At the center of the room, a tree trunk had been planted in the earth to stretch upward and help support the roof. Karyn looked up. There was no "upstairs"—not even a loft to escape to. Inspecting the ceiling, Karyn wondered how much rain would seep through when a storm flung itself at the pathetic shack. She felt the walls coming in on her. She had to get outside—to breathe.

Mr. Ritter was lifting her trunk out of the wagon, setting it gently on the ground. When Karyn stepped to the doorway he looked at her hopefully. When he spoke, his tone was apologetic. "It's not much like ho—" He corrected himself. "It's not much like where we came from, Miss Ensinger. That I know."

Karyn's thoughts went back to a few days ago when she and a dozen other girls had stepped off a train in Grand

Island, Nebraska, breathless with excitement and nervousness. They had answered a letter sent to Bremen, Germany—a letter that promised homes and good lives to women who would come to share a few years of hard work with a man they would choose.

The rules had been laid carefully. The girls would meet their prospective husbands at a church. There would be a meal and conversation, and if couples so desired, they could be married right away. But they would have to remain in Grand Island for twenty-four hours, after which any marriage could be annulled.

Karyn Ensinger had been eager to leave Bremen. She had lost her beloved Emil in a war that he had not wanted to fight. So long ago, it seemed, she had read the unbelievable news. So long ago, it seemed, she had stood by Emil's grave and wept.

And so Karyn had come to America, had nervously looked over the men who came to the meeting in Grand Island, Nebraska, had smiled to hide her fears, and had attracted Mikal Ritter. The other girls had tittered and whispered admiring comments about him. Karyn had thought him rather frightening. He was tall, with hair so blond it was almost white, and piercing blue eyes. When he spoke, his deep voice rumbled. He looked the slimmer girls over and passed them by. Karyn found herself wishing she was petite, that she could shrink back and not be so noticeable. But Karyn was tall. She was large-boned, with thick dark hair and huge brown eyes. After a cursory look at the other girls, Mikal had strode purposefully up to her and introduced himself.

"Would you sit with me, Miss Ensinger?"

And so, Karyn Ensinger had been captured to be carried away to what Mikal Ritter had spent the evening describing as a good farm with a promising future.

That had been a few days ago. That had been before the interminable ride over barren, endless land, seated alongside a stranger she must now call her husband. Standing in the doorway of the one-room house made of dirt, Karyn wanted to cry, She stared past Mikal at the vast, unbroken space.

She imagined her first letter home. Dear Sophie . . . America is a wonderful land, where the settlers live in dirt houses and burn buffalo droppings for heat . . . There are no eggs just yet and trees have yet to be invented . . . My husband is Mikal Ritter . . . He is handsome and blond and sleeps in a cave . . .

Standing alongside the cave that Mikal Ritter lived in, looking at the pile of manure she was supposed to use to cook a supper without eggs or utensils, Karyn succumbed to the weight of homesickness that flooded her.

The sight of tears coursing down Karyn's cheeks wrenched the last shred of optimism away from Mikal. Suddenly his life, his farm, all the toil of the last two years seemed meaningless.

Mein Gott, he thought, *for what have I been striving. If a woman looks upon my labor and weeps . . .*

He turned to walk away.

About the Author

Stephanie Grace Whitson lives in rural Nebraska with her husband of twenty-five years, four home-schooled children, and a very spoiled German shepherd. The Whitsons are active in their local Bible-teaching church. Stephanie is the author of the best-selling Prairie Winds Series: *Walks the Fire, Soaring Eagle,* and *Red Bird.*

To receive information about future works by Stephanie, write to her at:

Stephanie Grace Whitson
3800 Old Cheney Road #101–178
Lincoln, NE 68516

LOOK FOR THESE OTHER BOOKS IN THE PRAIRIE WINDS SERIES

Walks the Fire

This is the extraordinary story of Jesse King, a pioneer woman who is taken in by the Lakota Sioux after her husband and child are killed on the trek across the Nebraska prairie. As she teaches God's Word and adjusts to life with the tribe, she finds an unexpected peace and sense of belonging. She builds lasting friendships and finds love with a Christian Sioux brave, Rides the Wind, raising his son Soaring Eagle and their daughter LisBeth. The first in the Prairie Winds series, *Walks the Fire* is a tender and beautiful love story as well as a thrilling adventure.

0-7852-7981-4 • **Hardback** • **$9.99** • 312 pages

Soaring Eagle

The author of *Walks the Fire* continues with the story of LisBeth, Jesse's daughter. After losing her husband at the battle of Little Big Horn, she returns home and finds that she has lost her mother also. Without them, she must find who she really is and where she belongs. And on that journey, she will find her half-brother, Sioux warrior Soaring Eagle. The second in the Prairie Winds series unites three very different people — a young widow, a disillusioned soldier, and an angry Sioux warrior — to create a moving novel of romance and faith.

0-7852-7617-3 • **Hardback** • **$10.99** • 312 pages

Redbird

The third book in the Prairie Winds series finds Carrie Brown returning to Nebraska as an adult with big plans for the future. The biggest plan is one that includes Soaring Eagle, the Lakota Sioux she knew as a child. As she is forced to re-evaluate her life and relationship with God, a disaster strikes that changes her life forever.

0-7852-7484-7 • **Trade Paperback** • 288 pages